POISONED SOIL

A novel by

Tim Young

Harmony Publishing Company

Copyright

First Edition

Library of Congress Cataloging-in-Publication Data is available upon request

ISBN-10: 1479220213

ISBN-13: 9781479220212

Publisher Contact Information
Harmony Publishing
www.harmonypub.com

Acknowledgements

It's one thing to write a novel; to conceive a story, discover the characters and let the words flow unfiltered and, at times, in disarray. It's another thing to polish those words into a gripping, high quality novel. One in which readers can get happily lost without stumbling over mistakes in grammar, spelling and logic. My goal was to not only share a story with you, but to ensure the work was of the highest quality. To achieve that end, several kind and competent people poured over the manuscript and helped shape the final outcome of this novel. I owe them an enormous debt of gratitude.

Sharon Landress Hasting edited the final manuscript, corrected punctuation, pointed out inconsistencies and offered valuable developmental insights. She was generous with her time, accurate in her work and a real pleasure to work with.

After the editing round, I solicited a group of volunteer beta readers to assess the quality of the story, and to look closely for holes and inconsistencies. Amanda Higginbotham, Amelia McCain, Jill Perez, Eric Wagoner and my good friend, "Kupcake," read the story with interest, suggested phrasings to improve the flow, corrected spelling errors and pointed out areas where a reader might be confused. Their generous feedback allowed me to make those subtle but important tweaks, like adding the final handful of spices to the sauce that, I hope, will allow readers to become absorbed by the story. So to my editor and beta readers, please accept my most sincere thanks.

Finally, I owe the largest debt to my wife and ideal reader, Liz. She's the one I hope to impress the most, and she's the one I listen to most closely. Before sharing the manuscript with beta readers, Liz labored through the first draft and pointed out, shall we say...opportunities for improvement. On all points, she was right, and helped the story come to life. I love you, Liz!

As with everything I do, this is for Liz

Prologue

Baldev knelt on the damp, forest floor and wept with the knowledge that his remaining breaths were few. With tears in his eyes and rage in his heart, the Cherokee priest looked to the sky in disbelief. A flood of sorrow streamed down the crevices of his cheeks, weathered and red as the Georgia clay. He wiped his final tears, kissed the beads that hung from his neck, and prayed for the strength to do what he must. As he inhaled the sweet scent of pine that perfumed the forest, he rose to his feet.

There, in the midst of a vast wilderness, he stood among the sickly beasts—all that remained of his people's way of life. He surveyed the grief in the animals' faces, mirror images of his own suffering, as he shook his head with fury and utter disillusionment that he alone was the last of the seventeen thousand Georgian Cherokees. The tribe's livestock accepted their fates, just as the last of the Cherokee had, and stood prepared to surrender their flesh. Baldev vowed not to let their lives go to waste. Rather, he would sacrifice them in an enduring act of retribution against greed and oppression.

Summoning the strength of a nation, he raised his walking stick; its razor-sharp root spikes protruding like gnarly hair over the deranged face he had carved for its head. Pointing it toward the summit, he commanded the animals to the top of Rabun Bald, a mountain possessed by fire-breathing demons, according to his tribe's beliefs.

Atop the mountain, Baldev summoned a witch, the Raven Mocker, to torment and shorten the animals' lives. The Cherokee angel of death—most feared of all evil witches—appeared in the form of a shrieking raven and claimed the heart of each animal, adding their unused lifetimes to its own. As the witch tormented, Baldev mercifully sliced the throat of each animal and watched the blood pour out and stain a huge granite boulder, forever poisoning the soil. He murmured a prayer in reverence of the animals' sacrifice as the putrid blackish fluid seeped into the Appalachian mountainside. There, it would wait with eternal patience to punish greed and oppression. To punish, any soul not of pure Cherokee heart, who dared cohabit the soil.

For sixty years, no one occupied the mountainside and the evil lingered in the pitch-black soil.

Then, in the spring of 1898, a hardscrabble family of six in search of a plot to call home, veered north off Warwoman Creek and claimed a clearing on Rabun Bald. The father, Samuel Dixon, had come to Rabun County in 1867 at the age of two when his own father, a wool sorter from Bradford, England, came to southern Appalachia for its warmer weather and land to farm. It pleased Samuel to find a homesite just as peaceful as the one his brother Joshua had settled on nearby Rainey Mountain. He knelt and dug into the richest, blackest soil his lily-white hands had ever touched.

While Samuel harvested lumber to construct a small cabin, his wife, Sarah, and their four children tended to the small flock of sheep that Samuel's father had bequeathed him, as they planted the few herb and vegetable seeds they had.

They never got the chance to harvest a crop.

The first ominous sign appeared within days on three-year-old Rachel's hands. As Sarah examined the first few itchy bumps, she attributed them to poison ivy while she soothed her daughter's skin with the marshmallow root she carried for such ailments. Later that evening, a solitary, black bead of blood ran from Rachel's left nostril. Her mother wiped it away with her apron, only to unleash a river of blood from Rachel's nose. As she mirrored her mother's panic, Rachel's mouth opened wide to reveal a pool of blackish blood. Sarah's concern turned into panic as, one by one, each family member was afflicted with the same symptoms. By then, pus-spewing black ulcers covered Rachel's body—all but her head—and converged like summer freckles, cloaking the child in a suffocating suit of death. As the full moon crept over the evening horizon, Rachel lay dead in her mother's arms and black ulcers smothered everyone.

Distraught and hysterical, Sarah huddled the dying children under the roof of the cabin as the wind whipped through the unfinished walls. Nausea and fever took grip and enveloped the family in a nightmarish state. The woods seemed to come alive as frigid winds howled from the top of Rabun Bald, as if an angry God demanded repentant sacrifice. Samuel stood wide-eyed, his double-barreled shotgun in hand as he searched the darkness for a demon he could extinguish. A demon he could understand.

As the forest soil exhaled its deadly breath, Samuel's fever escalated to a state of panicked desperation. He gathered his stricken family and demanded they leave the cursed ground and follow the moon's light to refuge. They left Rachel's body behind and blindly stumbled through the mountain's dark shadows, all the while saying prayers aloud for salvation. Samuel came to a sudden halt and held out the palm of his hand to silence the others. He tilted his head as he began to hear the hushed whispers that taunted him from mere feet away, yet hidden in the darkness out of sight.

"D-E-A-T-H" was the long, drawn-out whisper that Samuel heard whistle through his ears. "D-E-A-T-H."

Samuel realized they had strayed into a thicket of soaring cathedral pines, tops towering over him as if they were ancient, disapproving gods. The canopy swayed fiercely, intoxicating and terrifying Samuel with strobing glimpses of darkness and moon-drenched shadows. His eyes grew wide, pupils the size of marbles taking in the dim light as he jerked right, then left, spinning out of control. As a wailing wind tossed pine needles at his head like darts in the blackness, the forest spirits possessed him, pushing his fear over the edge and commanding that he pull the trigger on the evil spirits that besieged him. Absent of conscious thought, he blindly obeyed. He turned to the four dark figures lurking, stalking and poised for attack, and watched his smoking barrels obliterate them.

The spirits quieted and smothered the winds, allowing an eerie calm to blanket the forest. The canopy opened and invited the moon to shine its light on the forest floor. Samuel's panic subsided as he stared at the moon, which now seemed a tranquil beacon of hope. He traced its searchlight from the heavens to an object five times his own height: a tremendous granite outcropping overhanging a natural spring. The boulder's weathered wrinkles reflected the moonlight throughout the pine cathedral.

Samuel's eyes fell to the spring at the base of the boulder, where four lifeless bodies lay, covered with black blisters and spewing blood into the cursed soil. Samuel loomed over them, mouth agape, staring at what remained of his family in the darkness. In a trance, Samuel stood still, unaware that his hands—or something else—had repositioned the choke of the shotgun just beneath his chin. He submitted to the soil's final command and pressed his thumb down on the trigger. As Samuel's body collapsed and draped over Sarah's, the echo from the shotgun faded and the evil crept back into the soil through the blood of its victims.

Baldev nodded in approval of the sacrifice.

Chapter 1

Ozzie jerked his head up in the darkness, his adolescent shaggy black hair standing on end. It wasn't the rain dripping on his head that had woken him so violently. By now, he had adjusted to sleeping through rain and oppressive heat. No, he had heard something. A drawn-out menacing moan from far below, a monster slugging its way up the mountainside, getting closer to Ozzie by the moment. He was sure he had heard it, but for now, the forest remained calm.

As the clouds began to clear, a wedge of moonlight shone through a rip in the shack's roof and landed on the dirt floor. Ozzie stared at the dust particles as they danced in the beam of light between the floor and the ceiling. Other than soft snoring from the three bodies that surrounded him, the forest was eerily quiet.

Until a deep, haunting whisper rose to him through the trees.

"Beware, my boy. I'm coming for you."

Ozzie bolted straight up, deadly still.

"I'm coming, little Ozzie. Coming to eat you. And then I'm going to eat your entire family too, put you all in my black, evil belly!"

Ozzie froze momentarily before he tugged at his brother. "Felipe! Wake up!"

Felipe rolled away from Ozzie. He never woke when Ozzie heard the monster coming. Other nights the monster had spared him, passing by just close enough that Ozzie could smell its breath—breath that stank like exhaust from an old rusty muffler. But this time it taunted Ozzie, called him out by name!

"I'm getting closer now, little one."

"Mom," Ozzie whispered before raising his voice. "MOM!"

"What is it, Felipe...Ozzie?" Isabella responded, voice deep and groggy with sleep.

"The monster's coming up the mountain! MOM!"

"Ozzie," Isabella said with her eyes closed, "It's no monster. They're just bringing us breakfast as they do every day. You know how you love your breakfast, Ozzie."

That was true. Even if it was just the same sloppy gruel every day, Ozzie looked forward to it. It was all that he had ever known, although his mother had shown him how to forage for some wild foods, mainly mushrooms and wild berries. But it didn't matter, as Ozzie had little room to explore. An electric fence three times his height kept his family, and countless others, imprisoned.

Isabella pulled Ozzie close to her and snuggled him. Ozzie's fear had caused his voice to escalate steadily until he let out a high-pitched, juvenile squeal.

"But mom, it said it's going to eat me...eat all of us!"

"What the hell is going on? The sun's not even up yet!"

"Nothing, Eduardo," Isabella said to Ozzie's father. "Ozzie just got a little scared, that's all."

Eduardo stood and stared firmly at Ozzie, furious that he had been woken.

"Dammit, Ozzie, you're not the only one who sleeps in here, you know. We all have to sleep together. You're almost grown now, and it's time you start acting like it! Now, go back to sleep!"

Eduardo didn't have the patience or the tact of a mother. With all they had been through, being held captive on this foreign land for so long, it was a wonder he had any patience left at all. As with most fathers, he felt it was his role to make sure his son grew up to become a leader—the protector and provider that Eduardo felt that *he* should have been.

"Shhh! Listen, mom...it's coming!" Ozzie said, being careful to keep his voice low.

"I don't hear anything, Ozzie."

Eduardo went back to sleep under their leaky roof as Isabella sat with Ozzie and listened carefully. Ozzie had a remarkable sense of hearing, nature's way of compensating for his extremely poor eyesight, Isabella reasoned.

Finally, Isabella heard the faint sound of the dilapidated old farm truck, Ozzie's enraged monster, grow louder, moaning along and grinding its teeth as it made its way up the makeshift mountain road. A road that existed on no map, to a destination that virtually no one knew existed.

Boom! Pow! Belch! The truck sputtered and backfired, the sound bouncing off the mountainside like cannon fire in a brick alleyway, as the black monster crept closer still. Ozzie had never seen it before and didn't want to see it. Always it came under cover of darkness, and every detainee knew to keep away until it left. Most just learned to sleep right through it. Ozzie never could, but as long as his mother was beside him, protecting him, the monster uttered not a word.

The truck inched forward in stops and starts, belching and grinding its way along the circular road, skulking ever closer to Ozzie's encampment. Ozzie dug into Isabella's side, bracing himself for the worst as the sound closed in on him. But then, as Isabella had assured him, the truck completed its rounds and slithered back down the mountainside. Ozzie cozied close to his mother as the sound of his monster slowly faded, and he drifted back asleep.

As his eyes fell shut the wind whispered down the Georgia mountainside, "I'll be back for you, Ozzie."

***

Ozzie climbed out of bed two hours after sunrise and staggered to the food drop. When he found nothing, he just stared dumbfounded and listened intently to see if the truck was coming back. He heard nothing, so he began exploring. Fifty yards away Ozzie found a cluster of oyster mushrooms spiraling up an oak tree. Starving, he ripped a mushroom off the tree and devoured it.

"Mornin' sweetie."

"Mom! I didn't hear you coming."

Ozzie walked over and rested his head on his mother's shoulder as he soaked up the warmth of her love. *Eduardo's right; he's growing up so fast*, Isabella thought. *Practically full grown now but still so innocent...so naïve!*

The sticky September air was deliciously humid, permeated with the sweet smell of anise. Together, Ozzie and his mother walked on the damp ground, sidestepping the three-foot high buckeye trees that had sprung up like root suckers and merged with other vegetation to create a dense forest understory.

Boom! Pow! Belch! Ozzie stopped suddenly and turned his head down the mountain in the direction of a faint sound.

"That's strange for them to come at this time," Isabella mumbled as her grin drained into a concerned frown. Ozzie picked up on the change in her demeanor and facial expression and moved closer. Isabella wondered if Eduardo was up and she glanced back home.

Home.

She couldn't believe that's what she called this ramshackle place where she was forced to sleep on the ground, without even a blanket to lie on. Just hard ground, so dusty when it was hot and dry, and so bone-chillingly cold when it was wet. Isabella got through most days by daydreaming about what had been, and what she feared in her heart would never be again.

Born near the ocean, she had lived with her parents and six brothers and sisters on a hacienda. Everyone knew and revered her parents, and that meant they would respect Isabella one day, too, since her Spanish ancestors had been there for centuries. To Isabella's eyes, their hacienda was paradise and had everything a body could want. Sun-bathed sloping grounds that yielded bushels of grapes and berries. Land overflowing with food: potatoes, tomatoes, beans and peppers. Rolling hills, oak filled forests, beaches, and an ocean to cool off in or to gaze over.

It was on a nearby farm that she first saw Eduardo with his thick black hair and bulging shoulder muscles. He grew up among five brothers, having no trouble putting them in their place when they needed it, and defending them anytime someone other than he wanted to tussle with them. Isabella knew right away that he was her soul mate. Their courtship was brief as they were eager to have their own family. Steeped in tradition, they wanted nothing more than to live simply and freely, just as their parents and grandparents had done for centuries. Their dreams began to come true as first Felipe was born and then, shortly thereafter, her beloved Ozzie. Life was unfolding just the way nature intended.

And in an instant their freedom was taken from them.

Her face burned with bitterness and rage as she replayed the night they were captured. She could still conjure the disgusting smell of the sweaty, armed men and their trained dogs that had surrounded and jolted them awake in the middle of the night. A man brandishing a knife held Felipe and Ozzie to the ground while three others cornered Isabella and Eduardo. Then the man grabbed Ozzie, merely a baby then, and flung him and Felipe into the back of a covered truck. Flung them! The men knew that Isabella and Eduardo would put up little resistance boarding the truck to protect their babies.

They were smuggled into a small, dark cargo room aboard a boat. As the boat raced away, she feared she would never set foot on her homeland again. An hour later the boat stopped, and the men shoved them onto the back of a large truck. The men hauled them through the night to a remote mountainside, where they understood nothing. Not a word spoken, not why they were there, and most frightening, not what fate had in store for them.

As Isabella looked back to the shack she saw that Eduardo was just getting up, but Felipe still slept. No surprise there, but from the distance, her eyes softened as she watched Eduardo mope around the shack. Day by day, she watched as he grew more dejected, which made her sad and stressed. When they met he was so full of life, so vibrant. Even when they were first captured he had such a determination to free his family and get everyone back home safely. To protect his family from these vicious men. But escape was impossible, even for Eduardo. Isabella begrudgingly accepted that early on and turned her attention to her children. Eduardo refused to accept that reality and spent days and months planning, plotting, and testing ideas on how to escape. With only the tools God gave him, he exhaustively tried to tunnel under the high voltage fence. He made progress in the hard ground more than once, but never had time to break through before the captors returned. When they saw the evidence of his digging the first time the men beat him brutally. When they caught him a second time they beat both Eduardo and Felipe with a 2x4. Ultimately, Eduardo was forced to acknowledge that there was nothing he could do without endangering Isabella and the boys and that realization steadily sucked the life out of him. He seemed beaten, utterly dejected, and it broke Isabella's heart.

Isabella couldn't afford the luxury of giving up. She had to make life as safe and happy as she could for Felipe and Ozzie.

The black truck continued its ascent. Isabella knew that other prisoners would get their food first before the truck continued on the circular makeshift road, something of a rutted cul-de-sac in the wilderness, with her family its final stop. Then the truck would rev its engine and burp exhaust in her face, providing an all too vivid reminder that her life stank.

"Why didn't they just leave food when they came a few hours ago?" Isabella asked rhetorically. Ozzie stood behind her.

The truck continued its rounds, sputtering and nearly dying every few minutes, stopping then pulling ahead, like a carrier delivering mail. A hooded man stood in the back of the truck and tossed bags of ready-to-eat food over the fence to a designated drop spot in each camp.

"Finally!" Ozzie softly whispered to his mother as the truck pulled up to its last stop. "I'm starving!"

Ozzie crouched behind his mother as she, too, hunkered down in the buckeye and privet understory, fifty yards from the drop zone. The truck cut its engine. Two men got out and walked to the rear. A third man in the back of the truck jumped the tailgate and landed in a mud puddle. The men surveyed the camp. Their eyes met Eduardo's.

"That's the one," one of the men said very softly, the left half of his cheek ballooned out by a wad of chewing tobacco. "That big ole black sumbitch." He spit a stream of tobacco juice in the puddle and wiped his lip.

They approached the thick steel gate, unlocked it, and walked inside a six by eight foot caged entrance they used for unloading newbies. They opened another gate that took them into Ozzie's camp, placed the food ration in the drop zone, and motioned for Eduardo to come inspect it.

Eduardo had learned the hard way to do what the men asked. Hoping, praying that he if gave no trouble, no resistance, then maybe they'd leave his family alone. As he walked, he started to glance in Isabella's direction and then thought better of it, not wanting to draw attention to her in case the men hadn't seen her in the bushes. He ambled the twenty yards to the men and stared at the pouches as they opened them, feeling relief to see no surprises. Just the same flavorless, ready-to-eat meal as every other day.

The men turned away and Eduardo looked once more toward Isabella, catching her eyes and offering a reassuring, loving gaze. As he did, a thunderous boom echoed throughout the forest that prompted every living thing to cringe. Blood spewed from Eduardo's mouth as his world plunged into total darkness. His eyes fixed on Isabella and Ozzie as his body crashed to the ground.

Isabella's eyes grew wide, full of shock and fear as her heart hammered into her chest. Ozzie stood paralyzed, not feeling the warm urine seeping down his legs. Eduardo lay in the mud, blood oozing from the back of his head where the bullet penetrated, convulsing and gasping on the ground as life left him, choosing for him this remote, desolate prison in which to die. There would be no sympathy cards, no flowers, no mourners. His death would go unnoticed. He would never be free, never see his homeland again.

Adrenaline thrust Isabella from the privet as if hurled from a trebuchet, flailing wildly toward Eduardo. The forest echoed with her shrieking screams as the sound of the gunshot still rang in the ears of all prisoners. Their camps grew alive with consternation and alarm.

The men anticipated the reaction and were ready for Isabella. She ran straight toward Eduardo, seeing him and only him, her one and only love, as if he were the light at the far end of a tunnel. He was all she could think of as she momentarily forgot about the three men, forgot about Ozzie and Felipe. She was crazed with disbelief, with hate and anger, driven to save her soul mate, to be with him once more. As she drew within feet of Eduardo, two men swooped in from the bushes to her left and shoved her hard in the direction of the gate. Knocked off course, she veered to the right and staggered to the gate entrance, hitting the ground nose first. Disoriented and now hurt, she tried to get up, but the men rushed up behind and pushed her into the caged vestibule that was no man's land between captor and captive, freedom and confinement.

Isabella screamed violently as they locked the door. She rammed the fence like a crazed lunatic bouncing off a padded cell room wall. She screamed piercing cries as only a frantic mother can.

Then, she stopped as suddenly as she began and grew hauntingly silent. She stood and helplessly stared through the cage into Eduardo's lifeless eyes, only then realizing what she had done. She had left Felipe and Ozzie alone with the killers.

Chapter 2

Blake Savage loved to do "the worm". And on the first Saturday of September, Blake Savage did "the worm" all the way from Sky Valley to Mountain City as he drove his black 2010 Harley Davidson edition F-150.

Ever since he had been a child, Blake had liked to pretend his hand was an airplane wing when he held it out the car window and let the moving air hit it. As he drove south, Blake rested his left elbow on the open window frame and pointed his hand forward as he kept the palm of his hand parallel to the blurry pavement. He slanted his fingers down, allowing the relative wind to hit the back of his hand and force the worm to dive, he imagined, before raising his fingers and letting the worm rise as the air blasted against the palm of his hand. A kid on the side of the road pointed and laughed as Blake rode by with his arm moving up and down like a flying serpent. Up and down, up and down, Blake's worm inched southbound on Route 441.

Blake put his hand back on the wheel as he banged a right on Wolf Fork Road at the sign that read *Black Rock Farm - Pastured Poultry and Grassfed Beef.* Wolf Fork Road divided the mountainous terrain of Black Rock to his left from the fertile valley farmland to his right. Acres of corn stood ready for the harvest, and Blake found himself wondering how the farmers would go about harvesting the endless sea of corn. *Too much to do by hand*, he figured, as he bit off a third of the McChicken sandwich he had just bought for a buck. He put the uneaten portion on the console and stared at the neat rows of corn and pondered. *Probably a combine or a bush hog*, he said to himself, *or something like that.* Growing up, Blake had been interested in only one thing, and it wasn't farming.

Past the cornfield was another type of farm. Ten large houses lay side by side, each much longer than a football field. About a dozen ventilation fans larger than Blake's truck were stuck on each house. Blake scouted the farm as he slowed his truck, but didn't see a single person or animal, just a hauling truck that was fully loaded with crates of chickens. It looked as if it was ready to pull out. Blake read the sign at the entrance:

McReek Poultry Farms

For Bio-Security Reasons

NO UNAUTHORIZED VISITORS

Blake drove for another half mile until he reached the home of Gus Wyatt, owner of Black Rock Farm. The F-150 pulled onto the gravel drive and Blake parked next to a metal building. He got out and didn't see anyone right away, but announcers loudly calling the Bulldogs game on the radio suggested that Gus was probably close by. In the field next to the house, Blake saw what looked like a flock of wild turkeys. Some were perched on a line of large, wooden cages that were neatly lined across the field. He walked over and was shocked that the turkeys not only didn't flee, they came right up to him. Bending over, Blake peered into the cages and began counting the number of plump white chickens that were crammed inside one. Forty-seven, forty-eight, forty—

"Blake!" Blake nearly jumped out of his skin. He turned and saw a man standing tall and leering over him, covered in blood and holding a knife. Blake exhaled deeply.

"Hey, Gus," Blake said. "I was just looking at these chickens and wild turkeys."

Gus laughed. "Those aren't wild turkeys, Blake. We raise them for folks to eat on Thanksgiving. They're called Heritage Turkeys."

Blake eyed one of the turkeys and thought that it looked like a prehistoric creature. "Hey, I got another load of bones in the back of the truck for you to grind for me," he said.

"Let's take a look," Gus said. They walked over to Blake's truck. Blake pulled a tarp back to reveal a truck bed almost overflowing with bones.

"Well," Gus began, "the grinder is already hooked up to the back of the tractor. Seeing as you're parked beside it, just throw the bones in the top of the grinder and I'll grind them into your bone meal after we finish killing chickens over here."

Blake climbed into the back of the truck and began tossing the bones into the grinder. The radio blared loudly from the shed as announcers discussed a player injury.

"You been listening to the game in Athens, Blake? Dawgs and the Gamecocks?"

"No. Been running around doing errands."

"Well, that Georgia quarterback got hurt pretty bad a second ago. Took him out on a stretcher."

Blake felt his tension rise. He shrugged at Gus and kept tossing bones.

"Yeah well—hell, he ain't half the quarterback you were, Blake. Couldn't carry your spit bucket if you ask me." Gus began walking over to a large walk-in freezer and looked back over his shoulder to Blake. "I'll get the coolers of chicken and beef ready for you to take to The Federal."

Blake clenched his jaw and looked down at the blood-stained bones. Grabbing a femur, he threw it as hard as he could into the grinder. The force of the impact shattered pieces of smaller bones.

Gus wheeled a couple of large coolers over as Blake jumped out of the truck bed.

"Let's just put those in the back seat to keep 'em clean," Blake said.

"Good thinking," Gus said. Blake hoisted the coolers into the back seat of the truck, closed the door, and hopped in the front.

"I gotta hit the road, Gus. Told Nick I'd be in Athens by 3:30 or 4:00." Blake hesitated a second. "Let me know when you need me to do any more deliveries for you." Blake put it in reverse and began to back up.

"Sure thing, Blake. I expect in a couple of weeks."

As Blake began to drive slowly forward Gus shouted, "Say, when you and that pretty wife of yours gonna have some young'uns?"

Blake looked back and shrugged his shoulders. He rolled up the window, gripped the steering wheel, and twisted his hands, as if he were trying to wring it out. He was in no mood to do "the worm." Instead, he ground his teeth side to side.

As he pulled out of Black Rock Farm and onto Wolf Fork Road, the truck hauling chickens cut in front of him and began shifting gears. A foul smell slapped Blake's nostrils open: a mixture of feces, feathers, ammonia and bedding. The heavy odor wafted forcefully into the truck as Blake rolled the windows up. As the windows closed, he grimaced and tried to decide if he had locked the smell in the truck. He rolled the windows back down, and his nostrils were pummeled once again with stench.

"Goddamit," he exclaimed. As he fought through the vile smell, his mind drifted to the things Gus had said. Innocent remarks and questions that induced a rage to stew and burn within. "It's none of his damned business if we're gonna have kids or not!" Blake fumed. But it wasn't the question about a baby that infuriated him. He just couldn't escape the reminders about football, about the fame and fortune of the NFL that was almost his. *Should have been mine!*

Blake gripped the wheel tightly as he stared at the dispirited birds packed tightly in the cages on the truck in front of him. The chickens lay placidly, either unable or unmotivated to move. The truck rounded a sharp corner allowing Blake to see the McReek Trucking logo on the side. As the truck picked up speed, one of the birds was thrown out and landed in the middle of the pavement with a splat. It tasted freedom for the first time and looked around with bewilderment.

Furrowing his eyebrows at the chicken, Blake swerved his truck. He lined the chicken up with his front left tire the way he often took aim at a discarded soda can. He stepped on the gas and ran straight over the hapless chicken, first with his front tire and then with his rear as his truck bounced down the road.

"Stupid chicken," Blake said, still fuming.

He glanced at the rearview mirror to see the bird's flattened carcass centered in the road, and cocked his head in surprise as a raven landed swiftly and hopped to stake its claim. Blake turned south on 441 and finished off his uneaten McChicken sandwich as he headed toward Athens.

Chapter 3

Angelica Savage marveled at the delicate silk teepee in the forks of Nancy's fig tree. Every spring the tent caterpillars emerged, just as sure as the daffodils and yellow bells, and every winter they left behind egg masses to overwinter. And each winter she failed to remove the masses, thus allowing them to hatch the following spring. She had no desire to harm them or anything else, for that matter, but she couldn't let them damage Nancy's Tree.

Smiling at nature's dew-covered masterpiece, she indulged in a moment of peace as she closed her eyes and thought about Nancy. There were no distractions in the sanctuary that Angelica had created, a secret garden in a forest clearing. The only access was a winding path from the house she and Blake had bought 300 yards away that was set well back off of Hale Ridge Road. She still couldn't believe how lucky they had been to get this piece of land three years earlier, twelve acres for themselves surrounded by almost 100,000 acres of federal land, mostly densely wooded terrain up and around Rabun Bald. *Might as well say it's all ours*, Angelica reasoned. It was far too much land for her to contemplate and she desperately needed a smaller place for herself, something akin to a pastoral altar. So she had painstakingly cleared the path by hand once she stumbled on the brookside clearing, just after Nancy...

"Oh Nancy," Angelica sighed. Her shoulders collapsed, like a brick set on top of a house of cards.

Angelica bent down with the grace befitting her name, picked up a small stick, and gently brushed aside the silky mass. Very tenderly, she placed each caterpillar in a cup. She stared

into the cup realizing, at least for the moment, that she was
their God, in control of their fate. She was their captor, they
were her prisoners. What must they think, having been abruptly
confined to something as unnatural as a cup, looking up at
Angelica's raven colored hair and eyes as green as the forest
moss? Maybe they thought she was an angel; perhaps one or two
worried that she was an evil monster with glowing, green eyes.

With her long, slender fingers, Angelica reached in and
picked out a chosen one for inspection. "Hello, little one," she
whispered before gently scolding the creature. "Now you and
your friends have to stay away from that tree, okay?" And the
little fellow was returned to the cup, eager to share the word of
his God. Angelica walked to the far side of the garden and softly
poured the contents on the ground underneath a mountain
laurel. "There you go," she said, before strolling back to Nancy's
Tree.

It had taken over a year for Angelica to be able to stand at
the tree without bursting into tears, hating herself, feeling
hopeless, helpless, and searching for understanding. Even
questioning God. But two years had now passed since she alone
had buried tiny little Nancy here. Now, finally, she had reason
to be hopeful again. Still, the memory of the miscarriage
haunted her. Twelve weeks, she had that time with Nancy
before the bleeding began. That fact alone was enough to strike
fear into any young woman's heart. Then the cramps arrived
and prompted a panicked trip to the doctor. Angelica feared the
worst all the way.

Why is it, she thought, *that anytime someone wants
something...needs something as badly as I wanted and needed that
baby, they can't enjoy the journey? Instead, they have to live in a
state of fear that they will be denied, that somehow they're not
worthy.*

The ultrasound lived up to her fears, revealing no heartbeat
and showing a fetus about the size of a nine-week old, meaning
that the fetus, Nancy, had probably died a few weeks earlier. It

was that realization more than any other that haunted Angelica; that Nancy had died, and Angelica, her own mother, didn't know and didn't do anything to save her baby. The emotional toll was almost unbearable. Angelica had never felt such a stew of emotions. The self-blame, the grief and the guilt were overwhelming. Sorrow penetrated every cell of her being, for her alone to digest.

She had no choice in the matter, she had to cope with the loss, but the worst feeling was how incomplete she felt. She had failed to do the one and only thing that nature asked of her: successfully reproduce. That realization, piled atop the remorse and the physical and emotional trauma, was overpowering. And then, Angelica did the hardest thing she'd ever had to do. She went home to have her miscarriage. Alone. She added the feelings of isolation and loneliness to her stew of haunting emotions.

The doctor had offered her something for the pain that he assured her would come. Something called DI-GESIC. Angelica refused. She didn't want to hide from the pain. She wanted to feel the pain, to not hide from the suffering.

She would regret that choice.

At first it was like a bad period. Just some spotting blood and a few minor chunks of tissue resembling torn bits and pieces of chicken liver. Was that all there was to it? All there was of Nancy? A few chunks of bloody tissue? Angelica didn't know what she was looking at, what to look for. How large could it be? Hadn't the doctor said the fetus starts shrinking immediately after death?

Death. The word slowly reverberated in Angelica's mind, admonishing her, denying her, haunting her. D-E-A-T-H. She just couldn't get her mind around the surreal nightmare she was living.

When she awoke the next day there was no bleeding, a sign that Angelica took that the event was over. She remembered everything about that day and remembered nothing about that day, as if she stood outside a snow globe of misery. She saw herself on the inside, curled up on the sofa, then standing over Nancy's crib twirling a mobile, singing softly to a baby that wasn't there. She did all these things, remembered them all, and remembered none.

The cycle began anew on day three with more bleeding and cramps, stronger than on the first day, but tolerable. The modest pain brought Angelica back to the moment, to the reality of her loss. But there had been no loss yet, she told herself.

Nancy is still inside me, isn't she? Maybe the doctor was wrong! Maybe Nancy is fine, just quiet!

From her deerskin pouch, Angelica removed a small, six-sided divining crystal that her grandmother had taught her to use. She prayed for insight and healing the way her Cherokee ancestors had. The fact that there were no symptoms on day four stoked Angelica's confidence, giving her false hope.

On day five, she lamented turning down the painkillers as it felt like (she assumed) she was in labor. She staggered to the medicine cabinet, desperately grabbing for something, anything. She fumbled with the childproof lock on an Ibuprofen bottle and emptied four tablets into her palm, but it was too late for it to help. Angelica fell to the cold hard bathroom floor, and for ninety minutes endured constant pain. No cycle of contraction and relief; only contraction. No one with her to help her, to comfort her, to tell her it would all be all right. She prayed that God was with her, but if he was, why had he allowed this to happen in the first place?

And suddenly it happened.

An explosive discharge as Angelica struggled to her feet to get to the toilet, instinct driving her there. With blood dripping out of her, she finally passed the large chunk she had feared. As she did, the pain subsided just enough for her to catch her breath and wipe the sweat from her forehead. She burst into tears, uncontrollable sobbing, needing to see what had just dropped out of her, but afraid to look. If it was Nancy, if she really WAS dead, then it was over. *It can't be over...it can't be*, Angelica had thought. She buried her head in her hands and allowed herself to cry for several moments before doing what she had to do for her daughter. Finally, she rose, turned around and tried to compose herself. Trembling, she overcame the fear and allowed her eyes to drop.

And there it was. An umbilical cord, clearly visible, wrapped around a thick, translucent sac. Inside the sac was Nancy. Tiny, precious, oh so precious, little Nancy, only an inch long. The doctor had told Angelica it was too early to determine the gender, but Angelica knew. It was a girl, and she had named her after Nancy Ward, one of the most respected of all Cherokee women. Now she would have to bury her, having never spoken to her. Having never kissed her. Having never nursed her.

Angelica burst out crying again, screaming hysterically and pounding her fists against the wall before sliding down in the corner of the bathroom. She wrapped her arms around her knees and wept loudly for no one to hear, immersed in her suffering.

At first she had no idea what to do with Nancy's remains. How could she know? She carefully gathered them, placed them in a Ziploc bag and put them in the freezer until she could sort it out. This had infuriated her husband Blake when he called home from an overnight hauling job to Savannah. *One that just couldn't wait*, Angelica thought, *leaving me to carry this burden alone.*

She said nothing more to Blake about it. Instead, she simply went to the hollow, empty nursery, sat down in the rocker and began to sew a tiny cloth bag from a yard of printed fabric she had purchased in Clayton. The fabric was intended to become Nancy's first Easter dress. Instead, Angelica would place Nancy in the bag, bury her and plant a fig tree to remember her. A tree that Angelica would nurture and protect from the grip of winter with a blanket so that it would flourish and have the life that Nancy was denied.

Family, friends, everyone offered sympathy. They were so sorry for her loss. They said they knew what she must be going through. They really said that! And then everyone said the thing that troubled her most of all. The thing they all are trained to say from the time they begin Sunday school, the thing that she too had believed all her life but in that moment, had begun to doubt.

"God has a plan." Or, "God works in mysterious ways." Those were the two empirical statements that her Baptist brethren would close with, saving them as trump cards in troubling times when no other words could console, explain or comfort. God has a plan. Yep, conversation over. Can't question that one...God has a plan.

"*What plan?*" Angelica recalled screaming at the time. "*WHAT PLAN?*"

Angelica was as much a believer as anyone, rarely missing a Sunday in the Sandy Creek Baptist Church off Warwoman Road. She was baptized there when she was a child for goodness sake! Reading the scripture, believing the scripture, consoling others in times of grief, hugging them and whispering comforting thoughts like, "He's in a better place" or "God has a plan." Oh, how she regretted saying that now. Did that really comfort anyone? God answers your prayer, gives you the gift of life within you, a baby, a child, and then rescinds the offer once you've bonded? Why? So you can pass some ridiculous test that He has for you? Angelica began to stew, partly at the maddening thoughts that ran through her mind, but mainly for allowing herself to remotely question God. At the time of the miscarriage, those emotions threatened to overwhelm her if she gave them the slightest opening. But she was spiritual, a believer in God and, at heart, eternally hopeful. No, she refused to question God's will.

Two years had now passed, and she came here to tell Nancy that she was five-months pregnant and that a brother was on the way. *Oh God, please let it be true*, she prayed silently, as she knelt to work a new raised garden bed she had built a few feet from Nancy's Tree. Angelica plowed her hands into the rich black soil that she had been nurturing since spring with grass clippings and last winter's leaf cover. She let the soil sift through her fingers, approving of its tilth as she reached for a bag of bone meal, holding it in her lap so that she could see the label. "Black Rock Organic Bone Meal," she mouthed softly. *One perk from Blake's work*, she thought; free, organic bone meal. Pulling the string, she opened the bag and closed her eyes as she worked it into the soil with her bare hands. She rocked her head from side to side in the gentle breeze, relishing the opportunity to nurture and care for the soil.

"There we go, Nancy, all done," Angelica whispered. "I'll have asparagus planted in here before the end of the September, well before the first frost." Angelica rose from the raised bed and looked over her secret garden, a place of peace, love, hope and solitude for her, but it was solitude that she didn't want. Blake had never even stepped into the garden and wanted no part of it once she told him of her plans for Nancy. He kept his distance from her secret garden and increasingly, from her.

She didn't know what he was going through or why, but it was obvious that Blake was changing. Every day he seemed a little more distant, a little angrier. At what, she wasn't quite sure. They had been married for eight years, and like many marriages, the first year was the best, when Blake was so grateful for the love and support Angelica provided just after his injury and car accident.

One blessing from the accident, if you could call it that, was that the settlement from the accident helped them to pay cash for their home and to start married life without debt. Blake stayed home recovering from his injuries and unable to work dependably for three years. Once he was able to work, he was forced to find something that didn't require him to exert himself. Even sitting more than a few hours in one position became excruciating for him so he spent another few years just doing odd jobs. As time went on, he became more anxious about what his identity would be.

Then, God had shown the way, Angelica believed, when a local winery on Lake Burton with struggling sales asked Blake to use his football 'name' to market and deliver their wine to restaurants in Athens, Savannah, and even Atlanta. Blake did have some connections, mainly with restaurant owners in Athens, and figured he could use them to start a small business. He contacted other wineries and farmers in the area and began selling to restaurants for a fifteen percent commission on all sales. The restaurants were happy, as were the wineries and farmers, but Blake wasn't.

"Chump change," he told Angelica. "This ain't money."

"We don't need much money, "Angelica told him. "The house and land are paid off, and I can grow and preserve most of the food we need. "

"What about money for vacations?" Blake responded. "Health care? Savings? Did you think of that?"

"We'll be saving money, sweetie," Angelica replied softly. "I can make a lot of the other household items we need. Soaps, shampoos, lard, medicines. My grandmother taught me how to do all of that. We can live a simple life and raise a family, the way our Cherokee ancestors did for generations."

"Hmm," Blake snorted. "Yeah, well, look where that got them."

Angelica longed for nothing more than her husband and a child to hold and care for, to share her life with. She had dreamed that now she would finally be blessed with the child and that it would bring Blake back to her, but he seemed to want more.

"We need some real money, Angelica. I ain't gonna be running through the woods with a spear chasing deer! Maybe we won't be rich, but we can't live on nothing neither. And so far that's what I'm making on these deliveries. Nothing."

Blake thought the deliveries were beneath him at first, Angelica recalled, but after the first month that changed. Something inspired him. He became so enthused, even ecstatic. It was right after he began selling to Nick Vegas at The Federal. Angelica thought it must have made Blake feel important selling to such a celebrity. She liked that; she wanted her man to feel important. But lately his enthusiasm had turned into stress. As Angelica watched Blake struggle with his identity, she felt that she had to give him some space. Her father had been a devout Baptist, and Angelica remembered the lessons from the book of Timothy concerning the role of man and woman in the household. Timothy 2:12 said, *I do not permit a woman to teach or to exercise authority over a man; rather, she is to remain quiet.*

Angelica knew how to be patient. She could be quiet. She knew that when the baby came, Blake would come back and be the husband she needed. The father that her baby needed. As Angelica stepped away from the raised bed, she felt a tiny kick in her left side, burst a huge smile, and began back down to the trail to the house.

Chapter 4

As the shot that killed his father rang through the forest, Ozzie's first thought was that the truck had backfired. But the truck wasn't moving or even running, and the men stood over his father who lay motionless on the ground. Paralyzed by fear, his entire body trembled as even his eyes were too afraid to blink. He stared through the dense brush at his father, saying to himself, *Get up dad. Get up!*

Ozzie flicked his eyes to Isabella, held captive in a caged area where she was forced to look at Eduardo and watch the men. Being careful not to look in Ozzie's direction, she fixed her eyes on Felipe, who had been startled awake by the ruckus and stood in his shack. Eduardo's bloody body lay in the mud between him and Isabella. With Isabella restrained, the men walked cautiously over to Eduardo.

"Make sure he's good and dead," the tallest one, Jesse, said to another young man wearing a Bass Pro Shop camo cap. "You know how them troublemakers in those horror movies always look like they're dead but they ain't. So go on now, and make sure!"

Shane removed his Bass Pro Shop cap and wiped his brow. He returned the cap to his head and walked to Eduardo, leaned in close, and placed the end of the rifle barrel to his back. He shoved the tip into him, poking him in several spots and stopped when he was satisfied that Eduardo wasn't a horror flick Houdini. Shane tried to hide his sigh of relief as he stepped back.

"This un's deader than a deep fried turkey," Shane pronounced. "Now what?"

Jesse looked at Isabella, seeing the fear in her eyes, but she was of no concern at the moment. She waited helplessly to see what would happen next, praying that the worst was over. *What could be worse than what happened to Eduardo?* She wondered.

"Well," Jesse said in a language that neither Isabella, Felipe, nor Ozzie could understand, "Let's just haul his ass out of here." Shane and the other fellow, Terry, each grabbed two of Eduardo's limbs and strained to lift him, while Jesse returned Isabella to her quarters at gunpoint before tossing his phone in the truck.

"Good God, he's heavy!" Terry said.

A tumultuous crash from behind startled them. Shane dropped Eduardo's deadweight against Isabella's cage, causing Terry to lose his grip. Eduardo's eyes were still open, his face pressed against the cage inches from Isabella as his body splayed prone in the mud.

"Shit!" Jesse exclaimed as he turned and saw Felipe barreling at the three of them, his eyes deranged and his intentions clear. Felipe's momentum slammed his body into Terry and pummeled him into the ground. Wild with uncontrollable rage, Felipe tore into Terry with all he had, looking to inflict pain on his taller adversary. Jesse and Shane, momentarily shell-shocked, stood by dumbfounded. Jesse came to his senses, ran and grabbed a 2x4 leaning against the shack, and slammed Felipe in the head, but not before he had bitten half of Terry's ear off.

"OH GOD!" Terry exclaimed, realizing at once that he could only fully hear his scream from one ear. "Jesus Fucking Christ, what happened? What the fuck happened to my ear?"

Jesse leaned down to look at Terry's ear. "Holy crap," he said, as he wiped the blood from Terry's ear on his jacket sleeve. "Looks like Mike Tyson done got a hold of you!"

Felipe rolled on the ground, dazed and moaning. Terry moved his bloody hand around the right side of his head and felt his ear in disbelief. "He bit my right ear off. Damn it, kill that sumbitch too!"

"NO!" Jesse barked. "Blake said what we're here to do. He wants that big un killed and that's it. For now."

"But he bit my ear off!"

Jesse thought for a moment. "Well...I s'pose we ought to learn him some manners then."

Felipe was helpless and barely on the verge of consciousness as Shane and Jesse rolled him face up. Jesse straddled him and looked at Terry while Shane helped hold Felipe in check. "Hand me your Bowie knife," Jesse said to Terry.

Terry had one hand to his ear, covered in blood. Ashamed of how much squealing he had done, he calmed himself enough to hand his knife to Jesse, who took the knife, flipped it upside down and held it in a hammer grip with the steely tip facing down. Without hesitation, Jesse put the tip of the knife on Felipe's forehead immediately over his left eye and drew a diagonal slit to the underside of his right eye. Felipe screamed in agony and tried to bolt upright.

"Hold him," Jesse commanded to Shane before returning his attention to Felipe. "I ain't done with you yet, boy." He then put the knife above the right eye and drew a diagonal slit to the underside of the left eye, forming a gruesome, bloody X right between Felipe's eyes. Blood spurted out onto Jesse's hands and blue jacket.

"Let that be a reminder to you, you black sumbitch. You tussle with any of us again I'll put a bullet right there," Jesse said as he touched the tip of the knife to the wound's intersection between Felipe's eyes. Felipe panted, his eyes were wide with fear. He was terrified to keep them open but even more afraid to close them. Isabella paced with disbelief inside the cage, not knowing what to do. Eduardo's dead eyes staring at her from her feet, Felipe beaten, screaming and tortured and poor Oz...

No! Isabella thought to herself as she saw Ozzie move. Panic had spurred him out of hiding, now standing out in the open fifty yards away, looking straight at the captors. *Please Ozzie, PLEASE, don't move!*

Ozzie looked around and shuffled his feet clumsily the way someone would do with two left feet. He was unsure of what was happening or what he should do. *The Monsters*, Ozzie thought. *They ARE monsters! They're trying to eat us just like they said they would!*

Isabella shrieked as loud as she could and rammed the cage violently, doing anything to get the men's attention off of Ozzie. Her maternal force knocked some of the fence clips off and partially dislodged the top of the cage. Jesse got to his feet, grabbed his 2 x 4, walloped the side of the cage, and drove Isabella back. Ozzie couldn't stand his mother being attacked, so he charged forward ten yards before fear stopped him cold.

With the shock of the bite subsided somewhat Terry said, "Looks like the little 'un wants some too. I'll teach him a lesson myself."

"We ain't got no time for that," Jesse shouted, but Terry was already off. Jesse let it go, figuring Terry had probably earned a little revenge of his own. Terry ran straight at Ozzie, screaming and wailing and trying to terrify him. It worked.

Terrified, Ozzie turned and bolted, running only fifteen yards back before he came to the corner of a tightly strung electric fence that was higher than he could ever jump. Ozzie turned right and sprinted along the back fence. Terry gave chase and stayed close, but Ozzie was fast. By now it had become entertaining for Jesse and Shane, who ran along just to see what happened. Ozzie concentrated on fleeing and not on where he was running. It wasn't until the last few yards that Ozzie realized the danger he had put himself in. He skidded to a stop mere feet before the rear corner and looked back to see Terry closing fast. Jesse and Shane moved in, on each side of Terry, to block Ozzie's path, forming a horseshoe in front of Ozzie with the fenced corner immediately behind him.

"Ha, ha, ha...got yourself in a pickle, don't cha?" Terry's mood had improved considerably. He eyed Ozzie as he slowly reached for his Bowie knife, taking a step closer in unison with

Jesse and Shane as if they were tethered. Terry moved within six
feet of Ozzie and waved the knife at him. Ozzie blinked and
had something of a flashback when he saw the knife.

Terry's patience expired. He stretched out like a baseball
player diving head first into second base as he dove for Ozzie.
Ozzie backed up until he was inches from the fence. Terry
grabbed a leg and tried to hold on tight, but Ozzie squirmed
from his grip and jumped two feet away. Terry got back to his
feet, held the knife in his right hand and swiped it at Ozzie.

Ozzie stared at Terry's hands, shuffled his feet and waited.
Terry faked a swing of the knife and, instead, reached with his
left hand to grab Ozzie by his head to pull him down. Ozzie
panicked and reacted like a frightened dog, snapping and biting
until he crunched through two of Terry's fingers on his left
hand, drawing a mouthful of blood. The knife fell from Terry's
hand to the ground and he stood straight up, screaming in
agonizing pain.

With both sides blocked, Ozzie saw an opening to dive right
between Terry's legs and started for it. Jesse read Ozzie's
intentions and sprinted toward the same spot, hoping to block
Ozzie's exit, but he tripped on a root just before he dove.
Instead of diving, he stumbled for a couple of steps before
crashing into Terry's knees, his arms tackling Terry as they
draped around him for support. Terry was thrown forward and
fell right onto the second wire of the high-voltage fence, his
weight pressing it to the ground.

Later, Ozzie would try unsuccessfully to recollect what
happened in the next eight seconds. The last thing he would be
able to recall was being trapped in the corner paralyzed by fear.
What Ozzie couldn't remember was that, for a brief instant,
Terry's body created a three-foot high opening in the fence. The
sound of the fence shocking Terry like a Louisiana mosquito
zapper added to Ozzie's terror and thrust his body into motion.
As if guided by a mysterious force (probably raw fear), Ozzie
jumped and landed squarely on Terry's back as he lay across the

fence and vaulted onto the other side, rolling in the leaves as he landed.

Shane sprinted to Terry's aid, grabbing his feet and yanking him off the fence and taking a strong shock in the process.

"JESUS!" Shane shouted as he tried to shake the pain out of his hands.

Terry rolled on the ground in excruciating pain, semi-conscious with a large part of an ear missing, two crushed and broken fingers and skin crawling with electricity. Jesse stood up just as Ozzie got to his feet on the other side. For a fleeting second, he and Ozzie regarded one another, confused, as each tried to get his bearings. The perspective was as it should be, a fence separating captor and prisoner, but the roles were reversed. Ozzie scampered down the fence line back in the direction of his home, calling his mother. Jesse realized the gravity of the situation and the personal repercussions if Blake found out he was the one that let Ozzie get away.

"GODDAMIT!" Jesse shouted. "Shit, he's out!"

There was no way through the electric fence, so Jesse ran toward the entrance with Shane in close pursuit. He swung open the gate and forcefully kicked Isabella out to the ground. Shane added a kick for good measure for all the trouble her family had caused.

"Leave him alone!" Isabella screamed in the language of her Spanish ancestors as she grimaced with pain. She managed to get to her feet and hobble to the back of the fence where Ozzie stood on the other side. Jesse got to the shut off switch, slammed the handle down and watched the light go from red to green.

"RUN, Ozzie, just RUN!" Isabella instructed Ozzie.

"Mom, NO!" Ozzie replied. "NO! I want to stay with you!"

Ozzie and Isabella stood face-to-face, inches from one another, but unable to touch for the first time in their lives. In that moment, Isabella realized how *lucky* she had been to be imprisoned all this time with Ozzie. Now they endured the worst kind of imprisonment either had ever suffered, the pain of being so close but denied from being together. With the fence off, Jesse and Shane had made their way back in and were coming up behind Isabella. She pushed her own fears aside.

"Listen, Ozzie," Isabella continued. "We don't have much time. Just RUN. Get as far away from here as you can. As far away from these people as you can, and never turn back. They killed your father and they want to hurt you, Ozzie!" Ozzie had only a second to read the fear in his mother's eyes before Jesse's rapidly approaching head loomed over hers. He saw the pure evil, the vicious hatred in the black depths of his eyes. Isabella turned and ran back to Felipe, hoping both to comfort him and to free Ozzie by doing the most gut-wrenching thing she had ever done, turn her back on him.

Sprinting down the fence line, Ozzie searched for a way in, having no way of knowing that the fence had been turned off. He looked back to see that the men were now on his side of the fence and chasing him. Racing down the back line, he continued past his encampment and along the back side of adjacent paddocks. The commotion from Ozzie's paddock had brought everyone out. Faces that had been there all along, that Ozzie had rarely seen, watched him run freely in the woods with two men chasing and yelling.

Ozzie could find no way back in. He stopped at the top of the ring of encampments for an instant when he saw a prisoner with bright red hair. In his entire life, Ozzie had never seen such a thing. Everyone he had ever seen had black hair. Unaware that Ozzie was being pursued, red-headed Tammy approached her side of the fence to introduce herself as Ozzie stared into her chestnut brown eyes.

"There he is!" Jesse shouted. The scream broke Ozzie's gaze and he jerked his head around to see the men running his way. Realizing he couldn't get past the men to his mother, he turned his head and looked into the thick, unfamiliar brush and trees that covered a steep mountainside. He desperately wanted to be back safely *inside* the fence with Isabella, but fear propelled him in the opposite direction.

With nowhere left to run, he stormed away from his mother up a steep bank in the direction of Rabun Bald.

Chapter 5

Blake fumbled with the radio, trying to pick up a decent classic rock station as he drove south from Clayton through Tallulah Gorge. He stopped when the dial landed on 97.1 and the sound of "Hells Bells" filled the cab in his truck. Blake's mood improved instantly, as it always did when he heard AC/DC.

Devil's music my ass, Blake thought. Angus did an interview with "Hit Parader" magazine and said "he becomes possessed when he gets on stage," and the religious purists had taken that literally. "See? He admits being possessed," they claimed.

What a crock, Blake thought. *That's when church stopped making any sense to me when they said stupid shit like* "you can't listen to AC/DC or you can't listen to Led Zeppelin because Robert Plant said he couldn't remember penning the words to "Stairway to Heaven", so he must have been possessed." *Hell, let 'em have How Great Thou Art, I'll take Metallica!*

Blake just shook his head, laughed and thumped the steering wheel. *This is just what I need, good old rock and roll therapy*, he thought. *Got the next hour to myself with nothing but blue skies, puffy clouds chasing the cold front, and kick-ass tunes*. He rolled down his window, cranked up the volume, and let his hand ride the wind as Blake did "the worm" all the way to Athens.

***

At 3:54 p.m. Blake pulled into the parking lot at The Federal, Athens' most distinguished restaurant. The glass facade on the exterior contrasted sharply with the earthy brick construction of its surroundings. Athens was, after all, a college town and showcased little of the glassy glamour and glitz like those the architects pumped out hurriedly in Atlanta. *That's probably what attracted Nick Vegas to open his first restaurant in Athens*, Blake thought. *Say what you want about his ruthless tactics, he was a shrewd businessman. Had Nick opened The Federal in Atlanta, it would have been good, but just another good Atlanta restaurant, nothing special. Put the same place in Athens and you've got something folks in both Athens and Atlanta will talk about.* And that attention is what Nick wanted more than anything.

Black brushed metal trim framed the towering glass windows, each showcasing tightly-closed plantation shutters, creating a pronounced sense of privacy. This made the entrance appear quite vertical and served to draw the eyes up to the words "THE FEDERAL", emblazoned in gold lettering in a substantive font like an old, impenetrable bank.

There were already a dozen cars in the lot, mostly cooks and staff, Blake figured, getting ready for the Saturday night diners who had no doubt made reservations weeks before. *Damn it!...Don't call them cooks*, Blake admonished himself, remembering that, for some reason, they expect to be addressed as chef. *Makes about as much sense as calling the owners of a car repair shop Mechanic Fred and Mechanic Barney*, Blake thought.

Blake frowned as he pulled on a sport coat, making himself presentable. He looked down to make sure there was no mud, or worse, on his shoes. *Can't have that now!* Comfortable with his appearance, he strolled to the entrance, opened the door, and walked through the black metal vestibule.

Frank Sinatra was already crooning, adding to the ambiance of the 60's era, upscale steakhouse that Nick strove to honor with The Federal. The hostess station stood empty fifteen feet directly in front of him. It was backed by a smoked-glass privacy screen, trimmed in rich mahogany. Behind the screen sat twenty tables on a sunken floor, each with four chairs. On both sides of the sunken floor were eight horseshoe-shaped booths, each upholstered in luxurious, black leather. The booths connected to one another in a long scalloped line with the open end of each booth welcoming two upholstered chairs, providing a comfortable setting for six. Dominating the divider between each booth section was a black iron bull, a nod to Nick's Spanish heritage and his love of bull fighting. In classic Nick style, each bull was slightly different. Some were covered with lampshades, some served as candelabras, some just stared, fiercely. They had all been, of course, custom made.

"Excuse me. I'm here to see Nick Vegas," Blake said to a young girl as she walked by the hostess station.

"Oh," she said as she raised an eyebrow and took in his blazer, jeans and scruffy Skechers. "Is...he expecting you?"

Blake caught her disapproving evaluation. Of course, she had no idea who he was. She was, what...twenty-one? Twenty-two? Probably wasting time at UGA, moved here from some worm hole and now had a big chance to work for Nick Vegas. She had no idea that Blake had *owned* this town less than ten years ago. Could go anywhere and not have to pay for anything, including at The Federal, which is where he had met Nick in the first place. When Blake and the Georgia Bulldogs were undefeated, Nick invited him to the bar on Saturdays after the home games knowing full well the affluent hobnobbers would be drawn in. They were.

"Yes. He's expecting me. Just tell him that Blake is here to see him."

Blake looked to the left at the towering, fake palm tree that partially screened the hostess station from the serpent-shaped bar and thought how ironic it was to have a plastic tree in a restaurant that Nick spent two million dollars to construct. Nick brandished that figure back when Blake was part of the "in" crowd, when he was an attraction rather than the redneck hired hand he now was. *It should be me dining here, throwing down hundred dollar tips at the martini bar with Angelica on my arm*, Blake thought. Now, everything to do with the restaurant reminded Blake of what he had lost. What he aspired to reach but couldn't. The notoriety of Nick's fame, the wealth that Nick and his affluent customers exuded, being one of those "in the money" rather than being a servant, like Blake. He hated going there.

Just let it go.

As he meandered along the wall, Blake stared at the framed clippings that Nick displayed in each of his restaurants, headlines that wove a trail of success among anything Nick had touched. Nick no longer bothered with the hometown praise from the *Athens Banner Herald* that he was so proud of in the beginning. Even the *Atlanta Journal-Constitution* was relegated to a montage of headlines recapping Nick's accomplishments in the past decade. "Athens Chef Wins Coveted James Beard Award." "Vegas Takes Winning Recipe to Miami, D.C. and Boston." "Author and restaurateur Nick Vegas Signs On With The Cooking Network." All that praise was displayed humbly in a small frame. The large illuminated frame, like a showcased Monet, was reserved for the cover of "Forbes". It featured a smug picture of Nick in front of his expansive Buckhead home. At his feet sat the Spanish bulldog he brought with him from Spain when he moved to lay claim to his American dream. The caption read simply "America's Wealthiest Restaurateurs." That's what Nick wanted; for everyone to see not that he was successful and wealthy, but *how* successful and wealthy he was.

"Set...hut hut!" Nick called to Blake as he strolled across the parquet floor, as if he was calling a play from the line of scrimmage. "How's it going, Blake?"

Blake turned and saw Nick approaching, his whitened teeth beaming brightly and contrasting starkly with his perennial tan. He already had his right hand extended, both to shake Blake's hand and, Blake figured, to put his gold Rolex on full display. Blake didn't recognize the man walking with him. "Hey, Nick. It's going all right." Blake offered Nick a weak handshake.

"Blake, this is Wade Ferry. Wade's been working with me since day one."

Wade Ferry was a name that Blake had heard from Nick before. He was the "Ferry" in Ferry/Jenkins, the largest executive search firm in the United States until, several years back, Wade sold the company he had founded for about $220 million. Evidently he missed being part of the "action" so he had taken to angel investing in a few ventures, mainly software start-ups. Even so, Nick was by far his most successful investment. It was Wade who bankrolled the two million dollars to get The Federal going. It was Nick who got the recognition, the awards, and even the series on The Food Channel, but Wade had a stake in everything. All ten restaurants up the eastern seaboard, the TV series, Nick's books, even the olive farm that Nick started in south Georgia to create authentic, Spanish-style olive oil. And Wade had lots of high-level business and government contacts from his years in executive and board level placements.

"Nice to meet you, Mr. Ferry," Blake said, without meaning it.

Wade looked about Nick's age: thirty-eight, forty, somewhere in there. Blake knew he was rich. He had heard the stories, but evidently Wade didn't feel the need to showcase it the way Nick did. He was dressed smart casual; khakis, black leather shoes, and a golf sweater that said Augusta National.

"Shoot, it's a real pleasure to meet you, Blake," Wade said in a slow and very authentic Georgia drawl. The kind you didn't hear too much around Atlanta anymore since hordes of transplants had descended on the city. "And you call me Wade. Heck, my family has had season tickets between the hedges for sixty years. I never missed one of your games. It was a real shame son, that injury of yours. A flat out crying shame."

Blake started to say something, but Nick jumped in.

"I thought Blake was going to make it back from that. I really did," Nick said, patting Blake on the shoulder. "But...he moved on to bigger and better things...didn't you Blake?" Nick kept his hand firmly on Blake's shoulder.

"A real shame," Wade said shaking his head and sounding as if he actually meant it. Blake had heard this a thousand times from folks and never knew what to say. At least Wade didn't say—

"Well, God works in mysterious ways, son. I'm sure he's got a plan."

Blake wanted to tell Wade what he thought of God's plan so far but thought better of it. "Thanks. I reckon so."

Had he been the one with all that success, Blake figured he might have just kicked back and enjoyed it. But not Nick. He just pressed the accelerator and chased even more glory now that the restaurants were on autopilot for him. That's when he and Wade concocted the idea for 50-Forks that they were now pursuing at breakneck speed. Blake knew it must be big money, real big. Enough for Nick to have dangled a quarter million dollars in front of Blake to deliver what he wanted.

"Let's talk over here, Blake." Nick headed past the plastic palm and walked alongside the bar, its top curved in the shape of a question mark. Nick walked past the bar to a smoked glass table surrounded by three red velvet chairs and pulled out a chair for Blake. He took the seat. "I hope you don't mind Wade sitting with us," Nick began. "We're preparing for an investor meeting and he was just here with me."

"Fine by me," Blake said, realizing there was nothing else he could say.

"You know, the kickoff dinners for 50-Forks are in six weeks," Nick said as his smile vanished. "The Food Channel is all set to televise it here in Athens and I want everything perfect. Are you all set on your end?"

Blake glanced at Wade and then back to Nick. Nick leaned back in his chair with his legs crossed and arms wide open as if they were gracing the armrests. He couldn't have appeared more confident, more in control. "Yeah, I'm in good shape," Blake said. "I'll deliver everything you asked for the week of the dinners." Blake eyed Wade again.

"Excellent, but not just here in Athens," Nick said, leaning forward. "You have to ship to all ten of my chefs."

"Yeah, I know," Blake answered. "I'll get the shipping details from you the week before."

Nick tilted his neck left, then right, cracking it both ways.

"How are the mountain sheds holding up? Everything working right, just like I laid it out for you?" Nick's line of questioning continued.

"Yep, all three are fully loaded and working fine. Blended right into the mountainside like it has been for two years now. You'd probably walk right past them," Blake replied, allowing the most imperceptible of smiles to skirt across his lips.

Wade couldn't hide his enthusiasm. "Heck boys, just like making 'shine in the old days up in Dawsonville."

Nick chuckled and relaxed just a bit. "Hmm. You gotta get up and see this spread," Nick said to Wade. "How big's the spread, Blake?"

"Twelve acres," Blake answered.

"Twelve acres," Nick continued. "But behind that close to a hundred thousand acres of nothing, just woods. And I mean absolutely nothing, not a trail anywhere and all federally protected land. You have any idea how much land a hundred thousand forested acres is?" Nick let the question linger for effect.

"I mean, a whole village could get lost up there and no one would find it," he continued. "Cool, mountain air, dense, tangled forest up over 4,000 feet. Absolutely perfect."

Wade listened awestruck as if Nick were describing another planet. "Yeah, we'll have to get up there, Wade," Nick continued. "We can stay at my place on Lake Burton, take Blake and his wife out to one of Clayton's finest restaurants while we're there. How's Angelica doing, Blake?"

Blake didn't care for the small talk. He just wanted to find out what Nick wanted, and get out. He could answer the tactical questions, but the personal ones just reminded him of how much of his life Angelica didn't know about...couldn't know about, and walking that fine line had taken its toll on him. He'd let off steam later though, not in front of Nick.

"She's doing fine, thanks for asking." Blake continued gingerly, not knowing how much Wade knew. "You know...if you come up, Angelica doesn't know...I mean, she knows nothing about what we're doing up on the mountain. She only knows that—"

"You're delivering for me," Nick interrupted. "I have you on the payroll delivering wine and produce, I know. Did you bring the chicken and beef from Black Rock? I have it on the menu next week."

"Yeah," Blake said. "Just need one of your guys to unload the coolers from the truck."

"Sabrina," Nick yelled across the room to the woman who had greeted Blake. "Have a couple of fellas in the kitchen grab the coolers out of Blake's truck." As Sabrina acknowledged Nick's order, Wade's cell phone vibrated. He excused himself and walked to the other side of the bar.

Nick lowered his voice. "So, you're on the verge of your big pay day," he said. "Close to a quarter million bucks for what you've done. You'll be debt free and have money to play with, what you always wanted, right?"

Blake didn't realize how pursed his lips had become, how tightly his jaws had clinched. He hated all this secrecy! He should have never...God, if he could go back and do everything over. Maybe Angelica had been right. But he was so damned hungry for money, to get out of the projects, to give Angelica more than she wanted or needed that he jumped at what he *thought* was easy money.

"Is that all you wanted from me—just an update?" Blake asked as he glanced at his watch.

The smile on Nick's face dissolved. Nick leaned back, extended his arms toward Blake and interlocked his fingers to crack his knuckles. "I need to be absolutely positive that you'll be ready next month." Nick's brown eyes stared at Blake without blinking. "I've promised this, among other things, to 500 members who joined 50-Forks and paid seventy-five grand each to do so. I won't let them be disappointed."

"I am, and it is," Blake said, keeping his voice low as he raised his eyes from the table to meet Nick's. "We're ready to go, just like we agreed."

After a long twenty seconds, the smile returned to Nick's lips.

"Good, but let me know if you have any trouble up there. Anything."

Nick softened his tone and smiled peacefully at Blake. "You know, what you're doing is really important, Blake. Just as honorable as the work my father did back in Spain. Maybe even more so since you're the first one here in America. A lot of people wanted to follow in my father's footsteps, and I predict a lot will want to follow in yours once they see what you've accomplished!"

"Thanks," Blake said half-heartedly.

"We're in good shape then," Nick said as he stood, providing the cue that Blake was dismissed. They shook hands, Nick promised to visit, but Blake knew he'd never set foot on the mountain. Blake wanted to sprint out, to get away as fast as he could, but he momentarily suppressed his anger as he walked through the vestibule and out the front door. He stood at the door of his truck and fiddled with the keys. Blake looked back at The Federal and pulled his sunglasses out of his blazer pocket. He put them on, turned right on Washington street and walked with purpose to the closest pub.

Chapter 6

Ozzie sprinted straight up the slope and away from the only home he had ever known with nothing more than raw fear guiding him. There was no time to think and develop a plan as he sprinted, his breathing already becoming labored. Had he had time to think of a plan it would have been simply to get ahead of the men and circle back to his mother. *How did I get out in the first place?*

By now he had learned the sights, sounds, and smells of this forest almost as well as any of the wild animals that inhabited it, but only from inside the fence that had imprisoned (or had it protected?) him. As he ran, he thought about how often he had wanted to break free of those wires and pursue his own freedom, the same liberties enjoyed by his captors and even the wild animals that often approached the other side of the fence. He even saw black bears lumber close to his fence more than once during broad daylight, examining Ozzie as if he were a zoo exhibit, but they hadn't frightened him. The only thing in the forest that had done that, other than the farm truck, was the occasional cries he heard. Horrific cries of anguish and pain that seemed to come from within the mountain itself, something between a woman's most frightened scream and a tortured baby's cry. Always they ascended from the depths of a ravine, and only on the darkest of nights. They never failed to send chills down his spine. He even saw his father cringe when he heard the cry late at night.

Why had he wanted to get out of the fence in the first place? Now, he wanted only to be behind the blanket of the fence's protection. *Just keep running*, he told himself, *lose these stalkers and go back to mom.*

But still the men came as they pursued him through a dense thicket along a featureless hillside in the midst of the massive wilderness. "We're gaining on you," Jesse shouted as he pulled off his light blue jacket in the early afternoon heat, tossing it on the ground. "You're done for!"

"Yee haw," Shane screamed.

Ozzie didn't understand a word the English-speaking mountain men said, but he understood the threatening tone. He ran on the wet leaves for at least half mile along a ridge, both the hunters and the hunted slowing to a pace they could sustain.

Jesse judged Ozzie's pace and realized the chase wouldn't end as quickly as he had hoped, but he had no choice. If he didn't catch Ozzie and return him, Blake would have his head, putting an end to the $5,000 bonus Blake had promised him that he'd earn the next month. $5,000 cash, all at once. Jesse became intoxicated by the number, vaguely aware of his surroundings as he saw only Ozzie running before him with a $5,000 caption suspended over his head. Jesse narrowed his eyes on Ozzie like an archer zeroing in on his target. He thrust himself ahead.

Ozzie sprinted alongside a thick line of mountain laurel and, once past it, turned sharply left. This forced Jesse and Shane to run the whole way around it, too, so they couldn't cut him off. Gravity and fear pushed Ozzie faster than he had ever run before as the ground descended steeply. The expansive forest looked the same in all directions, like trying to discern one wave from another from a raft in the middle of the ocean. There were no landmarks, trails, or singularly distinguishing features. Just ancient trees that towered above and required Ozzie to fend for himself in a life or death race over very steep terrain.

There was no need to look back. The sound of snapping twigs and heavy footfalls constantly reminded Ozzie that *they* were coming for him. Yet, the sounds weren't getting closer. Ozzie hadn't stopped moving for over half an hour, but he had greatly slowed his pace. It was pure torture running those hills, and now that he had left the ridge the underbrush had thickened. Privet, buckeyes and brambles popped up and Ozzie had to run through all of them. Jesse and Shane had fallen behind and were even more exhausted than the younger Ozzie, but still they came. Jesse in particular was motivated, as the $5,000 price still hovered over Ozzie's head, albeit in a smaller font.

Ozzie felt a sharp pain in his ribs from running so far, so fast. His leg muscles tightened and burned from the inside out, as if his blood were a sea of boiling magma spreading through his veins, in search of a vent. His mouth was so dry that he wondered if his body would reject water the way a thunderstorm washes off a drought-stricken hardpan. Breathing heavily, he crested a hilltop that flattened out as oaks gave way to a narrow stand of towering pines. He sprinted through a broad thicket of brambles, hearing only his labored breathing as soft pine needles muffled his own steps.

In the distance, Ozzie found a landmark that drew him in like a tractor beam. In the midst of the pine cathedral a massive granite outcropping beckoned. Ozzie had never seen anything like it, and the sight of it gave him a sudden burst of endurance. As he closed in, he focused his eyes on a protrusion overhanging what appeared to be a small cave opening. *A hiding spot!* Ozzie looked back, seeing that the men had still not crested the hill and were out of sight. His heart sank as he reached the boulder and saw it wasn't a cave. There was no place to hide. But it was water, fresh mountain water, and that was almost as good as a cave. It would give him some time to catch his breath and drink. Maybe sixty seconds until they were on him, but then they would have to rest too. *Wouldn't they?*

Ozzie took a long drink, almost choking because he drank so much, so fast. He burped loudly, drank some more and then plopped in the spring, cooling his whole body. He had run so long, so far, and only then did he think that he had no idea where he was. He turned his head back to the brambles, eyes closed, hoping that would erase the monsters. He opened his eyes and saw that still they came, closer now, each holding his side and running with great difficulty. Ozzie bent down quickly to take another sip, one for the road.

POW!

An incredibly loud and thunderous boom erupted and ricocheted off the boulder, causing rock dust to sprinkle into the spring just before him. Ozzie turned and saw the men only sixty yards away, almost on him. One of them pointed the black rifle at Ozzie. The sound catapulted Ozzie as if he were launched out of a cannon. He circled to the back of the boulder and ran flat out, zigging then zagging, out of the pine clearing toward the next thicket.

POW!

Bark flew off a hemlock tree just to Ozzie's right.

"Watch it!" Jesse said to Shane. "You don't want to hit him!"

"I wasn't trying to, but what difference does it make at this point?" Shane asked. "We'll never get him back without shooting him and we can't let him get away." Jesse wanted to disagree, but Shane was right. He stood bent over his knees, panting, and tried to catch his breath. It felt like a needle was being shoved into his left side just below the ribcage.

POW!

Another shot rang through the forest for no one to hear but the three of them. Ozzie was nearly out of sight now in a rising thicket, but he didn't know that the men had momentarily stopped pursuit when the bullet swished over his head. The frightening sound brought forth the image of Ozzie's father lying in the mud, eyes open and staring at him. What was the last thing his father had said to him? *You're almost grown now.*

Act like it! Yes, that was it. And his mother's last words to him? *Run, Ozzie, just run!* Ozzie said to himself, *run!*

Ozzie crested a hill, terrified but relieved to be alive, a good 200 yards away from the boulder. For just a second, he stopped to glance back. Shane used the boulder to support his 30.06 rifle. He had been following Ozzie for fifty yards through his scope but couldn't get a shot off. When Ozzie stopped and looked back it allowed Shane to zero in. Shane tried to catch his breath and control his breathing, but there was no time for the perfect shot. He squeezed the trigger, absorbed the recoil and then aimed his scope back at Ozzie. He found his target just in time to see Ozzie fall to the ground.

"Got him," Shane panted to Jesse, who was on his knees now trying to catch his breath. Shane had run long distance track the year before as a senior at Rabun County High and he was still in decent shape, but Jesse was really hurting. "Just get your breath," Shane said. "He ain't going nowhere."

Shane laid the gun on the pine needles and eyed the spring. *A gift from above*, Shane thought, *just in the nick of time.* A little piece of paradise, no bigger than a bathtub under this gigantic boulder, giving life to lush, fragrant rhododendrons on each side of the water. As he knelt before the water and prepared to drink, Shane felt almost as if he were at a Sunday church service. In the infinite blackness of the still water, he saw the reflection of the ancient, weathered rock, giving him the feeling of kneeling at an altar with God looming above as an everlasting boulder of strength. Shane knelt at God's feet as a humble, grateful servant. He leaned forward and cupped his hands to collect His gracious gift in this Garden of Eden.

Before putting his hands in the water, Shane paused as he caught the reflection of wispy clouds streaming overhead against a deep blue sky. The moment was perfect. So quiet, so peaceful. And yet...he felt something else, something disquieting. *What is it?* He thought. *Like...maybe I'm being watched. Is God watching me from above?*

A trio of pinecones fell beside him as a raven launched from a branch and descended to perch atop the boulder. It folded its wings close to its side as it peered deep into Shane's eyes.

"Well, I'll be," Shane said. "Look at that, Jesse."

Jesse remained hunched over, catching his breath. Shane looked down at the reflection of the bird and put his hands back to the water, still feeling as if he was being watched. *Is it the raven?* He asked himself. No. It wasn't the raven, he realized as he looked up into the bird's black eyes. Nor was it something he sensed from above. It was...something closer, he felt. Something from the side. Shane shifted his eyes to his left at Jesse, who knelt with his eyes closed and sweat dripping from his face. Jesse wasn't watching him. The hair on the back of Shane's neck began to prickle as he felt the staring bore into him. Something from...his right side. Slithering eyes upon him.

In the dead quiet of the forest, he heard the slightest twitch of a rattle. He jerked his head quickly to his right, just in time to see a coiled timber rattlesnake that had chosen this oasis to give birth to her young. Shane's eyes had time to open wide, but his scream couldn't escape as the five-foot long rattler struck fast and hard, her fangs piercing the right carotid artery of Shane's neck. Eden's serpent hissed and recoiled to her newborn babies.

Shane stood, screaming, as he pressed his hands to his neck.

"JESUS! Rattler! I got bit!"

Jesse saw Shane jump back. Ejected from the spring as if hell had spit him out.

"What the hell happened?" Jesse shouted.

Shane hit the ground, his face already flush and feeling like someone dug into his neck with a red hot poker. Jesse pried Shane's bloody hands off his neck just enough to see the marks on Shane's swelling neck as if a vampire had repossessed his soul. Shane clamped down on the pain again.

"Shit!" Jesse exclaimed. "Holy shit!"

Shane was in complete agony as the toxin started its work, weakening and disorienting him. He couldn't have been bitten in a worse spot. Jesse helped him past the rhododendron on the left side of the spring and leaned him up against the boulder.

"Shit!" Jesse was in a panic. He knew he needed to get help but—*Where the hell are we? Shit!* Jesse almost began hyperventilating. He tried to calm himself, tried to be the leader that Blake had told him he was of his clan. *Think!* he told himself. *It was a timber rattler, but they're not usually deadly if you get help.*

Then another voice emerged inside his head, a voice less confident. A voice that frightened Jesse.

Ah, the voice said, *but look at where the bite is. Right in the artery. D-E-A-T-H will be quick,* the voice said in a raspy, haunting whisper.

"Shit!"

Jesse looked back at Shane, who no longer screamed. His neck had swollen to almost twice its normal size and was horribly bruised. Shane's hands draped by his side. Jesse's mind tugged him in all directions. *Go get help. Stay and help. Save yourself. Comfort Shane. Kill that snake!*

"Shit!" Jesse didn't know what to do. There was no way to extract the venom, no way, not from that spot on his neck. He could carry Shane to help, but they had been on the hunt for hours. It was so far back, and even if he could carry Shane that far, even if Shane could make it that long, he wondered if he could even find the way back? Jesse grabbed the rifle and went around the bushes to look for the snake. He found the mother coiled up with three babies that had yet to squirm away. Had yet to slay their first victims. Jesse trembled as he took sight of the now defenseless creature and blew a hole right through her.

"Die, you bitch!" Jesse screamed as the rattler fell limp.

Jesse rushed back toward Shane but tripped on an embedded object at the mouth of the spring. He fell at Shane's feet. "Goddamnit!" Jesse shouted, looking back to see the rusty metal he had dislodged. "What the hell?"

His mind briefly diverted from Shane's suffering to the dislodged obstruction. He scraped wet pine needles away and clawed with his fingertips, using one finger to outline a smooth metal surface. Jesse darted his eyes back and forth looking for a stick, as he feared that the forest floor might be alive, slithering. The mountain soughed as the wind whistled through the pines. Jesse's senses had never been so heightened. His trembling fingers picked up a stick. He used the tip to outline a metal shape that slowly became recognizable as he unearthed over a century's worth of humus to free the rusty relic.

"Son-of-a-bitch," he whispered. "An old double-barrel shotgun. Son of a bitch! Hey, Shane!"

There was no response, and no response would come. Shane's chin dug into his chest as his lifeless eyes fixed on the poisoned soil between his legs. Jesse had been seduced by the moment and possessed by his archeological find at precisely the moment that Shane's life expired.

"Shane!" Jesse shook Shane, snapping his fingers and using his inadequate skills to revive him as he leaned the rusty shotgun against the boulder. "Shane!" There was no response and no pulse. Only a corpse remained that resembled Shane, except that his grotesquely swollen throat made it appear that he had two rotting heads stacked atop his torso.

"I'll go get help!"

Jesse knew that it was too late to help Shane, but couldn't believe it. Refused to believe it. He needed to do something, to take action, so he had to move—had to get help. If not for Shane, then for himself. In the midst of 100,000 acres of Rabun County's undeveloped wilderness, Jesse stood in a state of shock and tried to remember where he was, why he was there, and how he got there. He shook his head as he forced the cobwebs out and looked back through the pine thicket and back to the brambles.

"That's right," Jesse said, as if Shane could still hear him. "That's the way."

He took off toward the brambles and stopped after thirty yards to look back at the cathedral's lone landmark. The enormous granite boulder was now adorned with a man leaning against its side, motionless, as if sleeping. Shane Samuel Dixon didn't appear dead, only slumbering peacefully at the spot where Joshua Dixon's brother had died so cruelly in 1898 along with his wife and children. Now, Joshua's great-great grandson lay with them.

Jesse forged ahead. "I gotta get back...I gotta get help," Jesse said aloud, alone. Shane was no longer there to respond, but Jesse's inner voice was.

Sure you do, the voice said, *but can you find the way?*

Chapter 7

Blake stood outside The Olive Twist on Washington Street. He would have preferred a pub or sports bar, just for old times sake, but there was always the outside possibility that someone would recognize him, want to buy him a drink and tell him what a shame it was what had happened. He knew it wouldn't be likely since he wasn't topical in Athens anymore, but with glossy black hair and a six-foot, four-inch muscular frame, he might rekindle a memory. That's not what he wanted. He needed to unwind, alone, and to think. The Olive Twist was a more relaxed, upscale bar, and it would do nicely.

A green canopy channeled visitors into the bar. Blake pulled open the smoked glass door and walked in. He removed his sunglasses and surveyed the room. The lights were dimmed, and the darkness contrasted starkly with the sunlight that had so brightly reflected off the sidewalk. An immense antique mirror covered the wall behind the bar, catching some of the light that filtered through the smoky windows and reflected it to the dark wood floor. An array of leather barstools surrounded a horseshoe-shaped bar. The bartender stood in the center with a TV tuned to ESPN on each side of the bar. Two men sat at the bar nursing drinks and watching neither of the screens. Blake took the last seat on the right side, next to the mirror, directly across from the other TV and several seats away from the men.

"Welcome to The Olive Twist," the bartender said with a courtesy smile. Not an over the top smile and annoying chatter like you'd get at a chain restaurant. Just casting a line in the water to see how much, or how little, the customer wanted to talk, to open up to the therapeutic bartender.

Blake said nothing.

"What would you like?" she asked, sensing the mood as all good bartenders can. Still, she offered Blake a flirtatious smile as her blue eyes sparked in the sunlight that reflected off a glass jar on the counter. Blake glanced at the jar, which was the main feature on the bar top, a tall jar of Stoli Doli, a concoction of Stolichnaya vodka infused with fresh pineapple that had steeped for a week. He stared at the chunks of pineapple floating in the vodka and thought about the untold number of Stoli hangovers he had suffered from way back when. He turned his gaze back to the bartender.

"Belvedere up with a twist."

She placed a cocktail napkin in front of Blake, twisting her body ever so slightly as she did. The space between the buttons on her white blouse separated just enough for Blake to catch a glimpse of her right breast. The glistening softness of the image burned into him, commingled with the thought of the Stoli Doli to reignite the passion he used to feel after games in Athens. When he would be on the hunt for soft skin, exotic eyes, and defined curves. In an instant, he caught himself and looked away, but not before the bartender had caught him breaking her horizon. She smiled and left.

"Damn it!" Blake mumbled, shaking his head. "That's all you need, more trouble."

Glancing at the clock on the wall, Blake noted that it was 4:40 p.m. He could make it home to Clayton in about an hour and a half and wanted to be home by 7:30 p.m. at the latest. Any later and Angelica might want to talk and ask a lot of questions. Questions that would cause him to snap. Blake began to fume silently as he thought about it. He hated that he snapped at Angelica...at life! He felt like he was losing control. Everything seemed so unfair. *So fucking unfair!*

The bartender returned with Blake's martini. He looked up with a weak smile and nodded in thanks. She stood for an uncomfortable second before turning away, Blake's half-hearted smile dissolving as he stared down into his drink. Blake stirred the martini, not knowing why, but he figured for the same reason he swirled the wine in his glass when dining at a nice restaurant. It wasn't to release the bouquet or...whatever. It was because that's what he had seen people do when he watched TV as a child in the housing projects, people like J.R. on the *Dallas* reruns or Blake and Crystal on *Dynasty*. People who were rich, who knew what they were doing and who were living the life of luxury that Blake wanted so badly when he was young. So when he got to UGA and was introduced to life beyond his drunken father's alcohol of choice, Pabst Blue Ribbon, he did what J.R. and James Bond did. He swirled, stirred and mimicked the nuances of successful people.

Swirling the martini, Blake recalled the chicken he had squashed with his truck earlier in the day. He grimaced and felt utter remorse. *Damn it, what the hell is wrong with you!* The remorse turned to rage as Blake reflected on how quickly he now gave into anger, how truculent he had become. How out of control he felt. He took a deep breath and tried to calm himself.

The television flashed a series of highlights from the Georgia Bulldogs game earlier in the day, a humiliating home loss to rival South Carolina that dropped the Dawgs' record to 0-2. "Ouch," an announcer said. "Just look at this bone-crushing hit Georgia quarterback Buck Welch suffered in the third quarter." On the screen, a player lay motionless on the turf, surrounded by coaches and trainers. Blake mashed his teeth and was tunnel-visioned into the player's helmet as if he had taken that hit. His shoulders cringed, and he dropped his eyes to the bar. "Sort of reminds you of that career-ending hit that Blake Savage took several years back," the announcer said as a picture of Blake flashed on the screen.

Blake jerked his head to the screen and then looked around to see if anyone took notice. No one cared. He continued stirring his drink counterclockwise and lost himself in the eye of the swirling martini. His mind returned to his days at Rabun

County High School, where he had poor grades, a penchant for beer, and one hell of a throwing arm. That throwing arm landed him a football scholarship at UGA and an unheard of starting role as the Bulldogs quarterback in only his sophomore year. Athens went crazy for Blake—"Blakemania," the media called it, as fans body painted themselves while he led the Bulldogs to a 7-0 start. Then, on a crisp October Saturday, a safety from Vanderbilt shattered both his knee and his collegiate career on a blind-side blitz. In an instant, Blake's future was ruined. With their hero wounded and evidently quite mortal, the legion of Blake fans faded back onto campus and awaited their next hero. Blake lay in the hospital for twenty-six days, increasingly irrelevant in Athens with each passing moment.

Blake raised his glass, took a long sip, and savored it as he drowned himself in misery.

At first he had just denied the extent of the injury. As the reality set in, he focused his anger squarely on the running back that failed to pick up the block on the safety that put an end to his shot at the NFL. Then the blame shifted to the safety, who later became a first-round draft pick and claimed his fortune with the Baltimore Ravens. Then the doctors and therapists were to blame. Surely it was someone's fault. Somebody had to be accountable for costing Blake the only future he had planned on.

"I tell you, the Dawgs could sure use someone like Blake Savage these days," the announcer said. "But, I believe Blake is now residing in the 'where are they now' category". Blake turned his attention back to the screen. He raised his hand at the waitress.

"Hey, do you mind changing the channel?" Blake asked the bartender.

"To what?" she asked with a flirtatious smile.

"Anything," Blake responded. "News, whatever. Not sports."

"Not a sports fan, huh? Sure thing. Let's try CNN."

His face remained staunch, unchanged, but his mind relaxed and the drink instantly began working its magic. *Why the hell do they say alcohol is a depressant? Damn it feels so good*, Blake thought to himself. He didn't understand such notions too well, never was interested in learning about it in school or in life. Learning wasn't his thing. Getting to the NFL was...had been. Now, he wasn't sure what his thing was. He just stared at a crossroad every day doing what he did the day before, all the while digging himself a little deeper into a depression.

He took another sip of the martini and peered at CNN. Most of the time, he wouldn't have been able to hear it with all the bar chatter, but before 5:00 p.m. on a Saturday game day when most people were in sports bars, it was quiet enough, as Blake was fond of saying, "to hear a mouse pissing on cotton." Normally Blake couldn't care less about the news, other than ESPN, but the headline caught Blake's attention.

The graphic below a talking head read, "Secret Supper Clubs All The Rage," and Blake tuned in. A reporter said underground dinner clubs were the hottest ticket in major cities across the country. As she spoke, video footage played of private residences where hot and trendy chefs served up unlicensed five-star dinners complete with wine pairings. She said sometimes the dinners were held in warehouses, on farms and anywhere in between. It was all secret until it was announced a day or two before the event. There was no menu and no charge, according to the report. Had the chefs charged for the meal then it would be classified as a restaurant and would require a license, health permit, the works. Instead, the chefs suggested "donations" as well as an amount, usually one hundred dollars a person or more. No one ever dared to refuse the suggested donation.

"Can you believe that?" one man at the bar said to another, after both had turned their attention to the news.

The segment broke to a live interview with a retired, married couple, Kevin and Monica Colbert, of Sutton, Massachusetts from CNN's Boston studio. They looked like the "after" picture shots for a Charles Schwab commercial. Fit, gray, dressed sharply and now enjoying their success, just like the fairy tale ending promised to those who invest and save.

"We go anytime we can get in," Monica responded to the CNN reporter when asked if they attended the "secret" clubs. "Of course it's hard to get in. We never know where it's going to be until an email invite shows up giving the time that reservations can be made, but there's only room for thirty per dinner," she continued. "Most of time we can't get in even though we click right when it opens. We even synchronize our clocks with time dot gov just to be sure we're on time!" she added.

"Heck, we'd pay to be on the short list if there was one," Kevin blurted before the talking head could ask the next question. *Exactly*, Blake thought. *Don't worry; Nick will take your money with 50-Forks if you want in.*

The second man at the bar responded to the other man's question. "I not only believe it, I've been to one of those secret dinners! Right here in Athens, a secret dining club...well, it isn't really a secret. I mean they have a website and all, but you know, there's no schedule and you just get an email the week of the event, sign up on a Friday and if you get in the dinner's the next night inside someone's home," he said. "Four course dinner and everything! But that's IF you get in."

The CNN segment switched from the Colberts back to the talking head where the caption now read "Food Safety Questions."

"Joining us now from The Southern Nevada Health District is inspector Tom Masterson," the reporter said, "and from the Food Safety Inspection Service in Atlanta, Senior Compliance Investigator Clint Justice." An image of the guests appeared on each side of the talking head as the screen split into three sections. In a live interview, the reporter asked Mr. Masterson if these impromptu dinners were safe.

"Well, we just don't know. If it's a private event for friends and family there's no requirement to regulate, but the minute strangers attend or are invited we believe they should be regulated. But they're not, and if they're not regulated then we don't know where they get the food, or whether it's properly labeled, stored, inspected, or handled."

"Who is responsible for regulating these dinners?" the talking head demanded.

The health inspector repositioned himself in his seat and went on a rampage about local health departments, the USDA and the FDA, but the talking head summed it up best.

"So, no one inspects these dinners?" she asked the inspector directly.

"No, not exactly," he confessed.

"What about that, Clint," the reporter began, "does the USDA or FSIS inspect these dinners?"

"Well, that's not part of the USDA's jurisdiction. That's really a local health department issue. The Food Safety Inspection Service, or FSIS, ensures the safety of meat, poultry, and egg products. Our aim is to monitor inspections and require that all food items pass inspection with the resources we have."

"Resources you have?" the reporter asked.

Clint stared at the camera and said nothing.

"Can you elaborate on that, Clint?"

Clint shifted uncomfortably in his seat. Silos. That's what Clint called them, silos. Every entity to itself, no one working together. But he had been coached on what to say and what NOT to say so he measured his response.

"Well," Clint began, "it's just that we have our job at FSIS, which is ensuring meat is inspected at the federal level. Of course, each state can also oversee inspection for meats that don't cross state lines. But FSIS doesn't deal with the restaurants or supper clubs. The local health departments oversee that."

"What about the FDA?" the talking head asked.

"The FDA deals with product labeling, fruit and vegetables. They don't actually inspect dairy farms, the states do that. But, then again, the FDA must verify that they comply with regulations...does that make sense?" Clint stopped talking and held his best smile, which on camera looked like a perfectly straight line across his lips. *Different people, different standards, different agencies, different objectives, no communication. Silos,* Clint thought to himself as his face began to redden.

The producers switched to a split screen with the talking head on one side and the Colberts on the other. Monica was smiling at the camera as if she had been coached or had made a point to Kevin that *we must be sure to smile all the time because we won't know when the camera is on.*

"Mrs. Colbert," the reporter asked. "What do you think about the fact that neither the food nor the dining establishment is regulated and hasn't been inspected?"

"We trust the chefs," she replied. There was a moment of silence. Kevin's eyes darted around, seemingly unsure where to focus. Monica concluded that she hadn't said enough and added, "They're all James Beard award-winning chefs, you know."

The men at the bar looked at one another. "Who the hell is James Beard?"

The talking head seemed a little surprised by how lax Monica was about food safety concerns. She pressed harder.

"But—you don't know where the vegetables, dairy or meat came from? What if the milk is raw and not pasteurized? What if the meat wasn't inspected? What if wild mushrooms weren't properly identified?"

Kevin started to speak, but Monica leaned forward, signaling to Kevin that this was an opportunity for him to sit back and listen. "We all...everyone who goes to these dinners knows that stuff. That's part of the intrigue, that the chefs can use whatever they want, that they're not so restricted. One of the best dinners we went to featured Beluga sturgeon caviar and exotic truffles that you can't *legally* get here. The chef smuggled them over from France in some diapers that he—" Monica stopped as she realized that her mouth had sped ahead of her mind.

As Monica spoke the CNN graphic had changed to read "The Last Supper?" The talking head tried, unsuccessfully, to suppress a nervous laugh. "You ate food that was wrapped in diapers and smuggled illegally into the country?"

A few seconds remained in the two-minute segment, but it seemed much longer to Monica. She thought about saying something clever but concluded that she would look best if she just laughed nervously. That's what she did. The men at the bar laughed hysterically. "Oh man, she paid, what, a few hundred bucks to eat dirty diapers!" The other man chimed in. "Did you see the husband's face when she blurted that out? No doubt she'll blame him for that interview when she watches the recording, and he didn't say a damn thing!"

Even Blake managed a chuckle, but it was far too real to him. If CNN and these folks thought these little supper clubs were a big deal they had no idea. *50-Forks will make these little dinners seem like the children's birthday parties they are*, he thought.

His thoughts returned to Nick and to the stress and secrets in his life. *Just get Nick what he needs and walk away when you've met the terms of your deal. Then do what Angelica said and STOP trying to be someone you're not*, Blake thought as he drained the last of his drink and put his glass on the bar with a thud. He finished his silent pep talk to himself, asked for the check and looked at his watch. 5:30, perfect, he'd be home just after 7:00. *Hopefully some peace and quiet at home tonight,* he thought. He paid the check and walked out.

Chapter 8

Angelica took the black, cast iron skillet out of the oven as it began to smoke, just as her Cherokee grandmother had taught her. Put some lard in the skillet, put it in a cold oven and take it out when the oven hits 400 degrees or so, she recalled. "Make sure there's a good amount of melted lard in there, child," Grandma would say, "about an eighth of an inch or so. That way, the grease will push up the side of the pan making the cornbread crispy all 'round."

Anytime she thought of her grandmother, of the simple home life her grandparents had, Angelica smiled. Dinners together, not just on weekends, but everyday. Grandpa always there for every meal, or so she was told. He had died of heat stroke when she was only two. She loved the idea of the life her grandparents had lived in Dillard about twenty minutes away from where Angelica grew up south of Clayton.

"Then, pour the batter in and make sure it's sizzling hot. Bake it for about 25 minutes then dump it out of the pan right away child so that it stops cooking," Angelica could still hear Grandma coaching her with approval.

Quartered Yukon Gold potatoes from Angelica's garden simmered on the stovetop. The knife tip met with firm resistance when she pierced them. *Not ready yet*, she thought. She got the hand mixer ready anyway and warmed the cream so she could keep the mashed potatoes hot when the potatoes were cooked through.

The kitchen phone rang. She looked at the clock and prepared herself for it to be Blake telling her that he'd be late or was going out or...

She took a deep breath and answered the phone.

"Hi Angelica," her sister said on the other end of the line.

"Oh, hi Rose!" Angelica responded with genuine enthusiasm. "What are y'all up to?"

"We just got home from the Dawgs game," Rose answered. "We lost to South Carolina, but the girls had a good time."

"Oh no," Angelica said half-heartedly. Unlike Blake or Rose's family, Angelica didn't care for sports or anything she considered frivolous.

"Yeah, well, we tailgated after the game to let the traffic clear a bit." Rose said. "John turned the grill back on and heated some chocolate chip cookies for us. Yum!"

Angelica was somewhat jealous of Rose's life, but in a loving way. Rose always seemed happy and had married well, almost eight years before, to John McBride. She and John went to most UGA home games, wearing red and black and shouting "how 'bout them Dawgs!" along with the other crazed fans.

Rose worked in public relations the first four years after she graduated with a journalism degree from UGA. By the time the girls were born, WallCloud, the Web hosting company John started, had grown to over twenty million dollars a year in sales with no end in sight. With John and Rose owning all of the company's stock, other than thirty percent owned by a lone angel investor, they had plenty of security for Rose to stay at home with the girls. Angelica wanted the same thing for herself.

"What are you up to?" Rose asked, interrupting Angelica's dreams of a family.

"Oh, nothing. Just making dinner. Cornbread, mashed potatoes, cube steak, and cream gravy."

"Now don't forget to let that lard sizzle in the pan," Rose said with a smile in her voice as she recalled the memory of her grandmother. Angelica laughed.

"Guess what?" Rose asked.

"What?"

"We're going to the Bahamas!" Rose said, her excitement running across the phone line straight into Angelica's kitchen.

"My goodness," Angelica said. "Wow! When?"

"Six weeks. We're going for our wedding anniversary! Staying at a home on a private beach on San Salvador Island!"

"That's amazing, fantastic," Angelica said. "How long will you be gone?"

"Just a week," Rose answered. "That's why I'm calling. I was wondering if—"

"YES!" Angelica answered, interrupting Rose.

"You didn't even hear the question!"

"I know what you're going to ask Rose. You want to know if I'll watch the girls. And the answer is yes!"

"Thanks sis," Rose said. "It's a long time, I know. Are you sure?"

"No problem," Angelica said. "Absolutely no problem. It's only a week and the girls are no trouble at all."

Rose's voice became softer with a touch more sensitivity. "What about Blake?"

Angelica's smile dissolved, but only for a moment. "It'll be fine, Rose. He'll be fine."

"How are...things?" Rose asked as gingerly as she could.

Angelica paused and sighed louder than she meant. Rose knew her too well and could sense Angelica's mood the way so many sisters could tell about their siblings. She never let Angelica forget that she was the first born, and Rose always watched over Angelica, informally, even before their parents were killed in their father's small plane. Their parents had taken off after having breakfast with Angelica one autumn morning, seven years earlier. The Piper PA-28 Cherokee rolled down the 2,800 foot runway at Big Creek Flying Ranch south of Clayton as it ascended on a leisurely fall foliage flight over the mountains. They had hoped to touch down late morning at Sossamon Field in Bryson City in time to enjoy lunch in Cherokee, North Carolina before returning home that afternoon. They never made it to Bryson City and their aircraft was never located, even after an exhaustive search.

"Things are pretty good," Angelica said. She knew that Rose would see right through this and would probe for more. She didn't want to volunteer more, even to her sister, but she was ready to give in if pressed. She needed to talk to someone about her marriage, to get some direction. Rose was her confidant, but she would have to excavate Angelica's feelings.

"Angelica...it's fine. You can tell me. Are things okay between you and Blake?" The floodgates opened and Angelica sobbed like she hadn't in a long, long time. Trying to talk at the same time, coming across mumbling and as unintelligible as if she had a mouth full of peanut butter.

"It's okay," Rose assured, "Go ahead and just let it out. Take your time, sweetie." The more Angelica bawled the more Rose broke down and sobbed in the kitchen on her end. John took a step toward her to make sure she was okay, but Rose smiled through the tears and waved him off. He returned to play with the girls.

"He's just...not the same," Angelica began. "He's not here, he's never here. I don't mean physically. I mean...he's just so distant from me."

"I know sweetie, it's okay." What else could Rose say but to encourage her sister to talk, let her know that it would be all right? But, she had her doubts.

"He just has so much anger," Angelica blurted. "Everything, anything sets him off. He snaps if I do something, he snaps if I don't, he snaps at himself, he goes off on his friends."

Rose listened intently. She had known Blake for a long time, since her freshman year in high school. She had always had reservations about Blake, the way sisters or mothers always have reservations about the youngest in the family. No one was good enough for Angelica and Blake certainly hadn't passed Rose's test with his flashy smile and singular talent in football. But Angelica fell helplessly in love when he asked her to junior prom. She had never seen Angelica so happy as she was with Blake. Still, Rose thought Blake wasn't worthy of Angelica and that Angelica should be on a pedestal for Blake to worship along with the ground she walked on. Before Blake's injury, everything in his life had been all about him. He may have loved Angelica, Rose thought, but only as an adornment, something that completed *his* vision for his lifestyle. All Angelica seemed to care about was marrying someone who shared her Cherokee blood so she could pass that on to her children. Rose thought that her grandmother had filled Angelica's head full of Cherokee nonsense and she wanted Angelica to want more.

After the football injury and Blake's car accident, Rose was secretly optimistic. Blake was hurt both physically and psychologically. He needed to be cared for, to be helped. Angelica harbored a deep yearning to provide, to care and to comfort. Rose thought that event, although a minor tragedy (Blake would have disagreed with that assessment), could bring them closer together. For a time it did, but, along the way, something changed. Blake somehow lost his confidence. Rose didn't know what had happened, what the tipping point was that had caused Blake to feel increasingly more despondent and less capable, but it was a bad sign. Rose knew that women admire many characteristics in men. Some women like men short, some tall. Some fit, some round. Some blue collar, some white, but one thing women generally agree on is that they want a confident man. A man that loses his confidence isn't desirable to women, friends, employers, anyone.

"How long has this been going on?" Rose probed.

"I don't know. It's just been building, getting worse for a long time."

Rose had never known Blake to be short-tempered the way Angelica was describing. Competitive? Yes, but angry, violent? No.

"Was he like this before," Rose paused trying to decide if she should complete her question. "Before the miscarriage?"

Angelica thought for a second and composed herself enough to check the time on the cornbread. She could talk about this now. A year before and Rose would have known to not bring it up, but two years and another pregnancy brought renewed hope for Angelica. "He was starting to get real busy about that time working for Nick, the chef he sells to in Athens," Angelica began before Rose interrupted.

"We know of Nick," Rose said. "We eat at The Federal from time to time and John's angel investor is also an investor in Nick's business."

"Oh," Angelica said. She lost focus when conversations turned to business or money. The material world just held no interest for her. "Anyway," Angelica continued, "he was gone a lot back then but he wasn't—no, he wasn't angry back then. Just busy, like real driven to make money. He was going back and forth between Savannah and Clayton for about a month or so and was gone days at a time."

"What did he need to haul so often from Savannah to Clayton?" Rose asked.

"I—don't know for sure. Anytime I asked he just said it was nothing. I even asked if I could ride with him on one trip—" Angelica paused, thinking for a moment. "That was it. That was the first time he snapped at me. Became so heated, his eyes looked black when I asked him that. He even swore at me saying something like heck no and for me to stay home where I belong."

Rose's lower jaw tightened, her tension escalated.

"And you did? Why?"

"It isn't my place to question him, Rose," Angelica said, now calm as she stirred the potatoes. "You know the Bible as well as I do."

Rose bit her lip. Yes, she had been raised just as Angelica had but, over the years, her views had...evolved, she believed. When she thought about it, Rose attributed it to being in a more liberal setting where people think more progressively. Of course she still believed in God and in the Bible. She just...kind of figured it needed updating, especially the parts about the roles of men and women!

"And you know what grandmother taught us about a woman's role in the household," Angelica added as she covered the potatoes.

"ANGELICA!" Rose snapped and then caught herself. Her face burned at the recollection of what her grandmother had taught both of them. How she had shown them as little girls how to play the part of a woman by cooking, tending the garden, making pottery and soaps and so on. Girl stuff that most girls outgrew, except Angelica.

Rose sidestepped the issue.

"Angelica, how do you know he's really going on hauling jobs, that he's really even working?" Rose had taken the kid gloves off now. "Could it be something else?"

"Like what?"

Rose spelled it out. "Could there be another woman Angelica?"

The thought had never occurred to Angelica. She stared ahead and rubbed the beads of her necklace between her right thumb and index finger as she thought about what Rose asked.

Rose broke the moment of silence.

"I mean, you said you don't know for sure what he does. He went on frequent overnight trips and you're not sure where he went or why he had to go. Why all the secrecy?"

"That was a couple of years back," Angelica said. "He doesn't go on many trips now."

"*And*," Rose continued, "he has become increasingly distant from you and agitated with you when you do the slightest thing. And let's not forget that he wasn't even there for you when you had your miscarriage! Am I getting this right?"

Rose hadn't put together the pieces herself until she blurted it out. It seemed impossible to believe that someone who wasn't remotely worthy of Angelica's affection, at least to Rose's way of thinking, could cheat on Angelica! Rose was pacing in her own kitchen now, twisting and wrapping the phone cord tightly around her hand, strangling it.

"No," Angelica said. "There's no way that could be true. There's no—" Angelica stopped. Two bright lights hit the window in the living room coming from the driveway outside. A door slammed.

"I have to go," Angelica said. "Blake just got home."

Chapter 9

Jesse fought the same eight-foot tall brambles that he and Shane had come through just a half hour before. *Shane's dead! Shit!* Jesse couldn't believe it, couldn't believe any of it! The day had been a disaster all around, and now he had to get back, to get help.

Help for whom?

The voice was back, doubtful and speaking in a growling, condescending tone. Jesse regretted having watched so many Freddy Kruger movies. Freddy, who couldn't be killed, now became his inner voice.

Who you gonna help? Shane? Shane's dead...the maggots will take care of him, Jesse. I'd say it's YOU who needs the help!

The brambles bit into the flesh of Jesse's bare arms, his short sleeves providing no protection as he ran. He finally broke free, emerged on the other side and stopped. He placed his hands on his knees as he bent over and gasped while trying to remember the way. The voice quieted, letting Jesse choose his own fate.

Everything looked the same, singularly unique but indistinguishable in the crowd. Jesse turned on his inner DVR and closed his eyes to replay the chase scene that had brought him here. He looked back at the brambles to mark the spot they had originally entered then turned to re-create the line they had taken to reach that spot. He pointed ahead at it, convinced himself and took off.

Whatever you say, the voice hissed. *But I'd pace myself if I were you!*

"You ARE me, you idiot!" Jesse said and immediately regretted that he had taken this turn for the worse, arguing with himself. He stopped running after ten minutes and tried to remember the steps he and Shane had taken.

How many hills did you run over?

The voice sounded polite in Jesse's head, but it only served to send a chill down his neck and excite the hairs there to stand erect. Jesse spoke aloud in an effort to calm himself. "I don't know the way back for sure. I think it's that way, but—"

But you don't know, do you?

"STOP IT! Let me finish. Like I said, I'm not sure. So I could keep going that way and try to get back but I only have a few hours of light left, maybe less in these woods."

I'd say less.

Jesse was on the verge of snapping and realized he needed to keep his cool. If ever in his lifetime he had needed to stay calm, this was it. He sensed the danger of the situation and the more he thought about it, the more it scared him. "Damn it! What are my options?" he asked himself as he tried to assert his authority and suppress the voice. "I can try to make it back, but if I don't get back exactly to the truck I might as well be in the jungle. No one knows about that place other than Blake, Shane and Ter—"

Shane can't help you, the voice interrupted.

"OR," Jesse said, ignoring the voice, "I could look for another way out. I could look for a stream like everyone says and follow it to its source—"

But where you gonna find a stream?

"OR," Jesse continued, "I could just climb and try to get to the top of Rabun Bald. There's a lookout, people are there and I can get help."

That sounds like the winner to me. You can see everything from up there.

Jesse stood for the moment, safely lost in an endless sea of trees. He was about to make a choice that he knew could have life threatening consequences, but he still couldn't believe it.

"People don't just die in the middle of the woods. You never hear about stuff like that. I'm just overreacting. "

You know why you don't hear about stuff like that?

"Quiet! I'm trying to think!"

Because the dead can't talk, Jesse. Just ask Shane.

Jesse let out a deep breath and then took in another one, silently regretting that he had made so much fun of the Boy Scouts when he saw them in their dorky little uniforms. And then, he faced up the slope and began to climb.

***

Ozzie lay on the ground in shock, blinking. He looked up at a sea of straight pine trees that towered over him as if he was an ant surrounded by an army of erect toothpicks. *Where am I...how did I get here? Mom!* Ozzie's silent questions and calls went unanswered.

A throbbing pain from his right side diverted his attention from his surroundings to his body. He looked down, touched his side and felt blood. Ozzie's eyes grew wide with alarm. His mind replayed the sound of the rifle shot for him to hear again, which propelled Ozzie to his feet. He grunted in pain as it all came back to him. Looking back from the hilltop to the boulder, Ozzie thought he could see the two men standing next to the spring, but at the distance everything was a blur. He waited a brief moment until he was sure that one of the hazy figures moved.

They're trying to kill me, like dad! Run!

Scampering over the hill and down a steep hillside, Ozzie limped badly. His right side burned and felt as if it were pulled tighter than a drum, but the bullet had only grazed him. Enough to draw a steady trickle of blood, but not enough to kill him. *Maybe not this time*, he thought. *They'll keep coming until they get you.*

With the men no longer in close pursuit Ozzie stopped running and began walking, straight ahead, letting gravity assist him downhill whenever he could. Walking up hill was too arduous. After half an hour of trudging along he stopped to listen. There was nothing. No sounds other than his breathing. No birds, no scampering squirrels, no wind. No sticks breaking, no ruffling leaves. No men. Ozzie concentrated, hearing the faintest of sounds, something close to him. Something on the ground, a rhythmic terrestrial beat. He looked down. A newly fallen oak leaf was half covered in bright red blood. Ozzie watched as drops steadily dripped from his wound. In the absence of other sounds it was alarmingly loud. The only sound Ozzie could hear was his breathing and the spilling of his own blood.

They'll keep coming, Ozzie told himself. *Keep moving.*

He was exhausted and the fact that he hadn't seen the men recently took away some of the urgency, which allowed him to feel a little more relaxed. Left, right, left, he labored to shove his feet through wet leaves as it became difficult to pick them up. Ozzie was desperate to hear something familiar. Anything. The silence itself was more frightening than the sound of the men chasing him. He had never been alone his entire life. Even if he had to endure their chanting and their hateful screams, at least he wouldn't be alone in the wilderness.

In the lonely depths of the forest, light began fading quickly, but the dark was nothing new for Ozzie. Being without his mother, without his fence, was. Still he moved ahead, ever more slowly but ever onward until finally, as darkness grew closer, he heard a sound that he recognized. Faint and from his rear, in the direction from which he had come. He stopped and leaned his weary body against a tree to enjoy the sound that had comforted him many a night. Nothing but the playful yipping and howling of a pack of coyotes.

***

Jesse ascended the slope and slogged through tangled vegetation. Thick, thick growth of mountain laurel and rhododendrons, saplings, and thorny vines obscured a view of the ground just as the lush canopy blocked a view of the sky. The dense forest rapidly absorbed the daylight, but the dwindling light was secondary on Jesse's mind. What concerned him most was what might be crawling, slinking and hiding in the undergrowth that hid his view of the ground. Shane hadn't seen that snake and it had been right beside him.

Jesse picked up the pace. He felt safer rushing through the growth, telling himself that he could move too quickly for a snake to strike. He knew this was nonsense but he felt safer moving briskly, and of course he would reach the mountaintop faster.

The dappled sunlight that once permeated the forest began to vanish as darkness ate its way down the mountain. Jesse looked up to see dark clouds billow in and swallow the sun. The temperature dropped ten degrees in fifteen minutes, giving Jesse a chill and intensifying his anxiety. As Jesse's eyes fell from the cloudy sky to the forest floor he saw a hill crest fifty yards ahead. He picked up the pace and marched toward the spot where the slope leveled out. As he crested the hill he found that he stood atop a level mound that sloped away in all directions. There was no "up."

"*What the...*" He thought for a moment and then hung his head in exasperation. *Of course. There are lots of slopes, ridges, and ravines in the forest. Not all the hills go to the top, some just go to other hills*, he thought. Jesse surveyed his surroundings, peering through deep vegetation and towering trees as he tried to determine which direction was up. He nervously chuckled at that as he admonished himself. *You don't even know which way up is, dumb ass!*

He continued the way he had been going, reasoning that he had perhaps ascended 700 feet or so from where he began. He didn't know for sure how high he had climbed but he knew that it was getting much colder at this altitude. "I wish I had my—"

Jacket? Oh you're going to need that tonight, when the storm comes and you're all alone. Well...maybe not all alone, Jesse, but no one to help you.

"SHUT UP! Stop thinking that way!" Jesse smacked himself in the head with the palm of his hand. At the movement of doing so, something shiny and black wriggled quickly as a legless shape scrambled in the leaves at Jesse's feet and slithered under a downed tree. A tree in front of him that he had to cross.

"Snake!" Jesse shrieked.

Jesse's heart jumped right into his throat and stayed there as it choked his breath. He couldn't move for a moment until he realized that something, anything could be wriggling behind him, beside him, around his feet right now if he didn't move. Jesse danced around and lifted his feet off the ground in a motion that would have suggested to an observer that he was running in place. He was afraid to leave his feet on the ground, but couldn't keep in one place. He had to move on. He sprinted ahead and lunged for the tree, more afraid of what could be on the ground at his feet than what might be under the tree.

The downed oak stood about waist high, but the bottom was a foot off the ground, owing to the limbs and uneven terrain that supported it. Jesse picked up the pace and prepared to leap, hoping to land on top of the tree so he could survey his surroundings. He eyed the tree from twenty feet away the way a long jumper eyes the line, and took off on a sprint, hurling his flailing legs through the air toward the downed oak. His feet planted perfectly near the crest of the tree, but he should have landed just short of that mark. Waving his arms violently, he began thrusting his upper torso and head backwards as he tried to balance himself. Gravity lassoed him over the tree and pulled him to the damp soil. He landed nearly completely prone, but fear gave him enough arm strength to remain bent over just past the tree.

Coiled just to his left was a four-foot long Black Racer. Jesse and the snake eyed one other for a second, each petrified of the other. The snake made the first move as it slinked right across the hand that supported him. Jesse's heart raced as he picked up his hand, shaking it and his entire body as he tried to rid the feeling of the slithering snake. Fear drove him ahead at a breakneck pace through snarling mountain laurels that hid every view. He was no longer pursuing the mountaintop; just a cove or an opening would do fine. Anything as long as he could see around him, could see what's out there.

Oh, you don't want to know what's out there, Jesse.

"Shut—" His response to his inner voice was abruptly silenced as he tripped over a rock pile hidden in the vegetation. Jesse careened through a hedge of rhododendrons atop a bluff that overlooked a very small brook. Flailing his legs through the air, Jesse landed on one ankle with a thud and tumbled into the stream.

"Ow!" he screamed as he grabbed his ankle. The ten-foot fall was not enough to break his ankle, but landing with all his weight on the hard, uneven rocks punished him with a severe sprain. He sat for a moment in the stream grimacing with pain as he caught his breath. He knew he should move, should do something, but he just sat there and darted his eyes around to see if anything was wriggling around.

A bright streak of light high above illuminated the forest and shook him to his core. The treetops began swaying as the storm approached and motivated him to push himself up as he screamed in agony. After a few seconds, thunder rumbled in the distance, indicating that the lighting had struck on the other side of the mountain.

Shifting his weight to his left leg, Jesse hobbled to a nearby tree for support and to think. And to cry. He sobbed as he hadn't for fifteen years, since he was seven years old. He had held back the tears racing through the woods even when confronted by the Black Racer. Who cares if it wasn't venomous? He didn't want to see another snake as long as he lived. As he cried he tried to think coherently, but fear and confusion suffocated him, like damp fog cascading over a bridge. Indeed he felt as if he were in a fog, a horrible fog laced with suffering and death. Daylight was waning and now this storm? "Third one this week!" he said, finding that talking aloud kept his thoughts more rational, leaving any irrational thoughts for—

Me?

Leaning against the tree, Jesse panicked and finally gave way to the fear. "HELP!" He screamed as loud as he could and listened to his frantic cry echo through a sea of serrated ravines. "HELP! HELP ME!"

He slumped his shoulders and cried some more, knowing that no one would be able to hear him. Surrounded by sound-robbing, hilly vegetation, and drowning in isolation miles away from anyone, Jesse tried to calm himself and think his way out of his nightmare. *If I can just find some shelter until the storm clears or even until the morning if I have to, I can follow this stream down the mountain,* Jesse thought.

Limping, he looked around until he found a branch he could use for a walking cane and began hobbling downstream, letting the walking stick serve as his right foot. A strong gust of wind whipped through the trees and caused them to rustle more briskly. Hopping along, he followed the stream, keeping his eyes peeled. *Stay sharp and keep moving,* he thought to himself.

The dark green vegetation and black floor sucked up any light that managed to leak through the forest canopy. Jesse squinted to see, staying close to the sound of the bubbling brook, but discerned nothing. No rock overhangs, no caves...no Ramada Inns! The walls on each side of the creek slope began to steepen and the creek slowly increased its flow, a good sign, Jesse thought. But the storm approached, and as it did the wind moaned fiercely through the ravine Jesse entered. The wind howled and sounded somewhat like owls, but more and more it sounded to Jesse like—

Hushed whispers?

As Jesse walked something trailed softly across his cheeks. He swatted and found his head covered with tentacles, fingers...something sliding over his face and ears. He hobbled quickly through the fluttering vines that descended from trees above. "Jesus!" Jesse tried to compose himself and shake the feeling of spiderwebs and vines as his heart began to pummel his chest. Light faded to twilight as he forged ahead, able to see mere feet in front of him.

A monumental crack of thunder arrived with a terrific flash of lighting that brightly illuminated the forest, momentarily blinding Jesse, but not before...

"What was that?" he asked.

What? Did you see something?

"You know I did, just over there. What the hell was it? Something big and white!"

Jesse tried to decide if he was now hallucinating. He felt sure that the lightning illuminated something odd in the forest, no more than sixty yards from him, high up the left slope of the ravine. Something that seemed out of place. "I know I saw something there," he said aloud in an effort to reassure himself. In the chill of darkness he knew he'd never make it out of the woods that night. His only hope was to find shelter and make it until morning. He believed that what he *thought* he had seen might just be his ticket out.

***

The ravenous coyote pressed his black nose to the leaf and flared his nostrils as he inhaled the intoxicating scent of fresh blood. His three pack mates yelped wildly around him. *Blood, not carrion, not yet.* Only fresh blood, but where there was blood there was a wound, and where there was wound there was chase and then dinner. He knew that this was no woodchuck. It would be a big dinner. A feast.

The alpha male lifted his head from the ground and craned his neck to the skies. A prehistoric ghostly howl ascended from his soul to the heavens, inciting his lieutenants to moan a harmonious alarm to any nearby creatures in the darkening forest, especially to the one bleeding. To that injured soul it was a summons to surrender and give himself back to the mountain, to the soil.

They each took a turn sniffing the leaf, imprinting the scent of the target as they scampered and paced around the blood, riling each other up as surely as a quarterback boisterously slams a teammate's shoulder pads before attacking an opposing defense.

There was no denying who had earned the alpha male role in this pack. His bushy tail was as thick as a man's arm and resembled a furry club when held horizontal to the ground if he felt threatened or challenged. His eyes, the iris an ancient amber the shade of wet, Egyptian sand, encircled deathly black pupils the size of forest acorns. When challenged, he took on a wild appearance. He seemed able to command every mane hair to stand erect, looking like an agitated porcupine as he spread his ears, narrowed his menacing eyes, and opened his mouth to flash his most terrifying weapons. By simply opening his mouth and snarling, he invoked more fear than his counterparts did when they snapped their jaws loudly. His lower incisors, a single spear on each side of his mouth, rose like two pillars framing the entrance to hell. The razor-sharp crescent moons curved up to meet the upper incisors on each side that served as enamel nails sealing the doorframe. In preparation for battle, saliva dripped from his fangs and suspended in a thread that made him seem even more menacing, if that was possible. His scowl cinched back his upper lip, allowing a serrated row of teeth to protrude that filled the gap between his upper incisors. He was not to be tested.

The alpha male easily picked up the trail of blood that had spilled and spattered on the occasional leaf in an unwavering line leading down the slope. He trotted in that direction as quickly as he could while remaining certain of the trail. The pack followed closely, anticipating a successful hunt.

Three hundred yards ahead, Ozzie rested against a yellow poplar. The sun hung low in the sky and light began to wane sharply, owing in part to the ominous clouds that obscured the sun and hovered gloomily over Ozzie. He was utterly exhausted after trekking miles in the overgrown forest, up, down, over and around, all the while being chased. Now his injured body required rest as much as water. But those were not the thoughts on his mind. As he leaned against the tree, unable to fully comprehend the meaning of approaching coyotes that serenaded his subconscious, his mind focused on Isabella. There she was, with Ozzie, strolling together in the woods, eating wild blueberries, finding mushrooms, presenting her warm and loving shoulder for Ozzie to rest against. That's where Ozzie was at that moment. In his mind he wasn't against a tree; rather, he was against the warmth of his mother's love and protection.

The alpha male was getting close enough to allow a celebratory yelp that sent the others into a mood of maniacal celebration. He had detected a new smell a few moments before. Smoke. Burning. It was of no concern to him as it was beyond his target, and was a smell he detected from time to time. Ozzie, too, had picked up on the smell of smoke and burning and he was blindly heading toward it. Now he was close, very close he felt, but he could go no farther tonight. He would rest there, against his mother, and let the night rejuvenate him.

The alpha male almost skidded to a stop atop a hill crest. In the entirety of the forest, with all its trees, creatures, leaves, and pine cones, he zeroed in on a singular target, bleeding and resting against a tree forty yards in front of him. A tree close to the stream that they had been following before they had stumbled upon the blood trail. There he was, down, weak and theirs for the taking. The pack charged and communicated with each other with a primordial telephony that instructed them to spread out, circle the tree and enclose the target.

Ozzie looked up the slope. His gaze, lost in a daydream of Isabella's face, dissolved into the forest floor as her eyes gave way to two beasts charging his way. Beasts with jaws wide open, teeth flashing and narrow, penetrating predatory eyes. Adrenaline jolted Ozzie to his feet. He stood, paralyzed; only his head seemed able to move as he looked left, then right, as a circle of beasts danced around him as surely as the moon orbits the earth. They moved in a blur, making the circle seem impenetrable.

A flash of lightning lit up the forest and bounced off the coyote's eyes and reflected their crazed looks to Ozzie. Thunder crashed loudly and shook the forest. The fear Ozzie hoped had receded for the night reemerged as the circle of fur moved faster and came ever closer, somehow moving concentrically and closing in. Ozzie spun around as he tried to see each and every one of them, but they were fast. So fast! And Ozzie was tired, so tired. He just wanted it to all to be over. He wanted to sleep.

The eyes of the alpha male caught Ozzie's eyes and held him in a trance the way Dracula hypnotizes his victims with his stare. The gaze was broken by searing pain, a sharp bite to Ozzie's side that had opened and enlarged his wound as it spilled more blood on the dank forest floor. Ozzie jerked around. His mind was no longer in control as his body reacted helplessly and fought to survive. The coyote's jaws were dripping with blood, Ozzie's blood, as it raced off to rejoin the circle.

Another bite from his rear, this time on an upper leg. Then another, always from the rear, Ozzie kept turning to ward off attacks from behind. As he did, he constantly presented a new flank to the next in line. He was weakening fast and couldn't fend them off. Somehow he knew it. He needed time...he needed to block the rear, to keep them in front of him and in his line of sight. Sitting against the poplar and letting the tree block his rear seemed the answer.

The pack yelped and barked louder than ever, loud enough to awaken any souls that had ever cursed this land. Another boom of thunder, then another in succession as the storm closed in on Ozzie. Collapsing at the base of the tree, Ozzie plopped down as the alpha male stood before him, charging and snapping at his feet. Retreating and charging. The others circled the tree and ran to the leader at the top of the circle before reversing direction and circling the other way, but so far the tree protected—

Sharp pain emerged from Ozzie's left shoulder as a starving coyote reached around the tree and inflicted a serious, bone crushing bite. He tried to get up as he realized that the tree had failed him, but he couldn't rise. There was too much fatigue, too much thirst, too little breath, and too little resolve to mount another defense. The seconds seemed an eternity to Ozzie as he faded, his head bobbing and no longer able to see the forest or the predators. Now he saw only Eduardo's eyes, his father lying dead in the mud, calling to him. *Come with me son. Let go of your pain.*

Ozzie felt a wave wash away his pain as a final thunderous clap exploded right before him. The jolt pried his leaden eyelids open once more to see his hunter, the alpha male, staring into his eyes as a thread of saliva suspended from his fangs. Then, the coyote's legs collapsed as he crashed motionless to the ground at Ozzie's feet. Ozzie's eyelids sank again and he drifted away.

***

Jesse used his makeshift walking cane to press away from the creek, and began hobbling up the hill to the target he thought he had seen. "Sixty yards. I can make it," he said, encouraging himself to press on with each slow and torturous step. The wind had calmed momentarily. There was nothing other than the sound of his left foot planting followed by his cane swishing through the leaves. Each step about half a yard, over one hundred steps to go. Plant and swish, plant and swish. The beat was slow, but constant. Jesse stared only right in front of him. There was no need to look elsewhere, as the darkness gave him a circle of no more than ten feet to discern his surroundings.

He planted his left foot and prepared to move his cane, but a deep depression was right where his cane would have planted. He held the cane off the ground but, to his shock, he heard the sound of a walking stick swish through leaves anyway. It wasn't his stick. The sound came from above, just to his left. His heart stopped, his skin grew cold and clammy. He needed to calm himself...of course he hadn't heard that.

But, you did.

Jesse didn't answer and was scared to make a sound in the darkness. "Just find shelter," he mumbled to himself.

He planted the cane to the side of the depression and stepped forward, stopping only to listen. Nothing, save the sound he himself had made. He took two steps this time, trying to increase the pace on the second step and then stop suddenly so he could listen intently. Nothing, other than his heartbeat thumping loudly. Five steps this time at a steady pace, then a sixth step that ended with a support tree to Jesse's left, allowing him to stop abruptly there without lowering his cane. A half swish from his left, maybe twenty feet away, followed a second later by the snapping of a small twig, as if someone's feet were repositioned.

"Shit!" Jesse said to himself, his mouth drier than an August cotton field in drought.

The wind growled and crept out of the mountain's ghastly soul as it crossed the slope from his left. And the whispers came again, ghostly whispers saying something, saying nothing. As if every language ever spoken on this land had morphed into a forest opera of hushed voices speaking at once, commingling their words into a haunted stew.

Leave us, suffer, D-E-A-T-H—that's what I heard.

Jesse took the next step, his cane trembling violently as he moved and planted it. He tried to ignore the whispers and the howls as he moved his cane forward.

A brilliant flash of lightning jolted Jesse. Fear thrust his eyes wide open, turned his head left toward the footsteps he was sure he had heard. He saw nothing but—

He turned his head in front of him, catching the last of the lightning reflect off the target he pursued only a dozen yards away. It was bright white. An erect structure of some kind, tall, like a building in the woods. Definitely something that didn't belong. His head jerked back left toward—what was it he had seen? There was no one there, he was sure of that, a realization that allowed an audible sigh. But he had seen something.

Did you see that hideous walking stick leaning against the tree? The one with the gnarly root spikes on top?

Jesse's mouth opened, his breath stopped. He HAD seen it, a thick walking stick leaning against the tree with a spiky head. But, it couldn't have been...there was no one there. There couldn't be anyone there. He shook his head, prayed silently and aloud, using the words of the Lord's prayer to silence the ghostly sounds. Step, swish.

"Our Father, who art in heaven."

Step, Swish. Step, swish. The cadence of the beat increased until Jesse was within feet of his destination. He still couldn't make it out, but it was indeed white, the brightest beacon in the forest and at least twice his height. Maybe three times. He walked to it and placed his hands upon its smooth surface. Clank, clank, Jesse knocked gently on the object. "Metal? Here, in the forest. Metal?" Cloud-to-cloud lightning ignited the sky, allowing enough light to filter through the opening in the canopy above for Jesse to make it out.

"What the...an airplane? How the hell did..."

Jesse felt his way around the airplane, the image of its orientation imprinted firmly in his mind's eye due to the brief illumination, like a freshly snapped Polaroid developing slowly.

It was nose down, tail up, and wings extending from underneath the fuselage were still intact, somehow, spreading out at about the height of his chest. He made his way to the passenger side and found that the door was spread wide open. The plane wasn't perfectly vertical. Rather, it was closer to a forty-five-degree angle and rested against a large tree that supported it from behind.

"Just get inside and close the door," Jesse told himself. Jesse stumbled around the front, unable to see anything in the blackness. His hands moved slowly over the twisted propeller and trembled as they rounded the nose. He limped through the brush, following his hands until his hip crashed into the support arm of the passenger side wing. Jesse reached up for the passenger door.

And then he heard it.

Jesse froze, his spine stiffening tightly as he heard the most terrifying sound he had ever heard, that anyone had ever heard. A chilling, screaming cry from the depths below him that sounded just like a woman screaming. No, a child crying...something in between. And it was so close, down the slope near the stream where he had first seen the plane.

"Jesus! What the hell was that? Oh Jesus!"

You don't know what that is? Why that's nothing but a panther.

Jesse's voice trembled as he argued with the voice. "Isn't! There are not any panthers around here."

Well that thing that's not a panther, it's coming this way, Jesse.

Jesse grabbed the trailing edge of the right wing and struggled to pull himself up to the door. Again, a bloodcurdling scream that sounded humanlike, but not human. Wind howled too menacingly for Jesse to hear anything else. He pulled himself up on the support and threw his legs over the fixed landing gear that was interwoven with a tree limb, trying not to put weight on his right foot. His cane fell to the ground, but that was the least of his concerns.

The wind quieted, the sound replaced by thrashing leaves being scattered by footfalls, something rising up from the stream headed his way. The thing that was not a panther. Jesse grabbed the inside of the plane and pulled himself up and in. He scurried to the back seat, using the back of the front seats as his floorboard, and pushed back with his good leg as far removed from the forest floor as he could get. The wind howled again, but only the wind. No voices and no screams. Jesse sat, unflinching, afraid to move and afraid to breath. A loud creaking sound moaned from Jesse's right, the sound of the tree limb wrestling with the landing gear, forming a bridge between the fuselage and the tree.

"Saved! Oh thank God! If I stay in here, I'll be all right. Just stay put."

Sounds good to me, champ.

As he took a moment to calm himself and catch his breath in the safety of the cabin, Jesse couldn't believe what had happened. He was in a forest so remote, so expansive, that even a downed airplane couldn't be found. And yet, he had somehow come across it. His heart sank as he realized it meant he was lost in a place that even searchers couldn't find when they were trying to.

"Maybe there's a flashlight or something in here! Maybe even a gun!" Jesse moved his hand on the seat cushion, finding nothing since the plane had nosedived at such an angle. He felt along the floorboard and found nothing of substance, only some papers. He slid between the two front seats, his hand finding the throttle for balance. Jesse pulled his legs through and planted his left foot on the instrument panel just above the left yoke. Now completely in the front of the cabin, he felt along the floor. In the black chill of night he concentrated on what his finger tips were telling him. He traced smooth, knobby limbs that must have—

He paused and slowly moved his fingers along the surface of the limb he held until he came to the end and felt four long, cold, jointed extremities.

"SHIT!"

Jesse jerked back, trying to compose himself, realizing that whoever had flown this plane head first into the ground was still here with him, or at least his remains were. His heart felt as if it would beat completely out of his chest. He was sure that any creature around would be able to hear it.

Something did.

The most bone-chilling scream imaginable rose from just beneath him. The sound of claws scraping against metal raked slowly across the underside of the fuselage. Jesse groped, feeling for something, for anything. He felt along the floor on the passenger side and found something hard...headphones, he thought, as he tossed them aside. He continued rummaging in a panic and grabbed something oblong, somewhat round. He placed his fingers in three openings positioned like eyes on a bowling ball, only—.

"A fucking skull! Shit!" Jesse shrieked as he dropped the skull and shut his eyes, fighting through his terror. He continued to feel around for something useful, but found nothing but bones. He felt along the dashboard and raised his hands to the windshield, which was still largely intact. There he found fabric, a bag of some sort. He detected pockets along its side and a zipper on top. The pockets had papers...maps he assumed. *A flight bag*! Jesse tore open the zipper and fumbled inside feeling for anything hard. A gun, a flashlight. Anything. His fingers went to the bottom of the bag and felt something very cold and very hard. About six inches long, tubular. A fingertip felt for a switch, finding it. "A flashlight!" he said. He pulled it out and pushed the switch, but the light didn't respond.

"Damn it...c'mon!"

He smacked the light against his hand as he always did when trying to coax more life out of a dying remote control. He switched it on and a light flickered forth. His hands quaked violently as he steered the flashlight to his left. In the utter darkness, the light reflected brightly off the glass and plunged him into momentary blindness, but not before an image of what was reflected in the glass burned into his mind's eye. Two glowing orbs. Only, he hadn't seen them *through* the glass. No. They were reflected by the glass. Behind him!

As his vision returned he swung the flashlight around to the passenger door and reached for the handle, remembering only now that it still hung open. There, glowing in the blackness were two slits, yellow eyes, each the size of a silver dollar, perched on the branch at the door's entrance.

The night yielded one final blood-curdling scream, and it came from Jesse.

Chapter 10

Blake walked through the front door of his A-frame home just as Angelica hung up the kitchen phone. He breathed in the nostalgic smell of southern cornbread and smiled. Angelica's eyes dropped, her lips not returning his smile as she said simply, "Hi," with no discernible inflection.

Hmm, gonna be one of those nights, Blake thought to himself as he strolled through the kitchen. The kitchen opened into an extended family room with a stone-walled fireplace on the far end. The dark, hardwood floor throughout gave the kitchen and family room the shape and appearance of a long and narrow alleyway. Blake plopped on the sofa and grabbed the remote. "Who was that on the phone?" he called to the kitchen, hoping for an innocuous way to break the ice.

"Rose."

Blake didn't want any drama, any stress. Couldn't handle any more stress. In that moment he realized that he just wanted a sanctuary with Angelica. Just the two of them, the way it had been when they first got married. The way she said she wanted it to be and the way he—yes, he too now wanted. "Hey, you wanna watch a movie tonight?" Blake managed a smile with the question that Angelica couldn't see, but she picked up on the tone. She turned her head from the stove back to Blake.

"Sure!"

Blake admired Angelica's ability to forgive and forget as much as he was jealous of it. He hadn't found a way to do that in life no matter how hard he tried, but Angelica didn't even *have* to try. It took no effort and seemed unfair to him. "You can pick it out," Blake said partly to be generous, but mainly because he just didn't care.

Angelica drained potatoes in a colander over the sink. The evening was starting to get better and she thought of asking Blake if he wanted to help with dinner but quickly thought better of it. She put the potatoes back in the pot and cut off some home-churned butter, adding it to the pot with one hand as she grabbed the hand mixer with the other. On numerous occasions, she had thought of getting an electric hand mixer, but could never bring herself to do it. She just cranked her grandmother's hand mixer and slowly drizzled warm cream into the potatoes.

The phone rang. Angelica put the mixer down and answered since it was next to her.

"Blake, it's for you."

The stress boiled in Blake's gut and billowed to his chest almost instantly. He had no idea why he got upset so quickly, but tried to calm himself by taking a deep breath. He rarely got a phone call at home and sure as hell didn't want one now when he had mentally checked out for the day. If it was a telemarketer, Blake swore to God that he'd let him or her have it.

Blake walked to the phone, footfalls heavy on the hardwood floor.

"Yep," Blake answered. There was nothing on the other end of the line, only a faint scratching sound. "Hello," Blake said.

"Blake," the voice on the other end was out of breath and difficult to understand. "You got--a g-- -p h-re!"

"What? Who the hell is this? You're breaking up," Blake said.

"You gotta get – here!"

"Who is this? Jesse?" Blake tried lowering his voice, but there was no place to hide.

"No -t's Terry. I on-y got one b-r on my ph-ne. Y-u gotta get up --re now," he said gasping for breath.

"Damn it," Blake began, then tried to compose himself in front of Angelica. "What is it that can't wait til tomorrow?"

"Jesse and Shane are missing, haven't been back since midday," Terry shouted. "And that's not all—we got some escapees."

Blake fumed. "Where are you now?" he asked between clinched teeth.

"I'm," Terry began, "I'm – t-e wo-ds, at the sheds."

"I'll be right there." Blake slammed the phone on the cradle and dropped his head, preparing himself for disappointment both inside the house and out.

Blake was about to speak, but Angelica did it for him.

"I know," Angelica said, looking the other way. "You've gotta go. I'll leave your dinner on the stove."

***

Terry sat on a log in the darkness outside shed number one and watched the headlights from Blake's F-150 fishtail up the mountain road. Blake drove right to the shed, putting Terry in his high beams. Blake's farm truck was sitting there around the cul-de-sac facing down the mountain. There was no sign of Jesse or Shane.

Blake jumped out and looked in the direction of the main fence charger as he approached Terry. "Why is the goddam fence off?" Blake asked.

"What?" Terry replied dumbfounded.

"The green light is on," Blake barked. "Hell the fence ain't even turned on!" Blake threw the lever up turning the fence back on, the red light glowing. The fence was hot again. A five-joule charger was powered by a large solar panel that Blake had installed, which in turn juiced a bank of twelve-volt batteries. There was no electrical power on the mountain and no lights.

"Where are Jesse and Shane?" Blake asked as he stormed by Terry and headed back to his truck.

"Hell if I know," Terry snorted. "I got my damn ear bit off and was knocked unconscious for a bit. I came to about 1:00 this afternoon or so and nobody was here, but the truck still was. Jesse, he's got the keys. I don't know what the hell happened!"

Blake fumbled through his center console until he found a flashlight. He shined the light at the right side of Terry's head and grimaced. Dried blood painted the side of Terry's head like Gorbachev's stain, with the back center of his ear completely bitten off. His ear had the shape of the number nine.

"D-A-M-N," Blake said. Terry looked up, anger and disbelief in his eyes.

Blake went back and cranked the truck so that the battery wouldn't die as the high beams lit up everything in their path. He walked toward the old, beat-up F-100 farm truck. Just as Terry said, there was no sign of Shane or Jesse. Blake shined the light inside the truck. The keys weren't in it, but two cell phones were on the seat.

"Do you have your cell phone, er, do you have a cell phone?" Blake asked Terry.

"Yeah, got mine. It was in the truck with theirs and I used it to call you. I waited an hour before I even got a bar on it."

Blake walked along the fence and moved the light inside as the corner of his eye caught a large black mass on the ground. Eduardo lay dead, just as they left him. "Why'd you guys leave him here?" Blake shouted, almost instantly realizing that must have been when the trouble began. "Never mind," he said.

Terry followed Blake as they walked around the perimeter into the woods and followed the back fence lines. The fence was on and it was tight all around. Made no sense to Blake.

"You said some escaped," Blake said, "how do you know that?"

"When Jesse and Shane didn't come back I had some time to kill since I didn't have no way to get down the mountain,"

Terry said, "so I did a count. One black fella missing from this cell, one red head missing from up top. That's it."

"GODDAMN IT!" Blake said. "You know what'll happen to us if someone finds out we're holding them on this land? We can't take that chance!"

"You figure that's where Jesse and Shane went?" Terry asked. "To fetch 'em?"

Blake stared at Terry and wanted to tell him what a dumb shit he thought he was. How he was no different than that running back that missed the block on the safety, only this time the safety took off Terry's ear before trying to wreck Blake's life. Again. *Can't catch a friggin' break*, Blake thought to himself.

"Maybe they chased them and came out somewhere else," Blake said to Terry, seeking approval of his idea.

"I figured they'd have found a phone and called if they'd done that," Terry quickly surmised.

Of course they would have, you dumb shit, Blake said to himself.

They walked along the back fence line to the top of the encampment and shone the light into the woods. The harsh light made it surprisingly difficult to see. It brightly illuminated the face of each tree while plunging the backsides into utter blackness, casting long dark shadows on the ground. Blake took a few steps forward and Terry followed close behind, looking over his shoulder all the while to make sure he could see the truck lights. Blake realized almost instantly how pointless it was. He had no idea where to go, what to do. He stopped to think for a moment.

A shriek from above pierced their ears as a huge raven descended and swooped at them. Blake and Terry ducked just in time to see the raven fly into the headlights of Blake's truck before ascending, out of sight.

"Shit!" Terry said, already heading back toward the truck lights. "That scared the hell out of me!" Blake followed, knowing there was nothing he could do, not now. This was serious and he needed time to think.

"I'll take you to the hospital," Blake said, acknowledging the obvious but wishing there was another, any other way.

"What'll I tell 'em?" Terry asked. He knew he was sworn to secrecy; Blake had made that crystal clear when spelling out the terms of the three thousand dollars in cash he was going to receive the next month. Cash. More money than Terry had ever had in his hands. *Who needs to get a GED*, Terry had thought when Jesse hired him, thrilled that he had found a way to earn so much money.

Blake thought about it and figured a dog attack was the most likely answer, but they'd want to know where it was and what kind of dog so they could go after it. Then the doctors would call the police. Just more questions that he didn't want Terry to have to deal with.

"You know, hospitals are slow," Blake said as he led the witness. "What if I take you to someone who could clean that up for you without having to go to a hospital or to see the police?"

Terry wanted to say something but didn't know what to say.

"Tell you what," Blake continued. "There ain't nothing they can do for you anyway except put antibiotic cream on it. How about I go get you some from the drugstore and a splint for your fingers so you can doctor it yourself. You can tell whoever asks that a Rottweiler attacked you but you kicked him good. Just tell them it was away from here...over on Wolf Creek or something. That way we can finish all this up here and I can give you the three thousand bucks I promised you in a few weeks."

"Yeah," Terry said, hearing nothing other than the words three thousand bucks.

"C'mon. I'll take you home," Blake offered. "You'll have to show me where you live."

Blake and Terry descended the mountain in silence. This was serious, Blake knew that much. Terry's ear was nothing, the least of his worries. If any forest authorities caught sight of those escapees and were able to find out where they came from...that Blake was holding them captive on federal land! If something unspeakable happened to Shane and Jesse or, worse yet, even if they were all right but they spilled the beans on him...

It was only in that moment as he slithered down the mountain that Blake realized what a snake he was. Somehow, he had seen only dollar signs. He was no different from Jesse, no different from Terry just a moment before, and hadn't *seriously* considered the risks of what he was doing. At least he had the good sense to not tell Angelica about any of it so that he could keep her protected, but still...

All of Blake's worst thoughts and fears ran across his mind like an old fashioned ticker tape. His first thought was that he might not get the money he had worked so hard for during the past two years, the money he had counted in his sleep and dreamed of. Then he thought that maybe, somehow, he could be in trouble with the law.

"I'll go out first thing in the morning and look for Jesse and Shane," Blake said to Terry. "You just take the day off and recover."

"Fine by me," Terry said. "Hell, I'll need some time to mend up anyway."

"I never asked you, but how well do you know them fellas?" Blake asked.

"Shane and Jesse?" Terry answered. "Not at all. They're Rabun County High fellas and I live up near Sky Valley, closer to Highlands than Clayton. I just happened to see one of Jesse's posts on Facebook one night when he was was fishing for a helper. I shot him a message once I caught wind of it, that's all."

"So you don't know them at all? Their families, where they live...nothing?" Blake asked.

"Nope. Don't know jack shit about 'em."

Somehow hearing that put Blake at ease. Maybe he had overreacted. He'd probably find Jesse and Shane just fine the next day, but if he didn't, he was relieved that Terry didn't know their families or where they lived any more than Blake did.

"Them boys better hunker down tonight," Terry said as they drove north on 441 through Dillard. "There's panthers in them hills."

Blake chuckled. "There ain't no mountain lions or panthers around here no more," Blake said, his mountain accent coming on stronger every minute he talked to Terry.

"Well...ain't no mountain lions no more I reckon," Terry conceded, "but there sure is heck is panthers. We got pictures of them with our deer cam on the Sky Valley side of Rabun Bald. DNR tells folks they ain't no panthers cause if they admit it folks'll want to hunt and kill 'em. Then there won't be none."

Blake listened to pass the time, wondering as he drove the winding road up to Sky Valley what really did lurk in the woods on that mountainside...what came out at night. He had hunted the hills a fair amount growing up in Rabun County and felt pretty comfortable in the woods. Comfortable enough to know one thing for sure. He wouldn't want to be in those woods alone at night.

Chapter 11

Smoke wafted through the air and carried with it a symphony of odors. Yeast, burnt corn, fire: smells commingled with sounds, the crackling of a nearby fire, and the sizzling sound that accompanied another smell, bacon.

Ozzie's eyes twitched open and quickly blinked shut, not ready to accept the harsh, late morning sunlight. He opened them again, squinting, feeling as if he were in a dream. He was lying on the ground and everything appeared sideways to him. Rolling his neck to the right, he was able to take in more of his surroundings. Above was a wooden structure, the underside of a porch. A cabin. Ozzie tilted his head back to see an open door that went into the cabin. A hard, wooden floor lay beneath him as he turned his attention to what lay across him. It had been a long time since Ozzie had felt anything as soft as the blanket that someone had draped over him. Slowly he regained consciousness, not yet thinking of how he came to be there. Rather, just painting a relaxed picture of his environment. Like someone on a morphine drip, conscious to the world, but absent of reason. He let his neck roll to his left. A few feet from him a fire ring encircled a well-tended fire, above which a flat, metal surface rested. Smoke rose from the surface, as did the sound of meat sizzling.

"Howdy," a voice said from the other side of the fire. Ozzie's focus shifted from the fire to the man the way an auto-focus camera resets its focus on a distant object. The feeling of sedation began to wear off as Ozzie saw the man. He labored with great difficulty to remember what happened, how he got here, but was able to string together only memory fragments.

Hunting mushrooms with mom, running through the woods, getting shot! Coyotes! The fragments stopped there, not remembering Eduardo, Felipe, who this man was, or how he got here.

"The name's Hal," the man said. "Hal Skinner."

Hal leaned forward and stoked the fire, and then sat silently for a second, not sure what else to say. He had not spoken to another human being in almost five years. In all that time he had spoken to himself countless times, concluding ultimately that that was all thinking really was; someone talking to himself. He had tested his new theory once a few years back trying to see if he could think without a voice in his head speaking. He wasn't able to.

It surprised him a little that he was able to speak so easily to Ozzie. He thought of movies he had seen years before, in which people were stranded or isolated for years and almost forgot how to speak. Then again, Hal had never really stopped talking. He simply ranted to animals now. Of course, he hadn't forgotten his own name, but hearing himself say the name "Hal Skinner" almost startled him, as if he had come to believe his identity had been erased along with his physical being in the civilized world.

Ozzie stared at Hal, not feeling afraid and unable to act on his fear if he had. The frazzled hood of a wool jacket loosely covered greasy, scraggly hair that draped over the man's weathered blue eyes, the bangs shielding the dirt-encrusted crow's feet around his left eye. His unkempt beard, a scruffy mixture of rust, gray, black, and dirt rose to meet his hair, giving his face the look of a soiled egg. His cheeks were well worn, stained with dirt, age, and tears. Indeed, he had his reasons to cry, to live here alone in the woods and to leave the rest of society behind.

"You probably smelled that batch of moonshine I got brewing over there," Hal said. Ozzie said nothing and kept staring as Hal struggled to compose his next sentence. Ozzie understood none of Hal's words, but did understand his tone. He wasn't like any of the other men. He seemed kind, more like his mother.

"Got some bacon frying too," Hal paused, thinking of something to add. "Not pork bacon, mind you. Venison bacon. I don't—" Hal fought for words, not used to having to say anything. "I don't care for pork too much, you understand. Hell, can't get it much around here anyway. Isn't like there's a Piggly Wiggly in these woods."

Ozzie stared at Hal.

Hal looked at Ozzie then back at the fire, poking it some. "Hell, I figure you probably can't understand a word I'm saying," he said. "You ain't exactly answering back, but what the hell do I know? Do you know what I'm talking about?"

Ozzie stared at Hal and farted. Hal laughed for the first time in over five years, since before his wife's funeral. "Good idea," Hal said, and matched Ozzie one. Ozzie blinked, but said nothing. He rolled his head again to look at the door, staring at the top of the entrance. A strange inscription caught his eye and Ozzie tried to turn to make it out.

"TEOTWAWKI" were the letters that had been carved and burnt into the cabin wall.

Hal caught Ozzie looking up.

"Tee Ought Walk E," Hal said. "That's how you say that, you know. It means The End Of The World As We Know It. Tee Ought Walk E. That's why I came out here after," Hal blurted, his blood boiling as the memory of his wife rose to the surface. He paused, realizing that no one had forced him to bring it up. He had almost volunteered to bring it up. *Don't go there Hal, please don't relive that,* he counseled himself, too late as the cork was set to pop and spill his bottled emotions. Hal's grip on the poking stick tightened as he jabbed the fire and went back in time, unable to differentiate if he was merely thinking or talking aloud, as they had become one and the same to him by now.

"There was just nothing left to me, for me, after she died. Still isn't. It's like I'm trapped in a different world. Landscapes are in black and white, food has no taste, flowers have no smell. I see it all but everything is void of virtue," Hal blurted, without knowing it. He was in some place else now, that other place he went to so often, where he kept himself right after she died, the time and place where suffering and isolation was the greatest.

"I imprisoned myself the minute the funeral was over. Didn't take calls, allowed no one to see me, wouldn't even talk to her parents. Just shut down, shut the world out," Hal continued, spewing his stream of recollection as if on the sofa at a shrink's office.

Ozzie stared into the fire. The realization that Ozzie couldn't understand a word he was saying encouraged Hal to continue. "I took a month to get everything in order. You know, accounts, property, bills and all that bullshit. I decided I'd go into the woods and disappear. Don't really know why. Figured I could suffer and die here, I guess I wanted that most of all. Didn't have it in me to commit suicide. Just didn't feel that was my right. But I wanted it to all be over. The hate, the suffering, the anger, the loss."

Ozzie tried to reposition himself, but his pain was getting worse. He grunted and grimaced as he tried to move. Hal snapped out of his diatribe and realized Ozzie was in pain. "Careful there Ozzie, you've had a rough go," he said.

Ozzie stared at him, unsure of what to think.

"Oh yeah," Hal said, "I know your name. Right there hanging on that tag they stuck on you, like military dog tags or a prison tag. OZZIE, it says. Can't imagine where you came from though. Don't care none, neither."

Hal leaned over, grabbed his jug of corn whiskey and walked to Ozzie. His approach frightened Ozzie and he tried to get up, but a sharp pain from his rear made it impossible. He grimaced again. "Easy there," Hal said. "Like I said, you've had a rough go. Them coyotes clean broke your leg and bit right through it and your shoulder. I've been wanting to blast them suckers to smithereens for some time now. They was hooting and hollering up the ridge there not a hundred yards from here so I walked up with my shotgun and there they were beating you like you was Rodney King. Didn't look like a fair fight to me so I took two of them down. The other two scattered off and I brought you back here. That was...let's see...don't really know what day today is, but that was three or four days ago, I reckon. I've been keeping you fed on this moonshine to take the edge of that pain off."

Hal stopped talking for a moment to look at Ozzie's wounds.

"I had to leave these wounds open, son, to let them drain. Made you a bandage out of some sphagnum moss I took from a mountain bog not too far from here. They used to use this stuff in the Civil War, you know, when they ran out of sterile dressings. Healed wounds faster than the cotton did! That's cause this stuff doesn't let bacteria grow."

Hal let the moss bandage do its work and held the back of Ozzie's head to pour a little shine into his mouth. Ozzie drank it, vaguely remembering it. Hal gently placed his head back down and stroked it before returning to the fire.

"That right there's the whole problem with this world," Hal said, on the verge of a rant. "The answer to most things is right there in nature. But you can't put a patent on that moss so there ain't no money in it. Instead we just whip up some concoctions made of who knows what, put it in a pill, give it a stupid name so a pharmaceutical company can sell it. Only, if you listen to the fast-talking snake oil salesman on the commercial, it creates all kinds of side effects that need another pill. So people buy that pill! Ain't no need for none of it!" Hal concluded out of breath, his face becoming flustered. He thought for a moment as he checked the bacon.

"Bacon's done," he said. "I'll just put it over here. You can try some later if you'd like."

Hal sat back down, looked at Ozzie, and shook his head at all he had said in the last few minutes. He didn't want to talk, had become used to not talking, but the words just bubbled out as if someone had shaken the soda bottle violently before opening it. "I don't know what I was thinking," Hal said, his words still bubbling out. "I just didn't want to live without her. Didn't want to have to talk to anyone, hear them say shit like "oh we're so sorry" and "she was such an amazing woman" and whatever. Hell, I know how amazing she was. We did everything together, and I mean everything. Worked together, slept together, played together. No other friends, just her. And I was her one and only friend. And then...one of us is gone, leaving the other all alone."

Hal looked at Ozzie and realized that he too must be alone.

"Well, like I said, I just wanted to die, to be gone. But I couldn't pull the trigger. Couldn't jump off the bridge, if you catch my meaning. So I just hightailed it to the woods figuring if I had to be alone without her I'd just as soon be alone without anyone. Besides, the world's going to hell in a hand basket anyway. So I grabbed the things I needed to live out here and came and found my spot. To tell you the truth I figured for sure I'd be dead by now. Hoped I would, anyway, but death hasn't taken me."

Hal stopped, realizing that he had been talking nonstop, and wanting to extend an opportunity to Ozzie if he had something to say. Ozzie's eyes were sealed as the moonshine had coaxed his pain away and his body to sleep.

Hal continued ranting, half drunk now.

"Hey...I'm a quarter Cherokee, you know. Yep, Skinner, you can look the name up on the Dawes Roll of 1906, it's right there. My ancestors were run off this land, did you know that?"

Drool oozed from Ozzie's mouth as he lay on the porch.

"Back in 1838," Hal continued. "Made to march on foot about a thousand frigging miles, you believe that? White men like the other three quarters of me imprisoned them and took their land. A frigging crime!" Hal took a stick and stirred the fire as he continued his rant. "Then again, the Cherokee ended up keeping some slaves of their own, so I guess we're all either captor or captive depending on what day it is. Can't just let every creature live freely I reckon." Hal exhaled as he concluded his rant and stopped talking, realizing that he had put his first audience in five years to sleep.

Hal walked over to Ozzie and checked on his blanket. He had been badly hurt and would need time to heal, but for the first time in a very long time, Hal felt a twinge of purpose. For so long his life had no meaning and he wanted only for his body and soul to fade into the forest soil, becoming lost amidst the winter leaf litter. To just end it all already. Ashes to ashes, dust to dust and all that.

In Hal's barren field of despair a lone seed of hope now germinated, and its name was Ozzie. He had nurtured it for days, nursing it to its next phase of recovery, and he would continue nursing it. Hoping for it the happiness that eluded him and perhaps tasting a bit of happiness for himself once more.

Chapter 12

"Want me to freshen that coffee, sugar?" The Clayton Cafe waitress gave Blake a warm, Tuesday morning smile.

"Sure, thanks," Blake said. He felt calmer than he had in weeks, but was staring at a tough week ahead. With only four days until Nick's 50-Forks dinner he and Terry had plenty of work cut out to do. Blake cut into a biscuit smothered with sausage gravy.

"When?" A man's voice from the next table asked the waitress loudly as she relayed a story.

"About...3-4 weeks ago," she said. "Just flat out disappeared. Two boys that lived down on Warwoman just up and vanished, two best friends." Blake turned his head to listen. The waitress caught his gaze and turned her body to include him in the gossip group.

"How old were they?" The man at the table next to Blake asked the waitress, as if she had nothing to do other than relay the local gossip, which was probably true.

"20 and 22."

"Well heck, they probably just went a hoboing," the man seated said. He gave Blake a wink and added, "That's a good age to take off exploring."

"Maybe, but they didn't take a dab blasted thing with them," she said. "Not one thing missing from their house according to their folks, and not one word mentioned to nobody."

Blake tried to smile at the man as he turned to his breakfast, but he had lost his appetite. The discussion brought Blake back to the two boys who were possibly dead because of him somewhere on the mountain. Blake didn't want to believe it, but he did find Jesse's bloody jacket the day after he and Terry had found them missing. He didn't look much further out of fear of getting lost himself, and he didn't know what to do or say, or who to say it to. So Blake did nothing. He just swallowed the secret, piling it on top of the other lies that were beginning to poison his soul, and let the day pass. And then the next day passed. Then a week passed, then a few. As time ticked on, thoughts of the boys just slipped away from his consciousness as he came to rely on Terry to help get everything set for Nick's upcoming launch.

Blake threw a ten dollar bill on the table and left.

***

Terry was already on the mountain when Blake pulled up just before 8:00 a.m., having driven the F-100 that Blake now let him use. Terry hadn't asked one question about Shane or Jesse in three weeks. Blake couldn't decide if it was ignorance or apathy, but as the saying goes, he didn't know and he didn't care. Terry had been working hard and was thrilled that Blake let him drive the truck. He was even more thrilled with the fact that Blake said he would now earn $5,000 if all went well, since Jesse and Shane had run off and Terry had a lot more work to do. Terry celebrated real hard the night he heard that.

"Everything going okay this morning?" Blake asked as he stepped out of the truck.

"Yeah I 'spose, but a lot of these fellas are gettin' a might ill."

"Ill?" Blake snapped. "What do you mean *ill*?"

Terry waved his arm for Blake to follow and gave Blake the tour. "Looky there at that 'un," Terry said, pointing to Felipe, lying in his shed. Felipe rested on his side as blood slowly oozed from his nose and his mouth.

"Let's go in and take a look," Blake said as he walked through the entrance. Blake approached Felipe and got down for an inspection. He traced his fingers over his shoulders, which had swollen considerably. Just below Felipe's right shoulder Blake touched his right hand to a black, squishy ulcer and pushed it in and out, as he grimaced with disgust.

"What the hell is that?" Blake asked. Flies were already swarming around, more than usual. Blake lifted his hand from Felipe to scratch one off the back of his neck.

"Beat's me, but a bunch of 'em got it." Terry said. Terry took Blake around showing him the breadth of the illness that had popped up in the past twenty-four hours.

"Just came out of nowhere," Terry said. "Like the air is poisoned or something."

"Thanks, Dr. Terry," Blake said as he dismissed the simplicity of the kid's mountain logic.

"I'm telling ya, that's what it is," Terry said. "Looky over here by this tree." Terry walked Blake to a huge twisted oak tree beside Blake's truck and pointed to two dead squirrels and one dead skunk on the ground within thirty feet of one another.

"See?" Terry said. "Just up and died, not a scratch on 'em."

"Jesus!" Blake said, being careful to steer clear of the skunk.

They walked back in and passed Felipe. Blake had never seen anything like it. Body after body was hemorrhaging blood from the nose and mouth. Some had hideous black ulcers and severe swelling in the lower neck, chest, and shoulders. A few showed none of those symptoms, but just staggered around as if they were intoxicated. He didn't know what it was, but he knew enough to know it wasn't good.

"Some of 'em done died," Terry said. "Three of them real fat sumbitches."

"WHAT!" Blake said, staring firmly at Terry. "Where?"

Terry led him behind the sheds to see the three huge bodies that were so round they looked bloated to Blake.

"Jesus Christ!" Blake exclaimed. A stream of thoughts, all of them bad, washed over Blake, but his primary thought was of how much *less* money he would make if he didn't do something quickly to salvage what he could.

"Terry, I gotta go make a call but I'll be back to help you clean all this mess up when I'm done. You're gonna need it." Blake drove down the mountain and headed back toward Clayton. He stopped in the parking lot of the Sandy Creek Baptist Church once he picked up a good cell signal.

"Hi, you've reached the voicemail of Nick Vegas. Please leave—"

"Damn it!" Blake exhaled as he slammed the phone against the steering wheel. He looked up at the huge cross above the steeple, gathered his thoughts and listened to the rest of the message.

"—a message and I'll get back to you." BEEP!

"Nick, it's Blake. Need to talk to you about this weekend. I have a special treat for your dinner this weekend that I think you'll love. Give me a call."

***

Nick Vegas pulled into the parking lot of the Fox News Atlanta bureau on 14th Street at 8:20 a.m. The associate producer of the Fox & Friends show told Nick to be there by 8:30 for a segment on the morning show. It was an easy autumn morning ride, only taking eighteen minutes in traffic from his Buckhead home.

The cell phone in Nick's pocket rang. He looked to see that it was Blake calling, thought for a second, and sent it to voice mail. He left the phone in his black BMW 550i and walked inside the studios.

Nick was no stranger to the media. He had done countless magazine and newspaper interviews. He had even done several local TV interviews in addition to The Food Channel episodes, but this was his first live national television interview. The associate producer had asked Nick to appear in a panel that would discuss underground supper clubs, but when Nick explained his concept for 50-Forks and said it was launching that very week, the Fox & Friends team decided to do a full segment on it. Nick couldn't refuse, even though all 500 memberships were already sold out.

When Nick walked through the doors he expected to see a full studio. Of course he knew that the hosts of the show, Gretchen Carlson and Steve Doocy, were located in New York and wouldn't actually be there, but he expected to see producers, camera sets, camera crews with headsets receiving silent instructions. Instead, a young woman greeted him and walked him around a corner to a small studio with gray carpet, a single stool, and a camera on one end facing a wall with an image of Atlanta's skyline. She escorted Nick to the stool in front of the skyline mural, and began fitting him with the microphone and earpiece as he sat.

At once, Nick felt the fluttering of a butterfly in the hollow cavern below his heart, a rare and unwelcome feeling for him. He looked ahead at the camera and saw only a tunnel of darkness. He had expected that he would see a monitor of sorts—a flat screen showing what the home viewers saw so that he could see his hosts and, more importantly, see how he looked. There was only a solitary, uncaring camera.

"Morning Nick, this is Rachel in New York," a voice in his right ear said with crystal clarity. "I'm one of the producers and we'll go live to you in about two minutes." Nick's pulse quickened, alarming him. He smiled on the outside and disciplined himself on the inside, commanding himself to calm down the way he commanded excellence from his staff. He widened his smile, remembering that one is always supposed to smile on television, then tried to determine if his smile was too wide, too awkward. He raised and lowered his lips as he gave his smile the full range of motion until he found what he hoped was the perfect personification of success.

"Hi Nick, this is Steve Doocy." Nick instinctively looked around the room for the voice before he spoke into his lapel. "Hi Steve, this is Nick," he said, rolling his eyes at the obvious.

"Ten seconds, Nick." Nick stared into the camera as if waiting for it to attack. He realized that the smile had slumped so he scolded it to respond. The intro jingle began playing in Nick's ear, indicating the show was returning from commercial break.

"Welcome back." Nick could hear Gretchen speaking as he stared at the faceless camera. "We've got a great guest this morning. Nick Vegas, acclaimed chef and restaurateur, is with us from our Atlanta studio. Good morning Nick."

***

As Clint Justice drove north on I-85 past spaghetti junction, he visualized an aerial view of the overlapping intersection of two major Atlanta highways resembling a bowl of Ramen noodles. He hadn't eaten Ramen noodles in years, but as Senior Compliance Investigator for the Food Safety and Inspection Service, he knew they were safe.

It wasn't Ramen noodles that kept him awake at night. It wasn't even the gross violations the FSIS had detected and, for the most part, kept quiet. The fecal-coated intestines that were shoved into sausage grinders, the deep fried rats on fried chicken plates, the burgers at county fairs that were alive with more pathogens and harmful bacteria than they could count. For the most part, those violations were caught before they entered the food chain. For the most part. No, what worried Clint was pathogens that weren't identified at inspection or, worst of all, animal products that somehow entered the food supply without undergoing inspection.

Clint tuned his car's satellite radio to Fox News to keep up on news while he drove to interview an anonymous tipster about a meat processing violation in Gainesville. She had agreed to meet privately with an FSIS investigator and Clint got the call.

"We've got a great guest this morning. Nick Vegas, acclaimed chef and restaurateur, is with us from our Atlanta studio. Good morning Nick."

Clint used the buttons on his steering wheel to increase the volume.

"One of the hottest trends in the restaurant business is the concept of underground supper clubs," Gretchen began, "or secret dinners. You can find them happening in pretty much every city at this point and the routine is always the same. You sign up for an email list, the chef sends out an email announcing precisely when registrations will begin and diners have only seconds to secure a spot. The day of the event, those who are lucky enough to get a spot receive an email with the address of the secret location, usually a house or a farm."

None of this was news to Clint. He was well aware of these clubs operating all over the country, popping up in every little town as a way to operate restaurants without calling them restaurants and therefore not needing licenses or inspections. He didn't like it one bit, but it was out of his jurisdiction. That was the territory of local and state health departments. *Silos*, he thought.

"But Nick Vegas has introduced a new concept that takes these underground supper clubs to a new level. It's a membership only club called 50-Forks that combines supper clubs with executive-level networking. Can you tell us about it, Nick?"

Nick had been told moments before that this would be his first question. He knew he had thirty seconds or less to answer and had no idea what the questions would be beyond that. "50-Forks is about relationships," Nick began. "Each group is open to fifty high-level business executives, and each group focuses on a different area. For example, one group is called 50 Pharma, another is 50 Financial, there's 50 CEOs, and so on. Membership is by invitation-only and the goal is to encourage private conversations among business leaders, with exquisite dining experiences as the backdrop to facilitate the discussions."

"So when you say exquisite dining experiences as the backdrop, what do you mean? Are these held at your restaurants?" The question had come from Steve Doocy.

Nick smiled broadly, confidently at the camera. "No. Given our clientele and the objective of these business events they are held in private locations, not in restaurants. They—"

Gretchen interrupted. "Do underground supper clubs hold their events in private residences purposefully so that they can operate without the oversight of the health department or inspectors?" Clint thumbed the volume up a little more. Nick didn't care for the question. He agreed to the interview to discuss the concept of 50-Forks, not to get trapped in a made-for-TV news drama.

"No, of course not. In our case we operate ten restaurants, all in full compliance with all regulatory bodies. We're very comfortable operating that way. 50-Forks operates outside of that because it's a business club, not a restaurant."

"Nick, my understanding is that members pay $75,000 per year for membership. Just doing quick math on the napkin here, fifty members at $75,000 times ten clubs, that's closing in on $40 million per year in revenue." Steve Doocy had brought up numbers that Nick wanted people to hear, but didn't want to confess. Clint's eyes grew wide as he heard the number and veered left on I-985 toward Gainesville.

"We don't publish details about 50-Forks," Nick began, "but as I said, it's an exclusive club with fantastic benefits to everyone involved."

Gretchen took the lead again. "Nick, we know you're a very successful businessman, but that you're a chef at heart. Can you tell us about anything special you'll have...cooked up for your guests?" Both Gretchen and Nick smiled at the pun.

"Well, I wouldn't want to give away the surprises for our guests, but let's just say I've been preparing one of the dishes for two years now."

Nick couldn't see Gretchen and Steve look at each other with puzzled bewilderment on camera. Finally, Gretchen closed by saying, "There you have it, folks. A new twist on the world of underground dining."

Steve added, "And a new twist on the phrase slow-food! I can't imagine what the members of 50-Forks will get that took two years to cook up."

Clint stared ahead at the road that meandered north toward the Georgia mountains and wondered the same thing.

Chapter 13

POP! POP! Thumpa-thumpa-THUMP! Pop! Pop! It wasn't a smell that woke Ozzie from his nap. It was the rhythmic thumping that came on gradually as Hal's thumper keg began to heat up, like popcorn starting to pop. Ozzie peeled his eyes open and rolled his head to the right. Hal took a swig from his cup and began dancing to the beat of the thumper keg.

"Hey Ozzie," Hal said as he caught glimpse of Ozzie's eyes. "Watch and I'll teach you how to do the old thump keg waltz." Hal continued clogging like a man who was hoping to audition for a remake of the movie *Deliverance*. Ozzie noticed the lumpy shape draped over Hal's shoulders, but couldn't make it out in the darkness. "If this world goes to hell in a hand basket all I need is a bit of grain and this here moonshine still, Ozzie, and I can keep us fed."

Hal took another slug right off the worm of his moonshine still.

"Back in the old days, every village had themselves a preacher, a carpenter, a well-witcher, and a moonshiner. Hell, that's all you need for a community right there." Hal said, before adding the obvious. "I'd be the moonshiner. I figure Rex here would be the preacher. Which one would you be Ozzie? The well-witcher?"

Hal walked over and took a seat in the glow of the fire. Ozzie twitched his head and made out the lump on Hal's shoulders. Hal saw Ozzie's gaze and looked to his shoulder at Rex's head. "This here's Rex," Hal said, nodding toward the opossum that sat on his left shoulder with its tail draped around Hal's neck. "Hell, Rex here LOVES the 'shine! Sometimes

Bambi comes up and drinks the shine. I done told you Ozzie, this here's all you need to feed your family. Just ask these critters. They could eat anything in the woods, but they keep on coming back when they hear that thumper keg a'going."

Ozzie groaned and grimaced but managed to right himself.

"Atta boy, Ozzie!" Hal said with wild enthusiasm. "Let's drink to that!"

Hal gave Rex a few slurps of shine and then took a swig for himself from the same cup. He stood up, a little too quickly as it seemed to Ozzie that he had lost his balance, and then made his way over and plopped down next to Ozzie. Rex crawled behind Hal's neck, as he was unsure of Ozzie's character. Hal put the cup to Ozzie's lips. He took a small sip and was able to really taste it for the first time. Hal started to remove the cup to check Ozzie's bandages, but Ozzie wanted more.

"All righty then," Hal said. "Let's set you up, boy! Barkeep," Hal called to himself as he walked to refill the cup. He gave the full cup to Ozzie who, partly out of hunger, partly out of thirst, but mainly out of the need for remedy, slugged every last drop. Hal burst out laughing. Ozzie appeared a little dazed, as if he was either unsure what he had done or not sure what happened to the moonshine. He just stared into the empty cup.

"Hell, Rex, that boy can drink!"

"Looks like you're getting 'round better every day there Oz. Hell, it's only been...well let's see, don't much have a calendar 'round here. I'd say about five or six weeks from your death bed to you scampering around camp during the day. Yep, moonshine, moss, and rest, that's the recipe." Hal leaned over and poured Ozzie a little more 'shine, which Ozzie slurped with enthusiasm. "C'mon boys, let's have ourselves a party!" Hal said as he picked up his guitar and started picking. "We need us some women folk, though. It's a sausagefest around here—uh, no offense there, Ozzie," Hal said.

Ozzie didn't get Hal's meaning but it didn't matter. He had no words to describe the steady shuffling of the twelve bar blues that came from the Martin guitar, but he couldn't stop tapping to it. His entire body bobbed and shook uncontrollably, his eyes transfixed by the glow of the fire that cast its spotlight on Hal dancing and singing with Rex on his shoulder. The beat flowed into Ozzie's blood.

Da dum dum da dum dum,

da da da,

Da dum dum da dum,

"We need an electric guitar to rip a solo and get this party rolling!" Hal said, stopping just long enough to take a swig from his cup and to refill Ozzie's cup. The music kept playing in Ozzie's ears even when Hal stopped. Ozzie had never felt so good, so free. So alive! Warmth from the evening campfire, warmth from Hal's liquid concoction, and music that lifted his soul. Ozzie grinned his biggest grin and watched Hal make the amazing sounds. They had been hootin' and hollerin' around the campfire for hours, rendering Hal's voice somewhat raspy, but it was the best singing Ozzie had ever heard.

"Don't know why the hell they call this the blues," Hal said. "Hell, this will cure anybody's blues!" Hal ripped into the final chorus:

Well now they call me the breeze,

I keep blowing down the road

Ozzie bobbed and weaved to the beat.

Da dum dum da dum dum, da da da,

Da dum dum da dum

I ain't got me nobody,

I don't carry me no load

"Hot damn!" Hal screamed, wiping sweat from his brow. "That there's some mighty fine Lynyrd Skynyrd, ain't it Oz?"

Ozzie kept bobbing his head, the music alive within him, comforting him. Hal took his guitar off and leaned it against the cabin, sat down by the fire.

"Hell, that's all you need right there, fellas," Hal said to Ozzie and Rex. "Whiskey, rock and roll, and a couple of pals. Don't need none of that other bullshit."

Ozzie still heard the beat of the blues rocking in his head and kept bobbing as Hal spoke, his rant sounding much like singing to Ozzie anyway. He didn't know if it was the moonshine or Hal's voice, but the combination of drink and Hal's rambling captivated Ozzie. To him, this was the happiest place on the planet. Hal seemed so free and so carefree that Ozzie couldn't remember why he had ever wanted to go back home. Hal seemed to take his mother's place each passing day. Feeding him, protecting him and caring for him. *He's living the life!* Ozzie thought as he watched Hal. *All I want is right here!*

"Look at us," Hal continued. "Where's the heat? Right here in the fire. Where's the air conditioning? Right there in them leaves. Ain't no cost for HVAC and ain't nothing to repair. Ain't no cost for refrigeration neither, not with this cool mountain stream. Ain't nobody to pay taxes to. My flatscreen TV is up right up yonder on the Milky Way channel. Almost every plant out here is medicine or food. Don't need no General Mills or Johnson & Johnson. Hell, boys, we don't need a blasted thing!" Hal stopped for a moment and reflected on what he had said, was saying. He had uttered these thoughts aloud to no one for years. The last person he had shared these thoughts with was his wife, Connie, before she became ill. The flickering campfire lured him back to another world, a world that now seemed as surreal as an alien landscape. He knocked back a slug of 'shine and got lost in a memory.

He had owned a small business with Connie, a bakery in Athens. They got by fine for years, but as he got closer to retirement age he grew disillusioned with the government, the Federal Reserve's money printing machine, and how unfair everything seemed. Every time he earned another dollar it was offset by rising food or energy prices. Or taxes. Yes, retirement had begun to weigh heavily on him, although he took comfort in the modest 401K they had accumulated.

He didn't know it then, but within three months his world would completely collapse.

It was just after Christmas in 2008 when Connie first complained of a constant headache. At first she described it as a *normal* headache, similar to others she had endured as of late. Hal attributed those to stress from being tied down to the bakery 24/7 with no end in sight. Connie took acetaminophen. When the headache persisted, she switched to Aleve. On New Years Day the headache became so excruciating that Connie complained of a stiff neck and told Hal her vision was blurred. Hal quietly panicked and prepared to take her to the emergency room at Athens Regional Hospital. He *should* have taken her to the emergency room. But Connie was fiercely independent and afraid of hospitals. "I'll go to my doctor first thing in the morning," she had insisted. Hal sat on the sofa holding her, his fingers caressing her forehead. As Hal dozed off, Connie drifted to sleep in his arms. She never awoke. When Hal found her motionless, apparently lifeless, he shook her violently and screamed her name. "Connie! CONNIE! Wake up!"

To Hal, it was as if everything that happened from that moment on happened to someone else. An old, horrifying movie that Hal vaguely remembered watching as an observer, not a participant. The 911 call, the paramedics, the doctor's apologies, sympathies, and exhortations that "she should have gone to the emergency room when the headache persisted..."

She was gone. Hal was left to wander, sentenced to drift without a rudder in a sea of isolation and misery. He never made a conscious choice regarding his own fate. He felt an invisible hand guide him through the fog of Connie's funeral and open his eyes to how pointless his business of baking bread was. Hal put a "closed" sign on the door, walked away, and never returned.

As the nation's banks collapsed and financial markets plummeted over the next month to a twelve-year low, Hal watched his meaningless 401K dwindle to less than half its value while the government bailed out those too big to fail. It was all too much for him to take in, with or without the guiding hand. He cashed in what was left of his 401K and fumed some more when the government took its penalty for taxes and early withdrawal. All that was left for him was to make trips to a few stores. Army surplus for survival supplies, Barnes & Noble for some wilderness books, and finally a camping store. Hal drove north, unsure of his destination. The hand guided him to the mountains and down Warwoman Road where he found what looked like the most isolated and dense jungle on the planet. A place where he could hide, get lost and die, and be beholden to no one.

The doctors had offered no reason to satisfy Hal's need to understand Connie's sudden death. How could she have been here so alive, so much a part of him one moment and then gone, poof, the next? Just a ruptured aneurysm, that's all. It happens. More and more often, they said. One doctor even suggested the increase in incidents of aneurysms had to do with the factory farming methods that leeched essential minerals such as copper from the soil and, ultimately, from the bloodstream. Hal heard little of it, consciously. Subconsciously, the doctor's indictment against factory farming just piled on top of the bailouts, the finger pointing, the concrete jungles, and the sense of entitlement that increasingly everyone exhibited. Entitled to a job, entitled to a home, entitled to cheap food and fuel. It was an artificial world created by a parasitic invader—man. Hal was able to survive in that world with Connie because he and Connie created their own little world, their bubble. Without her, the bubble burst and deposited Hal in a world he wanted no part of.

"Ow! Jesus Rex, watch it!" Hal exclaimed. With the music stopped for the night, Rex dug his paws into Hal's shoulder to climb down and go exploring in the darkness. Hal looked across the dwindling fire to Ozzie, either asleep or passed out on the porch. His grin had faded, turned to drool as Ozzie twitched violently.

Hope he's having sweet dreams, Hal thought to himself, as he got up and decided to turn in himself. First, he allowed the piss mister to extinguish the fire.

Hal walked past Ozzie into the cabin with a peace he hadn't felt in a long, long time. Somehow Ozzie was healing him as much as he was healing Ozzie. Getting him back in touch with life and forcing him to process feelings he had never fully explored.

God, I love that little guy, Hal thought and drifted asleep as rain began to fall.

On the front porch, Ozzie began to dream. He dreamt that he was floating over the porch and spinning like a feather over the dying campfire. The heat pushed Ozzie above the forest canopy where he could look down to see a trail of smoke from Hal's smoldering fire climb through the treetops like Jack's beanstalk. Not far downstream, Ozzie saw a lush garden with an enchanting, black-haired angel standing in the middle with her arms spread wide. Overhead, he saw the swirling eye of an approaching storm, the sullen sky turning almost as dark as the mountain soil itself. Turning his gaze west, Ozzie drifted above another clearing where a winding road snaked up the mountainside. Below, he saw his mother lying on the ground alone, shivering and frightened. A lighting bolt singed Ozzie's nose, tracing a path from the storm above and striking the ground near Isabella. From the ashes of the lightning strike, a man rose and brandished a steely knife in her face. Ozzie screamed at the man, but no sound came. He flung his arms to fly and save his mother, but the skies opened and—

"Every man for himself!" Hal shouted in the midst of a moonshine-fueled dream of his own that jolted Ozzie awake from his nightmare.

Ozzie jumped up on the porch and looked around, not knowing for a moment where he was. He ran inside the cabin next to Hal, trembling, and crawled under Hal's bed. Before coming to Hal's, he had never had nightmares. Now, horrific nightmares came nightly.

Shaking uncontrollably under Hal's bed, Ozzie peered out the door hoping, praying to not see the men, the coyotes, and the swirling storm that he saw in his nightmares. He thought of his mother, alone, and his father murdered. The feelings tortured him, his love for his mother pulling him back to her, his fear of his enemies keeping him close to Hal. And he thought of Hal, who lived the life that Ozzie wanted. If only Isabella could be with him. But she wasn't, and Ozzie was scared for her. He closed his eyes tightly and cried himself to sleep.

Chapter 14

As the flowers in her secret garden glistened in the morning dew, Angelica regretted giving into her body's midnight craving and feeding it pork ribs. She knew that eating pork late at night was associated with bad dreams and poor sleep, but she devoured the ribs anyway, feeling sinfully gluttonous in the moment but unable or unwilling to refrain. *Baby's hungry*, she had said.

She slept miserably, tossing and turning and unable to stay asleep. It was hard enough sleeping with her belly bulging more each day, and she needed some rest. Morning couldn't come soon enough for Angelica, as she had hardly been able to wait to come to her secret garden, the one place that always gave her peace and comfort. Now, she gingerly fingered the branches of Nancy's Tree as she walked to a hammock that joined twin crabapple trees. She sat on the hammock and threw her legs up with more difficulty than the month before. Angelica pushed off, using one of the overhanging branches, causing the hammock to sway.

The garden was hauntingly quiet, the air not breathing, the birds not singing. Her eyes were too heavy to stay awake and contemplate the quiet. She needed rest and the hammock quickly soothed her into a deep sleep and she began to dream.

A drop of rain fell from the heavens and kissed Angelica's arm. Then another. She smiled at God's gift of rain and studied the drop curiously. The raindrop was as black as a cave's deepest secret. She touched the black drop and felt her skin rise, mushrooming into a searing black blister that spread along her arm before bursting and covering her in pus. In the dream, she searched the sky for answers, but instead of seeing God she saw a dark, swirling storm approach from the south. She peered closely at the menacing cloud and saw its shape contort into the shape of Blake's face. He frowned at Angelica and spewed his black rain over her secret garden. The toxic rain stripped everything it touched as fur, feather, leaves, and flesh melted from trees and drained into the soil.

Suddenly, Angelica found herself floating on a branch high in Nancy's Tree. As she reached to pick a ripe fig, its sweet scent faded, replaced by a putrid smell of rotten meat that gagged her. The figs began to rot and turn black as they fell from the dying tree with a splattering thud. Angelica tasted blood and wiped her lip to see blood coming out of her mouth. She looked to the ground and watched the blood wash down her legs, over her feet, drip from her toes, and plunge into the soil, as if the soil was pulling the blood from her. Her eyes grew wide with fear as she hugged her abdomen, realizing she was bleeding from between her legs.

"No!" Angelica screamed herself awake in her hammock.

***

Ozzie could hardly wait for sunrise. He crawled out from under Hal's bed and greeted the cool October air, the early morning sun casting long shadows over Hal's camp. The light was Ozzie's friend, a blanket of protection, he felt, from the horror of his dreams. Walking downstream, Ozzie wandered aimlessly in the safety of the light. After walking for an hour he stopped by the stream to think.

A thin fog had risen from the night's rain to cover the forest floor. Through the fog Ozzie saw a lush clearing at the point where the stream curved. He walked to it through the fog with trepidation and prayed there were no coyotes in the fog! Remembering the coyotes quickened Ozzie's pace. He ran into the clearing and stopped, able to see well around him.

Ozzie stared at all the trees, the flowers, and the plants. He had lived his whole life where there was little to eat. Now, he stood in the most beautiful place he had ever imagined, and the fog made him feel as if he were dreaming again. He found himself surrounded by food. Plants came from the ground, mushrooms grew on logs and food had fallen from the trees. He looked up at the first fig tree he had ever seen and was entranced. He dropped his head to see a ground littered deep with figs. They were overripe but it didn't matter. As Ozzie ate, he grinned and squeezed as many sweet figs as he could into his mouth. He lost himself in a trance as he filled his belly with the most delicious fruit he had ever tasted. A fruit that he figured must surely be forbidden.

"No!"

Ozzie snapped out of his trance as he heard a violent scream from a woman. He squinted through the fog to the other side of the garden. A woman shot straight up from a hammock and scared Ozzie back up the stream toward Hal's camp.

***

Angelica looked over her body and touched her arms to make sure there were no blisters. She felt her abdomen carefully. Realizing it felt precisely how it should, she breathed a sigh of relief and wiped sweat from her forehead. She threw her feet off the hammock, put her head in her hands, and cried. The tears ran like a summer downpour, there was no stopping them. She was horrified. *What did I dream? What does it mean? Is something wrong with my baby?*

The thoughts raced through Angelica's mind as the tears streamed down her cheeks. *Why was Blake there? Why was he creating the suffering?* Angelia closed her eyes and calmed herself as she allowed rational thoughts to overtake irrational tears. She felt her abdomen again and held her breath. She waited. The baby moved, ever so slightly, but she was sure. She exhaled. *He's fine*, she thought, as she rose to inspect her garden.

Since she had fallen asleep, the fog had descended on the garden, making it feel as if her Garden of Eden was indeed in heaven. She walked along the perimeter of her medicinal herb garden, inspecting the valerian, comfrey, feverfew and the St. John's wort. She rubbed her legs against her culinary herbs, releasing a bouquet of mint, oregano, rosemary and thyme into the fog to be lifted to the birds, to God. Angelica inspected the echinacea and the poke, the two plants she used most often in the tinctures she made to keep her immune system strong. She hoped that the benefits of nature's medicines would wash through her Cherokee blood and accrue to her son, although she had suspended taking the poke, due to its toxicity, the minute she found out she was pregnant. Bending slightly, she picked a few medicinal herbs and tucked them beside the crystals in the deerskin pouch that she wore at all times.

She walked to Nancy's Tree, captivated by the glistening foliage that hung from her branches. Nancy was growing into a beautiful young woman already. Angelica allowed her eyes to drop from the branches to the ground to take in the sea of fallen fruit, fruit that...had been almost completely eaten since she had walked by an hour before! Every single one, dozens of fallen figs, now mostly eaten, devoured.

He had been quiet, sneaky, whoever this fruit thief was. Angelica studied clues on the ground as closely as her Cherokee ancestors had two centuries before when tracking game over the same land. Her eyes focused on a small area of disturbed soil where Ozzie had dug in to race away when Angelica's scream scared him. She surveyed the spot and saw the prints where her intruder had run off up the stream. She smiled again. *A child of the forest, Nancy!* She thought to herself. *I hope he comes back!*

With the soft, morning light filtering through the branches, Angelica started down the trail to her house as she realized she should make coffee and breakfast for Blake. The house was clean, as it almost always was, but she wanted to straighten up a bit before Rose came by later in the morning to drop off the girls. After breakfast with Blake she would come back and sit in the corner of the garden and knit yet *another* baby sweater. The thought of keeping Rose's girls, of her baby that just kicked, of her new friend in the garden, these happy thoughts of others to care for and nurture lifted Angelica up the trail and washed away her nightmare. She was calm and at peace once again, other than a gnawing feeling below her level of consciousness that she couldn't put her finger on. Something to do with her baby, with Blake, with death.

Chapter 15

Ozzie ran halfway back to Hal's, slowing only when he was sure he was away from that screaming woman. Hal had befriended Ozzie, taken care of him, but every other person Ozzie met had chased him. He wanted to get back to the safety of Hal's camp.

Continuing along the stream, he approached Hal's cabin. The smell of the morning campfire, coffee, and bacon wafted downstream, telling Ozzie that Hal was up well before he got there. Hal was cooking eggs and venison bacon over the campfire as he saw Ozzie roll into the south end of the camp.

"Top of the morning to you there, Oz!"

Rex crawled under a fallen oak tree to hide from the sun and catch up on some sleep. It was good to be home, Ozzie thought. He wanted to tell Hal all about the figs, about his adventure, but before he could open his mouth he saw something that stopped him cold.

She walked out from behind the cabin and stood there, next to Hal, and stared at Ozzie. She didn't move. Ozzie didn't move. "We got a visitor, Oz," Hal announced. "I reckon you might know her."

Ozzie didn't know her, but he had seen her. Once, somewhere. She had wavy hair the color of a gingerbread cookie that trailed off over her shoulders, down her back. Her eyes were loving, carefree, and brown, her long and slender face was dirty, like she had been playing outside. Her nose was a little long, but not as long as Ozzie's, so who was he to talk about that. Yes, she was beautiful.

Her name was Tammy. Ozzie knew this immediately by looking at the prison tag she wore that spelled her name.

"TAMMY," just as his own tag spelled his name, "OZZIE." She must have escaped too, have been in a neighboring camp, but he had never seen her. Or had he?

Tammy made the first move, walking around Hal and the fire and up to Ozzie. Ozzie took one step back, stopped. She was a little older than Ozzie and more mature, having not been protected by a mother since her mother had died a long time ago. Tammy lived only with her brothers and sisters at the end of the cul-de-sac, far away from Ozzie. She had only seen him once, on the day he escaped.

"I'm sorry about what they did to your father," she said, hoping to ease into the relationship with Ozzie.

Ozzie was startled. The mention of his father brought back the memories of what happened, memories the moonshine had been scrubbing away that had become like a long ago dream. Now they came to the forefront again, presented real and true before him. But it wasn't just the mention of his father that startled him. She spoke to him in the language he understood, that he had learned from his Spanish ancestors. Ozzie hadn't spoken to anyone, hadn't understood anyone since his mother told him to run, to flee. He didn't know how to respond, what to say. Tammy sensed this and dropped her eyes from his, hoping to not intimidate him. Ozzie's heart was racing with fear, with excitement, with passion. With feelings he had never felt before. He calmed himself the best he could before uttering his first words to her.

"You have red hair." Ozzie reached out to grab the words he blurted, the foolish words that made no sense.

Tammy smiled. It was perfect. "Why yes, I do, Ozzie," she said, at ease as if she had not a care in the world. "Thanks for noticing!" Her ease calmed Ozzie and made him feel comfortable.

"Thanks," he said, "I mean for saying that about my dad. Do you know what happened to them, after I left? To my brother and mother?"

"No. I left just after you did. When you ran away, the men turned the fence off and chased after you. My brothers and sisters screamed when I did it, but I just ran right through the fence out into the woods. It was as if you freed me, Ozzie. I've been wandering around on my own all this time now, just finding this place this morning. I followed the smell of the campfire."

Hal saw Ozzie and Tammy talking quietly, moving closer together, and it made him happy. His life had been hollow and meaningless for years, having no more flavor than a stale rice cake. With Ozzie and now Tammy, there was life here. There was fun, meaning. Community. He didn't realize how much he wanted...needed the companionship of others. Hal smiled and flipped the eggs as his three hens hunted for bugs.

Tammy walked over to the stream. Ozzie followed and joined her, walking by her side. Tammy walked into the creek, feeling the cool stream rush by her legs. "Don't you just love it out here?" Tammy asked as she washed her face in the stream. "You can do whatever you want, eat whatever you want, go wherever you want."

"I suppose so," Ozzie answered, his indifference surprising him. He did love it out here, only...he loved it at Hal's.

"Well, you don't sound so sure. Don't tell me you're homesick. Any place was better than that place!"

Ozzie didn't say anything. He just doodled and dug in the dirt next to the stream, not saying anything, not really thinking anything.

"Why in the world do you miss *that* place, Oz?

"I'm worried about my mother. I'm afraid they're going to hurt or kill her."

"Well of course they're going to—" Ozzie's head jerked up as Tammy caught herself and stopped before she said anymore. She hadn't realized how innocent Ozzie was, how much his mother had sheltered him from what *really* happened there.

"Ozzie," Tammy began, more gingerly than before, "how long did you live there?"

Ozzie pondered the question for a moment. "I've always lived there!" he said finally.

"Ozzie, we were *all* brought there. We were all kidnapped and brought to that place. No one was born there and *no one* leaves that hell hole alive." Tammy paused for a moment. "Until...you Ozzie, you were the first one to leave there alive. You're the reason I'm free. You can never go back there Ozzie. Those men are vicious. They'll kill you and laugh while they're doing it. I've seen them do it."

Tammy stopped talking, her own horrific memories now trying to bubble to the surface. She squashed them in their tracks as she always did, suppressing her feelings the same way she and her family had been suppressed and held down. Tammy had watched them murder her mother, murder her father, only two years before. The men *did* laugh while they did it, talked about football and women while looking at her, smiling, when they slit her daddy's throat. As they bled him dry right before her eyes, Tammy's mind left her body and drifted far away from that place. It sought refuge in her own forest utopia where it roamed carefree and did what it wanted. Until, she now realized, Ozzie escaped and she followed him through the fence to *real* utopia. No, she would never go back to *that* place.

Ozzie studied her silence and thought about what she said. Tammy began walking down stream and Ozzie followed. Tammy changed the subject.

"Lets walk down the stream Ozzie!"

Ozzie walked just behind Tammy on the narrow trail. The trail widened and the sun shone brightly through the canopy. Tammy began spinning around.

"What are you doing?" Ozzie asked.

"Dancing in the sun's rays, Ozzie 'ol boy. Dancing in the sun's rays!"

"What on earth for?" Ozzie asked.

Tammy looked at him and cocked her head. "Because Ozzie, I can. I'm free! And last night I danced in the moonlight." Tammy left the trail and splashed in the stream.

"Come on in, Ozzie!"

Ozzie stared at her pensively but stayed firmly on the trail. He hadn't yet accepted his freedom and wasn't sure what he was supposed to do. Tammy, on the other hand, embraced her freedom. Nature provided almost everything she needed, just as Hal would point out that night and every night when his liquid rants echoed over the campfire. But it didn't provide everything. Unlike Hal, she didn't want to be alone. She wanted a family one day, and she couldn't do that alone.

By early afternoon they had made their way back to the clearing where Ozzie had found the figs. Ozzie stopped in the woods so that he was able to see the garden. He stood and stared. *If that woman is still there, she won't be able to see me,* he thought. Tammy saw the opening and wanted to go explore, but Ozzie cautioned her, telling her about the screaming woman. Tammy stayed back while Ozzie walked slowly toward the tree.

Angelica sat in a wicker chair in the corner of the garden. In front of the chair was two mullein plants, their yellow spikes towering over six feet high and obscuring most of Nancy's Tree, thirty yards away. With her hands, Angelica felt the heft of the royal blue yarn, the smooth, fuzzy touch of the fiber. She draped it over her skin, closed her eyes and visualized it warming her baby, her son, in the winter months. She tugged the half sweater she had knitted and approved of the tension. Without thinking, her muscles and ears took over, by now having memorized the movements and sounds to create the perfect rhythm of knitting. Her hands moved steadily, the metal knitting needles creating a soothing clicking sound as they struck together, the sound being precisely why she preferred them to bamboo. She watched her work when she wanted, but there was no need to concentrate on the task. Knitting in her secret garden calmed her the way yoga calmed others. It gave her peace and provided refuge from any stress that attempted to creep into Angelica's life. *All stress can be knitted away*, she thought, *and a garment made to take its place.*

Ozzie walked under the drip line of Nancy's Tree, entering from the forest this time. A few more figs had fallen from the tree. Ozzie pointed them out to Tammy. "It's safe," he whispered. "Come try one."

Tammy moved forward and tasted her first fig, deliciously ripe. She accidentally bumped Nancy's Tree, laughing as an overripe fig bounced off Ozzie's head. Across the garden Angelica saw the tree shake gently. She slowly leaned to her right and saw both Ozzie and Tammy at the base of the tree reveling in Nancy's gift.

Children of the forest! Angelica said to herself with a smile that ran almost to the back of her head. Tears welled in her eyes as she thought about the happiness that Nancy now showered on her garden and how much happiness had risen from that place that was so deeply sorrowful just two years ago. *I want to meet them!*

As she continued knitting she began to sing ever so softly, as if singing a lullaby to her newborn child. Her angelic voice lifted over the mullein, danced with the herbs and filtered through Nancy's branches down to Ozzie and Tammy. They ate, the singing a background noise as a distant wind that goes unnoticed. The knitting soothed Angelica. The singing soothed Ozzie and Tammy. Angelica let her voice rise ever so slightly, unable to help it anyway as if a spirit had lifted her soul. She wanted to belt out her love, her compassion, but didn't want to scare her new friends away.

Ozzie lost himself in the figs, but Tammy stopped and listened to the singing. She looked around unable to determine the origin of the voice.

"Ozzie, where's that coming from?"

Ozzie raised his head, half-chewed figs dripping from his mouth. He listened, hearing it for the first time, and turned around. There was no one in the hammock. He stared in that direction, his eyes sidestepping into the corner of the garden. The voice was coming from there, from the same woman, but he couldn't see her. It wasn't a screaming voice this time. It sang the way Hal sang, only...no one sang like this. It didn't make Ozzie feel like dancing. It made him feel joyous, peaceful, very nearly compelling him to kneel and bow his head. He felt as if he were a baby and his mother was singing to him, the way Isabella used to sing to him. The way all mothers sing to their babies.

Angelica stood up very slowly, smiled and looked right at Ozzie as she rose in the distance. Ozzie darted to the bushes and stopped with Tammy at his side. He looked through the bushes, able to see Angelica, but thinking that she would be unable to see him. Still she smiled, still she sang. Still she stood. She hadn't tried to harm him. Instead, she captivated Ozzie. Tammy looked at Ozzie, mouth agape as he peered at Angelica, her singing luring Ozzie into a trance that caused him to sway ever so slightly.

"Let's go, Ozzie. I don't like her."

Ozzie turned to Tammy, looking perplexed. "Why not? She's not going to hurt us."

"I don't like her," Tammy repeated, furrowing her eyes in Angelica's direction. She turned and walked toward the path by the stream. "I'm going back to Hal's."

Ozzie turned his head back to glance at Angelica. She waved at him. It startled Ozzie. He was sure she couldn't see him, could she? How could she see into the bushes?

As he began to follow Tammy, Ozzie walked into the open behind Nancy's Tree instead of following Tammy through the cover of the forest. Walking very slowly he looked straight into Angelica's eyes as she gazed peacefully into his. She smiled and sang to him as he continued walking out of the garden and up the stream.

Chapter 16

Some people's lives seem preordained at birth. As youngsters, they pass time playing with other children, absorbing what teachers and preachers have to say until they're old enough to accept their destinies. Sheriff Lonnie Jacobs was one such person.

He was born and raised in Rabun County in an area the locals called Chechero. His backyard playground was Rainey Mountain where he roamed the woods as a boy, learning to shoot by the time he was eight and hunting alone with his shotgun by the time he was eleven. Like most boys he knew, he learned how to use a gun responsibly and scoffed at the liberal media reports he would see from time to time that proclaimed guns as unsafe. He knew guns were safe, if treated with respect, and were deadly if treated with negligence. Just as a motor vehicle is, just as a knife is, just as baseball bat is. "Heck," he had recently told a friend over coffee at the Clayton Cafe when debating the subject, "the banjo is legally considered a deadly weapon under Colorado state law. It's true!"

Lonnie first learned the word *sheriff* from Mrs. Welch, a Sunday School teacher at the Bull Creek Baptist Church. She was reading a passage from the book of Daniel that said, "the king sent to gather together the princes, the governors...the judges...the sheriffs, and all the rulers of the provinces." Lonnie wanted to become one of those leaders, those rulers. Becoming a prince was out of the question and he had no interest in becoming governor since he'd have to move to Atlanta. Nor was he inclined to sit behind a bench, so he ruled out becoming a judge. He thought long and hard of becoming a pastor when he was a teenager, but also felt destined to become one of the sheriffs.

He had learned his way through the woods, knew how to hunt, how to track, what to eat, what to avoid. Lonnie also knew how dangerous the north Georgia woods could be to anyone unfamiliar with them. Fortunately, most folks in his county knew that all too well since most of them were born and raised there. No local in his or her right mind would just wander into the dense woods unprepared or without knowing how to get out. *Certainly two locals never would*, he thought to himself as he turned his new SUV into Blake Savage's driveway.

The sheriff's office had only recently begun using the SUVs, and Lonnie thought it was about time. Most of the sheriff's territory in Rabun County was rural and lightly populated. Old dirt roads, washed and rutted by rains racing down steep mountainsides, were the norm. Blake's driveway off Hale Ridge Road was no exception, but just getting there was the real battle.

Hale Ridge was one of the most isolated, least populated areas of Rabun County. The gravel road itself was in decent shape, Lonnie noted, with only a few bumpy ruts causing him to slow to a crawl. When it rained hard, however, it was a different story. Roads such as Hale Ridge became quickly impassable no matter what you were driving and were low priority for the road maintenance crews. Heavy rains would bring down huge trees, generally right over roads and power lines. To make matters worse, each side of the road was lined with terrain so steep a car could tumble off. If the drivers were sufficiently injured they may not be found or known about for a very long time, if ever. Hale Ridge road was wider than a one-lane road but not as wide as a two-lane road. It was rare for cars to meet on the road. When they did, they would each have to snake just along the edge of the road until they passed. Lonnie hated to think what that task would be like if the ground was waterlogged.

Lonnie knew Blake, but not very well. Like most folks in and around Clayton, Lonnie went to the Wildcat football games on Friday nights and had cheered as Blake dominated defenses until the rising star graduated in 2000. Lonnie himself had graduated from Rabun County fifteen years earlier before heading off to Georgia State College in Atlanta, where he majored in Criminal Justice. He hadn't cared for the city lights of Atlanta much and mostly kept to himself in his dorm, with one exception. Turner Field was within walking distance and he could buy tickets for Atlanta Braves games for only a dollar in the cheap seats, something he did several times a week when the Braves were in town. When Lonnie finished up at Georgia State, he headed back to his home on Rainey Mountain to pursue his life's calling just as he knew he always would. Ten years later he was elected Sheriff of Rabun County.

Lonnie parked in front of the house next to Blake's F-150 at 8:10 a.m., got out, and shut the door quietly, as was his practice. He straightened his hat and walked with purpose and authority to the door at the center of the A-frame, and rang the doorbell.

Blake sat on the sofa when the doorbell rang, having just finished a heated call with Nick to discuss the delivery Blake would make later in the day. He looked toward the door and exhaled deeply. *Angelica, if you've locked yourself out...*, he thought to himself with exasperation as he got up and walked to the door. As he reached for the handle he could see through the stained-glass door that it was not Angelica. The figure loomed large, with the morning sun casting a large shadow over its wide-brimmed hat. Blake's throat dried and his pulse quickened as he opened the door.

Lonnie gave a professional smile. "Mornin' Blake."

"Mornin' Sheriff. How can I help you?"

Blake immediately wished he hadn't said that. It was so formal, so distant. Not something you say to someone you know, someone you want to be friendly with, unless you want to appear uneasy. Blake had never been friendly with Lonnie. He was much older and Blake's gang in high school, while not troublemakers, had always steered clear of the law. Lonnie tuned in to Blake's demeanor and took the lead.

"Well," Lonnie began with a slow mountain drawl, "I just wanted to sit with you a minute and ask a couple of questions. That's if you don't mind, Blake."

In the second that it took Blake to respond, the worst thoughts raced through his mind. *What does he want? What does he KNOW? Am I in trouble? What should I do?* The rage began to boil within Blake as he knew that only someone who has something to hide would think such thoughts.

"Sure Sheriff, come on in."

Lonnie walked in and, to Blake, appeared to notice nothing other than the bar stool he sat on. But Lonnie was a trained observer, both in the natural world and in the manmade one. He took a quick inventory of the environment before him, noting nothing unusual. A flat screen TV, a shotgun on the wall and a handmade walking stick leaning next to the sofa. Everything was in order, Lonnie surmised.

"I'm looking for a couple of fellas that live around here, Blake. They've been missing for going on a month now and, well, I'm just asking around to see if anybody knows anything that might help."

"I ain't seen 'em, Sheriff," Blake blurted.

"Seen who?" Lonnie asked.

"Seen...whoever's missing. I assume you're talking about them boys I heard about."

"Well, what'd you hear?" Lonnie asked as he watched Blake wrench his hands.

Blake was nervous and was sure the sheriff knew it. He shouldn't have answered so quickly, so abruptly. He felt out of control, as if he was being interrogated in his own home. *SETTLE DOWN!* He told himself, the same way he used to when it was late in the game and he needed to lead a scoring drive.

"I just heard at the coffee shop that some boys were missing," Blake said. "Folks figured they ran off or something."

Lonnie nodded and reached into his shirt pocket, slowly retrieving a pen and note pad. He opened it and wrote a note reminding himself to stop by the hardware store on the way home. Blake watched the sheriff write and his pulse quickened even more. *What is he writing?* Blake realized he couldn't just stare at the sheriff so he surveyed the room, noticing the empty coffee pot. He realized he should offer the sheriff some coffee.

"Would you like me to make us some coffee, Sheriff?"

Lonnie looked up from his pad, and then looked at his watch. "No, thanks anyway. I gotta be heading back. Got some other folks I need to talk to on the way."

Lonnie stood up and began walking to the door. Blake breathed a quiet sigh of relief, walked ahead and opened the door for the sheriff. Lonnie walked through, stopped in the middle of the opening and turned to face Blake, their faces only a foot apart.

"Do you know them boys?" Lonnie asked. "Jesse Simmons and Shane Dixon?

"No," Blake said quickly and firmly.

"Hmmm..." Lonnie said, and then stood silently, his nose inches from Blake's.

Blake thought about what, if anything else, he should say. The moment dragged out just as the sheriff wanted and just as Blake feared.

"What?" Blake asked finally.

"Well...it's just that them boys don't live too far from here. Jesse's folks are dead and he lives with his uncle over on Sarah's Creek. Shane lives over on Earls Ford Road. His folks said he was doing some work for a farmer up on Hale Ridge, or 'round them parts. Ain't many folks that mess with farming up this way 'cept you, so I figured you might know 'em."

"I just deliver stuff for farmers and wineries to restaurants in Athens," Blake said.

"Yeah," Lonnie said, looking Blake squarely in the eye. "So you don't know them boys, then?"

Blake couldn't remember ever having felt so scared. *Oh shit, he knows! But, knows what? What is there to know?*

"No," Blake said.

Lonnie walked on through the door and pulled out his pad again to scribble a note. He glanced to his left at a woman walking up the path.

"Mornin', ma'am," Lonnie said as Angelica approached.

Angelica was surprised to see the sheriff, but not alarmed. She was generally happy to see anyone and would never suspect, or dread, that she was in any trouble. "Good morning, Sheriff," she said with genuine enthusiasm.

Lonnie turned back to face Blake.

"All righty then. Well, good talking with you, Blake." Lonnie glanced at Angelica before looking back at Blake, making sure she also got the message. "Let me know if you hear anything about them boys, will you?"

"Of course Sheriff," Blake said. *Now please LEAVE!* He thought.

Lonnie tipped his hat to Angelica, got in his car, and pulled away slowly.

Blake turned and stormed into the house. Angelica stood in the driveway. The peace and calm she had felt while knitting and watching Ozzie and Tammy gave way to unease. Seeing the sheriff and watching Blake storm off brought her morning nightmare back to the foreground.

She walked into the kitchen and closed the door. Blake sat on the sofa, his chin resting in the palms of his folded hands. His mind was elsewhere, unaware of her presence. Angelica turned on the water faucet, filled the coffee pot, and poured it slowly into the coffee maker. Opening the can of Maxwell

House, she put two measured scoops into the filter and turned the machine on.

Angelica stood in the kitchen and studied Blake, feeling in her gut that something was wrong but not sure how to approach him. He had become so distant, so irritable recently, that Angelica felt she had to tread cautiously when approaching him. Yet, at that moment, she realized how much she needed him. She didn't work or have any way of producing income. Blake provided almost everything. Angelica did inherit some money from her parent's death that she put alongside the money Blake's lawyer won him for the car accident. Together it had been just enough to pay cash for the house, furnishings, land, and Blake's truck. They had a great health care plan that would provide everything the baby needed if there was an emergency, but it was a plan that Nick provided to Blake by putting him on The Federal's payroll for a nominal salary. Angelica had been thrilled, even proud of Blake, when he explained that Nick had agreed to it as part of Blake doing so much for him. With no mortgage, no car payment, and no health care costs, Blake only had to earn enough to pay utilities, a little bit of food, and minor expenses.

But what if something's wrong? Angelica thought while watching Blake. *What if he's in trouble? What will happen to the health care? To the money that he makes to pay the bills? What would I do? What would WE do when the baby comes?*

Blake sat in silence, fearing the worst for himself. Angelica stood fifteen feet away, in silence, fearing the worst for herself and for her baby. The coffee maker stopped dripping and Angelica took a cup, filling it with black coffee. She walked around the bar and stood before Blake before speaking softly.

"Mornin' sweetie. Here's your coffee."

Blake looked up at the cup before him, at the woman before him. He saw what he had once seen, but had lost sight of. He saw an angel. He stared without expression into her eyes through the smallest of tears that threatened to flood his own eyes. *How could I have lost sight of her? Of our baby? Of what's important? What the hell is wrong with me?* Blake was in shock, both at Angelica's grace and beauty and at his own greed, his own stupidity. How had he gotten himself into this mess?

"Blake?"

He realized that Angelica was still holding the coffee.

"Sorry, sweetie," he said lovingly. It was all Angelica needed. She seemed to have no capacity to hold grudges, to stay angry. She had only the capacity to forgive, to comfort. To love. She smiled at the first truly kind words Blake had uttered to her in months. As she sat beside him, Angelica placed her left hand on his right knee. She wanted to know what the sheriff wanted but feared it would upset Blake if she asked directly, so she took another approach.

"Is everything okay, hon?"

Blake looked at her and quickly looked away. He felt himself losing control, tearing up, and didn't think he could keep his composure by looking at her. In that moment it felt less like she was his wife and more like she was maternal, someone who would understand, would comfort and tell him that everything would be just fine. That's all he wanted to hear, that everything would be hunky-dory but he knew that Angelica couldn't make any of his troubles go away. Only he could.

He sat beside her in silence and thought for a moment. He needed to tell her the truth and then to get out of the mess he felt he was in with Nick. To walk the straight path with her at his side, just as she wanted. She was right, he needed to go to church with her and he would, this Sunday, he told himself. Turning to Angelica, Blake took her left hand, opened his mouth, and prepared to tell her everything. To confess and give himself some peace.

"Angelica, I have to talk to—"

A series of loud knocks pelted the kitchen door, interrupting Blake. Blake and Angelica turned quickly to see the door rattle and to hear the voices of two little girls cry: "Auntie Angelica,

Auntie Angelica!" Blake stood and pulled his suit of armor back on. Angelica put her hand on Blake's shoulder.

"Everything will be okay," she said.

Blake walked to the kitchen and poured his coffee into a travel mug as Angelica walked toward the door. He turned and said, "I have to make a delivery to Nick. I'll be back in time for dinner."

Angelica opened the door and the girls rushed in, pink ribbons in their hair streaming. They nearly knocked Angelica down as she knelt to hug them. Blake walked past and out the door, seeing Rose walking in from the car.

"Hi, Rose," he said politely.

"Hi, Blake. Where you off to?"

"Athens," he said. He continued walking before turning around at his truck. "Oh yeah...have a good vacation," he added.

Rose smiled, but said nothing as she walked inside.

Chapter 17

After leaving the isolation and dense forest cover that overhung most of Warwoman, the small town of Clayton emerged as something of a rural metropolis after Blake snaked through the morning fog along Warwoman Creek. Turning south on 441, he drove past Regions Bank, Bi-Lo groceries, Chick-Fil-A, the new Super Wal-Mart and Home Depot, thinking of all the businesses Clayton now had where he could likely get a job. Places he would never have considered working before. He always thought he was far too good for them then, wanted way more out of life than they could ever offer. Now, they dangled everything that he wanted. Stability, honesty, security. More than anything they could provide a place to hide, to blend in, and be somebody by being nobody.

Blake drove under the nameless overpass that led southbound cars to Rabun County High School and recalled how he had once daydreamed that the overpass would be named after him. *You're now passing under the Blake Savage overpass,* he said to himself in a mocking manner, realizing how foolish and insignificant a dream that had been.

He continued on 441 past Tiger and Wiley, surveying all the businesses run by good, honest people. Respectable people. People doing what he now felt he should have done. But no, he had sought riches and glory. Fame.

After he was forced to surrender his football dreams, he became intoxicated with the notion of becoming a celebrity farmer, a ridiculous notion that made Blake chuckle when Nick had first mentioned the idea to him. Nick had told the stories of how his own father was a famed charcuterier in Spain, as was his father before him. Both had raised the revered black-footed pigs in the mountains, fed them acorns and cured the highly prized Jamón Ibérico de Bellota hams in mountain sheds, letting them hang for two years. Even in Spain those hams can cost over one hundred dollars per pound, Nick had said. Lured in by Nick's grand vision, Blake imagined doing in northeast Georgia what no one else was doing anywhere in America, creating what chefs across the country craved. Reproducing the mountain-cured hams from acorn-fed, black-footed pigs and selling to Nick's line of exclusive restaurants. He knew that Nick would get the glory, but Blake figured he would still be in the game, so to speak. And richly rewarded. Nick was as fascinated by the idea as Blake was, partly because there were hordes of pigs that descended from the Iberian pigs, right here in Georgia.

"When my people, the Spaniards, came through a few centuries ago," Nick had explained to Blake, "they brought the black-footed pigs with them and left them on an island near Savannah. That way, the next wave of Spaniards would have something to hunt, something to eat. At some point we stopped coming, and the pigs took over the island and thrived. All you have to do is get some off the island, raise them in the woods, and cure them in the cool mountain air."

Nick had made it sound so easy. So seductive. And he was so persuasive, partly because he was willing to pay a lot to get the real thing, not the inferior industrial version that other restaurants were able to get. Once the USDA had approved the process of allowing some Spanish hams to be imported they had basically been ruined. Sure, they had the name Jamón Ibérico and were quite good compared to American hams, but comparing them to his father's hams was like comparing drug store champagne to a bottle of vintage Louis Roederer Cristal. Both could claim to use the champagne method, but one taste of the latter would uncloak the former as mere toilet water. Nick wanted the absolute best for his restaurants and for his new 50-Forks club, and he was willing to pay for it to be made the right way. The way his father and his father before him made it, not the way the USDA would have it cooked and salted to death. But he needed an accomplice...*someone to do the dirty work*, Blake now realized. And Blake was only too eager once Nick did the math for him. Now, Blake began to do the math once again as he drove south, paying no attention to the SUV that had pulled into the lane behind him and now followed him.

I've got 200 hams hanging now, about fifteen pounds each. That's 3,000 pounds. Nick will pay me seventy dollars a pound when they're ready, that's just over $200,000, not counting the other parts...the shoulders, bellies and so on. Half the hams are ready now but they won't all be ready for another six months at least. I gotta get Nick to take everything now, or maybe take some to other chefs... Blake was immersed in his thoughts as he approached the Tallulah River. Delivering hams for the 50-Forks dinner was just the beginning. Nick wanted hams cured the way his father had done it and on a regular basis. And he wanted to make sure that no other chef had access to those hams, those rare black-footed pigs. Blake exhaled as he tried to figure a way out of having to continue working with Nick.

He glanced in his rear view mirror and saw a rack on the top of the car behind him. Blake looked more closely to see that the rack was actually the lights of the sheriff's vehicle. Instinct forced him upright. He corrected his posture and lifted his left hand to the wheel at the 10:00 position to face his right hand in the 2:00 position. He caught his breath and didn't exhale, his throat instantly parched. *What the hell do they want?*

The car stayed on Blake's tail about one hundred yards back, keeping its distance precise. Blake slowed a little and continued south. The sheriff's car slowed to match Blake's speed and stayed behind him. A trail of cars now followed the sheriff's car as no one dared pass, even though Blake was now driving five miles per hour under the speed limit. He looked at his speedometer and pushed the accelerator slightly, increasing his speed to fifty-five. The train behind him kept pace.

Blake saw the fog rising from the Tallulah gorge ahead of him indicating that he was close to crossing the bridge, where he would leave Rabun county and enter Habersham County, out of the sheriff's jurisdiction. *JUST GET OFF MY TAIL!* Blake screamed to himself. His pulse was rapid and his face was flush as he tried again to calm himself.

What do I have to be afraid of? What have I even done? Even if something happened to those boys, how is that my fault? I didn't do anything!

Blake tried all the logic he could muster, but his rational thinking was no match for his inner voice.

What about what's in the back of your truck that you're taking to Nick? How will you explain that if the sheriff asks?

In the mirror, the sheriff's car zoomed closer, right on his tail now as the bridge approached. Jesus! Blake crossed the bridge and entered the fog. He slowed and turned on his lights as the fog thickened. Slowly, he began the winding ascent up and around Tallulah gorge. Blake exhaled as he passed the sign for Habersham County and flicked his eyes to the mirror. The fog lights from the sheriff's vehicle stayed tethered to his truck, matching it curve for curve.

Jesus! What the hell does he want? Blake thought about pulling over at a gas station, a tourist stop…any place. Instead he continued, concentrating on the road. He took one hand off the wheel, wiped the sweat from his palm on his pants, and then repeated with the other. Blake glanced down at his pants to see the momentary stain left by the sweat and looked back in the mirror. There was nothing there. No sheriff, no cars.

What the—

Blake couldn't see where anyone had gone. The rapid curves and hills offered no more than a view of a hundred yards or so at many points without the fog. In the fog Blake was lost, alone. He just wanted out, to see that he was safe. He wanted

Angelica, to be by her side. He admonished himself again for letting his life come to this. *That's it...I've had it!* Blake pounded the wheel furiously. *I'm telling Nick that it's over. I'm done with all this! This Sunday, I'm going to church with Angelica and getting some peace back in my life.*

As he crested the last hill of Tallulah Falls, Blake accelerated out of the fog as 441 straightened. He drove the speed limit straight to Athens.

***

Vans and other vehicles crowded the parking lot of The Federal when Blake arrived at 11:02 a.m. Far more than usual, but then again this wasn't a normal Friday morning for Nick Vegas. This was the day before his opening series of the 50-Forks dinners that would be held simultaneously the following day in ten cities. Nick would be the host chef in Athens at a private residence, since that was where the Food Channel camera crew would be. The dinner would be the first installment of a new Food Channel series called Underground Chefs and would air weeks later.

Blake backed his truck up to the kitchen entrance and walked inside. He knew his way around The Federal's kitchen but always felt uncomfortable there. He passed the pastry prep area where dough was being rolled out and bread was being made, and continued walking into a sea of stainless steel. An orchestra of cooks...*chefs!* Chefs, sous chefs, assistants, line cooks, servers, and others without titles each attended to a task under the occasional direction of the conductor, the head chef. Pork bellies were being cured, fresh picked arugula was being sampled and inspected.

A local cheese maker had just come in with her assortment of cheeses for the Saturday dinner and the ensemble gathered for a team tasting. Yellow paste oozed from the white mold, raw-milk Camembert when the sous chef sliced into them, each cast member oohing and ahhing at the flavor, using descriptive phrases like "I can really taste the farm" and "it has the slightest essence of chocolate and lemongrass." The cheese maker, chasing fame in her own right, Blake reckoned, explained it was due to her farm's unique terroir. The chefs all nodded knowingly, as did the servers who would no doubt pass on that vague expression to diners so that they could feel better about parting with so much of their hard-earned money. Or inherited money, perhaps. Blake snorted to himself and continued walking. He saw two young busboys that weren't too busy and asked them for help. He watched them hoist several large coolers from the back of his truck and pack the contents into the walk-in coolers before returning the collection of coolers to Blake's truck. With the delivery unloaded, Blake strolled through the kitchen he knew so well to look for Nick.

"Can you tell me where Nick is?" Blake asked one of the sous chefs.

"Last I saw he was sitting at the bar."

Blake walked through the double doors and into the rear of the dining room. Past the plastic palm tree, he could see someone sitting at the bar talking on his phone. It was Nick. Blake walked around the perimeter of the room to approach. Nick saw Blake approaching. He buried his smile and ended the call.

"Blake," Nick said, looking at his Rolex. "What's up?"

Clearly, Nick had either no time or no interest for small talk, for an unscheduled visit.

"I need to talk to you for a minute," Blake said.

"Look, it's a bad time—"

"It won't take long," Blake interrupted.

Nick stood and crossed his arms in front of him.

"What is it?"

Blake drew a deep breath and prepared to go down the list he had practiced on the ride down the way a pilot might check items off a pre-flight checklist.

"I just dropped off your centerpiece for tomorrow night's dinner," Blake began. "I delivered the cured hams you needed on Wednesday and FedExed the others to the other nine restaurants on the same day."

"Yes, I know," Nick said. "I've spoken to the chefs."

Blake took another breath. "Nick..." Blake paused. *What do I want to say? What am I trying to say?*

"Blake, let's talk some other time. I have a ton to do before tomorrow."

"No!" Blake said, surprising both himself and Nick with his assertion of authority. "I mean...Nick, I'm done. Finished. I need to deliver *everything* to you as soon as I can. Everything. I'm done with all this."

Nick surveyed Blake, trying to detect what might be the problem so that he could choose the best response from his arsenal. He cast a line into the water. "What's wrong, Blake?"

"I'm just done, Nick. I can't do it anymore. My own wife doesn't even know what I'm doing!"

Nick saw his opportunity to take control and began to assert himself. "And *why* is that, Blake?"

"BECAUSE, Nick," Blake began and then quieted his voice. "You know why. It's illegal. Everything I'm doing up there. The animals weren't taken legally and the meat *you* had me cure for you hasn't been inspected. And, it's not even my land! You know that! I didn't want Angelica to have anything to do with that!"

As he stopped talking Blake realized he had blurted all of that naïvely, as if talking to himself alone in the car, something that had become habit. Nick said nothing. He kept his arms crossed and stared Blake down. Blake dropped his eyes and continued.

"It's over. Half of the hams are ready. I'm sure the others are good to go too," Blake said, "since they've been curing for a little over a year now."

"That's no good, Blake. They have to go through that second cool autumn and winter to fully develop, that's crucial. I'll take the hams when they are two years old, just as we agreed," Nick said. "And not a moment before."

Blake stood tall and prepared to call Nick's bluff. "Fine. Like I said Nick, I'm done. Take them now or...I'll offer them to someone else."

Blake hadn't meant for the demand to sound as threatening as it did, but it was too late now. Nick grinned slightly, slyly. He sat down on a barstool and appeared so relaxed, so completely at ease. He reached his arms forward, interlocked his fingers and cracked his knuckles as they pushed out toward Blake.

"You know, Blake," Nick began, "now that I listen to you describe what you've been doing, wouldn't that be considered a violation of the Federal Meat Inspection Act? It's just like that farmer in New York that got caught selling meat last year that wasn't inspected, isn't it?"

"Nick, you know what we agreed to! I'm selling you *live* animals, not processed meat. You don't need a permit or inspection to sell live animals. We agreed that I would cure the meat for you as a *friendly* service, but you bought the live animal and that's not a violation," Blake said, but not as confidently as he would have liked. The truth was he didn't know how the laws would be interpreted, and didn't want to find out.

"Hmm...maybe you're right, Blake. Except...I'm not sure the USDA would agree with you on that if they were to come in and ask us who we got the meat from. Oh sure, we'd probably tell them what you just said, but then again we as the restaurant wouldn't have any culpability. The responsibility for knowing and following the law is on the one who *sells* the meat. That's you, Blake. And that's what happened to that farmer in New York who sold meat that wasn't inspected. Let's see he's doing, what is it...eight years behind bars now, on top of the quarter million dollar fine they laid on him. Lost his house and his wife."

Blake listened and thought of how to respond to Nick's thinly veiled threat, but Nick continued.

"All I do is just write the check to you, Blake. Never checks larger than $5,000 at a time, just as you requested."

Blake clenched his jaw.

"Of course, the authorities don't come in and ask questions too often," Nick said, "but you never know when someone may make an anonymous call and a health inspector will show up here or a USDA investigator will show up at your place. By the way, if the inspectors ever do visit you, where'd you get those pigs from anyway? I suspect they'd want to know about that too."

Nick knew full well where he got those pigs, but, as if it had never dawned on him before, Blake realized that Nick had nothing to do with it other than planting the seed to germinate in the fertile soil of Blake's greedy mind. It was Blake who had found Savannah locals to trap the descendants of Spanish pigs for him for next to nothing. They were all too happy to make some money doing it.

"Island's overrun with them little black suckers," they had said. Hunts were held on the island every year just to eradicate as many wild pigs as they could, most of the carcasses just lying there and going to waste. After they were captured, it was Blake himself who had hauled them to the mountains. It was Blake who had built the curing sheds. Nick had told him how, sure, but otherwise he had nothing to do with it. Most important though, Nick was right; the meat wasn't inspected. Blake had talked to the USDA folks in Atlanta early on about getting licensed, but they said it had to be in a climate-controlled, stainless steel facility.

"That is bullshit!" Nick had said at the time. "Look Blake, if you follow all the rules then you're playing someone else's game and not your own. You won't accomplish anything that way."

"Look at this," Nick had said, pointing to his gold watch. "This watch cost me thirty grand. I have four of them. Pocket change. You think I've achieved everything I have by doing what others told me to do? Friggin' USDA! What the hell do they know about gourmet food? About tradition?"

Blake recalled how intoxicated he was at the idea of Nick's wealth. At the idea that he, Blake, could achieve...well, if not all of it, at least some of that wealth. In Blake's eyes, Nick could do no wrong.

"I want those hams to be from wild, black-hoofed pigs that range on acorns and are cured in the open mountain air. Just like we did it in Spain. None of these heavily salted country hams the USDA loves. I wouldn't feed that garbage to my bulldog. Otherwise Blake, no deal." Blake had hesitated for an instant, before Nick gave him his closing pitch. "But, if you do raise these for me," Nick had said, "you'll not only be richly rewarded, you'll be a legend, Blake. It'll be me and you together, doing something that no one else has done."

So Blake built the sheds and hid them in the woods the way the mountain moonshiners had done successfully during prohibition. Now, Nick was squeaky clean, Blake concluded as he stood there and thought it through, and Nick had no intention of letting him stop, of letting this be a one-time deal. Blake realized that he'd have to find another way out.

Hell, I'll just close up shop and not even tell Nick, Blake thought. *Get rid of everything to the highest bidder. Ain't a damn thing Nick can do then once I've shut it down. To hell with him!*

"You know," Nick continued, "come to think of it I can't remember if we ever asked for your tax identification number or your social security number to issue you a 1099. I'll have to check with my accountant to find out for sure. What did we pay you last year, Blake? At least a hundred grand I'd say for the fresh meat, wouldn't you?"

Blake stared and listened, hating what he was hearing, hating how much Nick knew about him, how much he controlled him. Most of all, hating what he had been doing. Nick was right. Blake had not walked the straight and narrow. He was nowhere close to the center of the road. He had veered off, deep into the woods, and now found himself perched on the edge of a ravine with a strong wind at his back.

"And I figure we'll owe you, what, another twenty-five, thirty grand for the shipments and deliveries this week. Broken up into checks for five grand each per usual, right Blake?"

Blake exhaled, looked at his feet.

"I wouldn't worry about anything, though," Nick continued, "I know you just added all the money I paid you to your tax return as the IRS requires, and that you will again this year. Besides, the IRS would have noticed if you didn't anyway, unless...well, unless you didn't actually deposit the checks in a bank account, but just cashed them instead. Of course you wouldn't have done that, and even if you did I suppose the only record would be the cleared checks that I have with your signature from when you cashed them."

Nick stopped talking and simply stared at Blake as his words hung in the air with the resonance of a jury's verdict.

Blake had driven to The Federal full of hope. Hope for a fresh start, hope to get back on the straight and narrow and renew his vows to Angelica. Hope for the simple life that he had once scoffed at and couldn't wait to get away from. Now it was all he wanted. Nick had just sucked that hope right out of Blake.

"Nick," Blake whispered softly, "p-l-e-a-s-e!"

Blake composed himself.

"Please let me stop. Let me have my life back. Please Nick."

Nick smiled, partly to calm Blake, but mainly because he knew his tactics had succeeded. He liked controlling things, owning things. Now it was clear to him that he owned Blake. He placed his hand on Blake's shoulder.

"My friend, it will all be fine. And you'll be handsomely rewarded, just as you wanted. Just deliver to me what you promised, when you promised. What we agreed to. We're both men of our word, Blake. You do what's right and I'll do what's right, my friend."

Blake knew he was not Nick's friend. And he knew there was nothing that he could do. He turned and walked away from Nick without saying another word. He continued walking through the kitchen, out the delivery door and to his truck, utterly dejected. He couldn't imagine how his life could get any worse.

Chapter 18

"Hold up, Tammy!" Ozzie called ahead to Tammy as she walked furiously beside the stream away from Angelica's secret garden. He raced ahead to get in front of her, his wounds finally healed enough to allow him to run freely. Ozzie turned and stopped, staring at Tammy.

"What's wrong?" Ozzie asked.

"Nothing. Just leave me alone. I wanna go back to Hal's." She moved to her right and lunged forward to pass Ozzie. Ozzie moved left and leaned into Tammy, blocking her momentum with great force. The impact angered Tammy.

"Get out of my way, runt!"

The hair on the back of Ozzie's neck stood up. "Who are you calling a runt?" Ozzie demanded. "What is wrong with you?"

Tammy lunged, this time right into Ozzie rather than around him. She wanted him to see her maturity, her determination. "I go where I want, when I want," she exclaimed. "I'm free and I'm sure not gonna have you telling me where I can and can't go!" She lunged into Ozzie with more force than before and hit him squarely in the chest, but despite being the one in motion, the impact knocked Tammy to the side. Ozzie barely budged. Instead he looked at her, puzzled, trying to figure out why his friend was so incensed. Tammy stepped back for a moment. She turned right and walked away from the stream, into the woods. The understory was thick, mostly a leafy patch of purple ferns and wild anise, but she liked the cool cover it provided. Ozzie followed her in and walked behind her for a few minutes with neither speaking.

"Tammy, what's wrong?" Ozzie was as much concerned as he was curious.

Tammy stopped and sat down, crushing the leaves of the sweet anise plant. "I don't know. Just something about that woman I didn't like, that's all." Tammy said.

"She seemed pretty friendly to me," Ozzie replied. "I like the way she sings."

"Yeah, I noticed. Couldn't keep your eyes off her!"

"What's that supposed to mean?" Ozzie asked.

Tammy didn't know why she was so upset. She knew she had no reason to be. But she was flushed; her face was on fire. "I just don't trust people in this neck of the woods," she said.

"What about Hal?"

Tammy thought for a moment. "He's all right," Tammy said. "I guess. But I don't need anyone else."

Ozzie said nothing, just stood and listened. Tammy lay on the ground looking up at Ozzie, at the trees swaying gently and freely above him, their leaves painted in October red, orange and gold. At the beautiful, impossibly blue sky. The movement of the trees inspired Tammy to move. She rose, allowing her body to rock back and forth to the motion of the treetops as she inhaled the intoxicating aroma of licorice from the crushed anise leaves. She looked at Ozzie and walked slowly in front of him. Tammy moved whisper-close to share the anise fragrance with him and nuzzle his neck.

Ozzie watched Tammy and tried to stand quietly, but his heart began to pound loudly. A warm flush overcame him as she brushed close to him, his body tingling and burning from deep within, so much that it scared him. It was a burning sensation he had never felt before. He wanted to run, to move, to somehow get rid of that feeling, but he couldn't move, couldn't take his eyes off her.

Tammy moved around him, leaning against Ozzie's back as she did, her warm breath falling softly on his neck. She walked right before him, stood there and presented herself to him.

Ozzie felt the strongest need to move, as if an earthquake would erupt from within if he didn't. He stared at Tammy's body, her eyes drawing him closer in an inevitable embrace. Ozzie stepped forward and dropped his head on her shoulder, his lips on Tammy's neck. Tammy uttered a deep moan as they closed their eyes at the same time, surrendering themselves to nature's will.

***

Rose slipped the DVD into the player in Angelica's living room and pressed play. Within seconds, Ariel entranced the girls as The Little Mermaid sealed them in an isolation bubble that was impenetrable to the kitchen conversation. Angelica poured coffee into Rose's cup and poured herself a glass of lemongrass tea, into which she stirred some honey and two droppers of echinacea tincture. She sat next to Rose at the kitchen bar.

"So, are you all packed?" Angelica asked.

"Oh yeah," Rose answered. "Even packed a bikini if I can get up the nerve to put it on. Maybe at night." Rose laughed.

"Now Rose, stop it. You have a great body and you know it," Angelica placed her hand on Rose's forearm to offer reassurance, although she couldn't imagine why Rose would need any. She needn't worry. Indeed, Rose was beautiful as well as smart. The sheen of her black hair matched Angelica's, though Rose kept hers shorter, never letting it drape over her shoulders. Like Angelica, Rose had inherited her mother's green eyes and they seemed to be able to see inside you, what you were thinking, what you were feeling. They gripped and held their prey until truth was revealed, and only then softened their grip.

"Hey, you wanna take some of my sunscreen with you?" Angelica offered.

Rose laughed. "I've got my sunscreen already packed, silly. But don't worry, it's SPF 50."

Angelica frowned at Rose. "Please tell me that you don't put those chemicals on your skin. Do you even know what's in it?"

"Now who's being silly?" Rose asked. "It's FDA approved, sis. You think they'd approve it to use on children if it wasn't tested? Safe?"

Rose cast her green eyes at her country bumpkin sister in both a loving and condescending way, as if to say, *"Poor Angelica. Didn't want to go to college and learn about scientific progress. Instead just kept her feet stuck in the mud back in the hills, going backwards in time instead of forward, clinging to Grandma's Cherokee traditions."*

Rose had fond memories of the mountains, but going to Athens and meeting so many new and enlightened people and professors at UGA had liberated her from the parochial views on religion, family, and science that had clouded her thinking as a child. Once she stepped out of that circle and opened her eyes, she found she couldn't move back, even when her parents were killed shortly after her graduation and she was so worried about Angelica. Instead, she had hoped to lure Angelica away, even offered her a place to stay in Athens. But Angelica was as stubborn as her Cherokee ancestors had been two centuries before, Rose reasoned, staying entrenched on her land, handcuffed by ancient religious beliefs, and refusing to surrender herself to progress.

"Are you taking the echinacea tincture that I gave you to boost your immune system?" Angelica asked. Rose reached into her purse and pulled out the small bottle. "Every day," she said.

"Good. Because wasn't that peanut butter sold in the stores FDA approved? You know, the stuff with the salmonella?" Angelica asked, without looking at Rose.

"Now wait a–" Rose began before Angelica interrupted.

"And wasn't that spinach approved...the bags coated in e.coli?" Angelica turned and looked Rose squarely in the eye. Angelica despised confrontation and almost never raised her voice, the only exception being if one of her dearest beliefs was challenged. She knew there was much of the modern scientific world she didn't know and didn't care to know. But she also knew what she did know, and that was the natural world and the Bible.

"Come on!" Rose said, glancing over her shoulder to see if the girls had been disturbed. They stayed under Ariel's hypnotic spell, so Rose continued. "Those are rare exceptions, Angelica. Accidents do happen, you know. The world isn't perfect!" Rose didn't like having to defend herself and preferred to squash questions as they arose so that she could then control the progression and content of the discussion.

"Nature is," Angelica said.

"Is what?"

"Is perfect. There's no waste. Everything is in God's landscape for a reason."

Rose rolled her eyes.

"Do you think people went out in the sun a hundred years ago...two hundred years ago?" Angelica asked. "Did you know that they knew how to protect their skin? Do you think there was widespread skin cancer back then?"

Rose was tempted to take the bait, to challenge Angelica to a debate. Instead, she chose to sit back and let Angelica have her moment.

"So tell me, little sister, what's in your magic skin potion?"

Angelica smiled, happy that any contention was over.

"Well, as Grandma would probably say..."

Both Angelica and Rose smiled, remembering the way their grandmother never followed recipes with precise measurements, instead relying on cute and cryptic phrases.

"A pinch of carrot seed oil, a hunk of beeswax, a smidgen of Shea butter, a dash of zinc oxide and some drops of vitamin E and lavender oils," Angelica said. "And then, I melt the oils, beeswax and butter in a double boiler and—"

"You mean in your cauldron over the fire pit, right?" Rose said with amusement. Angelica brushed the comment aside and continued.

"AND...I let it cool a bit, add the oils and zinc oxide. Then I push it into a container and, voila!

Angelica walked to the sink window that overlooked the forest and retrieved a newly made container of sunscreen.

"Here," Angelica said as she placed it in Rose's hand and narrowed her eyes on her, "Take it and use it. And here's a bottle of yarrow spray too. Directions are on it. Stop dousing your body and your food with chemicals, Rose."

Angelica walked back to the sink.

"Oh, before I forget," Rose began, "here's a gift card for McDonald's in case you want to take the girls in town for lunch and a play date, seeing as Clayton *finally* got a McDonalds."

Angelica turned her head slowly and bore her eyes directly into Rose's. "I most certainly will not take them to McDonald's, Rose. Please tell me you don't take the girls to eat fast food!"

"Oh c'mon!" Rose exclaimed. "You gonna tell me that's all unsafe too? You don't see their parking lots littered with dead bodies do you, little sister?"

Angelica cast a disapproving eye as Rose embellished the words "little sister" with as much sarcasm as she could.

"Stop calling me little sister. You're never going to let me forget that, are you?"

Rose crossed her arms and put on a smug grin.

"It isn't just the nutrition Rose, or lack of nutrition," Angelica said. "You KNOW how horribly those animals are treated in factory farms, and that's where their meat comes from."

As Rose opened her mouth to address that last remark, her cell phone buzzed in her purse. She reached in the side pocket and looked at the iPhone's display. "It's John," she said. "Hang on a minute."

"Hi, John."

"Hey, Rose. So...you w –to –ar–vacation a little ea–?" John asked.

"What? You're breaking up on me," Rose said as she looked at her phone and saw only one bar.

"Don't you guys have any towers around here, or are you afraid they're gonna kill you too?" Rose quipped to Angelica as she cupped her hand over the phone.

"I said, do you want to start vacation early?" John repeated.

"What do you mean?" Rose replied.

"My angel investor, Wade Ferry, just called me and invited us to a secret supper club dinner tomorrow night," John gushed with enthusiasm.

"Oh," Rose said, interested, but clearly not as excited about the idea as John was. John picked up on the tone and decided to sell the notion.

"This is one of Nick Vegas's special dinners, part of that 50-Forks thing we heard about on Fox News last week. It's only for the members of 50-Forks and even then you have to be invited to join," he added.

"How did you...we get invited?" Rose asked.

"A couple of members can't make it. You believe that? Shell out seventy-five grand and you can't make the first event?"

"Where will it be?" Rose asked.

"A house here in Athens. Not sure where. Wade said we'd get an email tomorrow morning telling us where to go. He said there's going to be amazing food that can't be found anywhere else. Sounds like a great start to the vacation to me!" Rose thought about it for a moment. She didn't care as much for the hobnobbing and social scenes as John did, preferring a more quiet life at home in front of a good movie with John and the girls. She pondered that for a second, realizing that maybe she and Angelica weren't as different as she had thought.

"Sounds like fun," she said, knowing how excited John was about it.

"You betcha!" John said. "Then Sunday morning we're off on our private flight to San Salvador, and a couple of hours later we'll be walking on Grotto beach!"

Angelica sipped her tea as she watched Rose on the phone. She couldn't hear the conversation but could hear the mumblings of John's excitement, of good news he had that he wanted to share with Rose. She picked up on Rose's sensitivity to John's needs, giving in when necessary and standing firm when necessary. A marriage based on loving give and take. She glanced over at Rose's girls, who were happily lost in a world of make believe. Angelica was thrilled that Rose was letting her keep her nieces for so long. She would take them out to the garden and show them another world, one that wasn't make believe, one that was real, alive, and wondrous.

Rose had it all, Angelica thought. Beautiful girls, a loving husband and security, although she had almost become a little too big for her britches just like pretty much everyone that went off to college. She had lost her way with nature and with God, but she had the children and a loving relationship that Angelica longed for.

Why can't I have that? Why doesn't Blake talk to me that way, doesn't spend time with me the way John does with Rose? John is much busier with his business and he finds time for Rose and the girls. He always puts them first.

"Anything new on tropical storm Isabel?" Rose asked John.

"They say it should pass south of Puerto Rico and go south of Florida," John said. "Don't worry about it. We'll know in advance if the course changes and we'll have plenty of time to leave if we have to. The pilot will be on call."

"Good. That's what I want to hear. All right, I'll see you tonight. Love you!" Rose said as she pressed the button to end the call.

"Did you get some good news?" Angelica asked.

"John got an invitation to a fancy dinner tomorrow night. He's all excited." Rose knew the dinner wouldn't interest

Angelica much so she skipped the details. Angelica smiled. As Rose figured, she didn't get what the big deal was. No dinner would be more special to Angelica than a home cooked meal with a husband and children that she not only cooked herself, but also from food that she grew, raised, and produced herself. The simple life was all she hoped for or aspired to.

"What storm are you talking about?" Angelica asked.

"Don't y'all get the news up here in Clayton? You know man walked on the moon too, has that news reached here yet?"

Angelica cocked her head at Rose and raised her eyebrows.

"Nothing, just your typical October tropical storm brewing in the Caribbean. They say it will become a hurricane, but John says it's going west into the gulf."

"Cuckoo-Cuckoo." The clock in the kitchen struck one and somehow managed to penetrate the girls' bubble. Their eyes marveled at the bird that came out and announced the time. The girls rolled on the floor and laughed with silly hysterics, the way that only little girls can.

"Oh jeez," Rose said. "I lost track of the time this morning. I need to get back to Athens. I've got to go by the post office and cancel mail delivery before our trip."

Rose got up to give her girls a hug. They accepted it begrudgingly as Ariel had captured their attention once again.

"You girls mind what your Auntie Angelica says," Rose said to the ears in the living room deaf to all sounds not from The Little Mermaid.

Angelica walked with Rose out to the car.

"Looks like the fog's about burned off," Rose said to Angelica at the car door, and reached her arms around her sister. Angelica closed her eyes and hugged Rose's middle as she normally did when Rose draped her arms around Angelica's neck. As she did, Angelica opened her eyes as...she felt something deep inside. She concentrated on the feeling and looked around to see if something around her was out of place or was wrong. It wasn't. It was coming from within, from Rose.

Angelica grew uneasy, but felt it must be silly. But still...something didn't feel right to her.

She pushed back from Rose and looked into her eyes.

"Rose," Angelica began, "be careful."

Rose smiled. "Don't worry, silly. We'll be careful and we'll see you in about ten days. Just have a great time with the girls!" Rose got in the car, buckled her seat belt and put the Honda Odyssey into reverse. She looked through the windshield at Angelica, waved goodbye, and left.

Angelica stood for a moment trying to put her finger on what she had felt. She turned to go in and get the girls, but had the most troubling feeling in her gut. A feeling she hadn't had since the last time she saw her parents alive.

Chapter 19

Blake sat in his truck in the parking lot of The Federal, paralyzed by fear. All of his worst thoughts and fears raced round and round, crashing into one another inside his head like unruly kids in bumper cars.

Slow down. Think!

He tried to calm himself the way he had done in college football when opposing fans would stomp their feet and scream, trying to make so much noise that Blake would be forced into a mistake. A hurried snap, an errant throw. But Blake had mastered those fans, those sweaty palms, time and time again.

Think! What could happen? What are you afraid of? He asked himself silently. *Money.* Money was the first worry that popped into Blake's head because it was what Nick had just mentioned. No...he had threatened it. Threatened to reveal that he had paid Blake a lot of money and that maybe someone should review Blake's tax filings. Nick knew that Blake hadn't reported that income, that he had cashed those checks instead of depositing them. There was no doubt that Nick had looked at Blake's signature on the checks, that he had kept them stowed away just in case he ever needed them.

So? What would happen if Nick did report me? Blake thought.

Tax evasion! He felt his body shrivel like an overripe blueberry as he thought about the real trouble he could be in. He didn't believe that Nick would *really* report him, but that wasn't what bothered him. What scared him, what infuriated him, was that Nick knew! He flat out *could* report it, as he had made painfully clear. Nick could do that today, a year from now, or hold it over Blake's head for years. The threat would just linger and follow Blake, keeping him awake at night, causing him to look over his shoulder in public. Causing him to dread going to the mailbox, to shudder anytime the phone rang. If Nick ever did report it then Blake would have to explain to an IRS criminal investigator what had happened to the money and why it wasn't reported. At a minimum, they'd slap a seventy-five percent penalty on him and he'd have to pay that, plus interest, from the first day he should have filed his return. He knew this because he had curiously looked it up when he cashed Nick's first five thousand dollar check a year and a half before. Since then he had cashed almost thirty of them and still had over ninety thousand dollars in cash tucked away at home that no one knew about, that he couldn't invest or deposit because then there would be an audit trail. Cash that he couldn't tell Angelica about, because how would he explain such an obscene amount of cash to her?

Sitting in the parking lot, Blake began adding and multiplying the best he could. If Nick ever reported him then Blake would have to explain, when all was said and done, about a quarter million dollars in income. Tax on that figure at thirty percent, would have been seventy-five grand. Add a seventy-five percent penalty to that and Blake figured that was well over a hundred thousand dollars due before the interest charges were added. But that's if the IRS found out *now*. The penalties would become more severe with each passing day.

If Nick reported that, years from now I'd be screwed, Blake concluded. They'd take the house, everything. I might even get jail time! Shit! The thought of jail time reminded Blake of the visit from the sheriff. The sheriff's vehicle trailing him out of Rabun County. *Maybe that was just a coincidence,* Blake thought. *Maybe they weren't trailing me.*

He didn't believe that. No, that would have been too much of a coincidence. A visit from the sheriff himself in the morning, and then less than a half hour later followed all the way out of the county by a separate patrol car? No, it couldn't have been a coincidence. *But what have I done?*

Blake thought about it, momentarily relieved that, he believed, he hadn't actually done anything wrong. *Even if them boys are found and they're dead, heads ripped clean off their bodies, what does that have to do with me? Even if the sheriff finds out they may have done some work for me, I didn't kill 'em. I didn't send them off.*

Blake started making his argument to the judge, to the jury, the way he had seen so many times on television.

Your Honor, what happened to those boys was tragic. An awful tragedy for the community to have to cope with. But, Your Honor, it was an accident. Those boys got lost in the woods on their own and couldn't find their way out because they was stupid. My client, Blake Savage, is as distraught about this as the rest of the community, your honor, but he is guilty of no crime. So just leave him the fuck alone! Case dismissed!

Blake exhaled after listening to his lawyer's well-reasoned defense. He didn't believe that he had done anything. So why was the sheriff after him? What had the sheriff said?

Do you know anything? Do you know them boys?

That's what the sheriff had asked and Blake had lied. That realization is what made the hair on Blake's arms stand up, the fact that, just that morning he had lied not once, but twice to the sheriff. If the sheriff found out he had lied about that then he would be under suspicion for...Blake didn't know. But for something else.

What if the sheriff gets to Terry? What if Terry blabs his mouth at a pool hall or something and the sheriff's men pick up on it, question him and come back to me?

Blake gripped the steering wheel with both hands, ringing the leather like he was ringing out a chamois cloth.

Crap! Blake tensed as he realized that he had forgotten what he had done with Jesse's jacket that he had found over a month before. *Holy crap! How could I not know where I put that? THINK! Where is it?*

He couldn't remember. *If they find that, can they link me to Jesse somehow? Is there a way to know that's Jesse's jacket? And it had blood on it! Crap! They'll think I killed him!*

Every thought led to a more sinister thought, like a series of opening doors leading Blake deeper into a snake pit. *Maybe I should go look for them? Maybe they're still alive,* Blake thought hopefully, but his optimism faded quickly. *It's been six weeks or so. Ain't no way them boys are alive in those woods. Ain't no way.*

Blake tried to think. He lifted his hand and rubbed his right palm on the back of his neck, trying to relieve some tightness, some tension. His fingers found some small bumps, a rash or something on the back of his neck. Blake figured it was a reaction to the stress, so he continued to try and figure a way out of his mess. He cranked the truck and put it in gear, feeling that he was in enough control of his senses, his emotions, to drive home. But his mind kept racing with fears, with ideas...ways out that only led to dead ends.

I wish I had someone I could talk to, Blake thought. *I'm sick and tired of being so alone, of having to figure out everything for myself.* But he knew full well he had created this mess. He had made these choices for himself. He would have to figure a way out. *How did I even get to this point?* Blake shook his head furiously.

He drove northwest on 441 and tried to find a radio station to free his mind from thoughts that haunted him. A salesman on the classic rock station shouted that he should "come on down!" and buy a Toyota from him. Blake switched instead to the NPR station in Athens at 91.7 and caught the announcer finishing the news at the top of the hour. "Widespread flooding can be expected throughout Puerto Rico as Hurricane Isabel, now at Category 1 strength, races toward the gulf. Forecasters say there's a slight chance the storm could turn in a more northerly direction and impact the Bahamas. This is NPR news."

Classical baroque music blasted through the speakers. Blake reached his arm to turn off the radio as he drove from Athens toward Commerce, the only sounds coming from his inner voice asking him questions, admonishing him and replaying his life for him, as if he were watching a game film on the Monday after a game.

The reel turned and played his life film on the windshield as he drove. There he was in high school, setting records in his red jersey and leading the Wildcats to their first and only state championship. Then he was in yet another red jersey, but with the same number seven as he led the Georgia Bulldogs toward a BCS bowl bid. And then...the hit. The safety, out of nowhere. He remembered watching it on ESPN while lying in the hospital, the blindside shot that his running back, his friend, his bodyguard, didn't even attempt to block. Blake collapsed with the hit, twisted like an empty tin can crushed underfoot, face first into the turf. His brightly lit flame snuffed out in that moment. Blake told doctors, fans, and friends that he'd be back, but he knew he wouldn't. He just tried to hang on to the fame, to the hope for as long as he could. With bad grades and an alcoholic father that had taught him nothing but hate and anger, he knew he was lost without football.

The reel fast-forwarded and stopped at the car accident, as a driver who had just left a bar crashed into the driver's side of Blake's car at an Athens intersection. When the accident was picked up in the *Athens Banner Herald*, Blake promptly received a call from a lawyer at Peacock and Associates who sympathized and suggested that Blake should be compensated for what had happened to him. "You're entitled," the man had claimed. Blake was furious at the world for the turn of bad luck that had come his way. He agreed even though he knew that, maybe...the accident wasn't the other driver's fault.

Blake knew that he had run that red light at night. That's why the car hit him. But he was furious with anything and everything then, and told the driver it was his fault. By the time the police arrived the two men were in a heated argument, but only one of them had been drinking, and it wasn't Blake. Police charged the other driver for causing an accident while drinking even though he had only registered a .06 on the Breathalyzer, paving the way for Blake to receive almost a one hundred twenty thousand dollar settlement after the lawyer took his share. It was easy money, something Blake did feel he was entitled to given his misfortune on the gridiron. He liked the taste of making so much money, so quickly. He returned to Clayton on crutches, with a load of money in his pocket, but not with what he really wanted and needed. Fame. Fans. The feeling that he had made it, that he was somebody. That he was important and that he was nothing like his old man.

Angelica had waited for him as she said she would, but Blake didn't really believe he would ever go back to Clayton. After the car accident he wanted to get back to her, to "close the deal" on Angelica if he could, to at least have that. She was there for him and she thought he was important. And she was exotic and naturally beautiful, like Pocahontas, he imagined. They married in Clayton and Blake put his money with Angelica's, spending virtually all the money on the home and a new truck since he knew getting a mortgage would be tough with no job and no prospects. Paying cash for an entire house made him feel successful, important, but once they moved in he had little cash left to spend. For years he laid low and did little other than feel sorry for himself. The pain in his back and legs was too great to exert himself too much, he told others. In truth, the pain subsided after the first year, but Blake had become addicted to the sympathy. He refused to do most "real" jobs like working at lumber stores—not because his body would give out, but because he felt it was beneath him.

Beneath you? Who do you think you are? Blake felt shame wash over him as he watched the film play on.

When the winery contacted Blake, it played right into his needs. It massaged his ego, letting him cling to his dwindling local fame by contacting successful people, pressing some flesh and getting back into the game. If not the game of football, then at least the hobnobbing game of knowing celebrity chefs and restaurant owners. After a few weeks of hustling farmers and wineries and delivering to chefs, he made a number of friends and earned, precisely, four hundred and fifty bucks the first month. Three thousand dollars of sales for farmers and wineries that he delivered netted him, at fifteen percent, four hundred fifty bucks.

That's bullshit, he remembered thinking. *Chump change. Even if I busted my hump and tripled sales, I'd earn about sixteen grand a year. I would have been earning more than that per WEEK in the NFL!*

Congratulations, Blake admonished himself, *you've made it right to the poverty level. Right where you left off. Dad would be so proud.*

Angelica had told him that they didn't need much money, that everything was paid for except daily living expenses, but he didn't hear it. Didn't want to hear it. Now he realized how right she had been.

The highlight reel sped forward and stopped in the parking lot of The Federal when Blake made his first delivery to Nick. Getting in to see Nick was easy since Blake had known him at UGA. Only now, looking back on the film, did Blake realize that Nick had manipulated him all along. Nick had brought him into the kitchen when Blake first called on him. Of course he would buy the wines, the fruits and vegetables. Whatever Blake had. "But you want more than that out of life, don't you Blake?" Nick had asked. "You're better than that."

That was it, Blake remembered. That's where it began, this winding road that led him to where he now found himself.

Nick had sat him down and told him the story of his father in Spain, how he came from generations of men who raised the famed black-legged Iberian hogs and slowly cured them in mountain air for two years. How it was an honored profession. How the Spaniards, and even the Italians and French had a food culture that was to be revered, unlike the fast food culture in America.

"Help me bring this here, Blake," Nick had said as he shaved thin slices of Jamón Ibérico de Bellota ham for Blake, almost spoon feeding the delicacy to him. "Join me and let's create a real slow-food culture here in Georgia." Whether he was seduced by the ham or the idea of being a part of Nick's team, of working hand in hand with Nick to create something really special, Blake couldn't recall. But he bought in, hook, line, and sinker. He swallowed hard as Nick laid out the plan, the simple steps that Blake had to take to set up.

"Don't worry about money," Nick had told him. "I'll cover your start-up costs. Won't cost you a cent. Then, when you get the hams cured in a couple of years, I'll buy all you produce at seventy dollars per pound." It seemed to Blake to be an insane amount of money until Nick explained how he sold the delicacy in one-ounce servings at fifteen dollars per ounce. "That's an affordable luxury for most folks," Nick had said, "but it works out to $240 per pound!"

Blake's eyes grew large hearing that as Nick laid out the basic math of what it would mean for Blake. "Two hams per hog, each ham about fifteen pounds, that's roughly $2,000 per hog. A hundred hogs equals two hundred grand, two hundred hogs is four hundred grand, and so on. And that doesn't include what you can do with the rest of the pork from the hogs, which we can use, or even the bones."

"What about the bones?" Blake had asked.

"Well, the people in my country never wasted anything," Nick said. "They showed respect for the entire animal, so my father would have the bones ground into organic bone meal. He sold it for fertilizer."

It seemed too good to be true. It was real money, LOTS of money. And he had the perfect environment right behind his house to conduct his illicit, covert operation. An operation that he increasingly convinced himself was legitimate as time went on. He even convinced himself that he had every right to raise animals and sell them live to Nick, just as Nick had suggested, and to cure them for Nick as a *friendly* service.

What an idiot I've been! Blake said, furious with himself. *It's just a stupid ham! Gold, diamonds, caviar, and now a stupid ham for people to obsess over and waste money on!*

The movie came to an abrupt end as the filmstrip slapped around one reel, flapping as the reel spun to remind Blake that the movie was over. The highlights of his life were over. And if he didn't do something to take control, his life was about to be over.

Chapter 20

The afternoon sun began to set, its remaining slivers of light filtering through the fiery autumn leaves as they lost their grips and parachuted to the forest floor. A yellow sassafras leaf pirouetted down from high above, tossing and twirling in the slight breeze until it landed gently on Tammy's face and covered her left eye. Tammy awoke, shook the leaf from her face, and felt beside her. Ozzie wasn't there. She sat up, looked around, and saw him standing in the bushes twenty feet away. He was looking off, at nothing it seemed, but deep in concentration. Tammy walked toward him.

Ozzie looked back and gazed at her for a moment, then looked away, continuing his contemplation. His gaze stopped Tammy in her tracks. It wasn't a spiteful gaze; nor was it a look of love or lust. And it wasn't the juvenile look she had seen him naïvely cast her way before, the look of wonder and curiosity he had usually worn. No, it was a calm, knowing look, as if he had undergone some sort of metamorphosis. She had slept and Ozzie had been transformed from boy to man, from cub to bear, from pup to alpha male. That she could understand this transformation, sense it from a single, momentary gaze startled her. But there was no question in her mind. She went to sleep more mature, more protective, more in command than Ozzie had been. She awoke with the roles forever reversed.

Looking back, Ozzie summoned Tammy with his eyes to come as he began walking toward Hal's. Tammy obeyed and walked just behind Ozzie, but not beside him. There was no hurry in his pace, no trepidation in his step. He was as guarded as he was confident, staring only at the trail before him, yet he sensed everything around him. He relied on all his senses to gather information, to sift through it all and tell him what was important.

The smell of the campfire lured them in. The sun set quickly and cast a blanket of inky darkness over the forest. The glow of the fire burned so brightly in the darkness that Hal considered wearing his sunglasses. By the time Ozzie and Tammy arrived he was already in full swing, having begun the party once Rex had shown up. "Well, look what the cats drug in," Hal exclaimed with a yip as Ozzie strolled into the campsite followed by Tammy.

Hal strummed the guitar, trying to find his voice as if doing vocal warm-ups before a recital. It had been a lazy afternoon for him and he had decided to start drinking early to celebrate the 4th of July, even though it was early October.

"Got any requests, Ozzie?" Hal asked, smiling at his friend. Ozzie walked past the fire, past Hal to his normal spot on the front porch and stood there. Tammy came up with him quietly, softly. Ozzie bowed his head to Tammy, not out of respect, but as an indication that she should take his spot on the porch. She obliged.

Hal watched and noticed Ozzie's peculiar action as he strummed. "Think I'm gonna find me a love song to sing," Hal said, sensing the mood.

Tammy lay on the porch and listened to the sounds, but not to Hal's words. She was happy, which was not unusual for her. But she was also calm and content, where before she had often been restless. That feeling had vanished along with Ozzie's adolescence, and was replaced with a feeling of belonging to a place and a time. A sense of knowing what she was *here* for, what she was *supposed* to do.

Hal stopped long enough to take a swig and pour a drink into the cup he placed on the porch beside Ozzie. Then he slapped the six strings some more and kicked his private party into high gear, the thumper keg now adding the percussion.

Ozzie looked down at the medicine that had nursed him back to health. The liquid that had warmed his body and freed his soul, allowing him to forget his past. To move on. He looked at Tammy and saw the life before him. He knew what she wanted. A simple life with children that, he suspected, would arrive sooner rather than later. He, too, wanted that life, would love living freely with her, maybe even close to Hal, although the daily party train that ran through Hal's camp was beginning to wear on Ozzie. It wasn't in Ozzie to forget pain and suffering the way that Hal had worked so hard to forget. The moonshine Hal served up offered an initial comfort to Ozzie, but the following sleep was laced with horrid nightmares from which he couldn't escape. Visions of his mother, of her suffering, both physical and emotional. Her feelings of hopelessness, capitulation, and despair. Her calls to him, beckoning him and pleading for salvation.

Stepping off the porch, Ozzie turned left to walk around the cabin. Tammy raised her head and prepared to rise and follow, but Ozzie jerked his head around and shot Tammy a look. Its meaning was clear to her. She sat back down and stayed on the porch, turning one ear to Hal's music and the other to the rear of the cabin where Ozzie had headed.

Fifty yards away the cabin silhouetted against the glow of the campfire as Ozzie looked back from Hal's garden. In that short distance the sound of Hal's strumming and singing, which was so loud from the porch, was remarkably muffled, having been absorbed by the trees, the forest floor and the darkness. Ozzie listened to the other rhythms of the forest and heard a band of coyotes yelp on the ridge underneath the mountain's haunting sough. Trees swayed in the breeze and caused distant branches to fall, some crashing with enough force to sound like cannon fire when they snapped. Winds howled in and out of steep ravines and caves, whipping up fallen leaves and incubating screeches that were faded and far away.

And still, cries rang out from high above that sounded like a mother and her baby were shrieking the excruciating howls of separation, their notes of despair rising up and over the treetops and sending a chill down the spine of every forest creature.

Ozzie walked past the garden, past where he had dared venture before and continued into the unforgiving darkness, summoned, he felt, by a force he couldn't resist. He walked upslope toward the ridge in the pattern of a serpentine curve to increase the coverage of his patrol. He stopped and listened to the sounds of man, hearing Hal's voice and music play steadily but more dully. Everything sounded as it should at the camp. Continuing his ascent toward the coyotes he had heard up the slope, Ozzie detected that they were now silent. But he felt their presence. Close enough to be a threat to Tammy, to Hal. Especially to Rex.

He reached the ridgeline, only one in the sea of endless, cresting slopes. He stood in the midst of a forest that was as much a familiar sanctuary for wild animals as it was a chilling prison for man. Unaware of Ozzie's presence, the coyotes had departed, likely scouring the forest floor for a meal from a freshly fallen soldier of nature; a raccoon, possibly, one too weak or weary to carry on. One that had hoped to purchase another sunrise, but found no reserves with which to do so. So it sheltered itself underneath the eave of a moss-covered log for a long slumber, its final prayer to morph into the soil before scavengers discovered and devoured its body, alive. The coyotes walked ahead and away from Ozzie, masquerading as angels intent on answering the fallen soldier's prayer. Ozzie turned south on the ridge to follow, his pace quickening but not hurried.

The still of the night was suddenly shattered with a deafening and rapid drumming. A ruffled grouse flushed from a mountain laurel just in front of Ozzie and flew past his face, filling the darkness with the resonant thumping of a military helicopter at low altitude. Ozzie stepped back, momentarily startled, and watched the bird ascend the mountain slope. He continued forward, unwavering. Ahead, a band of three coyotes heard the grouse drumming one hundred yards behind. They stopped, the recently anointed alpha male peering back down the ridgeline in the darkness and sensing a familiar smell. The smell of a creature that should have been the feast of a lifetime for him only six weeks before, another solider that should have fallen but somehow didn't. The male yipped rapidly and began in Ozzie's direction, his lieutenants close behind.

The yipping and yelping channeled horrible memories of suffering through Ozzie's ears to his mind. But the pain and physical suffering he was thinking of wasn't his own. Rather, the memory of the coyote attack reminded him that he had cowered and run. He had run away from the coyotes but had not escaped. He had run away from evil men and had left his mother and brother behind. He had been a child of the forest and fear had controlled him, but now, fear wasn't the primary emotion that Ozzie felt. It had been eclipsed by new emotions. Shame. Revenge. Rage.

Picking up his pace, Ozzie jogged toward the pack, the alpha male suddenly within sight. The pack leader stopped on the ridgeline as he felt an unfamiliar sensation. *He* was the one being hunted. The alpha male stood his ground with his mates at his shoulder to convey the appearance of a large predator. Ozzie came to a stop ten yards away and looked down. He saw the alpha male for what he was; a smaller adversary that could do him little harm, weak cronies at his side. As he swung his head from right to left, Ozzie oscillated his jaw, allowing the moon's rays to reflect through the branches off of his long and razor-sharp tusks for his opponents to fear. With sharpened hooves he pawed the ground, kicking dirt back and making his intention clear. He stood, prepared to defend what was his, but not looking for battle. Unless...

The alpha male lunged forward, charging at Ozzie and intent on extracting revenge for the brothers that fell at his feet the month before. Ozzie's eyes widened as he saw the three of them coming strong for him along the ridgeline. He quickened his breath, dug his hooves into the earth and sprinted forward, his conscience abandoning him as he prepared to confront all of his monsters, both real and imagined. And he saw and heard them all coming for him. The coyotes, the men, the menacing monster growling up the mountain, the yellow eyes in the blackness and shrieking screams in the middle of the night that tortured and taunted him. In his mind, Ozzie ripped into each and every tormenter, flinging them one by one into the bottomless ravines of death on each side of his ridgeline, towering above them as they fell, their screams fading with them until all had subsided.

Ozzie panted and heard only his breath and his pounding heart until his breathing slowed and the forest sounds rose to meet him. The notes were mostly calm and peaceful. Only the singing of distant frogs and crickets that sang their last songs of the Indian summer drowned out the last dying gasps of a trio of coyotes.

He looked to the sky. The full moon still shone its beacon brightly, and guided Ozzie home. As he began his descent to the camp he felt a chill, even though his muscles were flush from battle. A haunting chill as if a change was in the air. As if time was running out for something, someone. He trudged along and thought about his mother, as he lumbered past Hal's garden and around the front of his cabin. He stood and watched Hal wail. Hal looked, saw three of Ozzie, and smiled at the one in the middle. Tammy raised her head and looked at Ozzie, at the blood that stained his tusks. She called to him with her eyes.

Ozzie stepped up onto the porch, lying down close to Tammy and drifting asleep. For the first time since he had been with Hal, nightmares didn't chase him. Instead, Ozzie dreamed he was the one atop a mountain, looking over the expansive forest as he commanded the soil to wash away his enemies. To wash away anyone who meant to harm him.

Chapter 21

Rose walked out of the master bathroom and down the hall, stopping just for a moment to linger in the doorway to the girls' bedroom. It was the first night in six years, since their first child had been born, that she had been separated from either of the girls. John bounded through the kitchen and began climbing the hardwood staircase to the master bedroom.

"You ready?" he asked as he glanced at his watch. "Dinner starts in half an hour." Before Rose could answer, John looked up at her to see that she was ready. "Wow," John said, stopping on the third step from the top. "You look— breathtaking."

Rose tilted her head to her left shoulder slightly, just enough that her ebony hair flipped off her ear in a flirtatious way. She swept it back behind her ear with her right hand. "Thanks Johnny. It's so quiet without the girls here."

"Now, now," John said. "You don't want to change your mind, do you? Just a little R & R, me and you on the beach of a secluded Bahamas island."

"Of course not," she said, and smiled at John as he passed and walked to the bedroom to finish dressing.

The truth was that Rose would have been happy to stay home. The trip was John's idea, one to which she eagerly agreed, but not because she wanted to be away from the girls. She knew the stresses that John had in his job, the relentless pressure he was under to keep customers, to win customers, to find and keep employees. Even with all the success of WallCloud, John often spoke of the pressure in managing cash flow. Rose didn't understand the details the way John did, but she wasn't ignorant of business finance. She knew that the business could be profitable on paper and still have trouble paying its bills at the same time, the result of having to pay money out before receiving payments from customers. When the business was stable and not growing, managing cash flow was pretty easy, John had always said. But the past few months had seen rapid growth.

"We'll increase revenue by forty percent this year," John boasted the month before, after winning a number of new accounts. And the company was well on its way, but the new business meant that John had to incur expenses up front, in the form of hiring more employees, additional computing capacity, increased health care costs—the list went on and on. Costs that had to be paid now, even though customers wouldn't be on board until November. After waiting the customary thirty days to invoice them the cash wouldn't start rolling in from them until they paid thirty days later, in January. Rose had always thought it was peculiar that the faster John grew the business, the more strapped the business was for cash. But WallCloud was John's thing now. Rearing the girls and community volunteer work was largely hers. She knew that John needed a break from business even if she didn't need a break herself.

Rose sat at the hallway computer for a second while waiting for John. She moved the mouse to deactivate the screen saver and stared at the email John had opened. It was the invitation he had received earlier in the day to the dinner. Rose perused the email and noted the address and directions. Then her eyes drifted to the bottom of the email, which read to her like a legal agreement. "Hey, John, did you read this legalese at the bottom of this email?"

John poked his head out of the master bathroom, his fingers running styling gel through his wavy brown hair. "Which one? The dinner invite?" John asked.

"Yes," Rose said. "Get a load of this." Rose mimicked a fast-paced voice the way a lawyer closes a commercial on a radio advertisement.

When you attend a 50-Forks dinner you're attending a "dinner party" hosted by Nick Vegas at a private home. The home is not a restaurant, and has not participated in any health inspections. It is not subject to the standards required by law of a legally licensed restaurant. By attending the 50-Forks dinner you agree that you are attending a dinner party and not a restaurant, that you will not hold Nick Vegas or any member of 50-Forks liable, and that you willingly forfeit any right to sue any member of 50-Forks for any circumstances, including, but not limited to, food poisoning or any accident that may occur at, or as a result of, the event.

Rose paused and read the last sentence slowly in her own voice.

You're eating at your own risk.

"He's just covering his assets," John said with a wink, as he elongated the first syllable of "assets."

"Kinda takes the fun out of it," Rose quipped. "Sounds pretty scary, actually."

"Relax, honey. I don't think Nick Vegas would do anything to risk his reputation," John said. He pulled the chair out for Rose and took her hand as they walked down the stairs toward the garage.

***

John pulled the Lexus IS 350C around the gravel circular driveway that fronted the antebellum home, and parked after passing two dozen cars and two television vans that had already arrived. He walked around to open the door for Rose, a chivalrous act that Rose had resisted for years before finally relenting to John's loving gesture. She smiled and took John's hand as he helped her from the car. They walked, hand-in-hand, up the graded gravel drive and glanced into one of the vans as they passed. Three technicians were busy on high-end computers rendering real-time video of the visitors' arrival and the chefs' preparations. A cameraman stood at the base of the steps at the entrance and trained his camera on the two of them as they approached.

Don't trip! Rose said to herself as a cameraman filmed her climbing the stairs of the front porch.

"You okay there, hon?" John asked.

Rose smiled nervously, but continued looking at the stairs. "Just don't like these cameras," she whispered.

John patted her hand to ease her as they arrived on the front porch.

"What kind of house is this?" Rose asked as they stood in the breezeway. John began to answer, but a kindly face at the top of the steps asserted itself.

"Why, this here's a dogtrot, ma'am," Wade Ferry said. "Or a possumtrot, if you prefer." He smiled at John and extended his hand. "Howdy, John."

"Hi, Wade," John said, shaking Wade's hand enthusiastically. "Thanks so much for the invite, really." John looked to Rose. "Wade, you remember my wife, Rose, don't you?"

Rose extended her hand and smiled at Wade, knowing him as both a kind man and an investor in John's company.

"Well, sure I do!" Wade said. "I never forget the face of an angel." Wade was grinning ear to ear as he took Rose's hand and kissed it.

An image of Rhett Butler flashed in Rose's mind. She smiled, but didn't blush. It was a cliché response, but an appropriate one just the same, she figured. And it was a nice thing to say.

"Why do they call it a dogtrot?" Rose asked.

Wade turned and pointed his arm through the breezeway that ran from the front porch to the back porch. "Dogs were free to just trot down this here breezeway," Wade said. "Unless you lived out in the sticks. In that case possums might run through here so some folks call these homes possumtrots."

Rose smiled in amusement.

"Of course this is a modernized dogtrot," Wade continued as he pointed out the accordion glass doors framed in rich mahogany that could be closed to secure the breezeway and protect the six-inch heartwood pine floors that ran throughout the house. The enclosed rear porch had both skylights and ceiling fans that made sitting comfortable in the cushioned wicker furniture. The rear porch was crowded with the members of 50-Forks who had been invited to gather two hours earlier for their business discussion and introductions.

"Well," Wade said, "Mighty happy you both could make it. Y'all go now and enjoy yourselves."

John and Rose smiled and walked into the breezeway, taking in the lingering aromas of roasted meat and, Rose thought, candied yams. To the right and left were the main rooms of the 1830's home. The entrance to each had been enlarged to impart both the feel of separation and of being in one large room that swept the house.

In the breezeway all eyes were directed to a centerpiece table. High above the table hung four beautifully cured whole hams, each hanging by its black hoof. The star attraction on the table below was a whole roasted pig's head on a platter, eyes and teeth intact. The platter was stylishly decorated with forest flora and acorns from the north Georgia mountains. On an adjoining table behind the head was a fifth ham resting on a Salamanca, hand carved and made by Nick's own father. In true Spanish artistic design, the two-inch hardwood base of the Salamanca itself had been carved in the shape of a ham leg. A heavy, stainless steel open ring, secured to an arm that rose and curved a foot higher than the base, formed a cradle for the ham hoof. The butt portion of the ham rested on its own hardwood cradle on the opposite end.

About thirty guests stood around the table and in the breezeway, watching a very serious man expertly shave razor thin pieces of the ham with a long knife. Nick Vegas walked up beside him as he did so and held court as cameras zoomed in.

"This is an art form!" Nick began. "The man who wields the knife has to know precisely how to do this, how to shave thinly along the grain to extract maximum flavor. In Spain this man is known as a Maestro Secadero and he oversees the entire process of curing, grading, and slicing the ham," Nick added as he flashed his smile for the cameras.

By now, both the front and rear porches had emptied and Nick was surrounded in the packed breezeway by almost fifty guests, each of whom, other than John and Rose, had written a check for $75,000 to join Nick's exclusive 50-Forks Sales & Marketing group. "Look how thinly he slices it," Nick said, as he rolled his arm toward the ham in the manner of a maître d'.

Nick held up a translucent slice of ham and looked through it. Then, he rolled it in the shape of a cigar and savored it, kissing his fingers to his lips as he rolled his eyes. "Mmmmm!" he said, as he waved for his servants to plate small samples for each guest. "Sliced in this manner, at room temperature, the marbled ham will literally start to melt. Go on, taste it for yourself."

"Is this mold on the side?" one woman asked, pointing to a white powder that lined the edge of some of the slices. "Is it safe to eat?"

Nick smiled reassuringly.

"Yes and it's fine to eat," he said. "You'll be getting a lot of mold tonight. We have local, raw milk Camembert cheese featured in the first course and a local, organic blue cheese we'll use for the dessert course." The woman and a few other guests took the slice close to their nose first and inhaled the meat and mold as if their nostrils could instantly confirm Nick's stamp of approval. The cameras panned and zoomed, capturing the expressions of the guests, who both wanted to act as if they were the recipients of culinary bliss for the camera and, literally, were overcome with the explosion of delicate and complex flavors on their palates. The phrases uttered through the mouthfuls of one of the world's most prized meats varied, but conveyed the same satisfaction.

"Oh, wow!" one woman exclaimed as her husband simply mumbled, "Jesus!"

Another lanky man held his mouth open with apparent disbelief at the explosion of flavor. "Holy cow!" He said.

"No, this is no cow," Nick said with a smile. "It's a pig!"

The cameras caught the laughing faces as the group discussed the intense flavors and marveled at how very little salt they could taste compared to any ham cured in America. They walked closer to the centerpiece and pointed to the ham leg, asking questions of Nick as if he were a curator at a culinary museum. With everyone intoxicated by the taste of the delicacy on the table, Nick shared his vision for introducing a food culture to Georgia and the southeast.

"These hams, along with Kobe beef and Beluga caviar, are among the most prized foods in the world. The problem is that the *real* Jamón Ibérico de Bellota hams are only available in Spain and not available in the U.S. due to *your* U.S.D.A." Nick made sure he pronounced the U.S.D.A. as U.S. "*duh*" for the camera, eliciting a roaring response from the group.

"The U.S. duh does allow one company to export a cheap knock off from Spain, and they charge a hundred dollars a pound for that!" Nick said. "But it's garbage compared to the real thing. You see this black foot? You won't see that on their ham, as the U.S. duh forbids it to be imported anywhere in America." Nick pointed to the black hoof that pointed up to the ceiling from the Salamanca. "That black hoof is the only proof that you're eating the real thing," Nick added. "That you're getting the real pata negro or black-footed Iberian pig that grazed freely on acorns, or bellotas as we say in Spain."

The guests hung on each of Nick's words and marveled at the dark, ruby red slices of ham, seeing it not merely for what it was (the leg of a pig) but rather an exquisite human accomplishment of mankind, in a class with the Egyptian pyramids, Picasso, or even the space shuttle.

"We have taken a beautiful animal, a pig, and made it into so much more. Something far more elevated than what nature created." Nick said. "We have taken it and created art!"

"I'm not so sure the pig, or P.E.T.A. for that matter, would agree with that assessment, Nick," one of the unsmiling faces said. Nervous chuckles surrounded the centerpiece as eyes fell to the floor.

Nick turned his gaze to the man and then cast a mischievous smile. "I'm all for P.E.T.A." Nick said to the shock of his guests. "People Eating Tasty Animals, right?"

The group roared as the camera panned back from the lone vegan in the group to the carnivorous frenzy surrounding the pig's head.

"If the U.S.D.A. doesn't allow the black hoof to be imported, then where did these come from?" a woman asked. She was a senior vice president of marketing at IBM, and the $75,000 membership fee to network with so many other high ranking marketing gurus in this intimate setting hadn't been an afterthought in her multi-billion dollar budget. Nick had known that would be the case for each of the contacts that Wade had cultivated from his executive recruiting days, and that once a tipping point of membership was achieved, everyone would want in. That's exactly how it had played out, with all ten 50-Forks Clubs selling out within six months, each with its fifty paying members. Using the existing restaurant staff he had in each city, and with virtually no investment in the private meeting homes, Nick would rake in over $37 million dollars in membership fees the first year alone. He could afford to splurge on celebrity keynote speakers and extravagant dinners to create an over-the-top experience.

"Great question," Nick began. "These hams didn't come from Spain. They came from Spanish-breed pigs that were acorn-fed and cured right here in the Appalachian Mountains!"

Nick took in the wide eyes of his audience and continued.

"There's a little island off the coast of Savannah called Ossabaw Island. A few centuries ago, my people, the Spaniards, decided to do a little exploring and came over this way," Nick said smiling. "They brought pigs with them, the descendants of today's true Iberian pigs, and left them on the island for the next wave of Spaniards to hunt and eat. At some point we stopped coming, and the pigs learned to thrive on the island on their own. The locals call those pigs Ozzies, short for Ossabaw."

Nick stood in the center of the room with cameras both focused on him and on the faces of his guests. It was exactly where he liked to be, the center of attention, the focal point of culinary delights and connecting people to what he called *real* food. Not the tasteless garbage that he looked down on in America as people slurped and shoved paper bagfuls of trash into their mouths while driving, thinking they were eating.

"A farmer raised and cured these in the southern Appalachian Mountains," Nick added, "just like my father did in Spain, and his father before him." A producer for The Food Channel stood in the back of the room and signaled Nick, indicating they should sit. "Now please, let's take our seats and enjoy a marvelous dinner." Nick concluded. "We can talk more during dinner."

As the members moved to one of the two very long rectangular tables on each side of the house, Rose walked to the centerpiece with John and several others who wanted a final glimpse of the star attraction. Rose zeroed her eyes on the head of the pig, taking in its expression and trying to decide if it had been happy or sad when it lived. She was far from a vegan, but she knew that P.E.T.A. stood for People for the Ethical Treatment of Animals. Certainly any vegan would have sprinted far away from the centerpiece by now, she thought, as she eyed the lonely gentleman who had questioned Nick on the treatment of animals. As she thought of her conversation the day before with Angelica about factory farming, she leaned closer to examine the pig's head with John and others watching. A cameraman followed her right index finger as it touched right between the pig's eyes.

"What is this?" Rose asked herself and those around her. They all looked closely at the shape of the letter X that intersected right between the pig's eyes.

"I dunno," John said. "Maybe it split there during roasting or something." He had long been a vegetarian for health rather than for animal cruelty reasons, but John couldn't hide his grimace at the gruesome incision.

"Looks like someone marked it with a knife," another man said as he hoisted a glass of champagne to his lips.

"Well," John said, "I wouldn't want *that* job! Marking a pig while he was still alive. I mean, look at the tusks coming out of that thing's mouth. That thing could kill a man, easy."

John took Rose by the hand and led her toward one of the tables where the wine flowed freely and the servers stood ready to plate the first course. Naturally, much of the table's conversation touched on sales and marketing throughout the dinner, but John skillfully brought the discussion to family and personal issues as often as he could. Rose was grateful to John for yet another loving act that so many husbands wouldn't think to do or be able to do. Underneath the table she took his right hand with her left as she gushed about her girls to a new mother seated across from her.

Talking about the girls made her realize how much she cherished them and her life with them and John. She was eager to leave on vacation the next morning because the sooner she left, the sooner she would return to that life. It was that thought, and not the taste of the food, that put the Mona Lisa smile on her face as she deeply inhaled the moldy aroma and savored another slice of ham.

Chapter 22

Blake held Angelica's hand and walked across the blacktop parking lot of the Sandy Creek Baptist Church for the first time in a very long time. Since before the miscarriage, he concluded, as he tried to recall his last visit to church that wasn't on Easter or Christmas. It was a typical small country church, but plenty big enough for the Warwoman community. A white clapboard house of worship with a steeple reaching for the heavens from above the front entrance. Five, wide steps led up to the church entrance for those who could walk. For those who couldn't, a new wheelchair ramp sloped from the right side to the landing platform at the top of the stairs.

Two men of Native American descent stood at the base of the ramp and talked with an elderly woman who resembled Barbara Bush. One of the men dropped his head as Angelica cast a gaze upon him in passing. Charles Weaver, the eldest man, held Angelica's stare and nodded imperceptibly.

The elderly woman, Sylvia Jackson, spoke up. "Why the hush?"

Tom, a pudgy man with stringy gray hair and inflated cheeks, turned to Sylvia. "She's a witch," he whispered.

"Why, that's nonsense," Sylvia said looking as if she was in shock. "Well, that girl has been going to this church right on her whole life. She's an absolute angel, she is."

Tom kicked some gravel around and grunted. "Hmm. A witch I'm telling you," he repeated. "I could tell you some stories about her." Charles stared down at him.

"Why on God's green earth would you say that?" Sylvia pressed. Tom leaned over the railing to see if Angelica was within earshot. She and Blake had already walked toward the front.

"First off, her grandmother was a witch too!" Tom said.

"Hmm," Charles grunted as he cast an incredulous gaze at Tom.

Sylvia rolled her eyes and asked, "Oh, so now everyone's a witch?"

Tom raised a finger and pointed it directly at Sylvia. "Well answer me this. What kind of woman buries her granddaughter ALIVE?" Sylvia's mouth hung open as Tom continued. "Yep. Stuck her in a hole and covered her with dirt, gave her only a hollow cane to breath through. When she was only six or seven years old!"

Charles stared down at Tom and snorted with disapproval, "Hmm."

"Then," Tom continued, "old granny puts leaves on top of where she buried her own granddaughter, alive mind you, and sets the leaves afire. After the fire dies off, she yanks her granddaughter out of the ground and says now she's a Cherokee priest with supernatural ability!"

"That's—that can't be true," Sylvia said.

The elder man, tall and very weathered, spoke up. "That part is true," Charles said. "That girl is my great niece. The grandmother Tom speaks of was my sister. But the girl is no witch."

"Is too," Tom said. "I seen her one time use her magic to save a boy from drowning, right here on Warwoman Creek." Tom pointed up the road toward a widening in the creek.

"That doesn't make her a witch," Charles said, folding his arms across his chest.

"Does so," Tom continued. "We's having a potluck dinner up the road. We'd had a ton of rain and this boy slipped off the bank. Them rapids took him under and swept him clean over them boulders. Everyone was in a panic but I watched that witch. She walked right over to the edge of the river and stared straight at that boy. She took her fingers and started twirling some magic beads on her neck and kept on chanting a spell."

Sylvia was now trying her best to record every word in her memory so she could command attention at the following week's gossip circle. Tom continued the story. "I watched her and that girl didn't blink once. Nary a time. And you know what happened? Just then a tree leaned over and hung some branches right down in front of that boy so he could grab a hold of!"

Sylvia's mouth fell open again.

"Well," Sylvia said. "My word. I guess that could be just a coincidence that you're misreading. That don't rightly make her no witch. Sounds more like an angel to me if she saved that boy."

"She was casting a spell, I tell ya. She's a witch," Tom said.

"She isn't a witch," Charles repeated and grimaced at how loud his voice had become. He stared at Tom in a manner that suggested it would be wise to no longer suggest otherwise. "Witches do evil," Charles continued. "What you're describing is conjuring spells that the Cherokee people used for good, not evil. They used lots of verbal formulas, or chants as you say, even some to conjure up weather. And they used herbs for medicine. Witches used herbs for poison, and evil witches like the Raven Mocker took lives instead of saving them."

Sylvia very nearly fainted.

"My sister was only doing what was done to her as a child," Charles said. "She wanted to help Angelica become a Cherokee priest. To do that, she had to bury her first so she could say her old self was dead and buried. After the leaves were burned she rose as a priest. That's the way it's always been done."

"Why—why on earth would your sister want to do that to a child?" Sylvia asked.

Charles dropped his voice. "Because that girl, Angelica, is an identical twin, and the Cherokees believed twins had supernatural powers. They often became priests, especially the younger twin, which Angelica was."

"Is she a witch...I mean, a priest?" Sylvia asked.

"Hmm," Charles snorted. "That's old superstition. The kind of thinking my sister held with. Not me, which is why I don't see my great niece often. She doesn't approve of my lack of faith."

"What about them beads she carries?" Tom asked.

Charles had grown tired of the conversation. He exhaled and looked down at Tom.

"Beads and crystals were used for divination," Charles said. "A priest would hold a black bead in the left hand to signify death or disaster and a white bead in the right hand to signify health and happiness. The beads were moved slowly between the tips of the index fingers and thumbs. The strength of the motion told the priest if the outcome in question would be favorable or unfavorable."

The church bell rang and visibly jolted Sylvia. "Well, my word! That story and them church bells plum near stopped my heart!" She said. "We best get inside." Sylvia and the men walked in.

Inside, eight rows of simple wooden benches divided the aisle that led the eyes to the pastor's pulpit. Between the front pew and the pastor on the right side of the church were three more benches, each turned perpendicular to the nave of the congregation's benches. These were for the small choir, comprised of enthusiastic, if not harmonious, mountain voices, young and old. A door on the far end behind the benches led to a small room where Angelica had dropped the girls off for Sunday School an hour before.

On the left side of the church, just below the pastor's chancel, was a beautiful piano, a gift from the estate of the recently deceased Gladys Wilcox, who had been a member of the church for all of her ninety-four years. In that time she had reared three children, spoiled nine grandchildren, traveled once out of Rabun County and saved enough money in her snuff jars to buy the piano for the church as stipulated in her will.

Blake remembered thinking years before of how he would have made the church bigger, more fancy, if he had been consulted on the design. Even then he wasn't really religious. He never really "got it" and felt that people went to church because they were supposed to. Because they lived in a small community and, if they didn't, others would look down on them. So they went for the ham and egg suppers, for the potluck dinners, tried to stay awake for the sermons and wasted a good day each week, Blake thought. Some had even more time to waste as they went both Sunday morning and evening, and then again Wednesday night!

But they had something that money couldn't buy, Blake had begun to realize. They had each other and were there to comfort one another in times of need. Blake knew that this was his time of need. He also knew he had no right to ask for help, for forgiveness. He had given nothing to the community. Had shunned it, in fact, as he pursued his own dreams selfishly. He was always too busy, he had told Angelica with a straight face, because it was largely true. But the larger truth was that he wanted nothing to do with this or any church. Sitting there made him feel uncomfortable. Angelica led him to the second row on the right side and saved a spot for the girls for when they were dismissed. Blake sat next to the aisle.

He turned to his right and looked behind, recognizing most of the faces he had grown up among. Faces both familiar and strange to him at the same time. They nodded at him in a welcoming manner, inviting him to stay and visit often with their peaceful smiles. Blake returned the nods, returned the smiles as he took in the faces, in search of comfort and reassurance. Making eye contact with friendly faces allowed Blake to feel more at ease. He stood a little taller and turned left to look for faces on the other side. Memories flooded back to him from faces that had known him all along. Faces that he had abandoned, had forgotten. A calm swept over him as he welcomed them all, feeling like a security blanket that comforted him. His eyes finished their sweep when they met the preacher, seated with his Bible in his lap with an empty chair on one side of him and the pulpit on the other.

The music began playing asking for all to rise and sing to begin the worship. Blake stood and took Angelica's hand. As he did, the door opened from the Sunday School. The children walked out and found their parents or guardians. Walking behind the children, dressed in his clean and pressed sheriff's uniform, was Lonnie Jacobs. Blake inhaled and held his breath as his body tensed. *Shit!* he said silently, his mind forgetting where his vulgar mouth was.

The sheriff walked to the front and took the empty chair next to the pastor.

What in God's name is he doing here? Blake thought to himself, realizing the irony of his question given the setting. And then Blake remembered. Sheriff Lonnie Jacobs was also Pastor Lonnie Jacobs of the Bull Creek Baptist Church. Blake had completely forgotten, only vaguely recalling the fact that Lonnie had become a pastor before being elected sheriff.

Lonnie had made the highly publicized decision to run for sheriff when Blake was in junior high, saying that ministers were in the world to make a positive difference, and what better way than to use his understanding of God's word to take on societal problems and enforce the law. "The Lord has me here in this moment and this is how he wants to use me," Lonnie had said in his campaign interview for the Clayton Tribune. The Atlanta Journal Constitution also covered those words and the campaign, much to the amusement of the educated masses to the south. The message would have fallen on deaf ears in most parts of the country, and certainly in Atlanta for that matter. But in the rural belly of the Bible Belt the chords of Lonnie's calling rang true. He was elected by forty-seven votes, a landslide.

Lonnie's eyes surveyed the room with both compassion and righteousness. His eyes met Blake's, held them for a moment, and continued around the room. The pastor invited the congregation to be seated and began by saying what the others had already known. That they were honored to have a guest pastor that day from the other side of Rainey Mountain, who was here to spread the word of God and to deliver a special sermon. Lonnie thanked the pastor and stood before the pulpit. Blake didn't take his eyes off him, outwardly appearing to be supremely interested in what he was saying. Inside Blake's mind was another story as his worst fears zoomed and crashed into one another, occasionally interrupted by a poignant word or phrase from the sheriff.

Looming tall from the pulpit, Lonnie overlooked the congregation as he opened his Bible. "Can there be anything worse than isolation?" Lonnie asked the congregation as he began his sermon. "The feeling of helplessness, of being alone when confronted with crisis. With tragedy. No one that knows how you feel, if you're sick, if you've lost a close friend." He surveyed the room and parked his eyes on Blake before continuing. "No one you can confess to. Can tell the truth about what you've done."

Shit! A lump formed in Blake's throat, he was sure it was a massive, visible lump that parched his throat and suffocated his breath. Thoughts raced through Blake's mind of isolation, the feeling of loneliness he had. It was as if the sheriff...the pastor was speaking directly to him, about him. *How could he know anything about what I've done? What I'm feeling?*

"For each of you," Lonnie continued, "for all of us, we are not alone. We have the Lord to hear us." The men of the congregation spoke up. "Amen brother. Amen."

"We have each other to comfort us, to be there and share in the times of despair, whether they be of a singular and personal nature, as in the case of a grave illness." Lonnie's eyes fell to the loving family of an ailing elderly man seated on the front row, clearly attending one of his last sermons.

"Or in the case of a natural calamity that unites us in despair, such as Hurricane Katrina, or the horrible tornadoes that tore through the South in recent years, killing so many innocent children of God."

Angelica squeezed Blake's hand in a reassuring way.

"Imagine how much worse those times could be. Would be, if you had to endure them alone." Lonnie said. Heads nodded throughout the congregation. Blake's head dropped, his eyes falling from Lonnie. He realized this and popped his head back up, fighting against the burdensome weight he felt levied on his mind and his shoulders.

"Today, we live in a world of greed," Lonnie said. As he began the main thesis of his sermon, Blake felt connected via a tunnel directly to Lonnie, the people on each side fading as the message was channeled through a conduit directly from God through the pastor to Blake. *Or is the message from the sheriff himself,* Blake thought?

"Sometimes the greed is far away. On places like Wall Street, where unscrupulous souls worship and pursue material wealth at any and all costs." All heads nodded knowingly to a chorus of "amens."

"But the temptation isn't *always* far away. It's sometimes among us, my friends, luring us away from the Lord, away from Jesus," Lonnie said looking at Blake. "Away from the law."

"The book of Timothy is very clear about this temptation," Lonnie continued as he read Timothy 6:10. *For the love of money is a root of all evil: which while some coveted after, they have erred from the faith, and pierced themselves through with many sorrows.* "Pierced themselves, my brothers and sisters. Not the way these teenagers pierce their ears and body parts these days." Lonnie said with a affable smile. Eyes looked around the room as a couple of shaggy-haired teens on the back row hung their heads, waiting for the disproving attention to pass.

"No. Pierced like a lifeless hog on a spit," Lonnie said, using a visual reference that all could grasp. Blake's eyes widened in disbelief, unable to comprehend the uncanny irony of the reference.

"Today, I'd like to share with you a story from Kings chapter twenty-one, verses one through twenty-nine." Lonnie said. "I'll summarize the story in my own words rather than read it for you."

Angelica opened her well-worn King James Bible to the book of Kings and turned to chapter twenty-one. She laid it open on her left leg for both her and Blake to read. Blake dropped his head to look at the words on the page, relieved for the moment to have a reason to turn his gaze away from the sheriff.

"You see," Lonnie began, "Naboth lived on a vineyard in Jezreel next to King Ahab of Samaria. But Ahab wanted that land for himself to create a vegetable garden, so he offered to buy it. Naboth refused to sell the land because it was important to him since it had been in his family for generations. King Ahab sulked in his house and told his wife, Jezebel, the bad news."

All eyes were open and on Lonnie, nary a one looking at the Bible itself. Lonnie knew that the way to reach people was through stories and by making stories real. Sometimes the word of the Bible, particularly the translation of the King James Version, made that difficult for anyone other than Bible scholars. "But Jezebel came to Ahab with a plan," Lonnie continued as he furrowed his eyebrows, "pointing out that he, Ahab, governed the kingdom of Israel. I will give thee the vineyard of Naboth, she told Ahab."

Lonnie unfolded the rest of the story, in which Jezebel used Ahab's royal authority to arrange for two witnesses to falsely accuse Naboth of cursing God and the king. Naboth was then taken outside the city and stoned to death, thereby allowing Ahab to immediately claim possession of the vineyard. When the prophet Elijah learned of this and confronted Ahab with the truth, he prophesied a terrible fate for him and Jezebel. Once he heard the words of Elijah, Ahab removed his clothes, put a sackcloth upon his flesh, and fasted until he wasted away. As for Jezebel, she met the end that Elijah predicted, being eaten by the dogs at the wall of Jezreel.

"This is indeed a dark story of avarice," Lonnie said as he concluded the story. "As we see, greed isn't something new. It's as old and ever-lasting as the sand. As Christians, we must be on guard against it, help one another to resist it and cherish what is important in this physical world. As sheriff, I must help to root it out."

Lonnie spread his arms as if to reach and hug the congregation as a whole. "We are not alone, my friends, for we have each other. Our love for one another and for Jesus Christ," he said, "who died on the cross for us. It's this love that cost nothing and that's worth everything. Let us take this love for one another, for Jesus, and let it sustain us, fulfill us so that we want for nothing else."

Closing the Bible, Lonnie signaled for Mrs. Wyatt, the high school music teacher, to begin playing after the pastor offered the closing prayer. Parishioners wiped at their eyes on both sides of the aisle as the members walked toward the door, their steps light with the knowledge that they were walking straight down the center of the aisle, both in the church and in life. Blake, too, felt tears forming in his eyes. But his footsteps and his heart were heavy as he began to slowly slumber toward the exit. He caught himself walking on the edge of the aisle and not in its center. He no longer wanted to walk on the edge of any of life's paths so he began to move right. In his haste to get to the door to greet everyone, the sheriff hurried past as Blake tried to move right. He lightly bumped Blake as they met, and caused Blake to stray back to the left. The sheriff, the pastor, continued walking right down the middle.

Lonnie nodded at Blake as they passed.

Chapter 23

John sat in the left seat of the Beechjet 400A, feeling like a kid in a candy store as the pilot announced his intentions to the tower at Athens Ben Epps Field. "Athens Tower Beech Charter November niner one five eight Echo holding on runway two-seven, ready for takeoff." The African Rosewood doors that divided the main cabin's four leather seats from the cockpit remained open, allowing John to feel like a captain himself. The co-pilot looked back to John and Rose. "Heck of a Sunday morning isn't it?" she asked. John smiled and nodded. "Well, you two sit back and relax and we'll have you roaming the beaches of San Salvador in a couple of hours."

"Beech five eight Echo cleared for takeoff, runway two-seven." The lone flight attendant secured the cabin door in response to the tower's response just as the pilot's right hand pushed the throttle forward. The chartered executive jet rolled down the tarmac and climbed effortlessly at nearly 4,000 feet per minute. The captain began a shallow, sweeping turn to the right, coming around all the way to a southeasterly heading of 139 degrees.

John reached across the aisle for Rose's left hand, which was gripping her armrest. Her head rested on a pillow and her face was without expression as she stared out her window. John thought she might be a little nervous. It was understandable. Rose had never cared much for flying and the only thing she hated more than John being called away on business was if she, too, had to fly away. But they had agreed it was time for a nice vacation on their own away from the girls. Just the two of them for a week on a secluded Bahamian island.

When John told Rose that he had chartered the private jet from Athens, non-stop to San Salvador at a rate of $2,800 per hour, she thought the price was absurd until John explained that they only had to pay for the actual flight time. He figured the cost each way would be about $6,000, a steep price to be sure, but something John felt that they had earned with the success of WallCloud. Besides, he didn't want to have to drive Rose to Atlanta, go through all the airport hassle before boarding a huge commercial jet to Nassau, only to have to change planes and find a puddle jumper to get them to the tiny island of San Salvador. Still, he already regretted booking the flight so early in the morning. They had stayed at the 50-Forks dinner the night before far longer than they had intended and drank far more than they should. John had chartered the plane to take off at 8:00 a.m. so that they could have the afternoon on the beach after navigating to the beach house they had rented for the week.

As Rose responded by squeezing John's hand lightly, he reclined his plush, leather seat and fell fast asleep. Rose kept her head still, resting on a pillow as she looked out the window, staring at nothing. She concentrated on how she felt, knowing that something wasn't right, but unable to put her finger on what it was. Pulling her hand away from John's, she touched her forehead. Slightly warm, but only a mild fever if anything at all. Her stomach was sore, she thought, but then again maybe there wasn't any abdominal pain. Discomfort was a better description than pain, she thought. *Am I getting sick, or is it something else?* She concentrated on the question she asked herself as the plane leveled at 35,000 feet. *Could it simply be that I miss the girls?* She reflected on the many wonderful excursions she had taken with John before the girls were born. Cruises, Vegas, New Orleans, and beaches. She and John had loved every minute of it, of their time alone together. Now, she was a mother. Something had changed, she seemed to now fully realize for the first time, as she lost herself in the endless blue sky. She had no longings for exotic travel, no desire to drink daiquiris on a mega cruise ship. No, she was a mother now and she wanted only to be with her girls and to be with them all the time. Just the girls and John together, anywhere.

Is that it? Is that making me feel uneasy? The general malaise that comes from being homesick, away from who and what you love? Or is it the motion of the plane, the unnatural feeling of being in a tin can, moving on a seat at 450 miles per hour almost seven miles up in the air?

Something wasn't right. Rose knew it, but also knew she couldn't explain it. Just a mother's intuition, she told herself, as she tugged a blanket under her chin and tried to sleep.

***

Kevin Colbert returned weakly to bed in his Sutton, Massachusetts home with two glasses of orange juice and the Sunday Boston Globe. His wife, Monica, lay in the bed semi-awake, moaning, with the covers pulled tight. Kevin laid the newspaper on a chair, hoping he would feel well enough later to read it.

"Can you get me some more Motrin?" Monica groaned. Kevin sat the orange juice on the nightstand beside her and leaned over to feel her head. He wiped away the beads of sweat from her burning head and visualized a body emerging from a steam room. He stroked her head. "It's too early," he said. "We just took some three hours ago at 5:45 a.m."

As he stood back up, Kevin felt every part of his body ache. He trudged to the master bathroom and soaked a washcloth in cool water, wringing it out lightly as he looked up at the mirror. The man returning the gaze was blurred, disheveled, and in no way resembled the suave gentleman who had been on the CNN supper club segment the month before, or the debonair gentleman who dined with some of society's elite the night before at an underground supper club in an exclusive home in Dover.

Thank God we didn't get this flu yesterday, he thought to himself. *We would have never been able to make that dinner.* Kevin shuffled back to the bedroom and placed the cloth across Monica's forehead, having determined that there was really nothing else he could do. Of the two of them, Monica was the first to feel the symptoms come on, having awoken at 5:30 complaining of all-around body aches and pains. Kevin tended to her by giving her some juice and Motrin. He then used his computer to research the symptoms that Monica complained about—aches, pain, fever, and slight breathing difficulty—and found them to match the flu-like symptoms on the CDC's website. The recommendation was to stay home, drink fluids, get rest, and don't visit the emergency room unless you were in a high-risk category. Take ibuprofen or acetaminophen for fever if necessary, and have a family member look after you if possible.

That wasn't possible. As a precaution, John had sent a text to his only daughter, Kelly, just to let her know how they were doing. Kelly lived about an hour away, in Watertown, and had gone with her husband to Vermont for the Columbus Day weekend. She wouldn't return until late that night or the following morning...Kevin wasn't sure. He had not wanted to call her early on a Sunday morning so he simply texted her, "hope you guys are having fun! mom and I feel down today with flu so we're in bed. Turned phone off so we can rest. luv dad."

Had they lived in a more populated area, Kevin might have gone to a health clinic despite the CDC's recommendations. But they moved to their quiet and wooded home on Town Farm Road in Sutton for a reason. It was out in the boondocks, or at least as far out as you can be and still be close to Providence and Boston, and reasonably close to the Cape and the Berkshires. The only downside was that there was no medical clinic in Sutton and certainly no doctor's office open on a Sunday morning. The closest choices would have been emergency rooms at Milford Regional or in Worcester. There was no reason to make a big deal out of this, Kevin reasoned, so he turned off the computer and went back to bed.

Now, he had awoken with the same symptoms, and Monica had not improved. He crawled into bed to get his own rest. Monica's raspy breathing sounded like air was being sucked through a straw that was punctured with pinholes. Her lungs were trying to inflate, but it seemed like all the air wasn't getting in. Kevin went to sleep worried about her and hoping that he would fare better.

***

The taxi stopped in front of the Athens Regional Medical Center. "$6.50," the driver said. Megan Wilcox fumbled through her purse and squinted at the bill, trying to determine if it was a ten or a twenty. She shook her head in frustration at her blurred vision, which only succeeded at making her head pound even more. She tossed the bill in the driver's direction and grabbed the door handle.

"Hey, that's a twen—" the driver began as she closed the door. Megan looked up at the large red letters that spelled EMERGENCY in front of the huge panes of glass windows. She walked to the admissions station and stood behind an elderly man. Now *he* should be here, she thought. The admissions nurse pointed to a clipboard and nodded her head in the direction of the waiting area. Megan took the clipboard and walked to take a seat.

Walking slowly through the maze of interlocking, cheap, tweed-covered chairs, she looked for a place to sit where she could be at least a few feet away from the walking wounded, thinking naïvely that she wouldn't want to catch whatever they had. Not thinking at all that she might have something that they'd prefer not to have, thank you. As she passed, she took in the faces, some looking vaguely familiar to her even though that seemed impossible, given how far away from home she was. *I guess sick people all look the same,* she thought to herself.

She tried to focus on the form as she sat. Megan Wilcox, her trembling hands began to write with difficulty. It was difficult for her to see the form, even though she had perfect vision. She concentrated and tried to continue. 1445 Hutchinson Street, Armonk, NY, she wrote and then paused, trying to remember her ZIP code. Distracted, she glanced at the magazines on the table. *Always the same ones in these places*, she thought. *WebMD, Smart Money, Georgia Magazine* and *People.* She removed a copy of *Reader's Digest* from the seat beside her that featured the short stories of Edgar Allen Poe. On the cover, a raven held its mouth open and cast an ominous gaze. She tossed it on the table with the others as she returned to the the maze of questions on the form. Not reading any of them, just checking "no" to each one as she walked back to the desk.

"May I have your health insurance card?" the nurse asked. Megan sighed and reached into her wallet for the Blue Cross Blue Shield card and handed it to the lady. The health care coverage was the last thing on her mind. IBM offered a great health care plan, even if she was almost a thousand miles from home. No, the only thing she wanted was some meds, something to get rid of the chills, aches and fever that had come over her out of nowhere in the early morning hours.

"Here you go," the lady said, returning the health care card she had just copied. "The nurse will take you in now."

The nurse asked Megan to step on the scale and recorded her weight and height. She wrote down 127 pounds, 5 feet 6 inches on the form as Megan slumped on the scale and stared at the wall. "You can step down now," the nurse said, "and have a seat. Says here you're thirty-four years old, is that right?"

"Yes."

"New York," the nurse continued. "Long way from home."

"I'm staying at the Marriott here in Athens. Flying home tonight." Megan said.

The nurse popped a thermometer in Megan's mouth and recorded her temperature of 102 on the form. She sensed that Megan wasn't in the mood to roll up her left arm sleeve so the nurse leaned over and did that for her, strapping the blood pressure cuff over her arm. She pumped air into the cuff with the squeeze bulb as she surveyed Megan's condition. The nurse had already made up her mind that it was the flu. It was the fourth case she had seen in the past hour, even though it was months away from the heart of the flu season. After four years this job had become so mundane to her, other than the real emergencies that came in. But those generally went straight into the emergency room or prepped for surgery. The cases she saw were generally the same. The most exciting case she had seen this year was a beekeeper that was stung twenty times and was on the verge of anaphylactic shock. He couldn't speak and could barely breathe, so the doctor wasted little time giving the epinephrine injection. Other than that it was always people with cold or flu-like symptoms who came in and paid the exorbitant emergency room fees even though, she thought, everyone knew to not waste the emergency room's resources for common colds and flus.

She released the air pressure from the cuff and expected the blood pressure to be a little high, as it was with the other cases. The nurse recorded the numbers and then looked back to make sure she had seen them correctly. 162 over 114. The nurse checked the form to see if Megan had any family history of high blood pressure and recognized that Megan had blindly answered every question.

"Ms. Wilcox, do you have any family history of high blood pressure?" the nurse asked with a smile, not wanting to alarm the patient.

Megan had been leaning her head against the wall, her eyes closed. Now she opened them, but the bright florescent lights hammered spears right into her eyes and stabbed her temples. She closed them and said, "No. None."

The nurse squeezed the bulb again to take another reading. The result of 164 over 118 did nothing to assuage the nurse's concerns. "Ms. Wilcox, come with me and we'll take care of you." Megan tried to stand, but found she couldn't do it. The nurse took her right arm and helped her up. She walked her to a bed in the emergency room and helped her to take her shoes off and lie down. The nurse turned to get one of the doctors on duty and began to pull the curtain closed in her room. As she did she looked back at the admission form and turned back to Megan. Masking her concern, she smiled reassuringly and said, "Ms. Wilcox, can you give me the name and number of someone I can call for you in case we need to notify them of your condition?"

Chapter 24

The beach home sat alone on a southern point of San Salvador island surrounded only by sand, water, and sky. A wide, wood-planked porch wrapped all the way around the house. When Rose walked all the way around it, it gave her the feeling that she was on an island by herself, with no one in sight. A wicker rocking chair beckoned to Rose, one of two that sat beside the front door and faced the broad steps that led into the house. She sat down, cupping between her hands the tea she had just made in the home that she and John had rented for the week. Facing south, she stared out at the beach and the ocean. What else was there to see?

Surely there was more, so she challenged herself. There was wispy grass growing from gentle sand dunes between the house and water, but her mind had registered those as indistinguishable from the beach itself. But indeed, it was separate from the sand, something different to consider, if she was so inclined. She wasn't, so she looked to the sky, still dark blue overhead as it had yet to be fully illuminated. That was the event Rose had come out to see, the sunrise that would emerge from her left.

Pushing out of the chair she walked to the porch railing so that she could look overhead, seeing the darkness of the sky. Her eyes descended slowly to the eastern horizon and she tried to identify horizontal lines that distinguished the decreasing shades of darkness on the way down. The horizon was alive with energy and warmth. Above, the sky was cold and dark, not evil, but evoking no feeling of love. Resembling the coolness of death, not the warmth of life.

She couldn't discern where the changes in the sky's mood appeared. Instead, she could only notice the stark contrast from above to below, and her eyes settled on the horizon where the sun rose from the ocean so gently that it allowed her to stare directly at it. Two fishing boats were silhouetted against the giant orb and they appeared to be chasing it, pursuing it as if they could cast their nets around it and harness its energy. She wondered if John was on one of the boats.

John was so excited about the fishing excursion they had booked the month before, a private charter that would take him and Rose deep-sea fishing for trophy fish. When they had made their way to the beach house the afternoon before, Rose hadn't felt so well. She and John sat on the beach in front of the porch and listened to the soft waves, about all Rose felt like doing.

"I'll call and cancel the charter," John had said to Rose as they sat on the beach.

"There's no need," Rose replied. "We can't get our money back so let's see how I feel in the morning. There's no advantage to canceling now." By bedtime Rose had felt better. John was hopeful that they would be able to go after all and Rose didn't want to disappoint him. When they awoke this morning at 5:00 a.m. Rose did feel better, but she felt like a day at sea would set her back. Instead, she asked John to go to the Riding Rock Marina alone. John refused, and started to call the marina to cancel the trip, but Rose insisted.

"John, we've already paid for the boat. I'll be fine and you know as well as I do that we need a Wahoo on our wall," Rose said with a smile as she visualized the giant trophy fish.

John smiled and thought about it. Rose seemed fine and what she said made sense. Going to sea might make things worse for her, but why waste the trip?

"I just want to sit on the porch and read, John, so you go ahead and I'll see you tonight."

As the sun climbed and swallowed the darkness above, Rose walked back, this time choosing a wicker sofa on which to rest.

A morning breeze began to blow gently, enough to make it comfortable to snuggle under a light blanket. She positioned two pillows on the armrest and stared into the southerly sky at the high level mass of white cirrus clouds on the horizon. Gazing into the sea, she saw the smiling faces of her beautiful daughters and hugged herself tight, sending them her love. Other than missing them dearly she felt fine, at peace, as she fell asleep.

***

MONDAY NOON: BOSTON, MASSACHUSETTS

"This is WBUR, Boston's NPR News Station. A mysterious illness is being blamed for last night's death of a local married couple. Monica and Kevin Colbert of Sutton, Massachusetts, were found in their home by their daughter who told doctors they had complained of flu-like symptoms. The Worcester County Health Department entered the couple's homes wearing HAZMAT suits to remove bedding and take microbe samples. The initial cause of death has been listed as septicemia, but tests are being conducted to rule out whether or not avian or swine flu could be possible causes of death. This is Scott Sheldon for WBUR, Boston University Radio."

***

MONDAY 2:00 P.M: ATHENS, GEORGIA

"In local news, a thirty-four-year old New York woman died suddenly this morning at Athens Regional Medical Center from what doctors are calling flu-like symptoms. Officials at the hospital reported an uptick in patients complaining of flu-like symptoms, even though the heart of flu season is still months away. In local weather, expect fair and mild conditions for most of the week. The National Weather Service says that large ridges of high pressure, one over Texas and the other centered close to Bermuda, will remain in place, steering tropical air from the gulf to the southeastern states. For WUGA in Athens, this is Kimberly Blanchard.

***

At 4:00 p.m., John posed for a picture next to the fighting chair at the back of the boat as he held the tail of the sixty eight pound Wahoo he had just landed. The Ilander-skirted ballyhoo lure still hung from the Wahoo's lip, a rather unsatisfying last supper. Wind-whipped waves that had blown up in the past hour made it difficult for John to stand for the picture, but he was buoyed by his sense of accomplishment and smiled broadly.

He looked at his phone, hoping that somehow reception would magically appear. No bars. Not that he expected any twenty seven miles east of San Salvador island. "Oh, well," he said, knowing full well that Rose's cell phone wouldn't work at the beach house anyway. He just wanted to send her the picture, to tell her he was thinking of her and that he couldn't wait to see her that evening.

The captain turned the fifty-four-foot Bertram over-under around and began following the sun back toward San Salvador as the first mate took John's fish and put it on ice alongside the grouper he had also caught. Turning the wheel over to his assistant, the captain came back to speak to John. "Hey, that's a heck of a Wahoo you got there," the captain said to John, purposefully playing up his Bahamian accent for the tourist. "Especially this early in the season."

John smiled. "Yeah. Lucky, I guess." John knew the Wahoo really only started biting in October and that the winter months are when they were most active. Still, he had what he came for, and with a few hours of fishing left he was optimistic that he had yet to land the really big one. The captain had told him in the morning that he expected the best bite to be near sunset.

"So you may have noticed I turned the boat back toward the island," the captain said. "We got word that the hurricane in the Caribbean is turning north and they think it will head for the islands. We have to cut the trip short a few hours and head back. Just to be safe, you know, and to get our boat secured."

As he considered the captain's comments for a moment, John's initial thought was that the captain was pulling his leg since he definitely looked the part of the sunburned tourist who could be suckered. But the captain looked serious, so John glanced around at the waves and the sky. He had paid little attention to either during the excitement of fishing. The chop had picked up in the past couple of hours, but John thought that must be normal for being so far out at sea.

"Really? Are you—serious?"

"Yah man, we don't joke about hurricanes, not on the outer islands."

"What...when? What are they saying?" All of a sudden John needed data, information to help him make strategic choices, as if he was in a Monday morning meeting with his team around the conference table.

"They saying it'll take the path Irene took a couple of years ago when it went right through the islands," the captain said, "except they say it won't turn northeast. It's suppose to hit land somewhere between Florida and South Carolina, but that part ain't what concerns me if you know what I'm sayin'."

Suddenly the idea of fishing at all seemed ridiculous. John's smile faded as he surveyed the overcast skies and felt a light, steady breeze across his cheeks. Moving at twelve knots, he couldn't tell how much of what he felt was the wind blowing and how much was attributable to relative wind due to the boat's motion. The sea was littered with whitecaps. They were small and didn't alarm him so he turned his attention to the dark, small clouds on the southern horizon.

"When do you expect us to be back at port?" John asked. The captain sensed his concern.

"I'll get us back by 7:30 or so. Where you staying?"

"We rented a beach house on the southern tip of the island. We chartered a plane down here that's supposed to pick us up on Sunday, but I'll need to call them if we need to leave early. If I call tonight they may be able to get here by late tomorrow afternoon."

"Won't be no time for that. If Isabel is a coming this way like they say, it'll be here tomorrow night. Rain will be coming hard tomorrow morning and we'll lose power pretty fast. Always do. They'll seal the island off by morning. Irene knocked out power for a week." The captain and John stood and looked over the port side of the boat at the southern horizon. The captain smiled and placed his hand on John's shoulder. "Stay inside and batten down the hatches. Just some wind and rain, man, that's all."

As the captain turned to leave John stared at the sky in troubled thought. Something more than the weather bothered him. He spun around quickly before the captain left. "Captain," John began and then hesitated. "Is there a hospital on the island, or a clinic?"

The captain surveyed John for a moment. "Getting sea sick, are you? We might be able to give you a pill for that but closest hospital is in Nassau, 200 miles away. You won't be getting there anytime soon if Isabel's coming this way."

***

By the time the island taxi pulled up to the beach house at 8:30 p.m. the wind had picked up briskly. John estimated that it was steady at thirty miles per hour, probably gusting at forty even though the driver had said the hurricane wouldn't arrive until the following night. But he had confirmed that it would arrive, at least according to the hurricane prediction models. Same path as Irene, just as the captain had said, taking it squarely over the length of the Bahamas. Even though he was furious at the weather forecasters who had predicted that the hurricane would most likely steer south of Florida and into the gulf, maybe hitting Florida's panhandle, John was even more furious at himself. He knew that he should have known better than to go to a remote island without a contingency plan. Everything in his business life revolved around contingency plans. Back-ups, redundant servers and facilities, action plans if revenue didn't materialize, expansion plans if they did. For the past three hours he had labored under dreadful thoughts. Thoughts he didn't want to acknowledge, but had to. *What if the hurricane hits us directly in this little house on the beach. Where do we go?* The captain and the taxi driver assured him that they would be fine in their home, which was situated far enough back from the water to avoid any storm surge, but it did little now to assuage his fears.

"You won't have any power or telephones," the driver had said, "but you'll get by. Everyone made it through all right with Irene and that split down the middle of the islands."

But that wasn't what was bothering John, aching at his insides. What if Rose was ill or took a turn for the worse? That thought gnawed at him so much he was becoming sick himself. Time was moving so slowly for him, minutes dragging and cursing him with dreadful thoughts that could only be relieved once he saw that she was all right and held her in his arms.

John paid the driver and stepped out of the taxi. Wind from the southeast stung his face with grains of sand as he walked up the front steps. As he reached for the doorknob in the darkness he saw a mass lying on the wicker sofa to his left. His heart sank as he went to Rose, partially covered with a blanket, but lying there in the open as the sand pelted her cheeks. "Rose!" John fell to his knees in front of the sofa and picked up her head. "Rose!"

With great strain she opened her eyes, barely, groggily, as if she had taken sleep medication, but John knew she wouldn't have. He stood and slid his arms underneath her and picked her up, holding her close to him. Rose's body draped over his arms and offered no resistance, no support. Her arms lay limp by her side in his own arms as he walked to the door, using his body to shield Rose from the wind and sand. Turning the doorknob, John twisted his body to allow Rose's head to carefully enter the opening first. In a panic his eyes darted around the strange home as he walked straight to the bedroom. Again, he turned sideways as he walked down the narrow hall to protect Rose's head from hitting the wall. After navigating the doorway into the bedroom, John laid Rose onto the bed. A loud banging came from the living room and John raced back to close the door. He flipped on the light switch and silently thanked an unknown benefactor for the magic of electricity as he rushed back to the bedroom and turned on the bedside lamp.

"Rose!" John said firmly, yet softly. "Rose, can you hear me?"

Again her eyelids opened a sliver and looked at John. Her eyes had the energy to acknowledge him, but nothing else. She was shaking, shivering, her body trembling as if it had just been pulled out of icy waters. John tucked her into bed and pulled blankets tightly around her, pushing them around and behind her shoulders to warm her. He took the back of his hand and felt her forehead. *Oh no!* John said to himself as he felt the searing heat from Rose's head. He looked at Rose in the soft glow of the lamp, her sweat-soaked black hair sucking light out of the room. He looked for a clock to check the time. Seeing none, he took out his iPhone and had to wait for it to turn on since he had no reason to keep it on.

"C'MON!" John screamed to the inanimate object. Finally it turned on and revealed the time as 8:40 p.m. His mind raced wildly. *I need a doctor. That's all that matters. Find a phone book, the phone.*

John began to rise from the bed, but stopped halfway up in a crouched position. His nostrils had halted his progress as they detected something faint, but a smell that caused him to stop where he was until its source could be identified. He whiffed again, registering the smell and talking himself through the options.

I know that smell...it reminds me of...the girls...something about the girls....diapers!

John pulled the covers back from Rose and gently rolled her on her side. The back of her right leg was stained wet and brown. John looked at his left forearm where he had been carrying her and now saw the wetness on his arm. Obviously Rose had had diarrhea during the day and, evidently, was unable to get up to go inside. "Oh Jesus!" John said. "I'll clean you up in a moment, hon." Rose lay there, able to hear nothing.

"First I gotta find the phone!" John began walking to the kitchen with a sinking feeling that no one could help him.

Chapter 25

The sun inched over the mountains as Blake drove south on 441 in Mountain City back toward Clayton. He had just dropped off a bed full of pig bones with Gus, who would make a final batch of bone meal for Blake.

Terry had proven to be a real asset, worth every penny of the five grand that Blake paid him in cash the night before as he thanked him and bid him farewell. Hoping he'd never see him again, Blake had no idea what a kid like that would do with five grand, but he figured it wouldn't last long. Most importantly to Blake, he paid him in cash and there would be no tracing it to him.

Blake pulled into the Ingles grocery store just before Warwoman Road. A new Starbucks coffee shop had just opened inside and Blake wondered how "fourbucks," as the penny pinchers at UGA had called it, would do in this neck of the woods. But Blake had taken a liking to the dark roasted coffee during his Athens time and was glad to see the green logo appear a few weeks back. He walked through the door and marveled at the decor. Starbucks had taken something as simple as a cup of coffee and achieved with it what Blake had *tried* to accomplish with his own life. Elevate the mundane to the exotic, take a dirty seed and turn it into something the world admired. But underneath it all, once you stripped away the musical coffee house genre that they seemed to have invented, the fancy packaging, the curvaceous coffee mugs, once you stripped all that away you were left with what? A lone coffee bean grown by a lone, unknown, and unimportant farmer.

The dirty seed, as Blake now thought of himself, stepped forward to order.

"Welcome to Starbucks, what can I get you?"

"Hey, can I have a grande bold with no room?"

"Sure thing," she said. "Getcha anything else? A blueberry scone perhaps?" she asked with a smile.

"Uh..no ma'am, just the coffee, thanks."

"Okay, that'll be two twenty-three." The clerk turned to get the coffee and returned to the counter. Blake handed her a five and took change, leaving a buck in the tip jar. She smiled and handed him his coffee.

"Come back now," the clerk said before moving on to the next customer behind Blake. "Mornin' Sheriff!"

Blake cringed and jerked his head to the right. The sheriff stepped up a foot and stood beside him.

"Mornin', Mary Ellen," the sheriff said as he read the clerk's name badge. He turned his head to Blake. "Mornin', Blake."

"Sheriff!" Blake said before turning his gaze to Mary Ellen, not sure what else to say. He looked down to his shoes for a moment. "Well, so long, Sheriff." Blake turned and began toward the door. As he did, the sheriff left the line and followed him through the door.

"Blake, give me one second if you don't mind," the sheriff said as they stood outside. Blake turned to look at the sheriff, but said nothing.

"You don't have anything new to report about them boys missing, do you?" the sheriff asked.

Blake thought about the wording the sheriff chose. Had he asked "have you seen them boys" or "have you heard anything new about them boys" then the answer would have been an easy "no." But he had phrased the question differently. "You don't have anything new to report...do you?" He tried to figure out what the sheriff meant. Was the sheriff giving Blake another chance to report something...anything that he may have omitted before? Or was it simply careless phrasing on the sheriff's part with no specific meaning intended other than the obvious?

"No sheriff, I haven't heard anything about them." Blake's reply was measured.

"Hmmm," the sheriff said as he looked around, surveying the parking lot.

Blake stood and waited for the sheriff. The sheriff stood silently and Blake was faced with the option of standing poised or saying something to the sheriff, even if all he said was that he needed to leave. The sheriff succeeded in flushing Blake out of the pocket.

"Is there any news on them?" Blake asked.

"Not much," the sheriff began, "but we found some interesting pictures on one of the boy's Facebook page." The sheriff said no more.

"What kind of pictures...or is that private?" Blake asked.

"Well," the sheriff said, "a picture of one of the fellas in a wooded area in front of a whole mess of pigs. Then there was another of him standing in front of a shed of some sort. Couldn't make out the details but looked like some stuff was hanging in there."

Blake's pulse quickened. He sipped his coffee, so as to act nonchalant, but the caffeine would do nothing to help slow his heart rate. He said the only thing that he felt he could. "Hmmm."

"Yeah," the sheriff continued, "pretty strange. He was working on some kind of farming, 'round here I reckon, but nobody knows nothing about it." The sheriff looked at Blake, who said nothing. "You don't know anyone messing with pigs, do you Blake?"

He knows, of course he knows! There's no way he don't know, Blake said to himself. He didn't know what to say or what to do. He just wanted this to all go away so badly so he could start over. *I repent, I repent,* Blake said, only he said it to himself. Not to the sheriff.

The sheriff didn't wait for an answer.

"Of course, we expect to know more soon," the sheriff said. "One of his Facebook friends commented on the pics so we're gonna contact him. Already sent a subpoena to Facebook to get access to Jesse's account, the fella that's missing." The sheriff stood as calm as could be, allowing his words to sink in.

"I sure hope you find 'em, Sheriff," Blake said, "and I hope they're okay." He meant it. "Well, so long, Sheriff. I gotta get going."

"I'm sure I'll be seeing you, Blake."

***

TUESDAY 8:06 A.M: ATLANTA, GEORGIA

Clint Justice pulled into the parking lot of the parking garage on Alabama Street in downtown Atlanta for his 8:30 a.m. meeting with the USDA district manager. He parked the car and reached to turn off the ignition key, but hesitated so he could catch up on the local news.

"Support for WABE comes from WallCloud, providing dependable web hosting for mission critical applications. More at WallCloud.com. This is your home for Atlanta's classics and NPR News, the time is 8:06. Now the news. A spokesperson at Athens Regional Medical Center said a second person has died in as many days from what doctors are calling flu-like symptoms. The spokesperson said the hospital has experienced a spike in flu-like symptoms since Sunday, and are cooperating with both the CDC and Georgia Health Department, as many of the afflicted are from out of state. Yesterday, a thirty-four-year old New York woman died in Athens, as did a forty-two-year old Dallas businessman. Both died at Athens Regional Medical Center. In all, the hospital admitted over twenty people yesterday with flu-like symptoms. Neither avian nor swine flu has been ruled out. In weather, Hurricane Isabel is expected to hit the Bahamas this evening as a Category 3 storm. Forecasters predict it will continue to strengthen and make U.S. landfall somewhere between Jacksonville, Florida and Charleston, South Carolina by Thursday evening. This is John Mattock for WABE News."

Clint turned the key and sat in the car for a moment.

***

TUESDAY 9:10 A.M: SAN SALVADOR, BAHAMAS

Doctor Severino Ortega parked his jeep in front of the rented beach home and tried unsuccessfully to open the driver's door. The steady, southerly winds already exceeded seventy miles per hour even though the eye of the storm was almost nine hours away. Seve, as his friends back in Spain knew him, crawled over the center console and opened the passenger door. The wind flung it open violently, threatening to warp the door on its hinges. The doctor grabbed his bag and fought his way to the front door and let himself in. John heard the front door open and the winds howl through the house. He left Rose's side and went in to greet the doctor.

"Doctor," John said pleading, begging, "she's in here." Seve followed John into the bedroom. Wind-driven rain and sand pelted the side of the house and the windows. Seve looked at the windows vibrating as he walked into the room. "I hope those windows hold," he said.

"I couldn't leave her," John began, "so I didn't have any time to board the windows, and didn't have anything to use if I did. So I hung those blankets on the inside."

"Well, looks like the eye is headed for Nassau and will pass west of here," Seve said. "We won't get the worst of it but we'll get a wallop. And we'll be cut off from Nassau and the U.S." Seve sat his bag on the floor next to Rose and sat on the bed. He needlessly put his hand to her head but he could see that she was soaked with sweat.

"I'm scared, Doctor," John said, his voice shaking. "She was unresponsive all night. The last she spoke to me was about 2:00

a.m. or so, saying that both her chest and abdomen hurt. She has been a little delirious at times."

Seve took the thermometer out of Rose's mouth and made a note of the temperature of 103 degrees. He placed his stethoscope over Rose's lungs and listened closely. The wind whistled and battered the house, making it difficult to concentrate. What he heard through the stethoscope concerned him more than what he was hearing outside the house. He cupped his hands over his ears and concentrated on the continuous sound of the rhonchi that was reminiscent of constant, low-level snoring. It was a sound he had heard in patients before and it was never a good sign. As he removed his stethoscope Seve surveyed John. Other than being distraught, John looked perfectly fine. "On the phone late last night, you said you thought she had the flu," Seve said. "Why did you say that?"

"Because, that's what Rose said when we landed on Sunday. Just that she felt like she was coming down with the flu. Then she started feeling better and actually looked fine yesterday morning, which is why I left for the day. What was I thinking?" John started to ramble and get off topic. He had never been so scared. When he looked out the front door an hour before, the low clouds and crashing surf attacked him relentlessly. He shut the door and came to be with Rose, pacing the room frantically and waiting for the island's only doctor to get here after seeing other patients who just couldn't wait.

"You don't seem to have any flu-like symptoms." Seve said.

"What? No, of course not. I'm fine."

"Were you or your wife around anyone with flu?"

John thought for only a second. "No, I don't know anyone with the flu. Well, I'm not with Rose all the time. I don't know, maybe she bumped into someone at a store or something. How would I know? She was fine until we flew down here."

Seve knew that it wasn't flu season and he already suspected it wasn't the flu anyway. He wished it were the flu. "She doesn't seem to be congested. Did she have a runny nose at all?"

"No, I don't think so. No."

"Did she complain of dizziness?"

"Dizziness? She hasn't been up since I got back yesterday. She felt confused when I asked her questions last night. Couldn't concentrate, but I don't know if she was dizzy."

"How do you know she couldn't concentrate?"

John felt himself becoming infuriated, his face feeling as if it was baking in the sun. What the hell is wrong with her! That's all he wanted to know. Enough with all the questions! "Because–" John hesitated, "she–she couldn't remember the names of our daughters last night. She kept asking me their names and when I told her she–she forgot them instantly. Kept shaking her head and saying that wasn't right, then she'd ask me again." The lights flickered off and cast the room into utter darkness. John gasped loudly as he swore he saw a black, bird-like figure fly around the ceiling, circling over Rose. The lights flickered back on and remained on.

"Jesus...did you see that?" John asked. "Did you see something on the ceiling?"

"Yeah, we'll probably lose power anytime," Seve said, unaware of what John *thought* he had seen. Seve picked up Rose's left arm and placed two fingers just below her wrist. As he feared, he detected no radial pulse. He had begun to suspect that Rose may already be losing blood pressure, which is why he had asked about dizziness. Lack of concentration would be another symptom associated with low blood pressure.

"What did you do on Saturday before you flew down here?"

"Nothing. Just packed and went to a dinner Saturday night. Then straight back home. Why all the questions? Don't you just have something you can give her besides this stuff she's been taking?"

"What has she been taking?"

John showed Seve the two tincture bottles he had found in Rose's purse. One read "Echinacea Tincture: take daily in water for immune system health" and the other read "Yarrow Tincture: spray in nostrils for flu, in throat for cold."

Seve examined the bottles and placed them back on the table. "Did you do anything with these tinctures?" Seve asked.

"That's all we have here. Everything last night was closed. EVERYTHING! Like the whole island shut down. It took me forever to reach you, the ONLY doctor on the whole island. No hospital, no nothing!" John began pacing, his breathing labored. Outside the outer band of winds from a Category 3 hurricane slammed the house, but John heard or felt none of it. He was beside himself, furious that he had left the day before to catch a fish. A stupid fish! He left Rose to catch a stupid fish.

"It's okay, John. Back in my country people swear by those tinctures. You did fine, John."

"I—" John began and hesitated, "I sprayed the yarrow in her nose and in her mouth. I know it's stupid, I know. But that's what the label said and I didn't know what to do. I just needed to be able to do something for her. Her twin sister is really into that holistic kind of therapy stuff."

"John, you need to try and calm down," Seve said. "Let's focus on Rose. Now I have to ask you a few questions and I need you to answer them to help me. I can't treat her until I have a good idea of what I'm treating. All right?" Once again the lights flickered off and then on. John stopped pacing and looked at Seve. His eyes dropped to Rose, lying semi-conscious on the bed and breathing heavily.

"Okay," John replied.

"Good," Seve said. "First off, I don't believe she has the flu, John. She has no sign of congestion; you don't have any symptoms; there's no productive cough: I hear rhonchi in her lungs; you haven't been around people with the flu and it's the wrong time of year. That doesn't add up to the flu."

John paced and listened to Seve as blowing sand pelted the side of the house, sounding like hard rice hitting the sidewalk.

"Now, I have a theory about what this could be John, but we have no way to do any tests. The closest hospital is 200 miles from here and the only way to get her there would be a medevac. The U.S. Coast Guard would have to do that but they're not available just now due to the hurricane. They've been helping boaters in Haiti and elsewhere, so—we're on our own."

John stopped as he realized what Seve was saying. The gravity of the situation enveloped him. "Okay," John repeated.

"Before you came here, did Rose or you visit a farm at all? Do you live on a farm?"

"No. We don't live on a farm and haven't been to one."

"So there's no way she could have been around livestock, is that right John?"

"Livestock? What the hell does that have to do with—"

"John, I said I need you to stay with me."

John exhaled deeply. "No, she hasn't been around any farm animals. Jesus!" John thought to himself what a stupid island doctor he was dealing with. Back home they would have whisked Rose into a sanitized room, treated her with one of a thousand drugs, and she'd be up and fine now. Here it was as if he had gone back in time to be asked insightful questions from the tribe's medicine man. Questions like whether or not she had petted a donkey.

"Could she have been to a drumming event?"

"What kind of event?" John asked.

"Some place where they were playing drums. Or perhaps a craft fair where they were making rugs, shearing animals—anything at all like that?"

"NO! Nothing like that." John said.

Seve paused and looked back at Rose. He had seen these symptoms before in Spain. Too many times in fact, one of the many reasons he opted to sign up for a two-year sabbatical and become the lone physician on this island. Still, something didn't add up. What John was telling him didn't support his theory, but Rose's symptoms, without question, did. He hoped he was wrong, prayed he was wrong. He knew that if he were right then there was a high probability that Rose would be dead within twenty-four hours anyway.

"Does your wife happen to work for the postal service?"

John rolled his eyes and turned his head. "NO!"

"Any government agency at all?"

John bowed his head and shook it violently, placing his hands on each side of his head. The questions were too much for him and he was nearing the end of his rope.

So was Rose.

Chapter 26

Clint walked out of the conference room just after noon. He had hoped the meeting wouldn't eat up so much of his Tuesday morning, certainly not over three hours. But for the second consecutive year, Congress had approved the President's budgetary request for *reduced* FSIS funding, budget cuts that seemed ludicrous to Clint. Politicians wouldn't admit it, he thought, but they seemed to love it when that happened. Armed with a mandate for more oversight and a bigger budget, they'd outline huge spending programs and label them with grand names like the Food Safety Modernization Act, as if food safety measures prior to that had been operating in the dark ages. Congress would sign off and funds would flow for a couple of years until everyone forgot about the salmonella, the e.coli. *That's where we are now,* Clint thought. *No foodborne illnesses of any magnitude for the past few years, no more Jack-in-the-Box scares, no more spinach coated in e.coli so might as well lay off inspectors. Then when there's another scare hire some rookies, train them for a few years and lay them off just when they learn what they're doing.*

Clint walked down the corridor toward the exit. He looked into the break room at a few colleagues sitting down to lunch and watching the news at noon. Clint paused for a moment to watch the CNN update.

"CNN has learned of five mysterious deaths in the past twenty-eight hours from what doctors are calling flu-like symptoms." A talking head was reading the teleprompter but speaking directly to Clint, he felt. "Two deaths were reported just outside of Boston, two at the same hospital in Athens,

Georgia and one this morning, a thirty-six year old pharmaceutical executive near Trenton, New Jersey. NPR stations in each of those cities first reported on the deaths and CNN correspondent Drew Hunter pieced the story together and contacted each hospital. In all, there have been seventy-nine people admitted to hospitals in Athens, Trenton and in two hospitals in the Boston area, all from what doctors are calling mysterious, flu-like symptoms. Officials from the CDC have not acknowledged a connection between these illnesses. We'll continue to report on this story as details become available."

The words *"flu-like symptoms"* looped in his head as Clint walked toward the door. He paused at the front desk for a moment before continuing out the door and turned to the receptionist. "Carol, can you get me the number for CNN's newsroom?"

***

Lounging by the pool of his stately Buckhead home, Nick enjoyed what he thought might be the last warm day of the Indian summer. His view to the southern skies showed no sign of the storm he had heard was brewing in the Caribbean. It would make no difference to him if it came his way. Hurricanes were a threat to the coast, not to cities as far inland as Atlanta.

He picked up his phone to check his voice mail. Two minutes prior a blocked number had called, which Nick, of course, didn't answer. But, the anonymous caller had decided to leave a message. "Nick, this is Drew Hunter from CNN in Atlanta. I'd like to speak with you about a story I'm doing that's rather urgent. Please call me back at–"

Nick looked around for a pen and paper, but found none. He walked into the kitchen to retrieve them and replayed the message to write down the number. Nick grinned as he dialed the number, thinking that the reporter had no doubt seen him on Fox News or had otherwise heard of the success of 50-Forks and now wanted a piece of Nick for his own "urgent" story.

"Drew Hunter," the voice answered.

"Drew, this is Nick Vegas returning your call."

"Mr. Vegas, thanks for getting back to me so quickly."

Mr. Vegas. Nick liked the respect. He had worked hard for it his entire professional life. On days like today, when he took time off to enjoy the fruits of his labor, when he relaxed around the pool surrounded by his own palm trees, his own fountains, and had every freedom he could want, on days like this one he felt like he had arrived. He had earned the accolades, the success, and the respect. He could soak it all up now and savor it.

"You're welcome. Just call me Nick."

"Nick, I don't know if you've been following the stories of a number of people becoming suddenly and violently afflicted with the flu–" Drew paused, waiting for a reaction. Nick said nothing, waiting for Drew to continue, but a butterfly took flight in the hollow cavern between his heart and his gut. He hoped that the reporter had called the wrong person.

"Even several deaths," Drew continued. "Anyway, I've interviewed several of the victims and or their families in Athens, Boston and near Philadelphia–"

As the reporter spoke Nick's mind froze. Athens, Boston, Philadelphia...all cities where Nick owned restaurants. *Wait...what was this guy saying again...the flu?*

"–and the only thing I've found so far that they have in common is that many...most of the victims say that they ate at an underground supper club last Saturday."

Nick said nothing, could say nothing. The words sank in and meant nothing, meant everything. Drew gave his words a moment to register.

"Anyway, those cities are far apart so I dug into the supper clubs they mentioned and looked at the invitations from the chefs that were hosting them. I found that they were all hosted by chefs that work for your restaurants."

"Wait...what are you saying?" Nick, who had never before been speechless, now found himself without words.

"We're working on a story for this evening and we will report this information. Do you have any comment, sir? If you tell me where you are I can send a camera crew to meet you."

"Shit." Nick said this to himself. To the reporter he said, "I have no comment," and hung up the phone. He stared out over the pool for a moment as a cloud seeped in front of the sun, causing a dark shadow to cascade across his pool. His life, he feared. A gust of wind blew from the south and tussled his neatly combed hair out of place. Staring at his phone, Nick bit his lip and squeezed the phone tighter and tighter, as if he was testing his grip on a machine at a carnival. He looked back at the phone and dialed Blake.

"The party you have reached has not set up their voice mail system yet–" Nick rolled his eyes as he recognized the same message he had heard from Blake's phone for the past year. "Blake, Nick. Call me. Right now!" Nick pressed the disconnect button as hard as he could, walked to his computer and logged into his investment account.

**

Angelica sat down on the sofa beside Blake as he turned up the volume on CNN.

"Oh my," Angelica said. "Dear Lord, look at THAT! Why is he even out there in that?" Angelica wrung her hands as she watched the screen. The CNN reporter was standing on the balcony of a room at his resort in Nassau as the eye of Hurricane Isabel approached. The eye was expected to go directly over Nassau in less than an hour at approximately 9:00 p.m. It had already passed the southern and eastern islands.

"Power is out on all islands with backup generators expected to be the only source of power for at least a few days on the more remote islands," the reporter shouted through the roar of driving rain. The camera panned out to show palm trees bending like plastic forks underneath a broiler as horizontal rain pounded the island, seemingly much to the reporter's delight. "Just look at that surge," he said. "That's a hurricane right there."

No shit, Blake thought. *All these guys are actors now, seeing who can stand in the strongest winds, the hardest rains. Who can be right in front of the tornado when it passes. Idiots!*

"Do you think they'll be okay?" Blake knew that Angelica was worried about Rose and John. She had desperately tried to call them all day on Monday, but Rose had warned her that her cell phone wouldn't work. Angelica put the girls to bed a little early so they wouldn't ask questions about the storm.

"I wouldn't worry, hon," Blake said. "The islands are prepared for these storms. The TV stations dramatize it but I reckon it ain't nothing but wind and rain as long as you stay indoors."

"Maybe we should put it on the Weather Channel," Angelica said.

"I don't think they'll have anything more than this," Blake said. "Just better acting maybe." He meant what he said, but he had his own reason for wanting it on CNN. It took all of Blake's resolve to remain calm, to act peaceful with Angelica, after speaking with Nick late in the afternoon. Blake knew nothing about the sicknesses and told Nick so.

"Do you know anything that could have contributed to a food safety problem?" Nick had asked firmly.

"No." Blake replied. Nick told him about the CNN reporter and the report that would air later in the day.

"Well I'll tell you this, my friend," Nick said, "my chefs may be the common factor in those dinners but the only thing they had in common was you."

"What are you talking about?" Blake asked.

"You!" Nick said. "Every menu was based on local ingredients, every menu was different except for one thing. The ham that you provided. That's it. Athens was the only dinner to have the fresh pork you provided but all dinners had the ham. Other than that they have nothing in common. So if I'm the common denominator, you're the common supplier."

"So," Blake began, "what are you saying? Don't mince words Nick." Blake knew his relationship with Nick was over. He and Terry had already slaughtered all the pigs other than a lethargic sow they couldn't get to before light gave out on them. Blake would kill her himself later even though he knew he wouldn't get paid for it. He just didn't want any more evidence left on the mountainside. The two encounters with the sheriff, not to mention having the sheriff preach to him, had scared him to the core. It wasn't worth it. He couldn't risk the sheriff seeing him haul any of it, not with the Facebook pictures he reported seeing.

"I'm saying," Nick began, "that if they do come and ask me any questions, it will be you that I point them to. Your phone number, your address." Blake hung up on Nick. Hung up and then slammed the phone repeatedly against the palm of his hand.

The talking head on CNN continued reporting on the damage from the storm. "We have a report from the prime minister of the Bahamas who says that Hurricane Isabel has resulted in no deaths and, so far, no reported injuries as it has marched through the chain. He said the Bahamas is well prepared for storms and he doesn't expect any deaths but does anticipate widespread power outages."

"See?" Blake said as he reached over to touch Angelica's knee. She placed her hand on top of his.

The footage of the hurricane on the screen was replaced with a graphic that read "Foodborne Illness." Blake didn't want Angelica to know that this was the story he wanted to see, that he was afraid to see. That he had been controlling his fear and only appearing calm as he had learned to do when it was late in the game and his team was trailing on the road. But Blake's fear finally got the best of him. The words on the screen, combined with Nick's spoken words, panicked him. He pulled his hand away from Angelica's and leaned forward, his chin resting on his fists.

"This *just* in. CNN is able to confirm that Anthrax has been identified as the cause of death and illnesses in Athens, Georgia, Trenton, New Jersey, Boston and six other cities," the talking head said as she read the teleprompter. Blake's mouth hung open, air suspended somewhere between his lungs and the air in the room as he sat perfectly still, the word still resonating inside him. "A-N-T-H-R-A-X." The graphic behind the talking head changed to the capitalized word ANTHRAX, the motion graphic causing the letters to slowly expand and move away from one another to heighten the sense of drama. As if the word 'anthrax' itself, not to mention five dead bodies so far, necessitated more drama.

What the hell is anthrax? Blake asked himself. *I thought that was a weapon or something.*

"We turn now to CNN correspondent Drew Hunter for more on the story." As the talking head spoke, the camera panned to show a thirty-something reporter seated on the other side of the glass table, opposite the first talking head. As he began to speak, Blake zoomed into the studio with him from the privacy of his sofa in Clayton, just as Nick did from a dimly lit office in his Buckhead mansion.

"Details are only now beginning to surface, Candace," Drew said, before staring straight into the camera for a close up. "Five deaths and eighty-four hospitalizations have been attributed to anthrax thus far. The source of the anthrax is still under investigation, but the suspected cause is tainted meat."

Blake felt his heart stop and then explode as the graphic behind Drew changed to "Tainted Meat." He was sucked into a tunnel that connected him to the graphic, one that threw off his equilibrium like he was stranded alone, trying to make his way across a bridge in the vortex tunnel of a haunted house.

"What exactly is anthrax, Drew?" Candace asked.

"Candace, anthrax is one of the oldest diseases known to man," Drew began. "In fact, many Bible scholars believe that anthrax was the fifth and sixth of the ten plagues of Egypt."

"Do they know what causes it?"

"Yes, Candace, the organism that causes anthrax, Bacillus anthracis, can poison the soil for decades, even hundreds of years. In fact, it's so common to find anthrax in soil that deadly outbreaks among grazing animals occur frequently, although not so much in the U.S. Normally, humans contract anthrax only by coming into contact with livestock or infected animal hides and carcasses."

As the reporter spoke, footage scrolled on the screen of dead cows, pigs, and sheep lying on the ground. Stiff carcasses with their legs spread out dissolved into pictures of humans with gruesome, widow-black blisters that covered their entire arms or faces. Drew continued to narrate as the CNN horror reel played.

"There are three forms of anthrax, Candace. Cutaneous, gastrointestinal, and the most deadly and rare form, pulmonary or inhalation anthrax. Gastrointestinal anthrax generally comes from eating meat infected with anthrax. Conversely, when a person inhales the spores of anthrax they settle deep into the lungs, forming inhalation anthrax. Once there, the bacteria multiply rapidly and produce *very* deadly toxins. It's the inhalation form that's most associated with bioterrorism, as was the case in the 2001 attacks on the United States."

The background footage stopped and the camera panned back to show a third talking head join the other two.

"Dr. Chandak, do we know which form of anthrax caused the deaths?" A graphic appeared under the new talking head that read "Dr. Sachi Chandak, Neurosurgeon and CNN Medical Correspondent."

"Candace, we're told that it was inhalation anthrax that was the cause of death for the victims near Boston and Athens, Georgia, and for the fifth victim in New Jersey," Dr. Chandak said. "Now I'd like to stress that there is no evidence of bioterrorism and that anthrax isn't a contagious disease. You have to come directly in contact with it."

The graphic to the right of the talking head changed to read "Woolsorter's Disease."

"As Drew said," Dr. Chandak continued, "inhalation anthrax is the most rare human form of anthrax and is almost never seen in a foodborne illness since, normally, one doesn't inhale their food. It's also known in other parts of the world as Woolsorter's or Ragpicker's disease because, throughout history, the inhalation form was most associated with those who sorted wool. The most famous case of woolsorter's disease was in Bradford, England, where the disease killed many of the town's workers for decades throughout the 1800s. Today, the disease even shows itself sometimes at music festivals, when drums made from animal hides infected with anthrax are beaten, thereby aerosolizing B. *anthracis* spores that may be inhaled."

"What is the prognosis for victims that contract anthrax, Dr. Chandak?"

"Unfortunately Candace—I'm afraid that it isn't good at all for victims of inhalation anthrax. Most estimates show eighty percent to ninety-five percent *fatality* rate, even–"

"Ninety-five percent fatal?" Candace interrupted. The graphic behind the doctor changed to read: "DEATH IN 24 HOURS."

Dr. Chandak dropped his shoulders solemnly. "Yes Candace, up to ninety-five percent fatal even *with* antibiotic treatment," he said. "And inhalation anthrax acts very fast, sometimes killing its host within 24 hours. As for gastrointestinal anthrax, which would likely result from consuming tainted meat, the fatality rate is twenty-five to sixty percent. Cutaneous anthrax is very treatable and generally not fatal."

"Oh my! Drew, why do we suspect tainted meat?"

"Well Candace, it's very rare in the United States to get anthrax in any form, so much so that when we think of foodborne pathogens we think of salmonella, e.coli, listeria, campylobacter, even staphyloccus, but almost never anthrax. However, in this case over fifty victims or their family members have been interviewed and here's what we have discovered."

Blake waited. Nick waited. Both leaned forward in their chairs, breathless, over one hundred miles apart, connected through the conduit of television by this bearer of horrific news that, if he released the words that dripped from his lips would rain destruction on each of their lives.

"Every single one of the victims, both dead and those still hospitalized, ate at an underground supper club last Saturday," Drew said. "Now here's the strange part. The supper clubs were held in ten different cities across the country and were hosted by ten different chefs, but—here's the catch."

Nick picked up his glass of Maker's Mark and slugged it, knowing what was coming, knowing he was powerless to stop it. He tried to act calm, in control, even in the privacy of his study. His legs remain crossed, relaxed, as he tugged up his socks to be perfectly in place when the verdict was read.

"Every chef was employed by the same restaurant owner and the events were all part of the same club," Drew said.

"And who was that, Drew?" With the focus off the hurricane in the Bahamas, Angelica rose from the sofa to check on the girls.

"Candace, the chefs all work for acclaimed restaurateur Nick Vegas, owner of all ten restaurants that employed the chefs and founder of the recently announced 50-Forks Club. The dinners last weekend were the first for the new club's members."

Angelica stopped. "Nick Vegas," she said and she looked down at Blake, his head supported by his fists, his eyes locked with tunnel vision to the set. As he leaned forward his shirt collar pushed back allowing Angelica to see a pulsing black blister on the back of his neck. She tugged his collar slightly, the pressure still not distracting Blake from the television. Her eyes widened as she took in the hideous black lesion on Blake's neck. The oblong blister looked to be about the size of Blake's 9 MM pistol barrel and just as black. Angelica gently removed her hand from Blake's shirt and walked to the kitchen to straighten up the dishes as she continued watching the news.

"And have you spoken with Mr. Vegas?"

"Yes, Candace, but he declined comment or to be interviewed for the story."

Candace paused for a moment, either unsure what to say or waiting for a teleprompter. "But...but, isn't meat inspected? How would tainted meat get into the food supply?"

"That's the question that regulators and, perhaps even law enforcement officials, will want to have answered," Drew said. "My understanding is that the Food Safety Inspection Service is already working with local health department officials and the chefs to determine the source of the anthrax. I need to emphasize once more that this is still very preliminary and that all we know for certain is that health officials have verified inhalation anthrax as the cause of death in five victims."

"Doctor Chandak, have cases been confirmed for gastrointestinal or cutaneous anthrax?"

"No, not at this time. I suspect if they were going to find cutaneous anthrax then it would already have been reported, as it's easy to identify." As the doctor spoke, a graphic of a man with a grotesque, black boil on the side of his face appeared. Angelica looked at the blister and quickly turned her head to Blake, who didn't move.

"Cutaneous anthrax occurs when one comes into direct contact with anthrax, either in the soil or, most likely, by touching a sick animal or products from an animal that died of anthrax. It begins with a rash but quickly forms an ulcer with a black center. It would be hard to miss the visible signs, so if there were any of those cases I suspect we'd know about them."

Angelica stood at the kitchen bar only a few feet from her husband, but isolated from him. He was lost in the television, engulfed by news even though he rarely cared about, much less watched news. She looked back at the television set to see the final image of the segment, a magazine photograph of Nick Vegas with a bulldog in front of his stately Buckhead home that connected him, somehow, to Blake. The image of Nick disappeared and was replaced with the other top story, a satellite image of a fierce hurricane that covered all of the Bahama Islands and was intensifying as it headed north. Somewhere below that mass of clouds was a tiny island, and on that tiny island was her twin sister. Angelica glanced to the guest bedroom adjacent to the kitchen where Rose's daughters slept. She felt as if she was being presented with a puzzle. More than that. A test of some sort. The pieces were Blake, Nick, Rose, the hurricane and this wretched plague. And, she realized, every piece affected her. Was she supposed to act? To do something? To wait? She fingered the black and white beads that hung from her neck, rolling them gently between her thumb and index finger as she pondered the questions.

She would have to think about it later, perhaps in her secret garden. For now, she looked back at Blake who had dropped his head to stare at the floor, evidently swallowed by his own puzzle of grief. A puzzle, Angelica feared, that Blake may have created. A game of greed he wanted to make and play, only now it had turned deadly. It had grown into a frightening storm that threatened everything Angelica hoped for and cared about. She tried to remember a dream, a nightmare that she had had, but the details had slipped away. All that remained was a gnawing feeling.

As Blake slumped low to the floor on the sofa, Angelica's eyes fell to him from high above. She narrowed her eyes on him, but said nothing, thinking only of the tools at her disposal, at the gifts that had been given to her. Compassion, forgiveness, support, understanding, healing, tolerance, caring...these were the tools she had in ample supply. The gifts that God had given to her. Judgment was not one of her tools. That tool and responsibility belonged to God.

She looked once more at Blake's neck, the boil clearly visible as his shoulders collapsed, his hands supporting his forehead as if it were a dead weight. Something about the blister was familiar to her. Something to do with the plagues the talking head had mentioned. Walking to her bedroom, she retrieved her well-worn Bible from her nightstand and sat on the bed. With the Bible resting in her lap Angelica stared into her dressing mirror. Her rounded abdomen protruded in her reflection, showing the life that grew within her. She thought about her unborn son, due only three months hence, and wondered where he fit into the puzzle. Her vision for the life she wanted for him was so clear. To be raised honestly by loving parents with God and nature as the guide, embracing and honoring his Cherokee heritage. Through the doorway she saw Blake walk to the kitchen and return with a bottle to the living room. She sat quietly, her fingers caressing her belly, gently rubbing it in a counterclockwise motion with her fingers as she looked down. The same motion she had seen moments before as a hurricane spun its path of destruction. She stopped suddenly and began circling the other way. *"No, we're not victims son, she said aloud. We're not without power."*

Angelica opened her Bible and thumbed through the pages, her fingers somehow knowing where to go. She flipped the pages furiously until she reached the book of Kings. She began perusing the text like a speed-reader, searching for two specific words. In chapter twenty, verse seven of Kings, she found the words. "Boil. Figs." She read the entire passage with great care.

"And Isaiah said, take a lump of figs. And they took and laid it on the boil, and he recovered." She recalled reading the passage when she had planted Nancy's Tree, reading every mention in the Bible of figs. She found that figs were there from the beginning, in the book of Genesis, when Adam and Eve knew that they were naked; and they sewed fig leaves together, and made themselves aprons. And so she planted a fig tree for Nancy that had indeed flourished. Now she would call on those fruits that grew from the pain of losing Nancy to heal Blake's pain.

She laid the Bible on the nightstand, stood, and looked in the mirror, turning sideways to see the profile of her maternal form and the life that grew within. Always she had laughed in embarrassment when locals said she reminded them of Angelina Jolie. Blake had even insisted it was true when they were first married. As she stroked her belly and looked in the mirror, she smiled and admitted that she did resemble the actress she had seen pregnant on television.

Angelica didn't like this game, this puzzle that she was somehow a part of, but she believed it to be another of God's tests for her. She went to the medicine cabinet in her bathroom and retrieved gauze and tape. Then, she walked to the kitchen, opened the freezer and took out a bag of figs that she had picked from Nancy's Tree a few months earlier. She put three in the microwave to thaw. Blake sat at the sofa with a newly opened bottle of Jack Daniels whiskey already a quarter gone. When Angelica had left the room he was lost in the glass of the television. Now she returned to find him lost in the glass held between his two hands. He stared at it as if he were a lost soul. He lifted it to his lips, tilted the glass and slowly drained it, taking no pleasure in doing so. Without looking, his right arm reached for the bottle as he refilled the glass.

Angelica opened the cupboard door over the sink where she kept many of the medicines and tinctures she made. She retrieved the jar labeled "Four Thieves Vinegar" and reached for a soft cloth. She had grown each of the ingredients herself for the vinegar. The lavender, rosemary, sage, rue, wormwood and peppermint all came from her secret garden, as did the garlic. She even made the cider vinegar herself from her own crabapples and let it all infuse for two weeks before straining into the jar. She removed the softened figs from the microwave. Making sure they were comfortably warm, she walked to Blake, dipped the cloth in the Four Thieves Vinegar and washed the boil on Blake's neck. He became vaguely aware of what Angelica was doing, but couldn't concentrate on its meaning, so overcome was he with fear that he felt cerebrally paralyzed. Angelica washed, hoping the antibiotic properties would work their magic. She placed the cloth down and reached for the figs, gently placing them on the blister.

Blake felt their warmth, feeling for an instant that Angelica had found a warm blanket to cloak and protect him. He clung to that feeling of hope, the maternal reassurance that she infused him with as she secured the figs to his neck with gauze and tape. She took the cloth and patted Blake's neck dry and returned everything to the kitchen, dutifully putting everything in its rightful place. Then, Angelica walked back into the living room and stood in front of Blake. She reached over the coffee table and placed her right hand under Blake's chin, lifting it so that she could see the tears hidden behind his eyes. With her left hand on her belly she looked into his eyes as she said, "We love you."

And then, Angelica smiled and walked to bed.

With the talking heads saying the same things over and over, Blake sat and drank. And drank. As the whiskey swirled inside him and the footage of the hurricane raged on the screen, Blake slumped on the sofa, lying down to feel his back adrift on a raft in a wild sea from which there was no hope of rescue. He raked his mind for ideas of salvation, brilliant ideas that appeared as momentary islands of refuge, only to see the islands turn sour and become swallowed by the storm as quickly as they appeared, leaving nothing in their wake other than Blake, utterly alone. His head crashed on the armrest with the glass still in his hand as it lay on the floor. The very real visions from the television became horrific nightmares in his sleep. He dreamed not of being in the sea. Rather, he dreamed of being on a mountain. Of being handed a shovel from a demon on the mountain and being commanded in a twisted tongue to dig deep into the soil, to bury all the wrongdoings that he had done and to return to the soil what rightfully belonged there. To return all the poison that he had unleashed from the soil.

In the dream, Blake took the shovel and dug. He dug a hole deeper than himself, deep enough to bury the mountain of lies, greed and destruction that had poisoned his heart and his soul. The deeper he dug the freer he felt, the more joyous he felt. He dug to the haunting song of the mountain as a screeching raven perched high above. As he climbed from the hole he pushed everything into it that had caused him such suffering. The sheds, the fences, his truck, the lies, money, his football trophies—even Nick was shoved into the hole as Blake waved goodbye. He pushed and shoveled dirt back over the hole, filling it until he could stomp and dance on it.

When the music stopped in the dream Blake stood and smiled, surrounded not by what didn't matter, but only by what did. There was only himself, Angelica and his son.

Chapter 27

Lonnie arrived at his desk in the sheriff's office at 9:30 a.m. As he got out of his car, the humidity in the warm October air reminded him of a mission to New Orleans he had taken with members of his church immediately after hurricane Katrina. The moist air was tropical and smothered the mountains like a giant, wet towel.

"Mornin', Lucy," Lonnie said as he walked through the door.

"Mornin', Lonnie," she said. "Feels like we're on a tropical island don't it?"

"Yep. Don't go breaking out your bathing suit though, we got work to do," Lonnie said with a smile to his executive assistant. As he walked into his office and sat his Starbucks coffee cup on his desk, Lucy walked in to brief the sheriff on the day's schedule.

The D.A.R.E. poster hung prominently behind the sheriff's desk, taking fully half of the available wall space. Behind the desk in one corner was the Georgia state flag. In the other was the American flag. The desk itself was tidy, as usual. Pens in their holder, an empty inbox, a full outbox that Lucy would now empty. Other than that, lots of empty space for Lonnie to spread out whatever project he might work on.

"What do we got today, Lucy?"

"Nuttin' you can't handle, Sheriff. This package came in via FedEx a few minutes ago from Facebook out in California. And you got that luncheon at noon with the senior class at Rabun County High. Gonna tell 'em not to drink and drive, Lonnie? Or are you just gonna tell 'em to mind what ma says?"

Lonnie looked up to see Lucy's sarcastic grin. She emptied the outbox, turned, and walked away without giving him a chance to respond, even if he wanted to. She knew he didn't.

With precision, Lonnie sliced through the end of the 9 x 12 envelope with his letter opener, being as mindful as he would in examining evidence at a crime scene. He pulled out a thick stack of white paper that was stapled in the upper left corner. He estimated that there were probably sixty to eighty pages in the stack as he stared at the cover page.

CONFIDENTIAL

The information in this file is confidential material provided by Facebook solely in response to an officially sanctioned subpoena, court order, search warrant or other legal information request. The intended recipient is requested to handle the provided material in accordance with their organization's protocol for handling sensitive or confidential information.

"Good grief," Lonnie uttered to himself. "This'll take all day."

He flipped the pages, thumbing through all eight sheets of the subpoena itself before seeing the first page with any data worth looking at.

Neoprint for profile 149230525 taken on 2012-10-09 for dates (2012-07-01 thru 2012-10-08)

He read the details aloud as his eyes scrolled down the page. "Let's see...Name, Jesse Simmons. Recent Login IP address, email addresses, member since January 2008, born November 11, 1989, screenname is mountainman, relationship status is...none."

As Lonnie flipped the page he saw deputy Freeman Bishop walk through his door.

"Mornin', Freeman," Lonnie said, and returned to the document.

"Mornin', Sheriff. Just heard that the National Hurricane Center said the hurricane has strengthened and may actually make landfall near Savannah," Freeman said.

Lonnie dropped the picture of Jesse and looked up.

"Savannah? They haven't taken a major hurricane since --."

"1890s is what they said on the TV," Freeman said. "At least not a major one."

"What are they saying about this one?" Lonnie asked.

"Saying it's looking like it's gonna make landfall as at least a Category 4," Freeman said.

"At least?" Lonnie asked as he rose, thinking he must be missing something.

"Yep, maybe even a five," Freeman said. "They're already asking folks to evacuate the islands down there. That's a long way from here, Sheriff, but I figure a lot of folks will want to volunteer to help out if needed."

"Did you happen to see what path they're projecting the storm to travel?" Lonnie asked.

"Well, their map shows it hittin' the Georgia coast tomorrow late afternoon or early evening, then heading up toward north Georgia or western North Carolina early Friday morning. Course they say there's still a lot of leeway."

Lonnie stood stoically visualizing the storm's impact, both on the coast and on the mountains if the storm was really as strong as Freeman was saying.

"Them weather guys are always saying that, ain't they?" Freeman asked.

"Saying what?"

"That there's a lot of leeway. Lots of variables. That way they can be right no matter what way the wind blows."

"I reckon so," Lonnie said.

Freeman stood opposite Lonnie and looked down at his desk, seeing the picture of Jesse.

"Holy sh—" Freeman started and stopped, remembering that Sheriff Lonnie was also Pastor Lonnie. "What is that?" Freeman pointed to the picture.

"That, Mr. Bishop, is one of the missing boys we're looking for, Jesse Simmons."

"Yeah, but *where* is that? I mean, look at the size of that boar!" Freeman said. He invited himself around the desk to get a better look.

"Son of a–" Freeman began before biting down on his lip. "You don't wanna go messin' with them, Sheriff. I was huntin' 'em one time, them wild boars, and if you get yourself cornered they'll flat out kill ya."

Lonnie looked at Freeman's face. He was lost in the photograph the way a World War II veteran relives the horrors of Normandy when presented with an old black and white photograph.

"I been on some of them hunts," Freeman said. "Was on one when one of the boars, just like that 'un, killed a fella."

"What? Where was that?" Lonnie asked. He waited for Freeman to answer, but he remained lost in the photo.

"I don't believe that for a second," Lonnie said. Freeman looked up and and narrowed his eyes with an intensity Lonnie hadn't seen from him before.

"You better believe it!" Freeman said. "Arkansas. Five of us was on a huntin' trip 'bout twenty years ago. 1993 I think. We's all chasing after some pigs that had been ripping up cornfields. The fella that got killed was older...'bout 65 I reckon, and he owned that cornfield we were huntin'. Don't remember his first name but they called him Hopkins, which I sorta figure was his last name."

Freeman paused and reflected on the story. Lonnie stood and listened as he reached for his coffee. "We seen this big 'ol boar in his cornfield. I reckon he was 400 pounds if he was an ounce," Freeman continued. "I shot him with my 30.06 from about a hundred yards, hit him in the shoulder. Knocked him about a foot to the right then he took off a runnin'."

Freeman grabbed the sheriff's right arm and looked him in the eye. "I'm tellin' ya that was a dag blam 150 grain bullet and it just flat out bounced off his shield!"

"Shield?" Lonnie asked.

Freeman loosened his grip and remembered where he was. "Them boars grow these thick shields, Sheriff, 'bout a two inch plate of cartilage over and around their shoulders. That way the tusks from the other boars don't bother them none. Them shields can flat out stop an arrow, Sheriff, and if that boar's big and mean enough, it can stop a 30.06!"

Lonnie sat down and brought the coffee before his lips, but didn't drink it. He looked at Freeman's intensity and waited for him to finish his story.

"Anyway, I hit this thing and it took off into the cornfield. We had a fella with a huntin' dog and he sent it off after the boar. Then he and another fella chased after the dog while this fella Hopkins, me, and one other stayed back. After a couple of minutes we hear this scream from the cornfield and see that dog come running back. Then his owner's coming behind with that other fella helping, limping and bleeding badly. That boar tore up that fella's shin."

Lonnie didn't feel he really had the time for the long, drawn-out story, but it was too good to miss. He leaned back in his chair and looked up at Freeman.

"It was starting to get a little dark so we all tried to doctor up that fella's leg. All of us, that is, 'cept Hopkins. That old coot took off in the cornfield after that boar, all by hisself. Heck, we didn't even know he's gone 'til we heard this god-awful scream for help. Me and one other fella ran out to find him and he's just laying there, blood gushing out from just above his knee."

"We called the ambulance and it didn't take 'em more than ten minutes to get there. But that boar had hit a major artery and that old fella bled to death right there in his own cornfield."

Lonnie's mouth hung open as he heard the story. "Well I'll be," was all that Lonnie could muster.

"It took us two more days but we found that boar," Freeman said. "Killed him myself. And let me tell you, Sheriff, I stood twenty yards away and watched him die. He was good and dead for half an hour before I had the courage to walk over and check. This thing had two six-inch rippers...bottom tusks if you wanna call 'em that, coming out of his lower jaw plate, and two more six-inch tusks coming out the upper side of his mouth. They use them upper tusks to sharpen the lower ones and let me tell you, I ran my finger against it and them things is razor sharp! I felt that beast's thick, bristly hair and looked in them swirling dark eyes."

Freeman stood, shaking his head. "That thing, dead or not, nearly scared the life out of me. And he looked a lot like that thing right there!" Freeman put his finger emphatically down on the Facebook picture of Jesse standing behind Eduardo just after he had killed him.

"Where was that picture taken, Sheriff?"

"Don't know, Freeman. This here's a picture from the missing boy's Facebook account. They—you know what Facebook is?"

Freeman looked at Lonnie and exhaled as if he had just been asked if he knew where the ground was. "I ain't exactly no retard, Sheriff. I do got some kids, I'll thank you to remember."

Lonnie chuckled to himself, but was guarded to not let Freeman see. "Right," Lonnie continued. "Anyway, Facebook sent us this printout of his personal account and this picture here caught my attention. Where does it look like to you Freeman?"

Freeman leaned over and examined the black and white photocopy closely. "Heck, Sheriff, that could be most anywhere. Some thick woods it looks like but that could be from Alabama to Maine."

"Yeah," Lonnie admitted. "Not much in that picture to help us except the front end of that old pickup behind him. What's that look like to you Freeman? An old Chevy? C10 maybe?"

Freeman looked again. "No, that ain't no C10 sheriff. That's an old F-100. Probably 'bout a 1965 model." Freeman's eyes fell to the text underneath the photo:

> Created Saturday, September 1, 2012
> 11:24:19 EST. Comment posted Tuesday
> September 4, 2012 16:24:43 EST by
> WildPanther: "Glad we killed that sucker. R
> U coming back to work?"

"Who's this other fella, Sheriff? This WildPanther?"

"That, Freeman, is what we need to find out."

Lucy rushed through the door holding a piece of paper. "Sheriff, this just came in for you," she said as Lonnie and Freeman kept looking at the picture. "From the U.S. Coast Guard."

Lonnie looked up and grabbed the note and began reading it as he thanked her.

INTERNATIONAL

U.S. Coast Guard Responds to Medical Emergency in Bahamas

Wednesday October 17, 2012

Late on October 16, Operations Bahamas Turks and Caicos (OPBAT) operations center responded to an urgent request for emergency assistance from a doctor on San Salvador Island, Bahamas. The 7th Coast Guard District, headquartered in Miami, and Coast Guard Air Station Clearwater immediately approved the medical evacuation. An OPBAT helicopter is in route to San

*Salvador where the patient, Rose McBride, along with
her husband and a doctor, will be flown to the Miami
International Airport. A medical team is prepared to
transport the patient to Jackson Memorial Hospital to
receive treatment in the intensive care unit. Due to the
impact of Hurricane Isabel, all phone lines are down in
the Bahamas. The patient's husband, John McBride,
requests that you notify the patient's sister, one Angelica
Savage of 13 Hale Ridge Road, Clayton, Georgia of this
emergency as she is caring for the patient's daughters.*

Lonnie looked at his watch and saw that it was already 10:30
a.m. He took the Coast Guard note, grabbed the Facebook
package, and headed for the door. "Lucy, I have to run out to
Hale Ridge real quick with this Coast Guard message so I can
get back to the high school on time."

***

Tammy stepped off of Hal's front porch and walked slowly
past the ashes of the prior night's campfire. Hal had gone off
hunting again and evidently had taken Rex with him. One of
the hens came over and pecked at the ground in front of
Tammy. She continued walking out of the camp, hoping to
find Ozzie. Since his encounter with the coyotes the week
before, Ozzie had distanced himself from everyone. Hal, Rex
and even her. She didn't know where he had been staying or
sleeping, and suspected he had been sleeping during the day
since she often heard him at night rustling in leaves from the
ridge above, or chasing an animal off if something, anything,
came to close to the camp.

Tammy wasn't sure why Ozzie had taken to isolating
himself, but felt it wasn't her place to question it. He was just
doing what he was made to do, just as she was. There was no
reason to fight it, to go against the way nature made them.
Tammy knew what her role was and what she wanted more
than anything. She liked not having to think about it, but just

going with the rules of nature. Of course, she didn't know what it felt like to be Ozzie, to be a strong male, but she realized a curse of his assignment was the loneliness of isolation. She knew her role was to care, to nurture. Without question, Ozzie felt his was to protect and defend. That meant he had to stay on guard, to isolate himself and to be prepared. He did that not out of selfishness or a need for time alone. He did that for her, and she understood that.

She walked along the stream and studied the trail of trees and stumps that had large chunks gouged from their sides. Ozzie wouldn't be hard to find, Tammy realized, as she examined one tree injury closely. It was fresh and bright and smelled of fallen pine needles. She followed the trail through the woods and down the stream hoping to find Ozzie. Hoping that he would be happy to see her.

A couple of hundred yards before the fig tree in the garden, Tammy stopped to listen. In the distance, she could hear him, sharpening his tusks as if he were grinding an ax blade. Every day he had been sharpening his tusks on anything the forest offered. Mostly stumps, she observed, as he was now doing downstream forty yards from her, unaware of her presence. For a moment, Ozzie stopped and scraped his hooves on the rocks. They, too, were honed and well sharpened. Tammy stared at Ozzie, marveling at how much he had grown in such a short period of time. His arched razorback and physical size was impressive. Indeed, his long sharp tusks and bulging shoulder muscles intimidated even her. But he had grown so much more mature. When she had seen him escape from his paddock, she recalled, she had seen something akin to a scared teenager. A child that had just suffered the horror of seeing his father murdered before his eyes. That day now seemed so long ago, as if it was the final remnant of a vague and distant dream.

Staying well back from Ozzie, Tammy stepped off the trail and hid behind a mountain laurel. She watched and marveled at him. And she worried about him. This was no child. He had become his father, the protector, the defender. And yet, there was something else. He wasn't just preparing himself to protect. There was a restlessness in him as if he was searching for something, and Tammy was afraid of what it was. Ozzie turned and focused on a pine stump. He stared at it with the concentration a martial arts master applies to a cinder block he intends to slice with his bare hand. Pawing the ground, he began oscillating his head back and forth, opening his mouth and moving his upper and lower jaws in opposite directions to reveal his menacing tusks to the stump. Abruptly, he charged and rammed his head into the stump as if he in fact were a ram. Shredding the stump with his rippers and tearing it apart, freeing his rage over his mother's imprisonment as the shards of pine flew from the stump, leaving a soft bed of shavings on the ground where the stump had been.

Panting breathlessly, Ozzie stood with bleeding gums. He tasted the blood and got a crazed look in his eye as he looked around, searching the woods for anything, anyone that was a challenge, a threat. A man. His breathing slowed and he thought for a moment. He turned and continued walking downstream breathing in the faint smell of man.

Chapter 28

A harsh morning sun magnified its light through the living room window and landed squarely on Blake's right eye. He twitched his head and woke, instantly feeling the crick in his neck from sleeping with his head on the armrest of the sofa. He grimaced and threw his feet to the floor to right himself. The CNN newsroom still haunted Blake from the television and displayed the time as 9:34 a.m. EST in the lower corner. A team of weather forecasters stood in front of satellite images, discussing the devastation and path of Hurricane Isabel. The motion graphic read "Hurricane Isabel Upgraded to Category 4. Sustained Winds 123 MPH. Expected landfall Savannah Thursday late afternoon."

Blake rubbed his eyes as he tried to wake up. He couldn't believe he had slept so long, but the scrolling text at the bottom of the CNN screen brought the memories of the prior night into focus for him.

"Meat samples tainted with anthrax removed from restaurants."

Blake jumped up, fully awake as he looked for Angelica. Both bedrooms downstairs and the kitchen were empty so Blake ran up the spiral staircase and looked first in the nursery and then in the rec room. No sign. Evidently Angelica had quietly taken the girls out without awakening him. He felt the back of his neck and rubbed his hand over the dressing she had placed on his wound, realizing what it meant.

She knows! Did she leave me?

Adrenaline shot through Blake's veins as he considered the thought that terrified him. He moved quickly and walked out the door to see if she was outside. His truck was there so she hadn't driven herself anywhere. He walked around the house and circled back to the small lawn in the front. The only sound was the trickling of the brook in front of the lawn that flowed from the mountain above. There was no sign of Angelica or the girls as he looked and listened.

His eyes focused on the opening between two Cryptomeria trees that Angelica had planted a couple of years prior. They stood as pillars framing the path she had cleared, the path that Blake had chosen to avoid until today. He walked to the entrance, and as he looked down the winding path, a flood of painful memories washed over him. Blake remembered how inadequate he felt, how much of a failure he felt he was when Angelica called and told him about the miscarriage. She had sobbed on the phone and told him what the doctor had said while he was in Savannah picking up pigs that would later demonize him. While she sobbed out the details of their loss, of *her* loss, all Blake could think of was how he felt. As if somehow it was *his* fault. That somehow his semen was weak or had penetrated poorly because of his sorry Cherokee genetics. As a boy, Blake's father always blamed the Cherokee blood in their veins for their wretched life in the housing projects. "Me and you, son, have more Cherokee in our blood than anyone in this county," his father would cry in drunken despair. "And look at what it's brung us? This here's our own reservation of poverty, all because our English ancestors mixed with Indians!"

As long as he could remember, Blake had been bitterly ashamed of having Cherokee blood. The thing that Blake hated more than anything about himself was the thing that Angelica loved the most about him.

When Angelica told Blake about the miscarriage, he couldn't cry himself because Angelica was so distraught. She was the woman so *she* got to be emotional, he recalled. *She* was the one who got to feel inadequate, so Blake just shoved his feelings down as far as he could. And when she told him what she planned to do with Nancy's remains he lost his lid, unleashed his feelings of inadequacy on her, which he suspected she might have misinterpreted as something else. Like perhaps he didn't care. Now, Blake shook his head visibly as he tried to knock the memories from the forefront of his mind and bury them again. He had more pressing problems now to focus on.

For the first time he began down the path that meandered by the stream to the secret garden. The growth on each side of the path was dense and lush, but Angelica had kept the path itself neat and tidy. The winding path was peaceful and inviting as roots from trees on each side crisscrossed the path at the surface and formed something of a staircase for Blake to ascend in the sweet and humid air. After five minutes, Blake came to an opening so lush and full of life that the only word that came to mind was Eden. It was a sanctuary of life, a celebration of life, full of fruits, flowers and health. In the far left corner, near a bend in the stream, stood a lone and beautiful fig tree. "Nancy's Tree," Blake whispered to himself, his head nodding. Angelica hadn't spoken about it in a long time and Blake knew that was his fault. Close to the tree was a raised bed that Angelica had obviously built herself. He saw a flash of movement from the right and turned his head to see what he could have sworn was an angel and her two cherubs walking among her flowers, fingering their leaves and petals. Angelica looked and caught his humble gaze, and kissed a smile to him.

Blake stepped into the secret garden for the first time. He walked to Nancy's Tree, knelt and began to weep softly. At first, only a solitary gentle tear, as he was man enough to suppress the others. But then, the angel appeared and placed her loving touch on his left shoulder, opening the dam of tears to drench the soil. The angel knelt beside him as the girls played in the corner with a pair of frogs that Angelica had introduced them to. She draped her arm around Blake's shoulders, taking great pains to not press down on his neck. He collapsed his head in her bosom and reached around to hold her as dearly and closely as if she was the most treasured being in the universe. He tried to look up to her, to meet her eyes, but the lead weight of shame pushed his eyes down and kept them subservient. Still, he began to speak through the tears. "I'm so, so sorry, Angelica." The first words brought more tears from Blake, more stroking from Angelica, as she listened and tried to understand.

"I've just–" the tears took over, momentarily getting the best of Blake. This was no football game, no opposing crowd. He couldn't block this out, couldn't block out this pain. Most importantly, he couldn't shift the blame to someone else. He had to accept the tears and the remorse. "I've just—been wrong about everything," he said. "And you were right about everything, about how we should live our life. I've just done so much that's wrong." The stream of tears flowed as Blake was in the midst of a powerful confession, both confessing his sins and giving himself at the same time. Giving himself to God, he felt, but more important to him, giving himself to Angelica.

She held and stroked his head.

"There, there," she said, just as all mothers and caregivers say in times of comfort, "it's okay. It'll all be all right."

Blake fought through the tears, realizing that he hadn't told Angelica everything. Hadn't told her nearly everything. "You don't understand," he said. "I've done some awful things. I've been—on the mountain, just back up that ways a bit, I've been–" Blake broke down, saying no more and keeping his finger pointed high on the mountain where he had built the sheds, built the fences that held the pigs. Pigs that had now unleashed this deadly plague, this trail of death that led straight back to him.

"There, there," she said. Blake straightened up. He looked into Angelica's soft eyes. The hard part was over, he felt. He had confessed, he had told her. The secrets were mostly out, but not entirely out.

"Angelica, I feel like I am the one who unleashed this storm. Everything you saw on TV last night, all that stuff with Nick."

He paused; not wanting to say what he knew was true. "That was me," he said. "I just want to fix it, to get out of this mess so we can live our life just the way you want." He took her hand. "Can we? Can you forgive me?" Blake forced back the storm of tears that swelled beyond the dam of his eyes.

Angelica stood as Blake knelt at her feet. She stroked one of Nancy's branches with her left hand before turning her gaze back to Blake and taking his chin in her right hand. "Blake," she said, "sometimes God calms the storm and sometimes He lets the storm rage to calm the child."

She glanced at the girls to make sure they were content and looked back to Blake. "You do what you have to do, Blake, and God will sort you out. You need His forgiveness, not mine. I will be where I belong."

Blake rose before her and cupped his hand behind her head and stroked her hair. He pushed his tears back and looked at the tree. "So, this is Nancy's Tree?" he asked.

"Yes!" she said. "Isn't she a beautiful young woman?"

Blake smiled. He had troubles that lay before him, he knew that. But he now had a peace within him thanks to Angelica's amazing gift. "Yes, she certainly is," he said. "What's this contraption over here in the center?" Blake pointed to a large circle of stones at the center of the garden. Within the circle, thirty-six stones outlined four segments, creating pathways to the center.

"That's my medicine wheel," Angelica said. "I gathered the large rocks for the circle from the stream and planted various medicinal herbs in each of the four quadrants."

Blake pretended to be interested, but was already confused. "What's it for?" he asked.

Angelica smiled. "Oh you'd be surprised what I can use it for," she said. "Our Cherokee ancestors relied on these for a great many things, but this morning I used it to harness healing energies."

"Why?" Blake asked. "Heal what, who?" Angelica looked at Blake sternly and placed the palm of her hand against his chest. As she touched his heart she closed her eyes and spoke. "I feel," she said, "trouble brewing around me, Blake. And I will summon the help I need to repel it and protect the innocent and those I love." She opened her eyes slowly and pulled her hand from Blake's chest. Blake stood motionless, as if he had survived a spell.

"Uh...listen," he said, shaking his head in awe of Angelica, "I have one more thing I have to do to clean up this mess I've made. I have to take the farm truck and go now, but I'll be back for dinner with you and the girls." He leaned and kissed her on the forehead and began walking down the path. As he did, he turned to see Angelica standing in the middle of the circle, facing south with her arms held wide and her head tilted back. It reminded Blake of a human crucifix.

Hidden in the bushes thirty yards behind Angelica stood Ozzie, who had found his way down to the secret garden for reasons that were beyond him. He stood and watched the man and woman speak in twisted tongues, but the man had gone now and Ozzie began to wander. At the other end of the path Blake got into the F100 to ascend the mountain one last time.

Boom! Pow! Belch!

Ozzie stopped suddenly as he heard the monster cry, every hair on his back standing erect. Without hesitation, he spun around and sprinted in that direction. Blake gave the truck gas and ground the gears as he put it into reverse and took off down the driveway. Ozzie bolted out of the bushes and ran straight past Angelica, chasing his monster down the winding path.

Chapter 29

Ozzie burst onto the front lawn just as Blake turned left from the driveway onto Hale Ridge and began driving up the narrow road. As he heard the sound of the truck climb the road and turn left, Ozzie took a shortcut through the woods to intercept the monster.

Blake disappeared around a curve a half-mile above his driveway just as the sheriff appeared around a curve a quarter mile below his driveway. Lonnie turned into Blake's drive and parked next to Blake's 2010 F-150. Lonnie got out and knocked on the door. No answer. He knocked again. When there was no answer he walked around the house, but found no one. He looked at his watch: 11:10 a.m. Lonnie walked to the front door and took out his pen. He wrote the following note and left it pinned in the kitchen door.

"Angelica, please call my office ASAP. Sheriff Lonnie Jacobs."

He started walking back to his car. A mile up Hale Ridge, Blake turned left on an abandoned logging road. As he did, the old F100 backfired loudly. Ozzie heard the sound from only a quarter mile away and increased his pace, running through thickets with ease.

In Blake's driveway, Lonnie stopped at his car door as he heard the faint backfire from up the mountain. Normally it would probably not have registered with him, but it sounded like an old farm truck. He thought about the old farm truck he had seen in the Facebook picture less than an hour before. Lonnie got in his car, and instead of turning right on Hale

Ridge to return to Clayton, he turned left to climb toward Rabun Bald.

Blake's F100 moaned and groaned up the bumpy logging road. The left turn that Blake had made decreased the distance between the truck and Ozzie, allowing Ozzie to close rapidly. Blake made a quick right off the logging road onto a makeshift road that was barely visible to him and probably not noticeable to others. He ground the gears and began the final half-mile climb that would take him to a series of paddocks and curing sheds. As he drove along the bumpy road, if he could call it that, he took a moment to contrast it with the beautiful tranquility of the garden path to Eden that Angelica had created at the same time Blake had made this sloppy, sorry path to hell.

Lonnie drove slowly north along Hale Ridge, not sure what he was trolling for. He rode with the window down, but heard only the sound of gravel under his tires. In the woods the F100 spurted and stopped a quarter mile short of its destination. Blake turned the key. The motor whined, but didn't turn over. He tried again, but he knew the truck was finished. Sort of a fitting end, he figured, for the truck to breath its final breath on the mountainside where all of his own troubles began.

He grabbed his long hunting knife, got out, and began walking the final quarter mile.

Lonnie came around a curve and stopped where an old logging road veered off to the left. He shut off his SUV and listened. He got out and stood, listening closely for any sound. The forest was quiet, not even the rustling of a squirrel or the song of a bird to accompany him. He looked back at his watch and saw that it was 11:22. "Shoot, I'll barely make it to the high school," he said to himself. He got in his SUV, used the logging road to turn around and headed back down the mountain, making a mental note to return.

Ozzie bolted across the logging road and onto the other side. He could no longer hear the monster, but he could smell its breath. And he could smell man. But there was something else he could smell. Something faint, but very familiar. He could smell his mother.

***

The woods surrounding Isabella were silent. As Blake approached, she lay there in the mud, not rising for food, water, or shelter. For two days she had stared into the woods but hadn't seen the woods. She reflected on her life. Eduardo, so strong and vibrant, was with her, as was Felipe and Ozzie, both babies and both from her first and only litter. Felipe was the oldest, born a full four minutes before the younger Ozzie, and Felipe never let him forget it. Now they were all gone and Isabella was left alone, imprisoned. She knew her fate and just wanted it to all be over at that point.

Blake cut the power to the fence for the final time and walked to Isabella's paddock. She was a big sow. *Would have made some great hams,* Blake thought, as he took in her prodigious size. He would have preferred to shoot her, but couldn't risk a loud noise given all the attention surrounding him. She had to be dispatched quietly and then left to die and rot, morphing back into the soil and taking with her the final breaths of Blake's sins.

With his electric prod in hand, Blake walked behind Isabella, who lay still. He stuck her in the rump, the shock proving too much for Isabella to resist and forcing her to her feet. Still, she gave no resistance. With no difficulty he walked her into the entrance cage and used a half sheet of plywood to push her against the side. She slumped quietly and looked out through the open gate, already seeming as lifeless as a living creature could be. She had no desire to run, flee or live.

Ozzie approached the widening entrance of the cul-de-sac just as Blake slammed the board against his mother. He stopped just long enough to see Blake extract a long, steely knife from his side. The blade reflected the midday sun brightly into Ozzie's eyes, kindling a series of horrific memories. Memories that had always haunted and paralyzed Ozzie, but now, they fueled his rage. He pawed the ground and grunted a deep, menacing sound. Isabella tensed her body. Her eyes rose as she saw Ozzie, the mirage, charging from thirty yards away.

Blake felt Isabella's tension and turned to the sound crashing through the brush. His eyes and mouth opened wide, and so terrified was he by Ozzie's size and speed that the knife slipped from his quivering hands. Isabella, with all the strength a mother can muster, leaned against the plywood and pushed Blake back against the other side of the cage, momentarily pinning him with plywood. Trapped against the inside of the cage, Blake froze at the sight of the gleaming tusks on the wild boar that now blocked his exit. Every hair on Ozzie's body bristled and stood erect like an enormous cornered porcupine. But he was no porcupine. He was 350 pounds of solid muscle and tusk, deadlier and more menacing than any defensive end that had ever pummeled Blake into the turf.

Isabella moved to block the entrance to her paddock as Ozzie blocked the only other way out. With renewed life she stood there, her immense four hundred pound frame looming and holding Blake in place. She looked past Blake to her baby, her son who she feared was dead along with so many others. "Ozzie!" Isabella said, wanting to embrace him, to feel his warmth against her shoulder. Ozzie, too, had wanted the same thing for so long. But now, in this moment, he was not his mama's boy, and he didn't acknowledge Isabella. Instead, he guarded the cage opening, his shoulders taking up the width of it as he pierced Blake with his eyes. The man who had denied them their freedom, their lives together, now stood trapped before him.

"This is the monster," Ozzie told himself. "The monster of all monsters." Ozzie opened his mouth and flashed his gleaming tusks. Blake's eyes widened at the sight of the rippers. Tusks nearing six inches in length that looked sharper than any weapon Blake had ever seen. Ozzie moved his lower jaw left and right, back and forth. As he did, he tilted his head left then right as if he was in a trance, all the while never taking his eyes from Blake's. Back and forth Ozzie swayed his head, a pendulum of death that hypnotized Blake. He lifted his feet, his hooves, and pawed at the ground. Blake felt that he was being taunted. That if he made a move, ANY move, Ozzie would shred him. That if he stood there, Ozzie would attack him just the same.

With nothing else to protect himself, Blake held the flimsy half sheet of plywood in front of him. A mature, wild hog stood on each side of him. He knew the board was no match for one, let alone two. There was nowhere up or around to go. Looking down at the knife on the ground, Blake wished he had it, but had no idea what he would do with it now if he did. Ozzie saw Blake's gaze and took one step forward to loom over the knife, mocking Blake in a language that he couldn't understand, as if to say, "Is this what you want? Why don't you reach for it?"

Ozzie taunted him, dared him, begged Blake to make a move. He wanted Blake to charge just as the coyotes had charged. Blake pressed his back against the long side of the cage and felt his heart pound so hard that he glanced down to see if it had beaten through his chest.

A raspy, menacing breath came from Ozzie's mouth as he flared his nostrils at Blake.

"Ozzie," Isabella called, gently.

He kept his gaze on Blake, ignoring his mother's call. He was intent on tearing into Blake so badly, ripping him to shreds for what he had done to everyone. Feelings he had never had before brewed inside him like a hurricane of rage and hatred.

"Ozzie! Don't do it!" Isabella was louder now, pleading with him.

Ozzie stepped closer to Blake, close enough to touch the board with his snout. One half inch of plywood was all that separated Ozzie from Blake's legs, the half sheet only rising to just over Blake's knees. Ozzie stuck his snout a foot away from Blake's groin and sniffed.

Blake panicked. He raised the sheet and kicked the plywood hard into Ozzie's snout. Infuriated, Ozzie rammed right into the board, just as he had rammed into the stump, and penetrated the plywood as easily as a needle going into a balloon. Blake held on for dear life, taking splinters in his palms as he gripped with all his might. He looked down to see that one of Ozzie's rippers had come clean through the board and tore his pant leg above his knee. Blake felt a sudden burning sensation and saw blood seep through his jeans.

"Shit!" Blake said. He panicked even more, and lifted the toe of his steel-toe boot to support the board so he could push the board down to the ground. Ozzie freed his tusk and retreated slightly to reassess his attack.

A blurry black mass suddenly swooshed in front of Blake's face from above as a raven descended and besieged him, shrieking and tormenting him in his cage of hell. Blake tucked into a fetal position behind the board and found his face only inches from Ozzie's. His eyes widened at the sight of Ozzie's right ripper, the tip smeared red with Blake's blood. Ozzie tasted the blood, smacked, and began swaying at Blake once more as his breath smothered Blake's face. Blake lunged back against the cage.

The taste of blood crazed Ozzie. He pawed the ground and kicked up dirt.

"OZZIE!" Isabella pleaded once more. "We're NOT like them, Ozzie. We don't torture others. We just want to be left alone."

Isabella's pleas penetrated Ozzie's concentration. Ozzie broke his gaze from Blake and dropped his eyes to the ground. He snorted and turned his head slightly, enough to see both his mother and to see Blake.

"Let's just go," she repeated.

"Where's Felipe?" Ozzie asked sternly, keeping his gaze centered on Blake, who stood nearly breathless between two wild, black hogs that were grunting to one another, as if they were talking. As *if* they could communicate, share ideas, and plan an attack.

Isabella hung her head and began to cry. "He's dead, Ozzie! Everyone's dead! We're all that's left. But you can't—"

Ozzie fumed and started panting quickly. He turned back to Blake, to let him see the hatred in his swirling eyes. "But nothing, mom! This is the monster that killed my father, that killed Felipe." Ozzie pawed the ground and prepared to blitz.

"OZZIE, it won't bring back your father!" Isabella shouted. "It won't bring back Felipe. It won't bring anyone back! It will only make you like them."

Ozzie panted, pawed and swayed.

"Ozzie, I won't have it! I want no part of any more killing, any more oppression. Any more hatred! I'm leaving this place with or without you."

Ozzie fumed and lurched forward. Blake flinched and pulled back. Ozzie hit the board, but stopped, not ramming it with much effort as his mother's words had momentarily thwarted his attack. He was only toying with Blake, taking delight in scaring him.

Blake still had his head turned with his eyes flinched as Isabella pushed past him and shoved Ozzie back. She walked through the gate and tasted freedom for the first time since she was kidnapped from Ossabaw Island, almost two years before.

Ozzie lunged forward again and pinned Blake between the board and the cage. He turned to see his mother walking away, alone. Ozzie stood eye level to Blake's meaty thighs, easily within reach over the torn sheet of plywood. He looked up at the man who stood before him, seeing not a terrifying monster, but a terrified, quivering man. He looked back at his mother and slowly took a step backwards. Then another. He turned, walked through the gate, and stood on the other side, turning to shoot Blake a final look, a final warning.

Then, Ozzie walked into the wilderness with his mother.

Blake collapsed onto the ground. His hands shook violently but still clutched the board as he watched the pair lumber side by side into the woods. He looked at his hands, his knuckles white from gripping the board with all his might, and he finally loosened his grip. He looked back at the pigs, thinking that these two captured pigs had found what he was now in want of. Freedom. Refuge. Just to live simply and to be left alone. Blake felt that he was the one now imprisoned, only he had built the walls and incarcerated himself with his greed.

He remembered that there was a third, a red-haired Tamworth breed of pig out there somewhere, one of only three that he had been raising before he ever started messing with these wild pigs. Back when he raised only a few pigs for Angelica and himself. She, too, had escaped and was out there somewhere. They had each found a way to win their freedom.

Blake prayed that he could win his as he looked down at the blood soaking through his jeans.

Chapter 30

Clint pulled into The Federal's parking lot and parked next to the entrance. Even at 3:45 p.m. he would have expected to see many more cars on a typical Wednesday. He walked inside and continued past the vacant hostess station, pushing through the double stainless doors that led to the kitchen the way John Wayne might have entered a saloon in a Western movie. The kitchen was quiet other than the clanking of utensils by staff preparing dishes for the evening. The voices of those who manipulated the utensils remained hushed as melancholy eyes fixed on their tasks.

"Where can I find Nick Vegas?" Clint asked the group. A chef with a white hat closed an oven door after checking on legs of lamb that were roasting. The smell of the garlic, rosemary, and anchovies that he had masterfully studded into the lamb lingered through the air in search of praise, but finding none. The chef looked at Clint and held his arm to his left, pointing in the direction of Nick's office to the rear of the kitchen. Clint walked through the thirty-foot long kitchen between a line of cooks and preppers. He wasn't here to do an inspection. That wasn't his job. But he noted with interest the meticulousness of each task, the cleanliness of the work surfaces, and the tile floor. He noted the digital temperature readings of the coolers, etched in red at 38 degrees, and the readings of the sub-zero freezers. It wasn't the environment of a callous operator, of a body of people who didn't care about food or food safety. It had the appearance that Clint wanted to see in all restaurants, and it looked like the last place he would expect to find a lax approach to food safety.

He walked through the open door to the office in the rear. It was a small, rectangular room at the rear of the kitchen that may have been originally designed for storage. As he stuck his head through the door and looked to the right, Clint saw Nick Vegas seated at a desk on the far end. Clint easily recognized Nick from magazine and television images he had seen. Neat, thick black hair that was slicked back and perfectly combed framed a clean-shaven face that was tanned a luxurious shade of mocha.

"Nick Vegas?"

Nick looked up from his computer screen and turned his head left. The visitor looked vaguely familiar, but Nick couldn't identify him. Still, Clint's off-the-shelf two-piece suit and laminated FSIS name badge on his left lapel announced official business. Nick knew an official visit would come sooner or later. He was glad that it had come so quickly.

"Yes," Nick said with a placid smile.

"Mr. Vegas, I'm Clint Justice, Senior Compliance Investigator with the Food Safety and Inspection Service."

"Ah," Nick began. "I knew I had seen you somewhere. CNN, right? You were on that segment about food safety."

"Yes, last month," Clint said. "And I heard you as well on Fox News discussing your new club, 50-Forks." Nick smiled with the enthusiasm a mourner has when acknowledging a stranger's condolences. He reflected on the irony of the situation. Both men squaring off on two sides of the law, each having discussed similar issues on cutthroat, competing news channels.

"Call me Nick. How can I help you?"

"I'm here about the foodborne illnesses that resulted from tainted meat that was served by your chefs—"

"Tainted meat?" Nick interrupted. "How do you know that meat was tainted?" Nick crossed his arms and remained standing.

"We removed samples from each dinner location. I suspect you know this since your chefs allowed us access to the meat," Clint said.

Nick didn't respond. Clint continued. "The test results confirmed anthrax, both in the cured ham and in the cooked pork that you served here in Athens. Anthrax was in the white mold of the ham, which very likely contributed to the outbreak of inhalation anthrax." Nick sat down, but said nothing. He waved his hand to an empty chair, inviting Clint to sit if he would like. Clint remained standing and looked down at Nick.

"I need to know precisely where you got both the ham and the fresh pork," Clint said. "Purchase orders, receipts, vendor information, everything you have."

Nick looked up at Clint and delivered his response carefully. "Clint, those illnesses and deaths I've read about are tragic. But *if* they are a result of a foodborne illness, and I'm not saying they are, by your own admission those dinners were private events. They have nothing to do with The Federal or any of my restaurants." Nick had rehearsed his response many times in the past twenty-fours hours both to himself and on the phone with his attorney who assured him this demand would be forthcoming.

Clint took the seat. He leaned forward and rested his left arm on Nick's desk. "This issue is very simple, Nick. I'm here representing FSIS and I need the source of that meat. Unless you have something to hide then *they* are the ones responsible for the anthrax, since anthrax comes from the soil. Now, if you would prefer to not cooperate we will be forced to assume there may have been intended wrongdoing. In that case we'll have the FBI here tomorrow and at each of your locations."

Nick heard what he wanted to hear, that he wasn't the focus of the investigation. He pulled open a file drawer and retrieved Blake's file, writing down Blake's address and phone number on his personalized stationary. "Here," Nick said, handing the note to Clint. "This is the man you want to speak to."

***

Blake leaned with his back against a pine tree near the entrance to his driveway, his head cocked up and pressed against the bark. His eyes traced the long, straight pine that appeared to pierce the sky as if it were an arrow. Catching his breath, he looked once more at his phone that had registered no service for the past three hours. He was left with no choice but to hobble on his own down the mountain, leaving a trickled path of blood in the woods alongside the road. Twice he had heard a car coming down the road, and twice he had taken cover in thickets to avoid any encounters. To avoid answering helpful questions, such as "why's your leg bleeding so badly?"

The phone finally registered a single bar next to the time, 6:21 p.m. One single reception bar. Too late to be of any help as he knew he could make it the last few hundred yards. A message flashed on the phone indicating that he had one new voice message. Blake pushed off the tree and grimaced as his right leg seared with pain. He limped along the driveway, unable to move any better on the groomed drive than he had been in the uneven terrain of the woods. He brought the phone to his ear and listened to the message from the 404 area code.

"Mr. Savage this is Clint Justice, Senior Compliance Investigator with the Food Safety and Inspection Service. Nick Vegas has given me your name, number and address as a supplier of meats to him. It's about this matter that I must speak to you right away. Please call me back at the following number today or tonight."

Blake stopped and stood in the driveway. He turned and looked behind him to see if anyone was coming, even though he had heard nothing. Another wave of terror washed over him. Momentarily paralyzed, he was afraid to move forward, afraid that vehicles were already at his home, waiting to incarcerate him. He put his left thumb in his mouth and chewed on the nail, unconscious of doing so. He glided his thumbnail back and forth between his upper and lower front teeth as if attempting to floss them as he stared into the gravel drive and played out the scenario. He hobbled slowly through the woods next to the house as he imagined a team of snipers on his own rooftop, armed with long-distance listening devices trained on his direction. In his imagination the sound of the smallest twig cracking sent a barrage of bullets flying into the woods.

Through the trees, he caught his first glimpse of the house, a twinkling reflection from the windshield of his F-150. He was relieved that *they* hadn't come to repossess that, even though he had paid cash for it. Other than his truck, there were no other vehicles visible. He emerged at the edge of the woods and stood for a moment, looking closely around the house. There was no movement.

Blake walked to the kitchen door and opened it, praying silently that no one other than Angelica would be there. He opened the door and exhaled, momentarily releasing his tension and smiling at the woman who stood there. The woman who was the answer to his prayers.

"What happened?" Angelica asked. The girls were watching a movie that she had put in for them.

"Oh," Blake began as he searched for words, "just hurt myself in the woods. But it's all done. I'm done now. With everything." He felt himself wanting to confess more, needing to blurt out years' worth of secrets, of lies. Of deceit. Angelica took his arm and walked him to the bathroom. She helped him slide his pants off, supporting his beefy frame as he flinched with pain. Like any good nurse she showed little emotion when the two-inch gash was revealed just above Blake's knee. Still, the location of the wound alarmed her. "Oh goodness!" she said. "You're lucky this is a shallow wound. It just missed your femoral artery. And I mean *just* missed it!"

"Sit still. I'll be right back." Angelica walked through the sliding glass doors in the living room that led to the front yard. She snipped off several fresh yarrow leaves and went to the kitchen. She washed the leaves thoroughly in vinegar, rinsed them with water and returned to Blake. "Here," she said. She pressed the leaves on the cut, grabbed the medical tape and bandages and secured the yarrow to the wound.

"What happened?"

"I—I was working in the woods and took a stick through my leg," Blake said. Angelica looked up at him. Lying had become such a habit for Blake that he could no longer even recognize when he did it. He always told himself that he lied to Angelica about his activities for *her* protection. *Damn it! Is that what I'm doing now, protecting her? Just tell her truth, that a pig did it to you!*

"Keep this on for an hour or two until we're sure the bleeding has stopped," she said. Angelica walked back to the kitchen and picked up the note from the sheriff and brought it to Blake. "Look," she said. Blake jerked up at the sight of the sheriff's signature and winced at the pain. "When did this come? Did you see him?"

"It was in the door when the girls and I came in for lunch from the garden."

"Did you call him? What did he want? What did he say?" Blake was standing and felt a sudden urge to pack, to flee.

"No, I didn't call him," Angelica said while cleaning up the medical supplies she had taken from the cabinet. "I wanted to speak with you first. It's too late to call him now."

Blake read the note again. "Angelica, please call my office ASAP. Sheriff Lonnie Jacobs." *Why in the world does he want to speak with Angelica? To interrogate her? Thank God I didn't tell her anything. Don't start now!*

"I wonder what he wants," Angelica said.

Blake was shocked at how carefree Angelica was, but then he realized that she, of course, had nothing to hide. Nothing to fear. Why *shouldn't* she be carefree? She walked in to the living room and sat with the girls.

"Wanna watch some TV with us before dinner?" she called to Blake.

"Uh...no, not right now," Blake said staring at the note. "Tell you what, I'll get in touch with the sheriff first thing tomorrow and see what he wants. How 'bout that?"

"Sure," Angelica called from around the wall in the living room. She put her arms around the girls and pulled them close on the sofa, getting lost in one of her happy places. A place with family, simple pleasures, peace and quiet.

Inches behind the wall, Blake sat alone in misery.

Chapter 31

Blake woke up early. He had tossed and turned most of the night, partly due to the pain in his leg from Ozzie's tusk, but mainly due to Clint's message and the sheriff's note. He gave up fighting for sleep and arose at 5:40. He had been sitting on the sofa for over two hours watching CNN. He didn't know why he was still watching the news. After thirty minutes it seemed to just loop, saying the same thing in different ways, with different people sometimes, but the same thing nevertheless. Supposedly a strong hurricane was going to hit Savannah later that afternoon. A Category 5 hurricane that normally would have been the talk of the country. Maybe it was, for all he knew. But not for him.

His eyes stayed fixed on the ticker that tallied the trail of death and illness from the anthrax outbreak. A plague that he knew he alone was likely responsible for. The death toll stood at five, but now there were close to one hundred hospitalized. Ten or a hundred hospitalized made little difference to him at this point. The mountain behind him was claiming lives with a vengeance. First two boys missing, then the illnesses, now the deaths. Blake placed his hand on his right leg, lightly touching his injury. He realized how lucky he had been. So far.

On the table beside him his cell phone buzzed like a nest of yellow jackets that dared him to pick it up. He checked the time on the television: 8:17 a.m. Blake fumbled for the phone and dropped it on the floor. "Goddammit!" he said as he grabbed it and saw the 404 area code. He pushed the button sending it to voice mail. He knew he couldn't keep dodging the calls. A message popped up that a voice message had been left.

"Mr. Savage, Clint Justice again with the Food Safety and Inspection Service. I must speak to you. Right away. Please call me back before noon. If I don't hear from you I'll contact the sheriff and request his assistance in reaching you."

Crap! Blake stood up and paced the living room. *What do I tell this guy? I sure as hell don't want him talking to the sheriff!*

Blake went to the kitchen and wrote a note for Angelica. "Have to run see the sheriff and do some errands. Will be back later today but call my cell if you need me." He hesitated and continued writing. "Love, Blake."

He tried to remember the last time he had spoken those words, let alone written them. As he walked through the kitchen door he was met with a gust of wind that lifted his cap. He reached and caught it before if flew off. The high, overcast clouds he had seen before going to bed the night before now gave way to low clouds that streamed over the mountain like waterlogged sponges ready to be squeezed by the hands of God.

In his F-150, Blake fought the wind down Hale Ridge as the trees swayed on both sides of the road. Leaves flew off the autumn trees like dandelion seeds in a spring storm, darting in front of his windshield and obscuring the road. By now, Blake had memorized the curves of Hale Ridge road. Still, he had difficulty making out where the shoulders ended and where the steep drop-offs began. To make matters worse, his mind wasn't on the road...it was on the sheriff and Clint Justice. He needed a breather, a distraction, and his eyes were drawn to a forested abyss to his left, a ravine that funneled to a sea of rocks, trees and rotting leaves far below. The scene entranced him as swirling leaves formed mini-tornadoes and danced with and among the trees.

Blake looked back up and saw the road curving sharply to the right just in front of the hood, but he was continuing straight over the edge. He pushed back on the wheel, straightened his arms as he slammed the brakes, and then pressed back into the seat so hard he thought that it might break. The rear of Blake's truck fishtailed to the left as the brakes locked and the gravel shoulder gave way. The ravine loomed and gripped the truck's hood to pull him in.

The front left tire was the first to depart, sliding off the road as the tread of the back tires dug in with all their might. The front tire slammed into a small pine tree, snapping it in two and sending the top half tumbling down the ravine, but the tire rested on the swaying, broken spear. Blake's arms remained rigid. He pushed back from both the steering wheel and from the ravine, thinking that somehow if he pushed back he would be farther from the fall. Peering out his side window, he saw the drop just before him. Instinct guided his hand to the door handle, which he opened to see himself teetering on the shoulder. Blake released the seatbelt and placed his left leg out the door. Bending his knee to place his step as far back as possible, he grabbed the door jam and swung his body back, crashing to the ground. He crawled to the back of the truck, his right leg searing as his wound raked over the gravel.

Blake pulled himself up on the bumper and caught his breath. "Holy shit!" he said to himself, and then admonished himself in that of all moments to stop swearing. Blake walked around the truck to survey his predicament. The other three wheels were on the road. He looked down at his hands, trembling violently, as he tried to decide what to do. The wind whipped dusty gravel up the road, stinging his hands and cheeks.

Gingerly, he climbed back into the driver's seat and turned the dial to engage four-wheel drive. Slowly, he put the gearshift into reverse. He eased his foot off the brake and pressed the accelerator at the same time. The truck lurched back and the thin pine stump that bent under the weight of the tire rocked back, forth and snapped. With a thud, the front left end dropped as the running board landed on the shoulder, and the right tire tipped as it barely teetered on the road. Blake closed his eyes and floored the accelerator, pushing back on the steering wheel once more. The rear tires dug in and spun dirt up and past his window like a team of hungry dogs digging up a bone buried in the sand. The F-150 pulled back slightly and then lunged rearward as the front right tire took hold and pulled the front left tire back onto the shoulder. Blake slammed the brakes just before the rear right tire fell off the opposite shoulder.

He sat there, breathless. "Holy s—" He caught himself and swallowed his profanity. Blake began a series of three-point turns to get himself pointed down the mountain once more. Once he was centered in the road he paused and wiped the sweat from his brow and face as the wind rocked his truck back and forth. He took another moment to compose himself before shifting down into the lowest gear and admonishing himself to keep his eyes on the road.

***

Blake pulled into the parking lot at Ingle's and blended his truck into a sea of vehicles. He took out his phone to call Clint Justice.

"Justice," Clint said as he answered the phone.

Blake drew in his breath, disappointed that he had not reached voice mail.

"Yes, uh...hello?" Blake began. "Uh, this is Blake Savage calling you back."

"Mr. Savage, I'm conducting an investigation for the Food Safety Inspection Service. Do you provide meat for Nick Vegas at The Federal?"

Blake wasn't sure what he had expected. The tone was concise and not jovial. It was black and white, abrupt. Do you or don't you, did you or didn't you, guilty or innocent. "Do I need a lawyer or do I have rights?"

"I'm not a law enforcement official, Mr. Savage. I'm with the FSIS, which is part of the USDA. I'm simply asking you if you sell meat to Nick Vegas."

Sell. That was the word Blake heard and focused on. "I—deliver meat sometimes to him."

"Meat from where, Mr. Savage?"

"From farmers up here. I deliver all kinds of things." Blake felt himself having a good idea, felt the words beginning to form and flow with ease, filling him with confidence. He kept talking, feeling certain he could now talk his way out of any trouble he may be in. "I deliver fruits, vegetables, wine and sometimes meat from local farmers."

"What meats?" Clint asked.

"Oh, we got fellas up here that raise grass fed beef, pasteurized chickens—"

"Do you mean pastured chickens?" Clint interrupted.

"Yeah, pastured chickens, wild turkeys, raw milk cheeses, beef...you name it," Blake said.

"Okay, I will. Pork. Did you deliver any pork to Mr. Vegas or his restaurant? Specifically, any ham?"

Blake paused. He visualized himself on the final drive, the ultimate final drive. Instead of calling his plays carefully he had to choose his words with care, letting each word, each sentence move him closer to scoring. Victory in this game would be measured with freedom. A loss would...he didn't want to visualize that.

"Honestly Mr., uh, Clint, I don't usually know what I'm delivering. I just pick up them boxes from farmers and take 'em to him. If they're open where I can see tomatoes and what not then I know, but most time they're sealed and packed." Blake was turning on the country, redneck, hillbilly know-nothing accent, laying it on thick to make sure Clint knew this was a trail that led nowhere.

"Surely you—" Clint began.

"I suspect Mr. Vegas would have invoices that would show all the deliveries and what he bought," Blake interrupted, "because he pays the farmers for their stuff and not me. Ain't that what you wanna know?"

There was a moment of silence.

"Perhaps, Mr. Savage. Please keep your phone available today, as I will likely need to phone you back. By the way, I have your address as one 13 Hale Ridge Road in Clayton. Is that correct?" Blake knew from Clint's earlier message that he had his address, but hearing it said aloud made the hairs on his arm stand up. He felt the storm closing in on him, the noose tightening, even though he hoped he had just thrown the dog off his trail.

"Yes," Blake said. "That's right, but I'm not here—there today."

"That's fine," Clint said. "If I need to visit and have my search warrant it won't matter if you're there or not."

A lump formed in Blake's throat.

"I'll be in touch soon, Mr. Savage." Clint hung up. Blake sat in his truck and replayed the conversation. In Atlanta, Clint Justice made notes on his pad and did the same thing.

***

A white Econoline van with a Black Rock Farm logo pulled into the driveway at 13 Hale Ridge Road at 10:15 a.m. The driver got out and walked to the door, holding his hand against his face to block sand and gravel that the wind had launched in his direction. He banged on the door loudly thinking that since he couldn't hear with all the wind then no one else could. Angelica came to the door and greeted the driver with a smile.

"Howdy, ma'am. Name's Gus...got a delivery for your husband."

"Hello, Gus, I think we've met once before," she said.

"Right. Well, howdy again ma'am. Looks like we got some weather coming."

Angelica looked out at the trees swaying briskly in the wind. She had been immersed playing board games with the girls. "Sure does," she said. "Looks like a good rain's a comin'."

Gus looked at her with a sense of puzzlement.

"Rain? You been hearing what they're saying? 'Bout that hurricane?" Gus asked.

"Not since yesterday," she said honestly. "They said it may hit the Georgia coast I think. Has it changed?"

"Hadn't changed, just got stronger that's all. And coming this way too."

Angelica looked a little puzzled. "We can't get hurricanes up this far, silly."

"No ma'am, 'course not. But it's a Cat 5 storm and they got the eye tracking this way. Saying it's gonna bring a ton of wind and rain so you best hunker down."

"Well," Angelica said as she fingered the beads around her neck, "I think this mountain could use a good washing."

Gus gave her a puzzled look and then looked at his watch. "Well, anyway, I got a delivery here for Blake. He'd asked us to bring it tomorrow but we're rushing to get these all delivered on account of the weather. Where you want it?"

Angelica grabbed a light rain jacket.

"You girls stay put for a moment," she said.

"Hmmm...Gus, can we put the boxes in the garden shed over there?"

"You betcha, ma'am."

Gus backed the van up to the shed. Angelica walked inside to clear a spot.

"How many boxes do you have?"

"Let's see. Three full boxes of organic bone meal, ma'am."

Angelica surveyed the shed. Everything had a place and everything was in its place. She walked to a shelf that was just over the height of her head, about six feet high. There was a clearing on the shelf next to a couple of watering cans. She reached up to grab the cans. As she did she felt something soft brush the back of her hand. She pulled her hand down, mildly startled. A strong gust of wind slammed the shed with a loud bang and closed the door on the van with Gus in it. Angelica looked for something to stand on and found a milk crate. She

282   TIM YOUNG

turned it over so she could stand on it and raised her eyes to the shelf. Peering over the edge she saw a wadded-up piece of stained, blue fabric. She took it down and stepped off the crate. The door of the van opened.

"Almost got myself locked in here," Gus said with a smile.

Angelica smiled back. "If you don't mind, just put them up on this shelf next to these tomato cages." Gus took three plain brown boxes and stacked them on the shelf. He looked at how well organized the shed was and reached back up to align the boxes.

"There you go ma'am. Just sign here if you please and I'll be on my way." Angelica signed the form. "Nice to see you again, Gus. Come back anytime." Most customers in Rabun County were nice, Gus thought, but he was struck by how genuine Angelica's smile was. "It was my pleasure, ma'am. Y'all take care in this storm."

Gus drove away as Angelica unfolded the cloth. It was a blue jacket. A man's jacket, she realized, though she had never seen it. It was spotted with dark reddish-black stains. She examined them closely and scratched them with one of her long fingernails. "Blood," she whispered as she looked at the label of the jacket. "Large," she murmured. "Blake wears extra large." But it wasn't the size that puzzled her. It was the initials J.S. that were marked on the label in permanent, black ink.

***

Blake pulled into the courthouse parking lot just before 11:00 a.m. After the call with Clint he had driven up and down the strip in Clayton, hitting the Dairy Queen and going back to the traffic light, turning right down Main Street and circling back once he hit the bottom of the hill. Just as he had done countless weekend and summer nights in high school. Only now he wasn't cruising for girls, wasn't hootin' and hollerin' after a game. He was stalling. Thinking.

Leaning against the wind, he pulled the door to the sheriff's office open and walked in, the glass door slamming shut behind him. A steady rain had just begun and its sting surprised him since the hurricane wasn't expected to make landfall in Savannah for another seven hours, and the eye, or whatever was left of the system, wouldn't be near Clayton until the following morning. Blake looked out the door at clouds that seemed to be drooping and cascading down, smothering the valley. He turned and approached the woman at the front desk. "Is the sheriff in?" he asked Lucy.

"He is. Do you have an appointment?"

"Uh...no. Can you tell him that Blake Savage is here. If he don't have time that's—"

"Let me check, Mr. Savage. Just wait a moment."

Blake looked at the floor. At the ceiling. At the wall...anything to not make eye contact with anyone wearing a uniform. His eyes landed on the poster on the wall of Rabun County's Twelve Most Wanted, four photos across, three rows down. Four of the most wanted were black male. Curious, Blake thought, given Rabun County's overwhelming majority of whites. Three of the twelve were women. One in particular caught his attention. Her head tilted down in the mugshot, all badass, as if her eyes were saying, "You can't catch me coppers, not in a thousand years." Only, they did and here she was for all to see. Multiple fraudulent use of credit cards, theft of property, weight 137 pounds, tattoo on left ankle, brown hair, brown eyes.

Blake imagined himself fleeing. His mugshot would be in square number one, accused of raising pigs and, oh yeah, channeling anthrax through them to unsuspecting diners. *Like that was my fault.* He felt bad about the illnesses as he was sure everyone did. But, was it his fault? He didn't think so. It was an accident. That's all, just an accident. But someone always had to be held accountable, there had to be someone to point to and say "he did it." He was sure that Clint...probably even the sheriff wanted that person to be...

"Blake?" Lonnie said.

Blake turned his head to see the sheriff coming through the door with some papers in his hand.

"Hi, Sheriff."

"What can I do for you?" Lonnie asked.

"My wife asked me to see you when I came to town. She said you left a note for her. She's—not feeling too well."

Lonnie nodded and handed Blake the Coast Guard message he was holding. "Sorry to hear that. This came in yesterday. I wanted to deliver it personally."

Blake took the note and read it. "Jeez," he said. "I'll take this to her right away. Thanks, Sheriff." Blake stepped back and began to turn.

"Blake, can you take a look at this before you leave?" The sheriff handed Blake a picture of Jesse standing behind a huge boar, lying dead on the ground.

"What's this?" Blake asked, knowing full well what it was.

"You don't recognize him?"

"Can't say that I do, Sheriff." Blake looked at the scene, at the corner of the sheds and the front end of the F100 in the background. He felt his face turning flush.

"This here's Jesse Simmons, the fellow in that blue jacket behind the pig," Lonnie said. "You see that truck behind him? You know anyone down your way with a truck anything like that? That might help us find this boy for his folks."

Blake's throat dried. He concentrated not on the photo, only on trying to produce some saliva. He couldn't. He scratched his head, appearing to think for the sheriff. Blake was thinking all right, calculating. "I don't, Sheriff, but if I see a truck like that I'll be sure to call you."

He looked into the sheriff's eyes until he saw they were fixed on him. Blake dropped his eyes and then tried to prop them back up.

"Thanks Blake, you do that. I'd appreciate it. I know his family would too."

"Well, gotta be going, Sheriff. Thanks for getting this to us." Blake waved the Coast Guard memo as he began to leave.

"Sure thing. And be careful, Blake...there's a storm coming your way."

Blake kept walking through the door as if he was trying to flee not only the sheriff, but the sheriff's words as well. There's a storm coming *your* way, Blake repeated to himself as he climbed into his truck. He headed north toward Dillard, intent on circling around for a few hours, afraid to go home just yet. He still needed time to sort everything out.

Lonnie walked back into his office. As he entered he said, "Lucy, run me a report of all vehicles registered to one Blake Savage."

Chapter 32

Blake sat down at the bar in Red Dawgs just after 1:00 p.m. and ordered a sweet tea. "Sure that's strong enough for you?" the bartender said with a smile. "Want I should make it a double?" Blake tilted his head back and forced a grin. "Yeah, just tea, that's all."

He stared at the television in Clayton's only sports bar along with the other two customers in the bar. Everyone else had the good sense to be home. CNN had a camera set up somewhere in Savannah that showed a blur, mostly. Horizontal, driving rain and wind were already steady at over ninety-five miles per hour. The eye of Isabel wasn't expected to make landfall until 5:00 p.m. The talking heads fought for airtime, each thinking they had a unique perspective on the pending devastation. What they really wanted was airtime during the coastal cataclysm to pad their resumes.

Blake's phone vibrated. He looked and saw a 404 area code. *Shit!* He said to himself. He exhaled deeply and then answered the phone.

"Blake, Clint Justice again. I have spoken with Nick Vegas and I need to come visit with you." Clint hadn't spoken with Nick again, but he would. Something hadn't smelled right to Clint with Blake's story and he felt it was important to meet him right away.

"Okay," Blake said after a pause. "What for? When?"

"Now," Clint said. "I'm already on my way. Just passing Gainesville."

"NOW!" Blake said as he kicked the barstool out and stood. "Are you crazy? You seen the weather?"

"I'm on my way, Mr. Savage. Should be at your house in a little over an hour." Clint hung up. He had pulled over at a gas station at the Mall of Georgia exit on interstate 985. He hadn't passed Gainesville yet, as he told Blake. He should have by now, but the winds were already steady at over 60 MPH in Buford and getting worse.

"This is crazy," Clint thought. He put the car in gear and continued north. It was crazy but he thought it would be easier to pressure Blake into the truth than Nick, and Clint always birddogged the truth.

Blake threw down a few bucks to pay for his tea and headed to the door. "Heading out, Blake?" the bartender said. "He's calling an audible," one of the customers yelled as he lifted his beer into a salute. "Good call, Blake!" Blake ignored both men and pushed through the door, missing the text that began scrolling along the bottom of the CNN screen.

> "Anthrax claims sixth victim in Miami.
> Jackson Memorial Hospital has yet to
> release the woman's name."

Thick, tropical storm conditions had already settled in on Rabun County and the rain came down in sheets. The air was heavy and humid even with the wind blowing steadily out of the south at close to 60 MPH. Blake drove east down Warwoman Road, normally a lush, peaceful drive. Now, wipers couldn't clear the water from the windshield as angry trees swayed violently on each side of the narrow, two-lane blacktop. Blake widened his eyes to concentrate as he gripped the wheel firmly. He slowed to ten miles per hour as he snaked around a series of hairpin turns that he often navigated while pretending to be an Indy driver. The temptation was nearly irresistible to look at the trees above, to be prepared to dodge if they plummeted in his direction. He fought the temptation and resisted looking down the ravines to his right or up the steep banks to his left. He knew that many of those timber skyscrapers would lose their grip on the mountain if the wind and rain kept up like this.

Blake turned left on Hale Ridge and began his ascent. The close call from earlier in the day leapt out and took center stage in his consciousness. He drove slowly right in the center of the road, praying that he would meet no fool crazy enough to descend the mountain in these conditions. Autumn leaves fell as fast as the raindrops and clung to his windshield under his wiper blades. He resisted the temptation, barely, to look up at the trees that threatened to crash on his truck and smash him into the wet surface.

Finally, he came to his driveway and turned in, suddenly hitting the brakes and pausing to think. He put the truck into park and jumped out. Rainy bullets pelted his face as he leaned his shoulder into the 4x4 mailbox post until it wriggled free in the wet ground. When it did, he wrapped his arms around it, pulled the mailbox out of the ground and threw it in the back of the truck, taking with him the only indicator marking the entrance to 13 Hale Ridge.

Looking like a golden retriever climbing out of a dirty pond, Blake bolted into the kitchen at 2:00 p.m. and shook off the rain as Angelica and the girls played in the living room. "An indoor play day," she had told them.

"Hi, honey," she said with a tepid smile.

Blake exhaled, as if he had just successfully fled from a predator and needed to catch his breath in the safety of his den. "Hi. What are you gals up to?"

"We're playing Connect 4," she said. "And watching the weather." Angelica rose and looked at Blake. "I have something for you," she said. She walked into the kitchen out of earshot of the girls and reached on the shelf above the coat rack. She pulled down a blood-stained blue jacket and handed it to Blake.

"What—what's this?" Blake asked, shocked to see it, but knowing full well what it was. "Where did it come from?"

Angelica looked up at him in the center of the kitchen. Just as he towered over her physically, she towered over him morally and spiritually. "Well, I can assure you that I don't know, Blake. But I suspect you do."

"I don't kn—"Angelica interrupted Blake by placing her right index finger over his lips. She held his gaze sternly as she twirled her beads with her left thumb and index finger.

"He who makes it wrong must make it right, Blake. Otherwise, he will be found guilty and justice will be swift." An image of Angelica's grandmother flashed before her as she recalled what she had been taught about Cherokee beliefs. She repeated what she had learned to Blake. "Good is rewarded, Blake. Evil is punished."

Blake stared at his wife as she circled him, keeping her touch on his shoulders and catching his gaze each time she fronted him. He felt lightheaded and lost his focus, forgetting for a moment where he was and feeling somewhat hypnotized. Angelica stopped before him and offered a final warning. "This jacket has a home, Blake. Someone is looking for it. Find its rightful home." Blake stood dumbfounded with his eyes and mouth wide open. He had no idea what to say as he stood drowning in a sea of fear and confusion. He shook his head and tried feverishly to change the subject.

"I uh...I went by to see the sheriff. He had this note for you."

Angelica took the note from Blake. She read it carefully. "Miami? Intensive care?" Angelica said. She looked up at Blake and then turned to look at the girls. "What does this mean?" she asked. Angelica knew what the message meant, but it was her habit to ask Blake what something meant, just as it was her habit to defer to him on decisions. She didn't take responsibility for Blake's decisions. Nor did she feel she could control them. But she could react to them and make choices consistent with her own values.

"What should we do?" she asked.

"I reckon you should call the hospital," Blake said.

"I'll try Rose's cell phone first," Angelica said. "Oh dear." Angelica walked to the kitchen phone and lifted the receiver. Blake took off his jacket and hung it on the coat rack next to the door. She clicked the button on the wall phone several times. "Blake, there's no dial tone."

Blake took the phone, clicked it several times and found the same thing. "Phones are out," he said. He looked at his cell phone. No service. That wasn't a surprise as it was rare to get more than one or two bars in the best conditions on Hale Ridge. In this weather, no chance.

"We'll keep trying," he said. "It's too dangerous to go out now and it's gonna get a whole heap worse."

Angelica walked to the south-facing kitchen window and stared out. A solid sheet of water cascaded slowly over the glass, giving the impression of a flowing mirage. In her mind, the sounds of the house, of the girls, and of the storm faded, and she heard nothing, only silence. She peered deeply into the mirage and saw her twin sister lying motionless as strangers loomed over her limp body. Angelica concentrated as she tried to see if Rose was lying in a bed—or in a coffin. She stared out the window as if in a trance, thumbing the beads around her neck while murmuring softly.

When a flash of lightning raced brilliantly across the sky and shattered the mirage, Angelica didn't blink.

***

Clint saw the Dairy Queen on the left when he arrived in Clayton. He followed the directions on his navigation system, turned right, and went down Warwoman Road. Sheets of rain slammed the right side of his car as he drove east on the narrow road. Steep banks sloped down from each side. He had noticed very few cars as he came into town, although the RaceTrac station remained open.

The GPS indicated that he had eleven miles before he reached Hale Ridge. The GPS also said it would take another half hour, but after a mile and a half, Clint saw a line of cars stopped dead ahead of him. A huge oak tree, at least eighty feet tall, had fallen right across the road. The root ball was enormous and lay partially on the eastbound lane. Clint backed up, turned around, and drove to the fire station. He couldn't imagine there'd be too many fires to put out with it raining like this. He opened his car door and was soaked before he got out. The water was already standing at least an inch on the blacktop. He walked through the glass door and found a couple of fireman sitting at a table in the break room. They were both alert, ready for action. One of them, an older fireman, seemed genuinely happy to see him.

"Howdy," he said. "Help ya?"

"Yeah," Clint began, "I'm trying to get down to Hale Ridge road." The older fireman began shaking his head immediately. "My GPS says I have to go down Warwoman but I didn't get two miles and there's a huge tree across the road."

"There's a whole mess of them down," the fireman said. "We got a few calls before phones went down of trees across the road on Warwoman 'tween here and Hale Ridge."

The younger fireman jumped in. "Shoot I can't imagine what Hale Ridge is gonna look like. Might not even be there tomorrow," he said.

"Look I *really* need to get over there. Is there another way?"

The older fireman looked at Clint. "Son, there ain't no way you're getting there. In twenty-four hours or so, maybe you can take a boat."

The younger fireman spoke up: "You can get to the other side of Hale Ridge from up at Sky Valley or Scaly Mountain."

"Really?" Clint asked. "Where's that?"

"Of course it's likely to be a lot worse that way."

The older fireman looked down at his younger counterpart. "A heck of a lot worse," he said to him before turning his stare back to Clint. "Son, you ain't getting there. Do you have any idea what kind of road Hale Ridge is?"

"No...not really," Clint admitted.

"Well I understand it might look just like any other road there on your map. But it ain't. That's a narrow dirt road winding up, through, and around ravines on the backside of Rabun Bald. With this wind and rain, 'specially if it comes like they say it's a coming—that's the last place on earth you wanna be."

Clint said nothing. He walked over and looked at the large street map on the wall of Rabun County. The older fireman walked over to him. "You ought to go home yourself 'for it gets real nasty out there. After this storm passes the town will get the roads cleared, but a lot of towns are gonna be a mess for a while."

"Thanks," Clint said, and then walked out the door to his car.

He sat in the car and looked out his window at the amount of water standing in the parking lot. Leaning over the steering wheel, Clint looked through the sheet of water on the windshield trying to see the mountain peaks around him, peaks that were hiding in the cover of low hanging clouds. He tried to visualize the sheer volume of water that could funnel down those mountains if it kept raining like this. A loud clap of thunder shattered his concentration. He put the car in gear and started south on 441, heading for home and out of Rabun County. And heading right into the direction of the approaching storm.

• • •

Blake stared out the sliding glass door, barely able to see anything as the water pelted the glass and formed a thick, foggy sheet. The sky brightened with a terrific burst of light, followed almost instantly by a thunderous crash. Instinct thrust his right hand to shield his eyes as the lightning struck something close by. A series of pops rattled through the house as the television snapped off. All electric lights were snuffed out except for two small emergency lights that were plugged into outlets that came on when the power was out.

"Wow, did you see that?" Blake said.

The girls screamed and jumped into Angelica's lap, knocking the Connect 4 game on its side, spilling its pieces. "It's okay, girls," Angelica said as she pulled them closer. "Just nature throwing a little party."

Blake looked over at her. Most women—hell most men for that matter—would be scared out of their wits in these conditions, but Angelica seemed calm, at ease. As if she had long ago surrendered herself to nature, to God, and was now going through life as if watching a movie. Watching it happen and enjoying most parts, tensing sometimes at the scary parts. But this part, this torrential rain and lightning—this part didn't seem to scare her.

Angelica got up and walked to the closet. She pulled out two kerosene lanterns and lit them with a match from a kitchen drawer, adjusting the wick to get the light the way she wanted before placing one light on the kitchen bar. She took the other light with her to the living room. The girls' rosy cheeks glowed in the light as the flame entranced them the way only fire can hypnotize a child.

"This is how my grandparents lit their house," Angelica said to the girls, omitting the fact that they only did that for fun once in a while. Blake realized that if the storm knocked out all the power and it never returned, Angelica would be one of the very few happier people. No gas, no electricity, no telephones. Just the sun, the moon, family, God and nature. He walked over and sat on the sofa with Angelica and the girls. One of the girls moved over and jumped in his lap the way she would have jumped in her father's lap if he had been there. She curled up and laid her head against Blake's chest.

Angelica looked at Blake and smiled broadly. Blake clumsily reached his arms around the child as if he might break her. Angelica laughed. "Just hold her and love her," she said.

Blake did. He closed his eyes and felt the warmth of the child, the love of the child. She wanted nothing from him other than protection and love. She wasn't chasing him, taunting him, or pursuing him. Instead, she needed him. He pulled her close and stroked her hair as Angelica moved close to him and pulled a blanket over the huddled family.

The howling wind and pounding rain continued through the night.

***

Clint awoke Friday morning, but thought it was still night. Rain pummeled the driveway at his Sandy Springs home under skies as dark as soot. Looking at the clock to see it was 7:30, he was a little surprised that the power was on at all. After he got up, brushed his teeth, used the bathroom and went to the living room, he flipped on the television and turned to CNN.

The video footage on the screen was horrific. At first Clint wasn't sure if he was looking at a weather segment or a nature channel commercial. The camera angle was from the air, presumably from a helicopter flown by a brave pilot. The eye had made landfall over twelve hours prior, but the winds were still gusty. It looked as if the pilot was over the open sea, but debris was littered near and far. The caption read that the pilot was hovering over what *had been* Ossabaw Island, where the eye had crossed as the Category 4 storm made landfall just south of Savannah. There were hundreds...thousands of dead bodies floating in the water. Bloated, black bodies drifting aimlessly. Clint leaned to peer closely and realized that they were all pigs. The camera zoomed into a group of twelve piglets that were actually swimming toward the roof of a building. Clint watched as the piglets made it. They climbed up and joined at least a hundred other pigs stranded on the roof.

One of the reporters came back on and described what had happened. A twenty-eight-foot storm surge had hit the coast. Ossabaw Island, at only three feet above sea level, was wholly submerged, as were several other islands on the Georgia coast.

Downtown Savannah was a disaster. Video footage of when the 148 MPH winds hit the city showed every billboard being flung into the wind like a sheet of tissue in front of a fan. Skyscrapers stood, but nearly all of the glass windows were shattered or had altogether vanished in a rain of glass. Weaker buildings, especially along the river, collapsed completely. The helicopter flew over a swath of house walls that had been stripped of their roofs. Over eighty percent of Savannah was flooded. Roofing, sticks of lumber, tires, boxes, and bodies floated. The scene was too much for any human to take in, the destruction and loss of life and property too much to contemplate.

A chart displayed the track of Hurricane Isabel as it churned from the Bahamas and rapidly intensified, making landfall immediately southeast of Savannah. It spun its destruction northerly, just to the west of Augusta and the east of Athens. The eye of what was now Tropical Storm Isabel cast its destructive gaze upon Clayton, as the storm had slowed its forward progress. Record rains had fallen and were still falling in northern Georgia, eclipsing the effect of Tropical Storm Alberto in 1994, which had dropped over twenty-seven inches of rain in some places.

"Some parts of North Georgia will receive in excess of thirty inches of rain from this system," the reporter said, almost not believing his own words. "The devastation on the Georgia coast is unimaginable, but the flooding and damage in the mountains could be equally horrific," he added.

A panel of experts sat to discuss the impact of the storm. As with any hurricane, most of the attention was on the storm surge and the coastal impact, but a geologist on the panel spoke up and asserted himself. "I don't think we should underestimate the effect this storm will have on the Appalachian Mountains," the geologist, Michael Hammons, said. "Northeast Georgia and western North Carolina will be looking at major debris flows."

The moderator probed further. "Michael, can you explain debris flows?"

"Debris flows are very dangerous," Hammons said. "You're looking at a mass movement of soil and rock down steep slopes."

"Like an avalanche?" the moderator said.

"Sort of," Hammons said. "But with an avalanche, only the surface material moves, as in the case with packed ice and snow. With a debris flow, the earth underneath detaches as well. They have far more force than an avalanche...there's no stopping them. Anything in the path will be deeply buried."

As the geologist spoke, an animated sequence played on the screen that depicted the sides of mountains essentially washing into the valleys below.

"What triggers them?" the moderator asked.

"Very heavy rainfalls in short periods of time," Hammons said. "Just look at Hurricane Camille in 1969. It stalled over Virginia and dumped twenty-eight inches of rain in about eight hours. We recorded almost 4,000 debris flows that wiped out houses and killed over 150 people in one county alone."

"In Macon County, North Carolina, the county that borders Rabun County in Georgia, a 2004 debris flow detached material from Fish Hawk Mountain and it flowed over two miles."

The moderator was momentarily speechless, so the geologist summed up. "It's reasonable to expect the debris flows from this storm to be much, much worse than those."

***

For most of the night Ozzie slogged through wet leaves and standing water with Isabella as he tried to lead her to Hal's cabin, but the ferocity of the wind and rain drove them to seek refuge under the overhang of the granite outcropping in the pine cathedral. Even though it was almost noon, there was barely enough light to see deep inside the forest. Still, Ozzie was able to make out the body of the man who had shot at him.

Evidently the coyotes had gotten to him. He was dragged several yards away from the boulder, and what was left of him lay chest down on the forest floor. His head was completely removed, evidently chewed off by the coyotes. Ozzie scanned through the downpour but saw no sign of the head. Shane's arms and back were exposed, but virtually all the flesh was gone. A metal stick...a shotgun lay in the muck beside him.

Ozzie and Isabella jumped to their feet as the mountain roared beneath them. They looked quickly to the right to see an entire hillside begin to move slowly, impossibly. A tree lost its footing and fell backwards. Then another. The speed picked up and the entire slope behind them gave way. They ran out to their left, retracing the same path that Ozzie had fled that day that seemed so long ago.

Without knowing why, Ozzie stopped at the precise spot where he had been shot and looked back. The hillside flowed down like lava from a volcano. The huge granite outcropping split the flow and sent it to each side of the boulder. It rejoined on the other side and laid waste to everything standing in its path. Ozzie squinted to see the mountain swallow Shane's distant remains. Isabella and Ozzie turned and plodded in the direction of Hal's cabin and away from their life as the oppressed.

Far, far behind them, the mountainside awoke with a fury. The steep slope behind Ozzie's former home, his prison paddock, was among the first to seek its revenge for the painful oppression perpetrated on its soil. The slope erupted in a thunderous burst and washed down the mountainside. It devoured the curing sheds and the fences, burying their sins deep into its soil. The surge continued and spread as it slugged through hundred year old trees, swallowing them whole and mixing them with mud, leaves, and rocks in mountainous piles over makeshift roads and abandoned logging roads. A black sea of muck rolled over an old F100 pickup, burying it and Blake's sins forever from human eyes.

Ozzie's monster was finally laid to rest.

**

Hal shivered inside his cabin. His campfire had gone out early in the morning and his thoroughly soaked blankets were no match for the wind-driven rain. The only thing warm on his body was the back of his neck. *If Only Rex was big enough to cover my whole body,* Hal thought, *I'd be fine and dandy.*

The sounds around the cabin were deafening. Branches snapped loudly and crashed to the ground with increasing regularity. Hard, driving rain pounded the ground unmercifully, and the little stream that normally flowed peacefully fifty yards from his front porch now raged over his front steps.

Hal stood at the door and knew this was his moment. He had come out here to die alone, to be a burden to no one. Now death swirled around him, encircled him and tightened its icy grip until Hal had only the doorway to stand in. And now that it was here, it terrified him. He walked back inside and peered out the small window he had cut to see behind the cabin.

To the left of the garden lay a large Sycamore tree that had fallen the year before. Through the torrential rain, Hal peered at a red blob near its root ball. He stared pensively until he was sure he could make it out. Tammy lay on the ground and slept contentedly, riding out the storm and at ease with her survival instincts. Hal thought about how he had lived five years in the woods alone but, unlike Tammy and Ozzie, he was utterly at the mercy of nature. He needed shelter. And, he realized, perhaps too late, he needed companionship.

A bolt of lightning lit up the forest and blinded Hal just as if sunshine had reflected off a mirror into his eyes. He shielded his eyes and jumped back in the cabin as an earth shattering sound of thunder shook the cabin. A moment later he felt a bone rattling thud and saw a giant oak crash across his porch, ripping a third of his roof off in the process. His bed flew off the floor and crashed back down as Rex dug his claws into Hal's neck.

Hal shook uncontrollably, drenched and overcome with terror. He thought about Tammy, how she was a creature of nature and knew how to survive. He thought of Ozzie and figured he was just as safe...hoped he was just as safe. Mostly, he though of Connie, picturing her face as he shuffled his feet to what was left of his front porch and allowed the rain to wash away his tears and his pain. He had come to forest to die, to put an end to his suffering. He found that now, just as when he had come five years earlier, he couldn't embrace death. When push came to shove he realized what he wanted was to survive.

He stepped out of the cabin into rushing knee-deep water knowing that he had discovered that too late.

Chapter 33

Lonnie sat at his desk in the sheriff's office surrounded by his deputies eight days after Hurricane Isabel hit Savannah and a week after it dumped thirty-two inches of rain on parts of Rabun County.

"Well, all righty then, anything else before I head out with my church to Savannah?" Lonnie asked. No one spoke. Lonnie surveyed the expressions and paused as he became, for the moment, Pastor Lonnie. "Let us say a prayer before I leave," he said. Everyone bowed their heads and interlocked their fingers, none even questioning if an elected official could ask them to pray. Even the atheists and agnostics among them felt the loss and suffering that surrounded them and knew this was the time to remain quiet.

"Father—thank you," Lonnie began. "Thank you for reminding us of what we have. For showing us what we all can be by being here for one another in each of our greatest times of need. For allowing us to remember that we are here, Lord, not to enrich our own lives, but to serve you and our fellow man. Please be with us, Lord, as we set out to do that, in Jesus' name we pray, Amen."

"Amen," was shouted as men cried in the office, some uncontrollably. The losses they had witnessed first hand that week were permanently etched in their visions, as if a video game image was burned into an old television screen that was finally turned off. The vision would linger, forever.

Lonnie grabbed a bag and walked to the door. "I'll see y'all in a couple of weeks if all goes well," he said as he walked out the door.

"Oh...Sheriff," Freeman shouted, and walked to the door.

Lonnie stopped. "Yes, Freeman?"

"I—I heard from the medical examiner this morning," Freeman said. "He said it'll be at least a week, maybe more, before they get results on the dental records from that head— uh, the remains of that head that washed up down on Warwoman. They think it's a young man but they're not completely sure yet."

Lonnie turned his head away. "Well," he said with a quivering lip, "when you hear something, you call me and let me know, no one else."

"Understood, Sheriff. Good luck down there." Freeman reached to shake Lonnie's hand but Lonnie pulled him for a hug. Then the sheriff walked through the door and drove with members of his church to help victims begin rebuilding in Savannah.

***

Clint sat alone in the conference room at the USDA building on Alabama Street as the meeting ended. His supervisor, Clarence Green, walked back into the meeting and sat beside him.

"Clint—I'm sorry, but you got nothing on this guy," Clarence said.

Clint fumed and bit his lip. He shook his head as he felt his blood boiling. He threw his eyes at Clarence and then checked the door to make sure no one else was coming back. Clint grabbed Clarence's arm. "I know this guy is guilty, Clarence. I know it."

"You know what, exactly?" Clarence asked.

"I know he sold tainted meat that wasn't inspected. Hell he butchered those animals himself. I know he's responsible for those deaths and illnesses!"

Clarence shook his head. "Clint, we've been over this, and we've been over this. You—"

"Anthrax doesn't just come out of the air, Clarence! It comes from the soil, unless we're talking about a biological weapon. And we're not. What we are talking about is infected, tainted meat that wasn't inspected and was served to an innocent, unsuspecting public. That's a clear violation of the Federal Meat Inspection Act!"

Clint paused, before continuing. "People died, Clarence!"

Clarence removed Clint's grip from his arm. "Maybe you're right, Clint. MAYBE. But there's a difference between thinking something and knowing something. You don't know it, you think it."

"Ya but—"

"But WHAT, Clint? But you went up there to see him a few days ago and found, what? Oh, that's right, you found nothing. Absolutely nothing! A man living in a small house on a small piece of land where he couldn't possibly have raised and butchered a bunch of pigs."

Clint jumped to his feet. "You know good and well there's thousands of acres behind him that—"

Clarence stood, looked Clint in the eye and interrupted, "That has a bunch of trees in it. That's all I know. Most of 'em laid flat by that storm last week. Face it, Clint, you don't have anything on this guy. And we don't have any resources for you to go after him chasing a hunch. Hell, it'll take us months to figure out when all the restaurants and retailers are safe to reopen near the Georgia coast."

Clint looked down and tapped the conference table loudly with his fingers. "So that's it? We don't have the resources so we just let this guy slide?"

Clarence furrowed his eyes and pointed his finger directly at Clint. "L-E-T it go, Clint. You just focus on what we do know."

Clint looked up at Clarence and caught his stare.

"We do know that Nick Vegas served all the meats," Clarence continued. "And we know that the meat was, in fact, tainted with anthrax. Those are the facts."

Clint exhaled and dropped his shoulders.

"That's your target, Clint. Nick Vegas."

***

Nick sat in the plush leather window seat and stared down at the sights of Atlanta as the 767 climbed. Turner Field and the Peachtree Plaza hotel led his eyes to Buckhead. His sprawling home, which seemed so big to him, was lost down there somewhere. The Delta pilot flew over Stone Mountain and the flight attendant brought Nick another Jack Daniels once the chime indicated they had reached 10,000 feet.

Nick pulled the envelope out of the brief case in front of him that his lawyer had sent over that afternoon. "Just look this over this weekend and let's meet Monday to strategize,"the lawyer said. Nick had glanced it over. He had seen the $30 million class-action civil lawsuit carefully drafted by IBM's team of high-priced lawyers who had nothing better to do than to go after Nick. To make him a poster child for wrongdoing while making themselves look good to the public. Enhancing their image as sticking up for what they thought was right.

More than anything he wanted to stay and fight and clear his name, but everything transpired against him. Nick slugged the Jack Daniels and asked the flight attendant for more. To his way of thinking he had done nothing wrong. He really believed that. Mostly he wanted to break Blake in half for what he had done to him. For what Blake had cost him.

Yes, Nick wanted to stay and fight. But he'd lose and he knew it. So he transferred what money he could to banks in Barcelona. He'd lay low and fight the battle from there, hopefully holding on to the house and the restaurants but, if not, getting as much cash out as he could. And keep his freedom.

Chapter 34

Easter Sunday arrived on the last day of March, earlier than most years. The date made little difference to Ozzie. Nor did the day of the week or the event itself, for that matter. He walked down the slope after patrolling the ridge. He looked up as he walked and noticed that most of the trees were still bare. Leaves would be coming soon enough, along with all sorts of new life on the mountain. Ozzie walked past Hal's old garden to the pile of strewn lumber scattered about; all that remained in the woods of Hal and his cabin. Ozzie listened, hoping to hear the sound of the thumper keg, the sound of Hal's guitar. To hear Hal rant one more time. He heard the sound of silence.

A solitary, juvenile grunt from underneath the woodpile broke the silence. Then another. Then a chorus of them as six little piglets came out to greet their dad. Ozzie looked down at the motley crew. Three were soot black, just like him. Two were black with tan or orange spots. One little fella was bright, solid orangish red, just like his mom. He was the squeaky wheel of the bunch, always whining until he was fed first, always the one claiming there was a monster in the woods coming for him. They named him Rusty.

Tammy came out from underneath a cove of boards that she and Ozzie had built from Hal's old cabin. They pushed and shoved them around where his porch formerly stood just before Tammy had given birth two months earlier. She walked over and stood next to Ozzie and watched the little torpedos squirm around, snorting, sniffing and smelling everything in sight. Everything new and wondrous to them.

"Where're my grand babies?" Isabella called from beside the stream.

Rusty looked up and started running toward her. The others took off, racing as well, and passed him. Rusty came to a log lying down in his path, one that the others had magically hurdled over, but seemingly impossible for him.

"Wa, wa!" Rusty squeaked and squealed.

"Rusty, grow up!" Ozzie said, looking at him firmly.

Tammy walked to Rusty and glanced back at Ozzie, shaking her head. She put her snout under his rump and lifted him up. He ran sideways toward the stream and soaked up his grandmother's love.

***

The children raced out of the Sandy Creek Baptist Church as the Easter egg hunt was about to begin. "Not this year for you, little one," Angelica said as she tickled her three-month-old son's nose. "But you girls run along and have some fun," she said to Rose's daughters.

The girls ran off in the matching Easter dresses Angelica had hand sewn for them on her grandmother's Singer sewing machine. Bright yellow dresses with shoulder straps, hemmed on the bottom in six inches of pink fabric with red flowers. Angelica had put a pink ribbon in their hair that flapped now as they streamed toward the eggs.

"They're so beautiful," Rose said to Angelica as she walked out of the church and soaked up the midday sun with John. "I just wish they'd never outgrow them."

Angelica laughed. "Well, I want to see this little munchkin grow up," she said. Rose smiled as Angelica looked down to her newborn son.

"I just love the name Clayton," Rose said. "Surprising you never hear that name up here. I don't know anyone up here named Clayton."

"Well, now you do," Angelica said as she leaned down and put her face right in front of her son's.

Rose nodded as her eyes fixed on a tearful, middle-aged couple, dressed in black and kneeling to place flowers in the creek. "Who is that?" Rose asked.

"Mr. and Mrs. Dixon," Angelica said. "They live down on Earls Ford Road. Shane was their son."

Rose thought for a moment. "Oh God, you mean the remains of that boy that washed up, that head that—." Rose was unable to complete the sentence. The flood of memories overcame her. Her own near personal disaster, such a tragedy at the time that became eclipsed by the horrific losses that everyone suffered from Savannah up to Clayton and beyond. Everyone had a story of loss, a story of a hero who helped and saved. The grief was so great for everyone that they had to surrender and allow themselves to focus not on what they had lost, but what they had left. Rose stood beside Angelica and recognized for the first time that those catastrophic events had brought her closer to church and closer to Angelica.

Angelica stood and watched the kids scramble for eggs along Warwoman creek. Rose took her hand in hers. Angelica looked at her with a smile, which unleashed a flood of tears from Rose. She threw her arms around Angelica and hugged her as if she hadn't seen her in many years.

"I'm so grateful to you for caring for the girls last fall while I was sick," Rose cried. "I don't know what they would have done without you." Angelica pushed her sister back slightly so she could look into her eyes. "Don't be silly! We're just thrilled, so relieved that you're okay. When we heard that a woman in your hospital in Miami had died of anthrax and we couldn't reach you...that was the scariest moment of my life!"

Rose wiped her eyes and bowed her head. "I know," she said. "I couldn't believe that there were three of us in the same hospital who had all eaten at the same dinner. Oh God, it's such a surreal, horrible memory." Rose looked out at the girls running. She looked down at her nephew. "If that doctor on the island hadn't had experience with anthrax in Spain and known what to do...," Rose's lip quivered. "I don't know, Angelica, I know I wouldn't be here." Rose burst out crying.

Angelica thought back to the night of the storm, of staring out the kitchen window and seeing a vision of Rose. Of gingerly rubbing her beads and reciting a chant to heal Rose. A chant her grandmother had taught her that, somehow, she felt she had known for an eternity. She gave Rose a hug.

"Do you know he lost his sister to anthrax back in Spain?" Rose said. "That's why he came to the island – to escape from the memory of her loss. But because of her death he was able to save me."

Angelica smiled knowingly and ran her fingers threw Rose's hair. "We can make some good memories now," she said.

A hand landed on Angelica's left shoulder along with a whisper in her ear. "Hi, hon."

She turned around. "Hi, sweetie," Angelica said to Blake. "Whatcha been doing in there?"

"Oh I wanted to talk to the pastor for a bit about the sermon. Just enjoying some fellowship," he said.

Rose turned and smiled at Blake. She threw her arms around him. "I owe you a thank you, too, for being so good to the girls." Blake stepped back and smiled, still uncomfortable with moments of affection.

"Happy Easter," Rose said.

"You too," Blake said with a warmer smile. "Now...let's eat! What's for Easter dinner?"

"Well," Angelica said, "we all grew up eating Easter hams, but I decided to cook us a roast this year. I figure we're all a little tired of ham."

Rose nodded her head. "Amen, sis."

***

Nick Vegas sat at the tapas bar in Barcelona. The mirror before him reflected the image of dozens of Jamón Ibérico hams suspended from the ceiling over the bar. He looked straight up, able to reach out and touch the symbols of his passion, the symbols of his demise. The bartender poured him another glass of cheap wine as Nick returned his eyes to the Sky News business broadcast on the screen. The Forbes magazine picture of Nick and his bulldog splashed on the screen as the British reporter read the story.

"American authorities are still searching for Nick Vegas, the restaurant chain owner who is wanted in connection with the deaths of seven people and the sickening of over one hundred last fall in the 50-Forks episode, as the anthrax event has come to be known."

The bartender too was fixed on the screen and he turned to Nick. "Hey, you know I used to know that guy," he said.

Nick looked at him closely. "Who? The reporter?"

"No, Nick Vegas."

Nick took a hand and pulled his shoulder length blonde hair over his ears, giving himself a more scruffy appearance. It had been months since Nick had been clean-shaven or had worn neatly groomed black hair, but he still believed he looked like the man on the screen. As he fled the country, he managed to get a few hundred thousand dollars wired to his Spanish bank account, but within a week the Spanish authorities had agreed to cooperate with the U.S. and froze his assets. *All to protect the reputation of their precious Jamón Ibérico,* Nick assumed. Border authorities in the U.S. and Spain remained on the lookout for Nick, so with no place to run and no money to get there, Nick hid in the shadows.

"Is that so?" Nick said.

"Yeah. Spent a little time with him at The Culinary Institute of Spain. He headed to America and I ended up here."

Nick stared at him through his dark sunglasses.

"He always said he'd go over there," the bartender continued, "because over here he'd just be another good Spanish chef. Nothing special. But in America, he'd be one of a kind, so to speak. He said he'd make a lot more money because the market was so much bigger. He was always about the money."

The bartender chuckled as he put a plate of olives in front of Nick, "I like where I ended up better!"

The report continued. "Vegas is believed to have fled the country, but all of his assets were seized until the numerous civil lawsuits are settled against him. IBM lawyers are leading the legal efforts for all victims in remembrance for one of their own stars who was tragically lost. Indeed, IBM is the largest plaintiff in the wrongful death suits. Of course Vegas is also wanted by the FBI, which has issued a $500,000 reward for knowledge leading to his capture."

Nick threw a twenty-Euro note down on the counter and walked out.

**

Angelica unlocked the door at Cherokee Traditions in Clayton at 8:45 a.m. on Monday. She flipped on the lights in the store and took in the fragrance of the medicinal and culinary herbs on the shelves. The shop was neat and tidy, as she always left it, so there was little to do before she opened the doors at nine. Walking back to the door, she inhaled the scent of coffee from Grapes and Beans across the street, but it was the comforting smell of fresh baked croissants next door that lured her. She walked in and was swallowed by the aroma of bread baking in the brick ovens and the sound of J.J. Cale from the speakers.

"Morning, angel!"

"Well good morning, Hal. How was your Easter?"

"Lousy," he said. "Didn't have a drink all day! Preacher said I couldn't."

Angelica laughed. "Well, you should have had yourself a few drops of tincture, Hal. You do realize they're made almost entirely of vodka, don't you?"

"Hot dammit all, I knew there's something I liked about you other than the fact that you look like that girl Angelina Jolie. I'll trade you this here croissant for some moonshine tincture."

"Well...that's not exactly what I have," she said. "How about my Sweet Sleep Tincture?"

"Done!" Hal wrapped a croissant in paper and handed it to Angelica. "All righty, that'll be one Sweet Sleep Tincture," he said with a smile.

"I'm sure glad you stayed in Clayton and opened this bread shop Hal. We needed it...and you."

Hal dropped his head and shuffled his feet. He was more comfortable goofing off than being serious. A brief flood of memories washed over him. Of making bread with Connie before she died. Of living alone in the woods for so very long. Of the horrible storm and flood that very nearly killed him before he managed to follow the raging stream to a road. Of finding the remains of that boy's head and working with the churches on Warwoman to help so many who suffered in the horrific storm.

Mostly, he thought of Ozzie and wondered what happened to the little fellow. He reckoned he wasn't so little anymore and figured he was probably all right. But you never know...he'd never know.

"Yeah," he said, "I'm glad too. I like it better than Athens. Like this mountain air. And I'm glad you opened that shop of yours, too!"

Angelica took the croissant and smiled. "Monday, Wednesday, Friday, and Saturday, 9:00 a.m. until 1:00 p.m., she said. Come by anytime!"

Angelica walked to the door and looked back. "Bye, Hal!"

She opened the doors to her natural herb shop and walked to the counter. Her eyes caught an aromatherapy candle that she and Blake had made together two months before. She lit the candle and smiled, recalling the fun-filled Valentine's Day she had with Blake, making candles, watching movies and playing with Clayton. The candle flame began to burn brightly, but immediately—

"Oh no!" Angelica gasped, as the flame promptly died for no reason, leaving only a putrid trail of black smoke. Fumbling for the lighter on the counter, she placed the lighter over the flame, but even after two full minutes, the wick refused to light. Angelica looked around, feeling a twinge of unease that something was wrong. It reminded her of the feeling she had just before Rose went to the Bahamas. The same feeling she had at breakfast with her parents the morning their plane disappeared. She began to walk back to Hal's to make sure he was all right, but the bells chimed on the front door as a couple walked in. Angelica checked the clock, 9:13 a.m., and summoned a smile.

***

"You ready to help daddy work in the garden?" Blake asked Clayton. The baby smiled, or so Blake thought, as he tickled his belly. "That's my boy!"

Blake strapped Clayton into the infant carrier and walked out the front door. With the carrier in his right hand, Blake snaked his left hand through the air and showed his son how to do "the worm" as they walked to the garden shed. "Mama said we need to get the raised beds ready for tomatoes, little man," Blake said in the childish, baby voice that all adults use with infants. "Now you just wait right here a moment."

Before walking into the garden shed, Blake sat Clayton down at the entrance. Inside, Blake took a pair of garden gloves from a hook on the right wall and removed three tomato cages nested together from the overhead shelf, and then walked ten steps to place them beside his son. "We won't be planting tomatoes for a few more weeks but might as well go ahead and set these out, right little man?"

Clayton reached unsuccessfully for the cages.

Blake walked back in and looked at the three plain cardboard boxes stacked on the shelf. He reached his hand for the top one, but it was just beyond his reach. He moved his fingers to the side of the box and tried to slide it so that the top one would tip off. It wouldn't budge. "Hmmm. Whatever's in there sure is heavy," Blake said to himself and to the baby, if he was interested.

Looking around, Blake found a milk crate on the floor, placed it upside down under the boxes and stood on it. He looked over at Clayton, who still concentrated on reaching the cage that seemed impossibly out of his reach a couple of inches away. Blake landed the palm of his hand over the top box and pulled it toward him. It began to move, but stopped as the weight caused the middle box to crumple slightly, preventing the top box from sliding. He put a little more pressure on the side of the box and gave it a tug.

The shelf support to Blake's left snapped loudly. As it did, the shelf and all the boxes fell hard and fast, hitting him squarely in the nose and knocking him off balance. As he began to fall backwards the milk crate tilted forward, causing Blake to crash through the waist-high bench behind him. The last thing Blake saw before he smacked his head on the concrete floor and fell unconscious was boxes flipping on the way down. They landed hard on his chest and face and slammed his head into the cement slab. Bags of bone meal burst open and covered Blake's chest, face, and head in a thick cloud of moldy dust. He inhaled long and deep as he lost consciousness. Clayton's attention was distracted from the cage at the noise and the white cloud that billowed thirty feet from him. He looked at it and reached again for the cage. He kept reaching for the next forty-five minutes until his father finally came to.

Aarrck!

A screeching sound jolted Blake. He opened his eyes and looked at the ceiling. The white cloud had settled now, but Blake couldn't recall what had happened. As he reached back he felt a wet spot on the back of his head. He grimaced and closed his eyes, rubbing them and feeling the powder on them. Blake looked at his white finger and tilted his chin to see the thick powder that coated his chin. Alarmed, he inhaled deeply by instinct and began to cough immediately. He rolled over as he realized he was covered in dust and looked down at the torn bags of Black Rock Organic Bone Meal.

What? When did I put this here?

He snapped his head up in agonizing pain as he realized what the powder was, the ground up bones of diseased animals that had spewed death far and wide from the mountain's poisoned soil. Exhaling, he tried with all his might to blow all the breath out of him. The more he blew, the more he coughed.

Aarrck!

Blake jerked his throbbing head to the sound that came from the garden shed entrance. Clayton had fallen asleep in the carrier. Blake rubbed his eyes at what he thought he was seeing. "What the—" Blake mumbled. A raven was perched on the infant carrier handle above Clayton. Blake dusted himself off and stood up, pushing against the wall to steady himself. "Shoo! Get out of here!"

The raven flew off as Blake picked up Clayton, careful to hold him well away from his own dusty body. He walked toward the house with the carrier in his hand and saw a shadow on the ground of the raven circling overhead.

Inside the house, Blake stumbled and sat the infant carrier on the kitchen floor. Clayton was sleeping peacefully. As Blake's head pounded and his vision became blurred, he focused all of his concentration on unbuttoning his shirt. With great effort, he undressed and stepped into the shower where he scrubbed the powder off his body and out of his hair. Underneath the showerhead he coughed violently and spewed up blood. He couldn't stop coughing for over a minute as he bent over and watched the blood swirl counterclockwise down the drain, looking from above like the bloody eye of a deadly hurricane.

He toweled off and pulled a jacket from a shelf high above the washing machine, draping it over a t-shirt and sweatpants. Stumbling, he made his way to the living room as he fought off the coughs, telling himself to not cough the way a spinning drunk tells himself to not throw up, to hold it in. He crashed on the sofa and pulled a blanket around his neck.

His nose and lungs felt thick. Thick with powder, thick with deceit and lies. He felt all the symptoms rising within him at once. Nausea, fever, aches. He couldn't tell if they were physical or if they were imagined. If he was really feeling flu-like symptoms or if he was so run down from it all. More than anything he wanted Angelica and thought of calling her, but heavy fatigue gripped him. He was tired. So tired. His eyes made their way to the clock, 9:13 a.m. She'd be home in a few hours. He'd rest on the sofa.

Sleep, get some rest, that's all you need, he told himself.

The blanket slipped to the floor as Blake's breathing labored. He coughed loudly and his eyelids sank, sending him into a delirious journey to the darkest depths of a haunted forest. Alone he stood as the forest folded up around him. Trees inched closer; pigs squealed and stalked him with menacing tusks as coyotes circled concentrically while snapping their jaws. Jesse, Shane, Nick, Clint, and the sheriff held hands and joined the coyote's circle as a menacing raven swooped and tormented Blake. His demons taunted, shouted and spun as they all moved closer and closer. Blake turned and turned, watching his flame flicker as the poisoned soil opened its wicked womb and prepared to swallow him. As the raven shrieked and dove straight for his face he crouched and surrendered himself into a fetal position, cradling his head while offering a final prayer for salvation.

***

Angelica walked through the kitchen door and saw Clayton sitting in the infant carrier on the floor, happily bewitched by the ceiling light. The feeling of unease she had felt earlier in the morning vanished as she smiled, bent over, and put her face just in front of his. Clayton's eyes adjusted and focused on his mother's face, and a toothless smile beamed as his body shifted with uncontrollable glee.

Filled with love and bliss in her heart, Angelica rose and began walking toward the living room. After three steps, she stopped abruptly. Fear seized her, sending chills up her spine and down her arms as her eyes widened at the sight of Blake curled in the fetal position on the sofa. Within an instant, her gut swirled with worry and panic, supplanting every loving emotion she had felt only seconds before.

Quivering, she stepped forward and looked down, staring in disbelief at the blood-stained blue jacket that cloaked the lifeless body of her husband, her son's father. Slowly, her worry and panic began to fade as fury boiled within her.

She bit her lip and bored her eyes into a crucifix above the fireplace for answers, furious emotions stewing in her gut. A river of rage flowed down her cheeks as the realization set in that her dream of a simple life with Blake, an honest family life, was forever shattered. The tears turned bitter as Angelica stormed across the hardwood floor, narrowing her eyes on Blake as she feverishly paced back and forth. "Why didn't you just return the jacket and do what was right? WHY?"

She stopped and stood there, staring at Blake for a moment longer, finding no answers to her questions. Angelica turned once more to the crucifix, fixing her eyes upon it firmly. "Well?" she asked. "*Is* he in a better place?" She thrust her arms overhead in exasperation. "*Does* God have a plan?" Angelica held her breath and held a stern gaze upon the crucifix.

Movement from the kitchen distracted and disarmed her. She looked back to see Clayton's arms dangle excitedly over the edge of the infant carrier as he was captivated once more by the ceiling light. Her shoulders collapsed and her tension faded. As she exhaled, tears began to swell, and her sadness, her rage, morphed into forgiveness and understanding.

She walked to the sofa and stroked Blake's hair. Angelica thought of the day she first saw him. She thought of her junior prom date with Blake, and then thought of their wedding day. Turning her head to see the baby's dangling arms in the kitchen, she looked back at Blake and smiled as she thought of the day, only months before, when Clayton was born. Of how happy Blake had finally become. She pictured the little Georgia Bulldogs outfit that Blake had bought for Clayton and recalled the smile on his face as he placed it on the baby. For an eternal moment, she looked at Blake's face, caressed his cheeks, and smiled at him, one last time.

Then, Angelica leaned over Blake's body. She reached for her walking stick that was leaning against the sofa; its razor sharp root spikes protruding like gnarly hair over the deranged face that had been carved for its head long, long ago. Angelica kissed the beads that hung from her neck as she knelt on the hardwood floor, weeping with the knowledge that justice had been served.

Baldev nodded in approval of the sacrifice.

The End

(see next page)

Please Leave a Review!

If you're like me, you rely on the opinions of others when making purchasing decisions. We've all relied on word-of-mouth recommendations for generations, but one of the truly exciting aspects about the Internet is how easily we can share our experiences with others. In that way, we help them to make informed decisions just as they help us when they share their experiences.

But...it only works if you share. With that in mind, please take a moment right now, go online and write a review of Poisoned Soil. Let others know what you thought of it so they can determine whether or not they may enjoy it. Of course, be careful to not give away any spoilers!

Here are a few places where you can leave an honest review. Other readers will appreciate it and so do I!

amazon.com
goodreads.com
bn.com
iTunes bookstore
And please share a book link/review on Facebook, Twitter & your blog!

Just go to those sites and search for Poisoned Soil! If you write the review in one place you can cut and paste in each site.

Please do this, and thank you!

About the Author

While flying high over corporate America, Tim Young received a call he couldn't ignore. He shredded his business cards and said goodbye to the conveniences of urban life, to become a farmer and homesteader. Today, Tim is an award-winning cheese maker and author. He lives in Georgia with the most beautiful and caring woman in the world, and a little dog named Alfie that speaks to him in condescending, broken-English.

Other Books by the Author

THE ACCIDENTAL FARMERS

When Tim and Liz Young decided to leave their comfortable suburban life and become first-time farmers in rural Georgia, they embarked on a journey that would change their lives. The Accidental Farmers reveals how the couple learned that hamburgers, bacon, and eggs don't come from the supermarket but from real animals that forge emotional bonds with their human caretakers. Seeking a middle path between a meatless lifestyle and the barbarism of factory food, Tim and Liz created Nature's Harmony Farm, a sustainable oasis where rare breed animals and humans live together searching for something nearly lost by both humans and the animals...how to live naturally off the land.

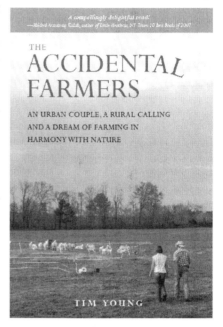

Rather than a how-to guide, this book is a personal memoir of the Young's journey to farming and is sure to delight those interested in moving to the country or simply learning more about the struggles of sustainable farming.

Buy and read it today!